Praise for the Jessica Darling Series

fourth comings

"Megan McCafferty's hilarious coming-of-age novels are getting better as Jess gets older . . . Acidly funny, imaginatively profane and, above all, a sharp reflection of the what-do-I-do-*now*, post-college dilemma."

—*Miami Herald*

"The books are a springboard for McCafferty's hilarious pop culture riffs . . . The series has won her a legion of fans, from teens and college students to twentysomethings, mothers, and the occasional grandmother."

—*Star-Ledger*

"Filled with humor . . . an authentic depiction of a time in life filled with changing relationships and tumultuous experiences."

—*The Princeton Packet*

"Every time's a charm . . . following intelligent and disgruntled Jersey shore teen Jessica Darling."

—*University Wire*

"Jess' wit has sharpened and deepened, and it's a joy to spend time in her company, especially when *Fourth Comings* doesn't end at all the way one might predict but practically assures us that a fifth serving of Jess' life is on tap."

—*Charleston Gazette*

"Jessica's voice is as honest and hilarious as ever . . . but in this book, for the first time, she seems to truly stand on her own two feet."

—*Home News Tribune*

charmed thirds

"*Sloppy Firsts*, *Second Helpings* and now *Charmed Thirds* may be about a young woman's amusing and rocky journey to adulthood, but they are smart and accomplished enough to delight all readers. Jessica's an original, but her problems are universal, and McCafferty is formidably adept at channeling her self-deprecating, wise-guy voice. If you don't see yourself in Jessica Darling, you're not looking hard enough."

—*Chicago Tribune*

"A witty, biting, and altogether true accounting of a girl's journey to young womanhood, complete with all of the cringe-inducing, hilarious moments of love, shame, and uncertainty that readers will remember from their own lives."

—Jennifer Weiner, author of *Certain Girls*

"It's Jessica, her wit and, especially, her utterly droll take on life, that draws readers (fans of the series include adult women as well as teens) into McCafferty's books. Entirely too smart for her own good, Jessica offers brilliant and cutting insights into the world of the adolescent about-to-be-a-woman."

—*Chicago Sun-Times*

"Megan McCafferty puts Jessica Darling through college in *Charmed Thirds*, and in the process turns her from a tart-tongued New Jersey high school philosopher into a heart-wrenching representation of all things uncertain. If she's not careful, she might end up with a heroine for our times."

—Ned Vizzini, author of *Be More Chill*

"A surprisingly mature and witty novel that should snag more than a few adult readers who well remember their college years."

—*Kirkus Reviews*

"Megan McCafferty rocks! Her sharp wit and keen satirical eye make her books must-reads."

—Meg Cabot, author of *Queen of Babble*

second helpings

"Boy, do I wish Megan McCafferty had been writing books about high school when I was young and foolish and insecure. But even now, at my advanced age, I get a huge kick out of the bright, wickedly funny and cheerfully off-color observations of Jessica Darling."

—*Miami Herald*

"High school sequel scores all A's . . . Jessica Darling returns for her senior year at Pineville High as irreverent and self-deprecating as she was in *Sloppy Firsts*. McCafferty tells the story from Jessica's perspective in the form of hilariously sardonic diary entries with cutting descriptions. McCafferty's debut novel became a crossover hit, equally touching teenagers and adults nostalgic about their youth. There's no reason this witty sequel, with an even more exhilarating and genuine take on teendom, shouldn't also reach the head of the class."

—*Boston Herald*

"Megan McCafferty expertly mines hallway and dinner-table politics to entertaining and insightful effect."

—*Chicago Tribune*

"McCafferty looks at teen travails with humor as well as heart."

—*People*

"Jessica Darling, the lovably cynical heroine of *Sloppy Firsts,* is about to begin her final year of high school. . . . Smart, tentative, and funny, Jessica is a likable and wry observer of the competitive, gossipy high-school world."

—*Booklist*

"The brainy and independent Jessica, author of this sequel's journal entries, is one of the more endearing offspring of these post–Bridget Jones years. McCafferty has the post-'90s teenage mind-set down to a tee . . . Sassy and packed with more plot twists than a *Real World* marathon."

—*Kirkus Reviews*

sloppy firsts

"Such a sharp, funny, poignant heroine, with an inner world we can all relate to. I love it."

—Sophie Kinsella, author of *Confessions of a Shopaholic*

"Comic and wise . . . Irresistible."

—*Miami Herald*

"Judy Blume meets Dorothy Parker."

—*Wall Street Journal*

"*Sloppy Firsts* perfectly captures the turbulent roller-coaster ride that is being a teenager. This is an intimate, painfully honest peek at a girl's coming of age. Getting to know Jessica was like meeting a new best friend. I miss her already."

—*CosmoGirl*

"A hilarious trip down memory lane. You'll laugh out loud—and cringe—as this first novel by McCafferty takes you back to the soap opera that was high school."

—*Glamour*

fourth comings

Also by Megan McCafferty

Sloppy Firsts

Second Helpings

Charmed Thirds

Sixteen (edited)

fourth comings

a novel

MEGAN MCCAFFERTY

This is a work of fiction. Names, characters, places, and incidents either are the product of the author's imagination or are used fictitiously. Any resemblance to actual persons, living or dead, events, or locales is entirely coincidental.

Published in the United States by Three Rivers Press, an imprint of the Crown Publishing Group, a division of Random House, Inc., New York.
www.crownpublishing.com

Originally published in hardcover in the United States by Crown Publishers, an imprint of the Crown Publishing Group, a division of Random House, Inc., New York, in 2007.

This book contains an excerpt from the forthcoming book *Perfect Fifths*, by Megan McCafferty. This excerpt has been set for this edition only and may not reflect the final content of the forthcoming edition.

Library of Congress Cataloging-in-Publication Data
McCafferty, Megan.
Fourth comings : a novel / Megan McCafferty.—1st ed.
1. Darling, Jessica (Fictitious character)—Fiction. 2. Young women—Fiction. 3. Periodicals—Publishing—Fiction. 4. Brooklyn (New York, N.Y.)—Fiction. 5. Chick lit. I. Title.

PS3613.C34F68 2007
813'.6—dc22 2007010818

ISBN 978-0-307-34651-3

Printed in the United States of America

Design by Ruth Lee-Mui

10 9 8 7 6 5 4 3 2 1

First Paperback Edition

For Christopher (again)

And for Collin

(who wanted to know if he was "in the book")

fourth comings

December 31, 2005

My dear Jessica,

I have but one request before you depart for Virginville, Pennsylvania: Don't forget to write.

Handwritten letters are going the way of the telegram. Landlines. VHS. It won't be long before we're all communicating via a wordless, emoticon-only language from a microcomputer directly implanted into our brains. Sci-fi writers have anticipated this for decades: a world in which language as we know it no longer exists, replaced by unpronounceable symbols that are instantly recognizable and incapable of being distorted by multiple interpretations. Maybe the written word will vanish altogether, and our descendants won't even comprehend the meaning of the word *handwriting*. It will be a baffling term one stumbles across in an old text, until all such texts crumble into so much dust.

(Dust is on my mind and under my skin. It cracks my eyelashes, sludges my nostrils, and muddies my tongue. Buddhists believe we're all dust, we're all everything. Here in the desert, I'm inclined to agree.)

I've always preferred laboring in longhand over swiftly skimming my fingertips across the keyboard, over dumbly thumbing messages short on characters and character. I feel sorry for future generations who will never know the pleasure of uncovering (recovering, discovering) old letters. I imagine myself far in the future, my knotty, gnarled fingers gingerly handling the delicate papers addressed to me from you.

You claim you're too impatient to practice zazen, and yet you stay still long enough to write and write and write. Writing is your preferred form of meditation. Hours slip away in seconds. The present is exchanged with the past. Time transcribed is time transformed.

(Translated. Transposed. Transferred. Transgressed. Transcended.)

And so, in addition to the eleven notebooks I've filled over the past two years, I give you this empty notebook as a simple going-away gift. I hope it inspires you to share your life stories with me, as I have with you. The tales we tell ourselves about ourselves make us who we are. To know them, dear Jessica, is to know you. And I want to know you always.

Forever, Marcus

notebook number one

september 2–5, 2006

saturday: the second

one

"Waiting sucks."

The voice was male and came from behind my right shoulder. I was so startled by the sound of another's voice rising above the undemanding Top 40 sound track, I nearly spazzed myself off my barstool.

The voice tried again, this time with an awkward paraphrase.

"It sucks, you know, to wait."

To have confirmed the source of the voice would have required me to turn away from the bar. I was the only one seated there, so I knew the voice was directed at me. And yet confirming this fact wasn't something I was particularly inclined to do. There was a swift movement, followed by a fresh whiff of citrus, sweat, and testosterone. The voice had taken the empty stool to my right.

"I hate being the first to show up anywhere," he continued, so sure of his hypothesis. "You feel like such a jackass."

The shift from first to second person was reflexive and unintentional. This is how his kind talk. To confirm, I refocused my attention away from my drink to his face. I was unsurprised by what I saw: a white, early-twentysomething male with a pair of mirrored aviator sunglasses resting on top of his head. His light brown hair was mussed in a calculated way that required far more product than neglect. He was broad-shouldered in his I'm-so-secure-about-my-masculinity-that-I-can-wear-pink Lacoste polo. A popped collar brushed against his ruddy rugby-player cheeks. Without looking down, I knew he had flip-flops on his feet.

Dude.

It could've been worse. Plenty of guys renounce Dude's scruffy preppy aesthetic and take to the sidewalks of this town wearing gaudy madras shorts, striped button-downs, and pastel sweaters knotted around their shoulders, like illustrations straight out of the first edition of *The WASP Handbook*. Earlier today on the way to the bar, I spotted a yachting, lockjawed specimen wearing green twill trousers (a corny word, but the only one that fits) with tiny ducks embroidered all over them. *Tiny ducks. Unironically.* I almost pointed and shrieked, which is something I hadn't done since first grade when I got smacked in the back of the head for screeching at a man with a cantaloupe goiter in the frozen-foods aisle of the Pineville SuperFoodtown.

Dude wasn't hot. He wasn't not. As with most guys of his privileged station and prep school pedigree, Dude was put together well—blandsome—which is all he needs to get laid on a regular basis. He was inspecting me inspecting him, a bemused expression on his face. He lifted himself up ever-so-slightly on his faded denim haunches, a gesture that indicated that he'd give me only a few more seconds before writing me off as embittered, boyfriended, or otherwise impenetrable.

"Hmm," I murmured. Then I sipped my drink and tried not to wince as the whiskey scarred my windpipe.

Dude settled back onto his stool. My indifference intrigued him, as all romantic impediments do. It's been scientifically proven. The harder the conquest, the more you want it. It's called frustration-attraction. (I don't think it's unfair for me to pipe in with this parenthetical: Frustration-attraction explains a lot when it comes to you and me.)

"So, you know, when we noticed you"—he thrust his carefully disheveled hairstyle toward a table in the corner, where three identically dressed dudes of varied races were pretending to drink beers instead of watching us—"we figured that one of us should come over and keep you company until your friends arrive." The fact that his friends were still sitting over *there*, instead of cockblocking him over *here*, suggested that money had exchanged hands before Dude made his approach.

"Twenty says I'll get her number."

"I'm in."

"Me *too*."

"Dude, you are so owned."

"Hmm," I said again.

"So where are they?" he asked. "Your friends?"

It wasn't an unreasonable question. I was, after all, a female sitting conspicuously alone in a college bar, drinking whiskey on a Saturday barely past one in the afternoon. Girls who look like me don't drink whiskey by themselves in bars barely past one in the afternoon. Granted, it wasn't the kind of dingy dive bar that ruins reputations, but a respectable Princeton institution that serves classic pub fare along with whatever is on tap. It's proudly decorated with orange-and-black paraphernalia and even sells a poster-sized version of a mural depicting Brooke Shields sitting in a booth across from Einstein, Toni Morrison, and other less instantly recognizable local luminary. Parents still bursting with pride were dining in the back room with their sons and daughters—freshmen and freshmeat who also arrived early for the pre-Orientation programming—enjoying one last lunch as a family before leaving their children alone to embark on their miraculous college journeys.

"My friends aren't here," I said. "Just me."

My first cryptic yet intelligibly human response made him break out into a smile. His teeth, it almost goes without saying, were thermonuclear white.

"I'm Dave," he said, extending a gentlemanly hand. "And you are . . . ?"

"I'm Jenn," I lied. "With two *n*'s."

"Two *n*'s?" Dude was emboldened by two multisyllabic replies in a row. "And how do you defend this blatant overuse of unnecessary consonants?"

Dude thought very highly of himself, and he considered this comment to be charming as all hell. As a female, I didn't have to play along in the same way. Just sitting there, seemingly agog at his patrician charms and in possession of a functional vagina, really was the only participation required on my end. And yet I couldn't stop myself.

"I need two *n*'s," Jenn-with-Two-N's continued in this facetious, flirtatious vein. "Because one's naughty and the other's . . ."

"Nice?" he offered.

"Or not."

Dude laughed really, really hard. He thought I was being ironic, which I was. But he was unaware of the full extent of this parody playing out before him. Ours was a multilayered mockery of a conversation, one occurring within a set of quotations within quotations within quotations. I was tired of having these types of conversations. I had a relationship with a philosophy major at Columbia that existed entirely within multiple sets of quotations.

"Why haven't I seen you around here before?"

"I don't go to Princeton," said Jenn-with-Two-N's.

"I didn't think so," Dude said. "By the time you're a senior, you feel like you know everyone even if you don't."

"Maybe it's because you all look alike," I replied, gesturing my glass toward the corner table. "That is, in your racially diverse way."

This also made him laugh. "I should be offended."

"But you're not."

"No," he said. "Because it's true."

I finished my drink in one long gulp. It was starting to burn less. Jessica Darling is a puker. But Jenn-with-Two-N's could handle her liquor. Dude lifted his finger to alert the bartender that we'd like another round. He was drinking Stella Artois.

"So you don't go here," he said.

"No."

"Work here? Live here?"

"No," I said. "And no."

"So if you don't mind me asking," Dude said, cracking his knuckles in such a way that required him to flex his lats, delts, and pecs, "what are you doing here?"

"I . . . don't . . . know." Each word a mystery unto itself.

Dude smiled because he thought I was joking. But it was a tight smile, one that betrayed his concern that I might be a bit of a nutcase, a drunken one-night stand not worth the psychotic hangover. He asked a question designed to get a better sense of what he was dealing with.

"So what *do* you do?"

"Breathe," I blurted in a bad German accent. "Eat. Fuck. Shit. Not necessarily in zat order."

I was quoting my landlord, Ursula, but Dude didn't know that. He looked over a muscular shoulder to the boys in the corner, perhaps wondering how he was going to get out of this bet but still save face.

" 'What do you do?' is the first question people in the States ask when they meet someone," I said. "No one asks that question in Europe.

It's considered rude. Over there, people don't want to be defined by their jobs. Over here, it's the only way most people define themselves. *I'm an i-banker. I'm a corporate lawyer. I'm in real estate*."

Dude's eyes glazed over, and not with booze. How could I ever expect this future titan of industry to understand?

"I'm in publishing."

It took a moment for Dude to realize that I wasn't speaking in faux first person anymore and that I had just informed him that I, Jenn-with-Two-N's, work in publishing.

"Oh. Like books?" Dude asked.

"A magazine."

"What magazine?"

"Well, it's really more of a journal than a magazine," I said. "I'm sure you've never heard of it."

"What? You think I don't read? You think I'm illiterate? I *do* go to Princeton, you know."

"I had no idea," I said dryly.

I also had no idea why I was still talking to Dude in this manner. Maybe it was because Dude was encouraging my antics by nodding his head vigorously, as if this whole conversation made perfect sense. Drunk is the universal language, the dipsomaniacal Esperanto, so he totally, *totally* got everything I was saying.

"So listen," Dude said, all business, all pleasure, all the time. "Since you're not waiting for anyone, maybe you'd like to join us."

"I don't think so," I announced as I stood up, smoothing out the wrinkles in my butter-colored Bermuda shorts with my palms. "I have to go break up with my boyfriend now."

Dude laughed harder than all his other laughs combined. He slapped his forehead in laughter, which sent his sunglasses falling to the floor. More laughter rang out from the corner table.

"Why are you laughing?"

"The way you said it," he replied as he not-so-stealthily gave my legs a once-over. " 'I have to go break up with my boyfriend now.' "

"I didn't think I was going to say it," I said, almost to myself. "It just came out."

"I have that devastating impact on the ladies," Dude boasted, pretending to mock his own sexiness.

I really hadn't intended for Dude to be the first to know. It only took a nanosecond for my mind to catch up to my mouth, but it was a nanosecond too late. It was a relief, in a way. Putting feelings into words makes them so. Once words are spoken (or written . . .) they take on a greater significance. With this slip, I suddenly felt that readiness I'd been missing all morning. It wasn't liquid courage, it was the real thing: *I'm here to break up with Marcus. That's why I'm here.*

I considered what could have happened next, if I wanted to.

I thought about lifting myself up on my tiptoes and leaning into Dude's face. I thought about breathing in his sweet-and-sour scent of citrus shaving cream and perspiration. I thought about his mouth opening to say something unnecessary and mine clamping over his to shut him up. I thought about a mushy kiss with a mealy banana mouthfeel.

Making out with Dude could've been a harbinger of all the horrible hook-ups to come. It could've proven that I wasn't looking to get involved with someone else right now, I was just looking to get out of the involvement I was already in. But I didn't need to kiss Dude to confirm this truth. Kissing Dude is something I might have done when I was in college (okay, something I *did* do in college), but I knew better now. So instead of making out with Dude, I made my exit.

"Wait! Where are you going? Can I get your number?" His cell was out and ready.

I walked away to the sound of Dude's halfhearted protests, leaving him behind to pay up for one piece of ass he shouldn't have wagered on.

two

I teetered out of the dimly lit bar and was assaulted by the sunlight.

It should be dark right now, I thought. It should be midnight and not . . . 1:39 P.M. Your first meeting had ended at one P.M. You had another meeting at three-thirty. I had one hour and fifty-one minutes left.

Official Orientation begins next week, and classes another week after that. But you were so eager to get everything you could out of your Princeton experience, you arrived early for the Frosh Trip, one week of hiking, kayaking, tent-pupping, and bonding with hundreds of other first-year students in the wilds of the tri-state area. You assured me that Outdoor Action is a very popular program, and I still can't help but wonder if its attractiveness to the majority of the eighteen-year-old attendees has something to do with its prurient sex-in-the-wilderness connotations.

I had no trouble finding your dorm because as undeniable luck would have it, you were assigned to Blair Hall—the oldest Collegiate Gothic dorm on campus and the most iconic. With its stone facade, imposing four-corner turrets, and famed archway, it looks like nothing less than a castle. It was impossible for me to miss, even in my somewhat inebriated state. When we'd moved you in earlier that morning, it struck me as absurd that students would actually live there, yet appropriate that one of them was you.

I was drawn to the noise of a volleyball game in progress on a stretch of sand near the castle that served as the campus beach. I envisioned row after row of nubile bodies in bikinis, as if this were a junior college in Fort Lauderdale and not one of the most esteemed and difficult-to-get-into universities in the world. As I made my meandering approach, I spotted you with ball in hand in the serving position—an impressive figure stretching several inches taller than any other player on the court. You were shirtless, as you often were since returning from the desert, and your lean, sinewy muscles were shiny with sweat. You're the rarest of redheads, unfreckled, with skin that turns red first, then browns in the sun. Your ropy dreads had grown past your shoulders and bounced along with your every move.

And then there was the Beard.

You had all but given up on shaving, and the result was a (forgive me) scuzzy, neck-to-nose beard/sideburns combo. At its best, the Beard was sort of bohemian and Ginsbergian. But it more closely resembled that which is usually seen on the faces of crazy homeless men or even crazier Islamic fundamentalists, or lately, the batshit crazy Mel Gibson. When it got too mangy and unmanageable, even for you, the Beard was attacked with a pair of cuticle scissors. A Weedwacker would've been more efficient. The Beard was, without question, aesthetically unappealing and hygienically unsound, two factors that distinguished it from the very deliberate and totally played-out hipster beards that plagued Lower Manhattan and certain Brooklyn neighborhoods in the mid-2000s.

Between the overgrowth of facial hair and the overlong dreads, I estimated that I could see only about one quarter of your face. Your kaleidoscopic eyes—always-shifting patterns of green and brown and hazel—still mesmerized, even from afar. Even when they were focused on the ball and not on me. Patches of sand stuck to your sweaty knees, forearms, and chest. I wanted to slide my body against yours until every grain succumbed to gravity, helpless.

Yes, the sight of you swinging your arm, serving the ball, made me dizzy. Even with the Beard. Even with the words I had just spoken out loud to Dude.

And I wasn't alone. On the opposite side of the net was a constellation of starry-eyed teenagers in shrunken prepster polos or cleavage-heaving camis, their tawny or milky white legs curled under microscopic denim, each one in full swoon over what it would be like to lose her virginity to you. And that included those who weren't virgins anymore.

I wanted to end the suspense. "He'll make you come the first time," I could've said with authority. "And every time thereafter." This wasn't exactly true, but it *felt* true, which was true enough. How many thereafters have there been? I lost count long ago.

(Sometimes when making love, I'd grip your face and force you to look at me just to confirm that you were still there, and I was still there, and that we were still there together. Sometimes I would gasp, "We're still here." And you would whisper back, "Yes. We're still here." You always knew exactly what I meant.)

Given what I was about to do, it was not unreasonable to think that you would eventually get around to having sex with one of these girls. I wondered if any of them were your type. I wondered if you even had a type. Your number hovers around forty, so I don't think I'm being an unreasonably jealous girlfriend when I doubt that you have a "type," unless "has a vagina" can be classified as a type.

I looked them over and tried to select the flower that would be first plucked from among this rosy bouquet. Her, I thought. It will be her. The sloe-eyed, pale-skinned dirty-blonde of indeterminate race. (Do you remember her? Do you?) She was pretty, but not at all perfect, with two ever-widening rings of armpit sweat soaking through the tissue-thin cotton of her shirt.

Yes, I thought. Marcus would go for a girl like her. This outcome felt okay to me. It was strangely comforting to know that my actions wouldn't devastate you, and that you'd be able to get over me and move on.

I was having trouble breathing, the air was so humid with pheromones.

The full weight of drunkenness was settling deep into my limbs.

The crowd cheered and the game was over.

You had served the winning point.

Hooray.

You loped over to me and pressed your mouth to mine with the fair amount of force necessary just to get through the Beard. Sometimes it was like kissing a scouring pad. My face from the mouth down was scrubbed raw and red, but I ignored the irritation.

"Hey," I said. I reached out for the sand trapped in the strands of your chest hair, which was darker than that on your face or on your head. I freed the granules with my fingertips. You made note of my touch with a smile, but you didn't bother brushing the rest of the sand off your body. You cocked your head in my direction and a single dread swung and hit my cheek. You reflexively soothed the spot with your thumb, eyebrows flattening in a silent, *Are you okay?*

I silently lied, *Yes, I'm fine.*

"Everyone, this is my girlfriend," you said. Your hand pressed the small of my back as you presented me to the crowd. "This is Jessica."

(Did you notice that you introduced me as your girlfriend first and Jessica next? Did anyone else?)

"Hey, um, everyone," I muttered. I wanted to keep the conversation to a minimum, to disguise that I was totally shit-canned in the middle of this brilliant afternoon. And also because I could not have cared less about getting to know Everyone. Everyone consisted of about a dozen eighteen-year-olds whose names I heard and promptly forgot, with the obvious exception of the freshmeat you would use to get over me.

"I'm Marjorie," she said, her heart-shaped face flushed with youthful ebullience.

(How is Marjorie these days?)

My clairvoyance made me feel superior, and I tried not to let on that I knew what would happen between you two.

I turned to you. "Can we go to your room?"

Giggly twitters agitated the air. The question "Can we go back to your room?" is tantamount to foreplay on college campuses. And even those first-years who had enjoyed certain freedoms because of boarding schools or absentee parents were suddenly reminded of one of the greatest promises of the next four years: *We can fuck whenever we want to!*

"Sure," you replied, unconcerned. Then to the children: "Later."

And they all enthusiastically agreed that yes, they would be seeing you later. You already had plans that did not involve me. As it should be. Would be. Will be.

You took my hand as we walked across the sand.

"They're all so young."

"They're all adults."

I snickered. "I'm twenty-two and I'm not an adult."

"That's you," you said, pushing open the door to your room. "Not them."

Your tone was light, and it reminded me how much I've missed hearing you talk.

I told myself then that I couldn't possibly miss your voice any more from seventy-five miles away than I did when you were walking right beside me.

three

We entered the wood-paneled carrel that will be your home away from home for the next academic year. Your roommate, an eighteen-year-old named Nathaniel "Natty" Addison who had come to Princeton, New Jersey, all the way from Mobile, Alabama, was sitting cross-legged on his bed, tapping away at his laptop.

"Hey, y'all."

I was born and raised in the Garden State, yet I have never, ever pronounced my homeland as "Joisey." But good ol' Natty proved that not all Southerners are Dixie Hicks, but some really do say "y'all." Young Natty was barely taller than me, and slight, which meant that he was dwarfed by you in every way. He had rosy cheeks, a sprinkling of freckles across his nose, and shaggy blond hair. I wanted him to spout off charming red-state aphorisms in his disarming drawl—you know, deep-fried wisdom about airborne bovines or armless skeeter-beaters that make no sense to Northern ears but sound just so goldanged adorable. I just wanted to sit and listen to him talk and talk and talk.

I met Young Natty's parents briefly that morning during the move-in. His dad was an alum, Princeton Class of 1970, a doctor whose substantial belly and crimson face were at odds with his profession. He looked more like a suckling pig on a spit than the go-to guy for medical advice. Young Natty's stepmother was about twenty years his father's junior, and most of her remastered face and body were significantly younger than that. Her lips were inflated into such a trout pout that I didn't know whether to offer lip gloss or tarter sauce. Mrs. Addison hadn't mentioned her career, but if this hot-rollered platinum blonde wasn't a former beauty queen—Miss Alabama Blackberry 1985—then she had tragically missed her true calling. Dr. and Mrs. Addison were professionally pleasant, and yet their rhinestone smiles couldn't hide the horror—oh, the horror—over their son's being randomly assigned to room with this hirsute and tattooed man of sketchy provenance and dubious sanitation who arrived on campus parentless, with little more than two dusty duffel bags and an unsmiling girlfriend. Perhaps Dr. Addison should have contributed a more substantive alumni gift to Princeton's coffers.

I gave you a look heavy with meaning. It's the type of look that only long-term couples understand, or half-understand in this case. You knew what I wanted you to say, but alas, not why I wanted you to say it.

"Natty?"

He looked up at you, then me, then again at you. I didn't get a gay vibe from Young Natty, but that wouldn't stop him from falling totally heterosexually in *luuurrrve* with you.

Young Natty caught on quickly. "Sho-wah thang," he said affably, but I'm pretty sure that he says everything affably. "Ah was a-baht finished up he-ah anah-ways." He slapped his laptop shut, grabbed his messenger bag, and headed out the door with a goofball grin. You offered a convivial pat on the shoulder as he passed.

"Thanks, man."

"Sho-wah thang," he said to you. Then to me: "Sho-wah was a pleh-shuh, Jess Darlin' . . ."

I blinked hard in disbelief.

Young Natty's words transported me back six years, to one of my first encounters with you, in the principal's office of Pineville High School. A cornball secretary, not usually graced by the presence of straight-A students with spotless transcripts, had just expressed surprise to see me. "Well, if it isn't Jess Darling!" Moments later, you—whom no one was ever surprised to see in the principal's office—mimicked her hokey delivery. "Ain't you Jess Darling?" But it came out sounding like "Ain't you jus' darlin'!" A drawling, Confederate mockery of my name.

Months later, when the Brainiac and the Dreg were talking every night on the phone yet still not acknowledging each other in school, you said my last name over and over and over again—*darlingdarlingdarlingdarling*—until it morphed into something else: Darlene. For a while, that was my nickname, which you claimed was a representation of my trashier alter ego. This was still a year before we slept together, and I'm sure you were using the powers of *nomen et omen* to hurry up and get inside my pants already.

I looked at you today, hoping for a mutual, miraculous remembrance that might have given me a reason not to fulfill the breakup prophecy. It was a futile wish, as I knew that such mind-melding was impossible, even among symbiotically entwined lovers, even among *soul mates*, as my thirteen-year-old self would have earnestly put it. And yet I was still disappointed to see no sign of the shared recollections, only you smiling at Young Natty's back as he bounded out the door.

"Marcus . . ."

"Jessica."

Then you dropped your shorts to the floor. You weren't wearing underwear, another luxury item disposed of during your retreat to Death Valley. So there was precious little to prevent what happened next and next and next: You placing your hands firmly on either side of my hips, and then pulling my shirt up over my head. Sliding down the length of my body, granules of sand roughing up my torso before falling away. Kneeling at my feet. Breathing hot on the sensitive gooseflesh around my navel. Unbuttoning, unzipping, and unburdening me of whatever clothing remained.

And me, surrendering to the last thereafter.

Middle-of-the-afternoon sex is notable for its complete lack of modesty. The window shades had minimal impact on blocking out the sun, and I was thoroughly and unself-consciously exposed in its light. I stretched my naked body before you, inviting you to do whatever you wanted, which was everything I wanted.

Your teeth nipping my lower lip. Your fingertip tracing the curve of my hip. Your tongue teasing the tender underside of my breast. Your nose nuzzling my innermost thigh. The Beard tickling nerve endings I couldn't locate. Cognition was overcome by sensation. . . . If I was thinking about anything, it was how I wish I wish I wish I could live my whole life within those exquisite moments of dumb pleasure right before I come. . . .

You murmured softly, not a word exactly, something untranslatable. The sound brought my brain back to my body. And once the corporeal/cognitive connection was restored, there was no way I would return to that blissful, dumbfucked state.

"Jessica?"

I knew what you were really asking. *We're still here . . . aren't we?*

No.

We were not. *I* was not.

I was elsewhere. And I wanted the erotic interlude to be brought to its end. What's more, I wanted it to end in a dramatic way, one that could've justified my intentions.

four

I don't hear the *click-click-click* of the lock.

Or see the door opening.

Or Young Natty's parents getting a clear, Kama Sutra view of you neck-deep in my nether regions.

"Ohhhhhhhmaaaaaaahhhhhhhhhhh!!!!!!!!!!!"

"Jayyyyyyysuuuuuuuhhhhhhhhhsssss!!!!!!!!!!!"

I freak *("OOOOOHHHHHFUUUUUUUUUUUUUUUUCK!")* and scramble under the sheets. You calmly remove yourself from my crotch and cover up with a pillow.

If you recall, when I walked in on my own parents catching lumpy humps on the couch at their condo a few years back, I still had the presence of mind to put aside my gut-churning horror and slam the door shut on the image that would haunt me for the rest of my life. In this dramatic scenario, Young Natty's parents don't have the sense to shut the door. No, they gawk and gawk and gawk some more, as if we are the first humans in recorded history to do what we are doing, as if no one before us has ever thought to unite mouth and vagina for the purposes of female pleasure, as if we have, in fact, just put our perverted minds and bodies together to invent the act of cunnilingus. And can you blame them? Because sometimes it *does* feel as if we have invented it and all intimacies. Our bodies surging and retreating in innumerable positions and countless combinations for us and us alone . . .

I imagine Dr. and Mrs. still *just standing there*, with no sign of bringing the awkwardness to its desperate end. No, only you can do that.

"Dr. and Mrs. Addison," you say in a surprisingly dignified tone considering the only thing separating Young Natty's parents from your formidable boner is a small foam-filled pillow that, quite frankly, is not up to the task. "Would you mind leaving us alone?"

I'm awestruck by your ability to collect yourself so quickly. But then I remember how my parents were so shamelessly unflustered when they reopened the door with their clothes on. I take this as a cue that those responsible for the interruptus have more reason to be embarrassed than those engaged in the coitus. Dr. and Mrs. Addison reach a similar conclusion and suddenly get all tangled up in a flurry of apologetic "Pahdons" and "Ahm so sorrys" as they make their (belatedly) hasty retreat from the room.

Young Natty gets much mileage out of the "On My First Day of College My Parents Busted My Roommate Going to Town on His Girlfriend" story. As a getting-to-know-you gambit on campus, that story is tough to beat. And just when the story starts getting old at Princeton, and he's told everyone he can possibly tell, he recycles it for his high school friends when he returns to Alabama on breaks. Oh yes. Such a tale can be told many times over.

five

But that's not what happened. That dramatic scenario only exists in my mind. (And now in this notebook.) As it really happened, the erotic interlude ended not dramatically at all, but modestly, with a whisper.

"Jessica?"

You had fully extracted yourself from my body and were sitting up in the sheets. I had no idea how long you'd been sitting like that, looking at me. You were slightly out of breath, and when the exhalation hit my face, my stomach twisted in recognition of the brackish scent I knew as my own. I turned my head away, disgusted.

I'd already decided that when I returned to Brooklyn, I would tell Hope this story, the real one, in its entirety. I wouldn't even censor the nasty bits. I've always refrained from discussing the most delicate details of our sex life because my love for you transcended dishy fuck-and-telling. But there was already a shift in my brain that said, *Nothing is sacred anymore*.

So I couldn't fall back on a histrionic deal breaker like the previously described dramatic scenario. I had to rely on the truth.

"I don't think I can do this."

You rested in the sheets, eyes closed, mouth open just wide enough to slip a pinkie finger inside. I couldn't see the airflow, no telltale rippling of nose hairs, but I imagined that you were breathing in one nostril and out the other like a master yogi.

"I don't think I can do this," I repeated in a momentary lapse of courage.

One eye winked open to give me a look that asked, without actually asking, *You can't do what?*

"I can't . . ."

"You can't do what?" you said, this time out loud.

(If you had any idea what I was about to say, it didn't show in your eyes. And I was looking carefully. Did you know? I was searching for a hint anywhere on your face that revealed that you'd seen this coming. That you, too, thought it was inevitable and the best thing to do under the circumstances. But all I saw was you, unexpecting, and eager to hear what I'd say next.)

"I can't be . . ."

The words hung there, suspended by an argument-in-progress that passed under the open window.

"Ninja, dude. *Ninja.*"

"But, dude, wait. Seriously. What if . . . ?"

"What if I don't give a shit? *Ninja.*"

"What if they fought on the open sea?"

"For the love of fuck! A NINJA WILL KICK A PIRATE'S SWASHBUCKLING ASS EVERY GODDAMN TIME."

I paused. It wasn't the dramatic scenario I'd had in mind, but it would suffice. This overheard inanity perfectly supported what I was about to say.

"I can't be the girlfriend of a college freshman."

You considered this for a moment. Your smile dimmed but had not faded entirely from your face.

"Jessica, you'd be the girlfriend of . . ." You pursed your lips in contemplation before finishing. "Me." Then your face crumpled under the awkwardness of the phrase. Was this the longest sentence you'd uttered all day? All week? In a month? Eight months?

"And *you* are a college freshman," I said. "A twenty-three-year-old college freshman."

"That's not all I am."

"Of course that's not all you are," I said. "But it's going to be a big part of who you are until next year, when you're a twenty-four-year-old college sophomore, until the year after that, when you're a twenty-five-year-old junior—"

"I understand, Jessica."

"I don't think you do." And then more firmly: "You don't."

And you sucked in your breath as if you had just been tackled by someone twice your size.

"I know what's going to happen here, Marcus."

"You do?"

"Yes," I said, "I do."

"Enlighten me," you said with a tease to your tone.

"You're going to find that there's a certain cachet to being the old guy on campus."

"Jessica . . ."

"Seriously, Marcus, you'll get a campus nickname. Like 'the Buddha' or something. And when you walk around campus, other first-years from Outdoor Action will point you out, like, 'Hey, there goes the Buddha. He's twenty-three years old and he's a freshman.' And everyone will be really interested in the whole Marcus mythology and how you ended up here. Like, 'Hey, did you know that the Buddha meditates twice a day? And he did this silent meditation where he didn't speak to anyone for like *years*, including six months on a ranch in Death Valley? And he screwed his way through high school and was like this undiscovered genius, and oh shit, yeah, I almost forgot, he spent time in drug rehab when he was like seventeen, and he's just like the coolest fucking dude, you know?' "

I knew I was right. It wouldn't take much to become a legend here on this preppy little campus in this quaint little town. Columbia is in New York City, a place that isn't exactly lacking in distinctive characters. While I was there, a guy known as Bathrobe Boy gained notoriety simply because he couldn't be bothered to get dressed for class. Then there were the Carman Twins, who achieved no small measure of campus popularity simply because—you guessed it—they were genetically identical. And you certainly had a lot more noteworthy and/or notorious aspects of your personal history to get tongues wagging.

But you were unmoved. You fiddled with the silver ring hanging from the leather string around your neck. You pressed it over your eye and wore it like a monocle as you read the hidden words soldered inside: MY THOUGHTS CREATE MY WORLD. You had made it with your own hands, out of an old quarter.

Finally you spoke.

"I'm not a Buddhist. I'm a deist who practices Vipassana meditation."

"Buddhist! Deist! Whatever!"

"Are you drunk?"

"No," I said too quickly. "Maybe."

You sighed. "I tasted it when we kissed."

I felt guilty, knowing that the only alcohol you've touched since sobering up at seventeen is that which stubbornly clings to my own tongue. Your observation was apropos of nothing. And, well, everything. And so I responded with another non sequitur.

"Why Princeton? Why now?"

I had wanted to ask this question since late last January, when you first told me about your acceptance.

"It's one of the best schools in the world. And I'm not too far from my parents, and with my dad . . ."

My gaze dropped to the floor, as it always did when you mentioned your dad, which wasn't often.

You continued with a shrug of your shoulders. "So why not?"

"I can think of many reasons why not," I replied. "It doesn't make any sense that you're going here."

"I got in. It makes sense."

You smoked out most of your brain cells before you were seventeen years old, and yet you still have enough left over to outscore 99 percent of standardized-test takers. (Myself included.) And your, shall we say, untraditional background must have appealed to Princeton's admissions officers, who have been trying for years to undo the school's reputation for being a bastion of WASPiness. And they succeeded, according to the headline in one of the local papers: CLASS OF 2010 MOST DIVERSE IN UNIVERSITY HISTORY. And yet if Dude and his friends are a fair representation, it's a homogenous kind of diversity, which makes you a shoo-in for next year's catalog. It will be you, a dark-skinned female, an Asian male, and another female blinging a Star of David—a multicultural quartet clutching weighty academic tomes and rocking tiger-themed finery on loan from the bookstore.

So yes, you were accepted early decision to the number one school in the nation when applications were at an all-time high. You deserve to be there. But, as you know, that's not what I meant about not making sense.

"You being here is like an extensive form of performance art. Like you're going to be *'Marcus Flutie, twenty-three-year-old Princeton freshman.'* In italics, wrapped in quotations."

You rested your head against the pine-paneled wall. "Don't we all live our life in italics, wrapped in quotations?"

I thought about Jenn-with-Two-N's.

"Well, I don't think I like this version of me," I said. "The one in which I'm your *old* girlfriend, old in both meanings of the word."

"You're not old."

"To these eighteen-year-olds I am! I'm like a campus cougar. . . ." I curled my hands into claws and *grrrrrrowled*. "Prowling Princeton for some hot young tiger tail."

Your abdominal muscles squeezed and released in low-belly laughter.

"And you won't want to visit me because you hate the city."

You opened your mouth to protest, but I wouldn't let you.

"You know it's true! It *is* true. You hate the noise. The dirt. The pace. You were miserable whenever you visited me in the city. . . ."

"I had other reasons to be miserable."

"I know," I lied.

six

The truth is, I don't know much about your misery at all.

You knew all about your dad's illness when you miraculously reappeared on my parents' doorstep last Christmas Eve—the proverbial lost shepherd in a wool peacoat and ski hat—almost two years to the day since I'd last seen or spoken to you. You knew all about it when we made love less than twenty-four hours after that reunion. You knew about it four days later when Hope and I departed for our monthlong road trip.

In retrospect, there was something tentative about the way you handed over my going-away gift. I was struck then by your shyness, something in the way your eyes skimmed the sidewalk, the sad, downward slope of your shoulders as you presented the red raw silk box containing this blank notebook and eleven others, the Death Valley diaries, filled with your observations of life in the desert without me. I had assumed you were grieving a little bit about me, over saying good-bye again so soon after our sweet reunion. But I was wrong. Your morose mood had nothing to do with me, but with the secret of your father's sickness, which you only reluctantly revealed upon my return. I can't understand why you waited, or why you have rarely spoken of it since.

So I was lying when I said I knew why you were so miserable. I have no idea what it's been like for you for the past eight months, living at home in Pineville, helping your parents cope with the diagnosis and its aftermath. I don't know because you wouldn't tell me.

seven

You hadn't made a move. Sun sliced through spaces in the blinds, and the light slashed in diagonals across your naked torso.

"You keep encouraging me to tread the middle path, but I know from our past that you, Marcus Flutie, are an all-or-nothing proposition for me." I cleared my throat. "I'm tired of only seeing you a few weekends a month. I don't want that kind of relationship anymore."

You gave yourself a few moments of deep breathing before finally responding.

"You don't want to visit on the weekends."

"No."

"Then move here and be with me every day." You clasped your hands behind your head. Problem solved.

"Move?" I snorted. "*Here?*"

"We can live off campus—"

I cut him off. "I'm not giving up my life in New York just to be your girlfriend. I've finished college, Marcus. And if I wanted to relive the experience, I would have applied to grad school."

(I am a liar. And a bad one at that. I would love to relive the experience. I am desperately envious of everyone who is currently living or reliving the experience.)

There was a pause. Then a puckish smile played on your lips. "You say you can't be the girlfriend of a college freshman."

"Right."

"There's another choice."

"I know," I said sadly. "Which is why I made this difficult decision. . . ."

"*Another* choice."

And that's when you slipped out of bed, got down on one knee, and took my left hand in yours.

"Don't move here just to be my girlfriend," you said.

You pulled the leather necklace over your head and slid the silver ring onto my fourth finger. Then you said two words I never I imagined I'd hear from anyone, let alone Marcus Flutie.

"Marry me," you said.

These are the most absurd words I have ever heard.

eight

I have never been the type of girl who dreams about this moment. I have never been the type of girl who envisioned the love of my life getting down on one knee on the observation deck of the Empire State Building. Hiding the diamond in a crystal dish of tiramisu. Skywriting. JumboTron. Rose petals spread across a hotel bed. I have never entertained fantasies about any of those once-clever, now-cliché ways for a man to ask a woman to marry him. You already know this about me, which is why you could so easily satirize what most females consider a sacred act.

A betrothal, even one as simple as yours, is a pretty theatrical gesture. And you love theatrics. I think of you at seventeen, fresh out of rehab and standardized-tested into the realm of misunderstood genius, making your debut in our junior honors classes wearing an über-nerdy jacket and tie. You've always gotten a lot of shock value out of embracing, and thereby subverting, the mainstream. Young marriage has come full circle, from an act of tradition (marrying to unite family assets), to an act of rebellion (marrying to escape the family), back to tradition (marrying to have a family), and now rebellion once more (marrying because why the fuck not?). What's more punk rock than getting married? Why else would so many barely legal celebrity skankbots make and break so many engagements?

So that's *all* your proposal was to me at that point, just another entertaining act in the ongoing performance art of being Marcus Flutie.

"Marry me," you repeated.

"Sure!"

"Sure?"

You were skeptical of my speedy acquiescence.

"Sure! I'll marry you and we can adopt Young Natty and raise him as our own!"

"I refuse to be fazed by your sarcasm," you said. "Marry me, and we'll work out the details later."

"Okay, Marcus. Har-dee-har-har. Game over."

"This isn't a game."

"You're trivializing what was not an easy decision for me. . . ."

"I wouldn't call a marriage proposal trivial."

"It is when you're asking me to marry you just so I won't break up with you!"

"I'm simply following your all-or-nothing rule."

"What are you talking about?"

"Let's choose all over nothing."

You wanted to get a reaction out of me and you were succeeding on a biological level. My palms were sweating, my pupils were dilating, my nostrils were flaring. And goddiggitydammit, my heart was booming.

"Don't take this the wrong way . . . ," I began.

"I'll try not to."

"But I can think of a bizillion reasons why marrying you is the worst idea ever."

"Now, how could I possibly take that the wrong way?" You smiled. "Just give me five."

"One: You are a twenty-three-year-old college freshman. Two: I don't want to move to Princeton and you hate New York. Hello? It's 2006, not 1956! That makes three. And you're only asking me to marry you because you don't want me to break up with you. Four. And then there's number five." I took a bracing breath. "I don't even believe in marriage."

(Not only do I not believe in marriage, but when I looked down at my newly adorned finger, I couldn't stop myself from conjuring morbid till-death-do-us-part metaphors, like *The leather string hangs from the ring like a slackened noose*. How's that for romantic?)

When it was clear that you were just going to keep smiling at me, I was forced to fill the silence with stupidity.

"I mean, there's a reason it's called the *institution* of marriage. . . ."

You mercifully cut me off before I finish the hackneyed joke about the mental instability of brides and grooms.

"Okay, you can think of—how many was it, a bizillion?—reasons why you shouldn't marry me. But I can think of one reason why you should."

"And what is that?"

The sun had shifted through the slats, adorning your serene, smiling face with an orangey-gold halo.

"Forever."

You said it without hesitation. "Forever" is how you have signed most of your correspondences with me, from your short entry in my senior yearbook ("There is nothing that I can write in here that I won't be able to tell you in person. . . .") to the dedication to this very notebook. But it's the as-of-yet unwritten FOREVER that immediately sprung to mind.

nine

Your postcards are tacked to a corkboard beside my bed, picture-side up. The seven images are:

1. A medical eye chart
2. A starry sky
3. A globe with the words *nuestro mundo*
4. Brassaï's *Couple d'amoureux dans un petit café* (Paris, c. 1932)
5. Sands slipping through an hourglass
6. ©
7. The National Organization of Women logo

The underside of each postcard is hidden from view. If you were to remove one card from the wall and turn it over, it would reveal one word in your feminine cursive. If you pulled out all the pushpins from all the cards, flipped them over and lined them up in the order in which they were received, it would reveal the message that eluded me during your silent years, a message you built one word and one postcard at a time:

I WISH OUR LOVE WAS RIGHT NOW

The eighth card is not with the others up on the wall because it's not mine. It's yours, the only postcard written to you from me, with the significant word in my own sloppy scrawl.

AND

"AND" represented my faith that there would be more to come for you and me, even if I didn't know what it was. I mailed you that cheapo promo postcard from an A&P supermarket outside Virginville, Pennsylvania, the first (and final) stop on Hope's and my cross-country tour of creatively named cities. I sent it not knowing if you would even be waiting for me in Pineville when I returned at the end of the month, or if you would be off meditating on a mountaintop halfway around the world. Either outcome seemed both probable and even preferable in their own way.

I remember sprinting to the mailbox as Hope honked impatiently in the parking lot, her ninety-nine-cent Ambervision sunglasses slipping down the bridge of her nose, a strawberry Twizzler dangling out of her mouth. Hope and I had a lot of highway to cover in Pennsylvania, having already set our sights on its cities named Blue Ball, Muff, Dick, and finally, at long last, Intercourse. Of course, we never made it to any of these sexually suggestive destinations, because less than twelve hours after you handed me this notebook, and only a half hour after I stuck the stamp on that postcard, our car got jacked and our trip came to its infamous end.

You *were* there when I got back, thirty days ahead of schedule. That's when you finally told me about your dad, and explained why you couldn't stay with me in the city for more than a weekend at a time. And for the next eight months, I tried (oh, I tried) to make good on my postcard promise, to let our relationship evolve in the open-ended spirit of AND.

Is it any surprise that you would want the final word?

FOREVER.

A rabble of butterflies swarmed inside my stomach.

FOREVER.

How could I possibly follow up FOREVER?

BUT

HOWEVER

UNFORTUNATELY

?

ten

I stalled.

"Aren't Buddhists against forming attachments?" I was flailing. "Because . . . uh . . . attachments lead to longing . . . which is . . . uh . . . the cause of all human suffering?" I smiled weakly.

"Yes; samsara, or suffering, is caused by clinging to something that should be free," you explained patiently. "But I'm not a Buddhist."

"I know!" I retorted. "You're a deist who practices Vipassana meditation."

"Right."

"What about the Four Abodes?"

"What about them?"

"I thought you were totally into the Four Abodes. . . ."

(I said it exactly like that, too. *I thought you were totally into the Four Abodes.* As if you had suddenly switched allegiances from teenybopper pop to hardcore hip-hop. *But wait! I thought you* were totally into *Ashlee Simpson!*)

"Well, I think we could all learn from them. They're guidelines for living that anyone can follow. Buddhism is very humanist in that regard."

As much as this kind of talk usually irked me, it was a relief to see you having *so much fun*. Not even the Beard could mask the childlike exuberance of your smile, one I hadn't seen in a very long time. I could see what you looked like when you were Marin's age, a daredevilish four-year-old sprinting away from your poor mother in the most crowded shopping malls, or clambering up the tallest trees to limb-dance on the highest branches.

Before we could commence our psycho-theological discussion, there was a knock at the door.

"Hey, y'all!" Young Natty called from outside the door. "Ah foh-gaht mah say-yell phone."

"It's our boy," Marcus said.

"Har-dee-har-har." I hopped out of bed, grabbed my T-shirt and shorts.

"Y'all finished up in they-yah?"

You were still unclothed, still on your knee, on the floor. Only the awkward pose didn't seem funny or fake. Your nakedness made you appear more real, more vulnerable, and more profoundly human than ever.

"Almost," I croaked.

"So?" Marcus asked.

There was something about this absurdist comedy of a conversation that stirred up my most sentimental longings for us as a couple. Maybe it's because this was the longest uninterrupted conversation we'd had in months. Despite the fact that there was only one logical answer to this question, I couldn't say it.

"I think I need to think." I took off the ring-on-a-string and handed it back to him.

"Just don't think too much."

"That's like telling me not to breathe too much," I argued.

You sighed as you often do when there's fresh evidence that I couldn't find the path to enlightenment even if the Dalai Lama himself planted a GPS device in my (nonexistent) soul.

"Observe emotions objectively as they rise and pass," you suggested. "Don't turn away from unpleasant feelings. Be receptive, but not reactive. . . ."

I tried not to roll my eyes at all this meditation talk. None of it has ever made much sense to me. I can't stop my mind from thinking what it thinks, I can only stop myself from sharing those thoughts with others. Isn't passing *silent* judgment a cornerstone of civilized society? This is why I've kept my journal private all these years.

(Until now. But you asked for it.)

Another knock from Young Natty. *"Helloooooooo?"*

You chewed on the leather to undo the knot that usually rested on the nape of your neck. You removed the ring from the necklace, took my hand, and put it back on the fourth finger of my left hand.

"This always belonged to you."

"I was just thinking that . . ."

My voice trailed off, shamed by the memory of me childishly thrusting that ring back in your face.

" 'My thoughts create my world,' " I had seethed. "I'm so tired of being scrutinized through your goddamn third eye!"

That fight, as you know, precipitated your two-year disappearance. During my junior and senior years at Columbia, your contact with me consisted solely of those enigmatic postcards. You started keeping the Death Valley Diaries, of course, only I didn't know that then.

All that time, you wore the ring, my ring, around your neck. You wore it in my absence, and then after our reunion. You wore it knowing that it would one day return to its intended, when the moment was just right. (I WISH OUR LOVE WAS RIGHT NOW . . . AND . . .) The history of the ring lent a sense of preordainment to this spontaneous proposal. Had you planned it? And for how long?

"A week," you answered as you stepped back into your shorts.

At first I thought you had read my mind again. But then I realized my mistake.

"You'll be back from your trip in a week."

"A week."

I envisioned you mouthing this new mantra over and over as you manned a raft full of eighteen-year-olds downstream.

"Y'all?"

"I'm leaving now!" I said to Natty. And then to you: "I don't see how your proposal will suddenly make sense seven days from now."

"Jessica," you said, taking my face in your abraded hands. "I love you."

(For you it really is that simple, isn't it?)

"I would hope so," I replied, clinging to the humor in all this. "You just asked me to marry you."

"I'm serious about this."

"So am I," I replied. "Which is why I can't say yes."

You leaned in and locked eyes. "It's also why you can't say no."

Before I could defend myself, you lowered your lips to suck on my earlobe. My clavicle. My parted lips. Your kisses scrambled my brain. They manipulated the solar system. They returned Marcus Flutie to the center of my universe. I was defenseless against your pre-Copernican pull.

"Y'all still in they-ah?"

We parted. I shouldered my bag and opened the door.

"Sho-wah was a play-shure meetin' ya, Jessica!"

I ignored Young Natty and focused on you.

"I love you, too."

But this hopeful farewell does little to bring peace of mind, even now. Loving you has never been the problem. What's troubling me is how loving you may never be enough.

And I have a week to find out why.

sunday: the third

eleven

When I woke up this morning, the first thought that registered was my position. I was on my stomach, legs splayed wide across sheets, arms reaching up and around my pillow. It's my preferred sleeping pose, one that is impossible to achieve when I'm squeezed into my twin-sized mattress with you, as I found out when I fitfully kneed and elbowed you through the seven nights leading up to your departure.

This sleeping position required the left side of my face to smoosh up against my pillowcase, which prompted the second thought in this particular sequence, in which I remembered my mother's stern warning that sleeping on my face would destroy my skin's elasticity, causing deep nasolabial creases and adding years, nay, decades to my appearance.

My customary first-thought-of-the-morning—*Goddamn, it's bright in here!*—was bumped to the third spot. As you know, Hope and I have dubbed our sublet bunk bedroom the Cupcake because it is decorated in the juvenile style preferred by its usual tenants, twelve-year-old twin girls whose preference for supersweet 'n' creamy pastels brings on excruciating visual toothaches. I imagine there's an ongoing flame war on ParkSlopeParent.com about how these sugary hues reinforce the gender stereotypes that are at the root of all female oppression. I don't know them, but I love the twins' two mommies for not giving in to the neighborhood dictum, even if that decision makes for unpleasantly cloying wake-ups.

The significance of the ring on the fourth finger of my left hand was, in fact, my fourth thought of the morning: *Marcus asked me to marry him*.

I slowly rolled over, looked up, and smiled. Grinning right back at me was none other than Kirk Cameron, so dreamy with his brown puppy-dog eyes, his signature mullet puffing up and over the popped collar of his acid-washed jacket. Kirk had a personal message for me, scribbled with a Sharpie.

JESSICA:

NO "GROWING PAINS," NO GAINS!

XO, KIRK

I love these messages. I look forward to them the way I used to look forward to getting Hope's daily e-mails, weekly phone calls, and monthly handwritten letters—the Totally Guilt-Free Guidelines for Keeping in Touch, as they were known—when she moved to Tennessee.

I thumped the top bunk with my foot.

"*Hope?*" I whispered to counterbalance the kicking, bringing the annoyance factor of this wake-up call down to a more forgivable level. But there was no sign of life coming from above.

I returned my gaze to Kirk's molten chocolate eyes. Hope and I had only recently inherited a whole archive of late-eighties teenybopper mags—*Teen Beat, Tiger Beat*—from my sister. They date back about fifteen years, to Bethany's middle school days, and were in one of the last boxes dragged out of long-term storage after she settled in Brooklyn Heights with her family. As a thirty-three-year-old wife and mother, Bethany determined that she was too grown up for "10 Things You Don't Know About Ralph Macchio," and it was finally time to let go of these remembrances of first lusts. Hope and I, at twenty-two, had no such delusions of maturity.

When we hauled them off, a wistful, slightly worried expression dinged my sister's delicate beauty. She regretted her decision to give them up. She tried to distract herself from the truth by pinching imaginary lint off her crisp pin-tuck capris, or fingertipping stray blond highlights back into place—both hereditary tics passed down from our mother.

"What's Ralph Macchio's favorite color?" Hope asked. "Anyone? Anyone?"

"You have visitation rights," I assured my sister as Hope and I lifted the cardboard box.

Bethany nodded brusquely before providing Hope with the correct answer.

"Ralph Macchio's favorite color is blue."

Hope originally said she wanted the magazines because she had some vague idea about using them in a collage commenting on teen celebrities as commodities and the fleeting nature of fame. My motivation made less sense. None of these former heartthrobs mean anything to me, not the teen-idols-turned-has-beens like Kirk and especially not the obscure never-weres like Scott Grimes. And yet I'm sort of fascinated by how important these "hunks" once were in my sister's life. She's eleven years older than I am, and I've always appreciated her generation's cheesy contributions to pop culture—the movies, the music, and now the magazines—more than my own. That tenuous pop cultural connection kept me from drifting away from my sister throughout the decade or so when our only other commonality was a nine-month stint in the same uterus.

I kicked again.

"Hope?!"

When she didn't answer, I bumped the volume up a notch.

"Hope? You there?"

I already knew she was there because a mass of orange curls dangled off the edge of the mattress. Even in the gentle early-morning light, Hope's genuine coloring resembled something not found in nature, like the chemicals added to any fake-Cheddar snack product.

"Hope?"

After my third attempt with no response, I decided to let her sleep. Hope needs all the rest she can get. She's working as an assistant for an event photography firm called Capture the Moment, so she's gone every Friday night, and usually double-booked on Saturdays and Sundays. Her weekdays are spent going over proofs and helping clients put together the albums that will help them remember that special day for the rest of their lives. All this work puts a major crimp in her own social life, but it's enabling her to pay her way through graduate school. In two years she'll have a master's in art therapy from Pratt, and she's planning to make a career out of working with physically and mentally disabled individuals of all ages. If Hope wasn't so damn likable, her do-gooding would make her the most annoying person I know. And in this city, sheer numbers make it impossible not to know a lot of annoying people.

When Hope's not dealing with psychotic brides, bat mitzvah brats, and not-so-sweet sixteeners, she and two other almost-starving artists share a so-called Swing Space, thanks to a grant provided by the Lower Manhattan Cultural Council. In this makeshift gallery/studio on Maiden Lane, once the site of a former office building, Hope is working on a series of paintings she doesn't want to talk about until her group show on Friday night—her first Friday off in three months! This reticence to discuss her works-in-progress, as far as I can see, is one of only two manifestations she exhibits of the tortured-artist cliché. The other is her full immersion in her work at the expense of food, sleep, and fun. Her breakneck creativity amazes and exhausts me.

Art spaces like these are obviously hard to come by, and even harder to hold on to, and I greatly admire the council's efforts to preserve and protect the city's creative class. The five boroughs are quickly being bought out by slumming fauxhemians, i-bankers, hedge funders, and their moneyed spawn. One day, not too far in the future, Hope and her poor, arty brethren might find themselves the last of their kind, left behind by those who have fled New York City for artistic colonies in the greener, cheaper pastures of Santa Fe, Portland, or Paducah.

But for now at least, Hope is here with me, snoozing away in the top bunk in our Park Slope sublet. Our bedroom—the Cupcake—is only ours for a year at most, after which it will return to Claire and Chloe. We are reminded of this fact every time we walk in the room because the twins' names loop into the flowers-and-vine design stenciled in strawberry mousse script onto the angel-cake walls.

I just nudged the mattress again.

I fell asleep before she came home last night, and didn't wake up upon her return. I suppose my impenetrable slumber was aided by the sleeping pill washed down with booze. Now, before you get too alarmed by the suicidal implications of my self-medicating, let it be known that the pill was all-natural melatonin from the organic pharmacy and the alcohol barely qualified as such because it was pink and came out of a box with an expiration date because that's all we had in the fridge. As an across-the-board abstainer, I know you worry about my use of mind-altering chemicals. But I doubt anyone has ever OD'd on a combination of herbs and "flavored wine product."

A car alarm bleated from across the street. Hope stirred, and flung a long leg over the side of the too-small mattress.

"Hope?" Another kick.

Nothing.

twelve

I gave up and got up. I pressed an ear to our bedroom door, listening for signs of life. When I didn't hear anything, I opened the door a crack and listened again. I determined that my housemates were either still asleep or not on the premises, so I tiptoed toward the kitchen, stupidly shushing the loose planks in the wood floor that creaked under my weight.

I leaned against the linoleum countertop, content that the only sound inside the apartment was the slurpy gurgle of the coffeemaker. I said my morning prayer: *Don't let them come until I finish my first cup.* Despite the rarity of such moments of solitude, I love my apartment. And not just because I thought my post-graduation mailing address would read something like: Jessica Darling, Kitchen-Aid Refrigerator Box, Flatbush Avenue, Brooklyn, NY 11215.

I am extremely fortunate to live in one of two bedrooms in an actual apartment with real (i.e., not cardboard) walls, located in the basement of a gorgeous brownstone. It's rent-stabilized and usually rented by an academic family whose matriarch is currently on a one-year sabbatical in Europe. And it even comes equipped with a colorful landlord character, Ursula, a fortysomething half-Swede, half-German former fashion model who considers it her lot in life to point out Americans' many flaws in vivid prose. For example, when I delivered the rent check the other afternoon, Ursula informed me that my eyebrows were all wrong. Besides plucking a few strays here and there, I've never given much thought to my eyebrows. But I dropped my head in wait for the wisdom Ursula could wield like a guillotine.

"Zey are like two desperate sperm trying to impregnate your eyeballs!"

The blond giantess turned on her boot heel and pounded up the stairs. I retrieved my head and carried it back down to the basement.

Maybe I've got a bad case of Stockholm syndrome, but I'm captivated by Ursula's cruel humor. I'm not surprised that you feel differently. When you were targeted by one of her insights/insults (something about dreadlocks and cockroaches?), you referred to Ursula as "Jotun."

"What?"

"Jotun. A fearsome Norse demigod, like those that suffer in the Asura realm in Buddhist culture."

I had no idea what you were talking about. But you had my rapt attention, as you always did whenever your sentences consisted of more than a three-word subject-verb-object construction.

"They mean well, but always do more harm than good."

I saw your point, then and now. Even when Ursula is on to something—and in the case of my eyebrows, I have noticed a certain spermy resemblance—her methods hurt more than they help. Still, I just can't help but love someone who could say something like that.

(How about you? Could you love someone who would say something like that? Oh, that's right. Whether you like it or not—and that's not even a question, now, is it?—you already do.)

thirteen

Knowing it won't last forever enhances our apartment's many pleasures. (I'm doing a commendable job of not worrying about finding a new place in exactly nine months and twenty-eight days.) Hope and I confirmed the first and best of said pleasures last spring as we sat on the front stoop waiting for our prospective housemates to arrive, before we had even set foot inside.

"According to this historical marker," Hope said, examining a small bronze plaque affixed to the front door, "this building really was home to the Swedish American Men's Sporting Society, more commonly known as S.A.M.S.S."

"SAMSS," I pronounced. "More familiarly known as Sammy."

Within thirty seconds, even before we had crossed the threshold, Hope and I had already invented a nickname for our future home. Though Hope and I had never before given much though to Sweden or its fine people, we were entranced by the prospect of living where muscle-bound Brooklyn Vikings once worked themselves into a sweat.

"Do you think Ursula is really serious about the fifty-percent rule?" Hope asked. "Will I be quizzed on all things Swedish?"

The academic family has been officially on the lease for fifteen years—and they still are. Ursula could have terminated their contract when they left for sabbatical in Europe, and made some minor renovations to jack up the rent to its ridiculously high market value. But Ursula, despite her hostile exterior, does have a heart. She's loyal to her renters, and sort of sees their family as an extension of her own, so she agreed to sublet the apartment for the next year under one strange condition: Fifty percent of the occupants had to come from Swedish stock. Apparently, such pro-Scandinavian discrimination isn't considered xenophobic when it's in the name of historical preservation and rent stabilization. It's one of those strange New York stories that I would never believe if I were not personally involved.

I spun around. "Quick! Who's your favorite Swede?"

"Hmm," Hope said, giving the question its due consideration. "A toss-up between Ingmar Bergman and Astrid Lindgren."

"Oh." I knew Bergman, of course, having studied his suicidal black-and-white films for a fun fun fun seminar titled "Cinematic Expressions of Existential Crisis." I had no clue who Astrid Lindgren was. I'd find out later that Astrid Lindgren was the author of the Pippi Longstocking books. I never read them, but Hope loved them as a kid, mostly because she and the titular character are both redheads. At the time I didn't get the chance to ask about Astrid because Hope had already volleyed the question right back at me.

"Who is *your* favorite Swede?"

"I'm not the one representin' Scandinavia," I said. "I'm gonna big-up to all my Anglo-Scotch-Irish boo-boos in the UK!"

"Holla," Hope said like the honky she is.

"Favorite Swede," I mused, tapping my finger to my temple. "Favorite Swede . . . There's just so many to choose from." Then after a moment I snapped my fingers. "I got it!"

"Who?"

(Do you, Marcus, know my favorite Swede? Take a guess. Don't peek. I'll start on a fresh page to keep up the suspense.)

fourteen

"The Swedish Chef."

(Did you get it right? Or did you guess another Swede? Did you guess Max Martin? Max Martin was the mastermind behind the catchiest late-nineties teen pop. He wrote contagious hits for all the boy bands: *NSYNC, Hum-V, and yes, the Backstreet Boys. "Quit Playing Games with My Heart." "Show Me the Meaning of Being Lonely." "I Want It That Way." We all owe a great debt to Max Martin for these audio viruses and so many more.

You were wearing a Backstreet Boys T-shirt outside the principal's office when you drawled *Jess Darlin'*. I *think* you were wearing that T-shirt, or that's how I remember it. If you were to ask me to name my favorite Swede, I would say Max Martin because you used to come to school with Kevin, Nick, A.J., B-Rok, and Howie D. on your chest. You were wearing T-shirts ironically before anyone in our high school even realized that one *could* wear clothing ironically. I was alone in my appreciation of the joke. Yes, for you my answer would have been Max Martin. But you're not the one who asked.)

For the next few minutes Hope and I tested the limits of childishness by singsonging nonsense like the cleaver-welding Swede from *The Muppet Show*.

"*Yorn desh bern, dor reett dor geet der du,*" sang Hope.

"*Urn deesh, dee bern deesh, dee urr,*" sang I.

"*Bork! Bork! Bork!*" we sang together.

"*Sprangten unga teem der muken* Swedish pancakes?" I asked.

"*Der muken* Swedish pancakes?" Hope asked.

And then I reminded her, in English, about the Swedish pancakes her mother used to make whenever I slept over her house.

"My mother never made Swedish pancakes."

"Yes she did! They were sort of like crepes. Thin and golden brown with crispy edges. And she would dust them with confectioners' sugar—"

And then I suddenly stopped myself. Hope's older brother used to snort sugar off our pancakes with a curly straw, flinging his rangy frame around the kitchen, banging his body into countertops and appliances in imitation of a crazed, coked-up *SNL* cast member. Six months after the last time I remember him doing this routine, Heath was dead from mainlining a bad batch of heroin. Had it been insensitive for me to so casually mention the sugar? Did the memory of her dead eighteen-year-old brother leap to Hope's mind at the time? Of course, it's too late to undo a conversation from four months ago.

And if the memory had stung, she didn't let on. She stopped humming "Dancing Queen" only long enough to correct my mistake.

"My mother made German pancakes."

She was perched on the bottom step like a frog on a lily pad, her long legs bent and splayed out wide as she hunched over the ever-present sketchbook resting between her feet. Her hand never stopped moving, her eyes didn't lift from the half-finished sketch of a homemade rain-smeared sign taped to the nearest corner stoplight. In the sketch, as on the sign that inspired it, the central image was blurred beyond recognition. Only one word was legible: **LOST.**

"Really?" I asked. "Are you sure?"

"*Ja,*" she replied.

"How are German pancakes different from Swedish pancakes?"

"I have no idea," she replied, tapping her pencil. "Maybe they don't have as many sex partners?"

"And they're really bureaucratic. . . ."

Memory is a strange thing. I distinctly remembered those pancakes as being Swedish. Why would my mind randomly swap Swedish for German? After we discovered that our landlord was, in fact, Swedish-German, there was a brief, embarrassing moment where I thought my memory slip might really be evidence of an underdeveloped form of ESP. And then I literally smacked myself on the forehead for being suckered into one of the human brain's most common contrivances, one that gives deep significance to mere coincidence.

"I think that if we get to live here, we need to be more respectful of the many contributions the Swedes have made to our culture," I said seriously.

"We will sing 'Dancing Queen' and other ABBA songs," Hope suggested.

"And Ace of Base. . . ."

"And we will eat many Swedish fish. . . ."

And so it went. The apartment had already become a part of our history.

Instant inside jokes were reason alone for renting the place, even before we found out that our basement apartment had served as the *bowling alley* for the Swedish American Men's Sporting Society, which explains why it's very long and very thin. And also very dark, since Swedes are genetically accustomed to getting little sunlight.

Sammy comes completely if unimaginatively furnished by the Swedish geniuses from IKEA. Behold our overstuffed Olga couch with the celery green Fjeliin slipcover! Our Nökskaagen steamer trunk/coffee table and stainless-steel Måkdorrpvat bookshelves! And Sammy boasts a washer and dryer stacked on top of each other and located in the bathroom in what would normally serve as a linen closet. I don't have to subject myself to the indignity of dragging my dirty duffels to the Laundromat! Imagine! Who knew such luxuries could be afforded to someone so desperately in debt?

The only possible downside to our apartment is the neighborhood.

In this overwhelming, real-estate-obsessed metropolis, you are your neighborhood. People make instantaneous assumptions about who you are based solely on your address. Everyone does it. It's a necessity in this city of eight million, an instant ID badge that defines you as a member of a more select community among the masses teeming in anonymity.

It reminds me of what I've heard about huge public universities, where first-year students feel pressured to rush a fraternity or sorority because it's the easiest way to develop an on-campus identity. (Well, easy if you don't mind consuming grapes that have fallen out of your pledge brother's ass crack.) You get a bid from Sigma Whatever and everyone knows that you're an alcoholic jockstrap. You pledge Kappa Kappa Fill-in-the-Blank and everyone knows you're a rich girl whose inbred equine features kept her out of the sorority for rich *hot* girls.

The same holds true here in the city. What's more, we all go around preaching our allegiance wearing the post-college equivalent to Greek letters (Gawker T-shirt, YSL ski goggle sunglasses) and pledge pins (skull pendant, Tiffany solitaire).

Some quick and totally subjective free association:

UPPER EAST SIDE = ARISTOCRATIC

UPPER WEST SIDE = ACADEMIC

LOWER EAST SIDE = ADDICTED

These are totally biased observations, of course. Certainly there are welfare moms on the UES, college dropouts on the UWS, and tri-athletes on the LES. (Then again, maybe not.) I should really make a better effort not to stereotype, especially since I fall victim to such casual assumptions. We happen to live in a very desirable neighborhood, but not one that comes close to accurately reflecting who we are, because:

PARK SLOPE = BREEDERS

Yes, the Slope is known for having more sidewalk-hogging sancti-mommies than any other neighborhood in all five boroughs. Whether this is really true, I don't really know. It seems to me that annoying mommies are hardly limited to the confines of Fourth Avenue, Prospect Park West, Flatbush Avenue, and Fifteenth Street. Still, Ursula has lived here for twenty years, and often waxes nostalgic about the good old days, when "zere were more dykes den tykes."

The Park Slope Mommy is a peculiar, oft-ridiculed mommy, one who is stereotyped as both crunchy *and* uppity. Oh woe to the straggler who stands between her double-wide Urban Mountain Buggy and the seminar on sustainable permaculture at the Food Co-op. And when it's a dozen Maclarens deep at Tea Lounge, do not even think about apologizing if you accidentally brush an elbow up against the shrieking red bundle slung across her body. The Park Slope Mommy will mow you down and Croc-stomp your ass, because *Park Slope Mommies don't play.* (Seriously. They don't. They engage their children in "multidisciplinary explorative colloquia.")

Again, I don't know how much of this is really true. But childless singles like myself swap PSM stories all the time. Creating these urban legends is a big part of this neighborhood's appeal because New Yorkers just love to one-up one another in their tales of metropolitan woe.

In that vein, I get a lot of mileage out of the fact that I'm sharing a bedroom for the first time in my life, and bunk-bed style at that. But at least I've got the bottom bunk, and the top bunk is Hope's. And really, at only $550 a month, all grievances are moot. Considering my income-to-debt ratio, I'm lucky to be living anywhere at all, let alone in relative comfort in one of the more desirable neighborhoods in one of the acceptable outer boroughs. I love this apartment so much that it almost didn't bother me at all when I heard the biggest drawback to living here unlocking the front-door dead bolt before I was even halfway through my first cup of coffee this morning, my silent prayer unanswered.

"Good morning," said the biggest drawback as she half-walked, half-shuffled toward me with a weary grimace, as if she resented the very idea of complying to the laws of gravity, of actually having to *lift her limbs* off the ground.

"Good morning. Uh. Manda."

fifteen

I've defended this choice before, and I'll do it again.

Yes, I'm well aware how the only thing more unlikely than Hope and me sharing the rent with Manda Powers, our promiscuous Pineville High classmate, is sharing the rent with the promiscuous Manda Powers and her lesbian girlfriend, Shea. Or rather, her *genderqueer boifriend*, as Manda prefers, that is, if I *insist* on using *labels* because I am *brainwashed* by the *heteropatriarchal paradigm*.

For someone so devoted to hedonistic pleasures of the flesh, Manda sure has a knack for lecturing us in a self-righteous tone that instantly drains the fun out of everything. Case in point: On that very first afternoon outside the apartment, she showed up in her I HAD AN ABORTION T-shirt and asked, "Would you be making jokes if it were the African American Men's Sporting Society? The Puerto Rican Men's Sporting Society? What is it about the Swedes that makes it okay for you to be racist with impunity?" Manda has subverted the classic female dilemma by being both holier *and* whorier than thou. And yet, as you've repeatedly pointed out, I am voluntarily and hypocritically living with her.

The city's stratospheric rents make for bizarre living arrangements. And I know you'll disagree, but by New York standards our story is not at all unusual. One of the twins' two mommies is Manda's aunt, the out-of-the-country academic. Manda and Shea met posing in an all-nude photo shoot for *Rut*, "the high-minded hard-core magazine for the Rutgers University community." After graduating in May, the former sexhibitionist offered the latter the opportunity to share bedroom #1. For a little more than a month, the second bedroom (ours) was occupied by a barista of Swedish stock and his vegan-chef boyfriend, until they suddenly decided that they'd rather tour the country promoting alternative fuels in a VW bus pimped out to run only on recycled vegetable oil.

News spreads fast around our small hometown, especially around college graduation time. All parents want proof that the diploma they paid for was a smart investment, and they need to find out whether the neighbors' kids have better post-college prospects than their own. My mother will shamelessly grill any Pineville mom on how and where her child is making a living, which is fairly infuriating because my parents stopped paying for my Columbia education after my sophomore year. But if it weren't for that Pineville parent-to-parent gossip hotline, it's unlikely that Manda would have discovered that Hope and I were tired of living with my sister (me) and crashing on floors and futons (Hope) and were looking for an affordable (ha!) apartment just about anywhere in the city. Manda texted me: **apt 550 mo. r u/hope swdsh?**

Yes, I needed an apartment. And $550 was a price I could sort of afford, that is, until my student loan payments bumped up to match my "elevated earning potential," as the loan officers very optimistically put it. But was I or Hope . . . what? Single White Divorcees Seeking Husbands? Swinging Women Doing Sexy Homos? Single White Dick Sucking Heteros?

It's indicative of my desperation for affordable housing that I didn't ignore Manda's cryptic and possibly kinky message altogether.

ok. wtf swdsh?

After Manda explained Ursula's Swedish clause via e-mail, I called Hope in Rhode Island to give her the bad news.

"We can't get the apartment unless you just so happen to be part Swedish."

"I *am* part Swedish," she said. "On my mother's side."

"No way."

"Yes way," she said. "Her maiden name is Johansson."

I loved that I didn't know this about her, as it hinted at all the other things I had yet to discover about my best friend of ten years.

As I just documented, one week later Hope and I traveled to Brooklyn and fell in love with SAMSS. We were nervous about the prospect of moving in with Manda but figured it was safer than finding someone through Craigslist. ("Better the nympho you know," was our motto at the time.) We moved in two weeks later, constantly joking about how Manda and Shea might try to seduce us into their omnisexual union.

Manda and Shea work the eight P.M. to four A.M. shift at Cave, a hipster sinkhole in Bushwick known for hosting a retarded carnival of pointless posturing known as Fuckyomomma.

WILLIAMSBURG = HIPSTERS WITH TRUST FUNDS

BUSHWICK = HIPSTERS WITHOUT TRUST FUNDS PRICED OUT OF WILLIAMSBURG

I have kindly declined Manda's invitations, but I've bled out the eyes as she's shown me digital picture after picture of wannabe or slumming Williamsturdburgers trying too hard to outdo one another in their kaffiyeh neck scarves, scraggly crustaches, and Jheri-curl mullets. This morning Manda was wearing the omnipresent terry-cloth headband with a red velour strapless booty-short romper. It's an altogether frightening standard that's being set when this American Apparel–Nymphette getup comes across as one of the less exasperating aesthetics du jour. I don't need to pay a twenty-dollar cover charge to suffer ocular hemorrhaging in person. No. Thank. You.

(I know. I'm forgoing the Four Abodes. Dissing the *dharma*. Deepening my *dukkha*. For someone who doesn't claim to be a Buddhist, you're damn good at *dokusan*. But come on, if I can't hate on ridiculous hipsters, who can I hate on? Now, that's a Zen koan worth riddling.)

Manda's and Shea's jobs require them to lead a nocturnal lifestyle. They spend most of their daylight hours in bed, but not always *sleeping*, if you get my horrified drift. This is why *I* rarely work from the apartment even though working in one's pajamas is supposed to be one of the greatest benefits of being a freelance editor. (Though I'd trade that in for medical benefits because on January 19, 2007, I turn twenty-three and will be officially removed from my parents' health plan. Without that protective coverage, I am destined to contract a hantavirus on January 20.) Manda also works some afternoons at Planned Parenthood while Shea works similar hours at a video store. If I do my editorial work for *Think* from Ozzie's coffee shop all morning, then go straight to Bethany's to babysit Marin in the afternoon, I can time it so Manda and Shea are heading out the door for work just as I'm coming home. I've arranged my schedule so I hardly ever see them, which is the only reason our roommate situation works. As for how they spend the rest of their nonsleeping daylight hours while I'm out of the apartment, I don't really want to know. It apparently requires a lot of lubrication, as indicated by the Post-it reminder stuck on our bathroom mirror: *BUY K-Y*.

The one thing I will say about Manda is this: She's always been an unrepentant sex maniac.

sixteen

Shea sullenly dragged herself in behind Manda and greeted me with a dip of her baseball cap.

"'Sup."

To which I replied, "Hey, Shea."

And she said nothing else as she headed to the kitchen table and huddled over the Automobiles section of the *Times*. Even in her hooded sweatshirt, calf-skimming cargo shorts, and dingy white Vans slip-ons, Shea isn't exactly butch. No, I've come to the conclusion that her gender-blending aesthetics and attitude are modeled after those of a sixteen-year-old boy. She looks no different from the dozens of teenage skaters grinding all over Prospect Park, fueled by ADHD and megadoses of caffeine and testosterone. She even smells like a high school boy, a ripe combination of a fermented hamper and AXE deodorant body spray. So it's no surprise she acted just like a surly adolescent when Manda took off her baseball cap and playfully nuzzled the charred-black buzz cut beneath.

"*Daaaaaaamn*." Shea has a talent for stretching four-letter words into four syllables. "Dinja gettanuff lasniiite?" Her tone could only by the very loosest definition be considered affectionate.

"Mmmmm . . . Never . . . ," Manda cooed.

"*Daaaaaaamn*. Why you gotta be such a pain-in-the-asshole rapeface?"

Shea also has a talent for such wonderfully scatological outbursts.

(Though I can hardly blame you for not embracing *cumchugger*, though I swear she meant it as a term of weird endearment.) I'm not at all freaked out by Manda's Sapphic tendencies, but I do think it's peculiar how her pangender partnership with Shea exemplifies the kind of cruel misogyny this self-described "fourth-wave feminist" has so aggressively fought against since high school. Manda would have never dated a guy this offensive back then, and is only dating one now because *she's really a girl*. Let me put out an apology to the entire GLBT community, but I just don't get it.

And yet I kind of can't blame Shea for being so . . . pissed off. I mean, all but the most genetically blessed go through periods of squirmy discomfort in our own skin. But there's a big difference between *my* kind of discomfort ("Boo-hoo! I don't have any boobs!") and Shea's ("Boo-hoo! I have boobs! And where the hell is my penis?").

"Where's Hope at?" Shea asked in a slightly more pleasant tone, opening a jar of peanut butter. Shea is always very interested in Hope's whereabouts. If only Hope were right here, right now, we'd all be *that much closer* to having an orgy. Or so Shea would like to believe.

"Sleeping."

"She need comp'ny?"

"I doubt it," I replied. I then watched as Shea scraped out what was left of the peanut butter with her forefinger. I was placing bets on how long it would take Manda to start licking it off.

"How's Marcus?" Manda asked.

The sudden interest in my life was unprecedented. I hadn't prepared an answer I'd be willing to share with Manda on this subject.

"Uh," I replied.

"Shiiiiiiiiiiit. You buttplugs break up or what?"

"*What?*" I asked. "Why would you ask that?" I hadn't given Shea or Manda any indication of, well, anything.

"Oh, I don't know," Manda said. "It just seems like you were having some troubles right before he left."

"He has troubles with New York," I said, repeating a familiar excuse. "Not with me."

"All the more reason why I thought you might be having second thoughts about the long-distance thing," Manda said as she overfilled her mug, spilling coffee over Mary Wollstonecraft's ceramic portrait.

"Oh."

"Sooooo?"

I didn't want to get all touchy-feely in a figurative or literal way. So I figured the best strategy was nonchalance.

"Well, I was thinking that it might be easiest for both of us if we just do our own thing. . . ."

"Break up," Manda clarified.

I was still very suspicious. Manda and Shea were way too interested in my emotional life. "Well, I tried to break up with him, but he wasn't convinced and . . ." I stopped there. Manda and Shea could not be the first to find out about your proposal, even if it was an elaborate inside joke.

"And . . . ?" Manda asked.

"And I'm taking time to think."

"So you're technically still together?"

"Yes," I said. "More than technically. We are—"

"Hellyeah!" Shea slammed down the peanut butter jar and leapt up from the chair to engage in an elaborate touchdown dance: her baggy pants thrust up and down, one hand flat on the floor and the other smacking an imaginary ass.

I asked the only logical question. "What the hell?"

"Hellyeah! Hellyeah! Hellyeah!" Now Shea simulated wild, rear-entry copulation with an imaginary strap-on.

"We had a bet about your breakup," Manda said. She beamed as she said this.

"You are so owned! You thought Marcus was breaking up with her! Ownage! Ownage! Ownage!" She was still thrusting her pelvis.

"Puh-leeze, I am so not owned!"

"Ownage! Ownage! Ownage!"

Living with Shea is like living with the zitty, Ritalin-tweaked little brother I never had. Only she's twenty-three years old. *And she has a vagina*. Oops. There I go again, getting all caught up in the hetero-patriarchal paradigm. Shame on me.

Manda squealed and positioned herself in front of her boifriend to complete the faux-porno tableau. "Give it to me! Give it to me! Give it to me!"

I retreated back down the hall before the simulated act could be authenticated.

seventeen

Hope was sitting straight up in the top bunk when I opened the door.

"I'm *so* sorry," she said.

"Are you kidding? People pay good money to watch what I just saw for free."

"I meant about you and Marcus." Her head hung low, but her curls still teased the decorative squares pressed into the tin ceiling.

"Oh, you must have heard wrong," I said.

"Heard *what* wrong?"

"Marcus and I didn't break up," I explained.

Her head jolted with this news. "Really? I thought . . ."

"Manda and Shea had a bet about our breakup."

"I know that," she said. "They actually asked if I wanted in on it."

"What were the stakes?" I asked.

"You don't want to know," Hope replied, a wry smile sneaking across her face. "But it involved something called a Jaguar Harness."

"A what?!"

"I told you that you didn't want to know!"

And then we both laughed. Joking about the sexual imprimaturs paying half our rent never gets old. The oppressive mood had been lifted, but I was still surprised by how rattled Hope seemed by the prospect of us breaking up. Perhaps she needs to believe in us because it helps her feel better about her own long-distance relationship with Wynn.

I love Hope and Wynn. Just the very sound of them is so positive. He won't be around much anymore because he's living with his parents in Pittsburgh while he earns his M.F.A. in Multimedia/Visual Communications at Carnegie Mellon. This should make my sleeping arrangement less pervy than it was all summer. There won't be as many opportunities for third wheeling, that is, suffering in the bunk alone, excruciatingly aware of the entwined lovers above or below.

I always had a single at Columbia, so I was never subjected to the various collegiate indignities suffered when one roommate is getting laid and the other is not. Since we're older now, and this isn't a dorm, Hope and I tried to put a "no sex" rule into effect during third wheelers. As you are well aware, you and I violated that rule last week. In our dubious defense, we did check and double-check to make sure Hope was asleep before the bunk started its rhythmic squeaking and creaking. But I can't say with any real certainty that she was really out cold, or just too embarrassed to say otherwise, as I was all summer long when Hope and Wynn whispered and moaned in the dark. Horny twentysomethings hath no shame.

"So you two are still together," Hope said slowly, carefully, as if she were trying to find the upper-right corner of the sky in a five-thousand-piece jigsaw puzzle.

"What would be the polar opposite of breaking up?"

"Um . . . staying together?"

"The *ultimate* commitment."

"I don't know," she said, her voice wandering off in search of the answer. "His'n'hers tattoos?" She politely laughed at her own joke.

"Marriage," I said. "Marcus asked me to marry him."

I had expected Hope to respond with a joke. Something along the lines of "But what about Kirk? Won't he get jealous?" Because what did this sound like but the grand setup to some great big joke? But she just blinked at me from the top bunk.

"I'm not kidding," I said, wiggling the fourth finger of my left hand. "He got down on one knee and everything."

THWACK! Hope smashed her head against the ceiling.

"Holy shit! Are you okay?"

"Sort of," she said, rubbing her curls. "Are *you* okay?"

"I don't know," I confessed.

(*Confessed* isn't really accurate, is it? Is it possible to confess the obvious? Would I be writing in this notebook if I were certain of anything, even my own okayness?)

"I mean, this isn't something I ever thought would happen," I said. "Especially not yesterday. And I'm still not sure what to make of it."

"I don't blame you," she said. "Tell me everything."

I climbed up to the top bunk and obliged.

"And so," I said, finishing up, "he wants an answer when he comes back from Outdoor Action on Saturday."

Hope's eyes popped out of her face. "You didn't come right out and say no?"

"Uh, no."

Hope rattled her head in disbelief. "Jess!"

"What?"

She shut her eyes and screwed her mouth tight.

"Hope," I said. "You've been my best friend since seventh grade. And you've known Marcus even longer than I have. You can't say the wrong thing."

Hope was about to respond when I heard the unmistakable sound of muffled whispers right outside our door. I shushed Hope with my hand, climbed over the side of the bunk, then crawled across the floor to the bedroom door. I flung it open so quickly that the two interlopers tumbled cartoon-style right onto the lemon-curd carpet.

"I dint hear nuttin'!" Shea lied.

"But I did!" Manda said, pushing her way past her pangendered partner in crime.

"Invasion of privacy?"

"Oh, puh-leeze," Manda said. "If you want privacy, you gotta pay more."

She had a point. Meanwhile, Shea preened behind Manda, winking and wagging her green-stained Sparks tongue for Hope's, uh, benefit.

"So come on," Manda said, tapping her foot. "Let's see it!"

"See what?"

"The rock!"

"There's no rock," I said, holding out my hand so she could inspect the silver.

"No rock? Puh-leeze!" she said, dropping my hand as if it were something toxic. "What kind of engagement is that?"

"I wouldn't have expected someone who has exchanged clit rings to be so traditional."

Shea guffawed.

"What?" I asked.

"Huhhuhuhuh," Shea chuckled. "You said *clit*."

This proves it: I am living with Beavis and Sluthead.

"Well," Manda said, "it's slightly less humiliating than the three-carat solitaire Sara bought *herself*."

"Ah yes," I said, recalling our Pineville High classmate's condition. "A carat for each trimester . . ."

"When's she due, anyway?" Hope asked.

"Two weeks ago," I answered.

"Ouch," Hope and Manda said at the same time.

eighteen

I haven't seen Sara in about six weeks, not since the babymama shower. I was the only one in Sammy invited. As you might recall, Manda and Sara were former BFF's, the cornerstone of the Clueless Crew back in their Pineville High heyday. But Manda hasn't forgiven Sara for so gleefully informing all of Pineville that the former had turned into a *quote* carpet muncher *unquote* in college. And Sara hasn't forgiven Manda for so gleefully informing all of Pineville that the former had dropped out of college after getting knocked up after two minutes of unprotected passion in the Bamboo Bar parking lot.

I was not an obvious invitee. High school graduation brought with it many liberations, including my emancipation from the alphabetical guarantee that D'Abruzzi, Sara would be assigned to sit in front of Darling, Jessica in homeroom *and* every single honors class from seventh through twelfth grade. Since I threw my mortarboard into the air back in June 2002, my relationship with the guest of honor has consisted of rare, random run-ins around Pineville. I was only dragged to the shower by my sister, who felt obligated to attend because of her husband's ongoing business partnership with Sara's father, the Jersey Shore Junk Food King, Wally D'Abruzzi. These two families have gotten insanely wealthy off Americans' insatiable desire for frozen custard and deep-fried dough, having opened up twenty-five new drive-through Papa D's Donuts/Wally D's Sweet Treat Shoppes in the past year alone.

Wally D spared no expense on his daughter's celebration of accidental fertilization. But I don't need to relive the *gitchy-gitchy goo-goo gag-me* details because it was hardly any different from a typically torturous baby shower. Not that you, Marcus, would have any idea, since you were lucky enough to be born with a penis. The only significant deviation was how there was more talk about the bride-to-be than the fetus-that-already-was.

"Omigod! You should see my Vera Wang!" Sara brayed. "It's so *quote* Jessica Simpson *unquote*."

"Scotty proposed?" I asked. "Uh . . ."

"Congratulations!" my sister chimed. "That's fantastic!"

Sara flinched, then quickly recovered. "Well, we're not technically *quote* engaged *unquote*," she said brightly. "Not technically. But it's like everything but technically. We're living together, and he totally wants this baby."

My eyes bulged in disbelief. Bethany elbowed my ribs to shut me up.

"It was *practically* his idea to have it! Any other guy would have wanted me to *quote* get rid of it *unquote*. But he was all like, 'Do you want to keep it?' and I was like, 'Yeah, I totally do.' And I know he totally wants to get married, so I'm just, you know, helping him out, getting things started because he doesn't have a lot of money and I do, so . . ."

So Sara—unemployed college dropout and daughter of self-made millionaire Wally D'Abruzzi—bought herself the three-carat solitaire diamond that she will start wearing as soon as her ring finger shrinks to its prepregnancy size. Nothing Sara said could make me believe that this was anything other than a devious get-married gambit. By purchasing her own ring, Sara had put a new and demented twist on the classic Impregnation Equation:

ENGORGEMENT + ENTRAPMENT = ENGAGEMENT

"Think of all the bad girls who have been transformed by marriage," she said at one point during her insane, estrogen-spiked monologue. "Christina Aguilera. Avril Lavigne. Pink. Omigod! Getting married is, like, the best makeover ever."

There was only one little *quote* glitch *unquote* to getting hitched: Scotty hadn't proposed. And despite this minor setback, all this wedding talk was only occasionally interrupted by the cranky unborn human who had taken over Sara's uterus.

"Ow!" She winced, groaned, then admonished her stomach: "Destiny, settle down in there!"

Destiny?

"Omigod! We're naming the baby Destiny Estrella. Did we tell you that?"

No, she had not.

"It's because Scotty and I totally think it was *quote* destiny *unquote* that brought us together."

Really? It wasn't the Natty Lite?

(If the Dalai Lama were there, he would've made the same joke. But being His Holiness and all, he probably could have gotten away with saying it to her face.)

"And Estrella means *quote* star *unquote* in Spanish. . . ."

"Uh," I said, this time out loud. "Didn't you take Spanish for four years?"

"Yeah, so?" she huffed.

"So you should know that the Spanish *l* isn't pronounced."

"What do you mean it isn't pronounced?" Sara sniffed.

"The *l* in Spanish doesn't sound like *l*, it sounds like *y*," I explained. "So it's Es-STRAY-ya. Not Es-STRELL-A."

I was trying to spare Sara the embarrassment of mispronouncing her daughter's middle name for the rest of her life. And you know what I was thinking about when I did this? What you told me about the Four Abodes of Buddhism: kindness, compassion, joy in others' joy, and levelheadedness. The Four Abodes are just great, Marcus. Really. They make sense to me. They kick the Ten Commandments' ass. I mean, you'd have to be a total dick not to be down with the Four Abodes. And yet whenever I speak with the Four Abodes in mind, I still sound like a bitch.

"Whatev," Sara said. "I like it my way."

"It's a great name," Bethany said, snapping my bra strap in admonishment.

"Omigod! I know! It was gonna be *quote* star *unquote* in Italian, you know, because of my heritage and all, but *star* in Italian is *quote* SteLLa *unquote*," Sara said, going out of her way to overpronounce the *l*'s. "And Stella is, like, an old lady's name. Like someone with drooping boobs who pushes a mop for a living."

I followed my sister's cue and nodded vigorously.

Sara covered her mouth, then burped into her hand. "And *star* has a deep significance for us as a couple because there were all these stars out the night that we, you know, *quote* conceived *unquote*. But Destiny Star is, like, a porn name. Destiny EstreLLa is, you know, *quote* classy *unquote*."

Oh, yes. The mangling of foreign words is always considered the epitome of genteel refinement. As is referring to oneself as "classy."

Sara burped again, only this time she didn't bother covering her mouth. "Scotty and I have known each other since kindergarten, you know, but we never even thought to hook up with each other until we started meeting up at the Bamboo Bar on breaks and we realized that we had so much in common, like the same core values. It was destiny. Destiny . . ."

So it was *destiny* that got Sara knocked up. Not the drunken, unprotected sex under the stars in the Bamboo Bar parking lot. Got it.

(I'm sorry, Marcus. This is how I really think, despite my failed efforts to think otherwise. Isn't it better you know the truth than live with the illusion that I am a kinder, more evolved person than I really am?)

And just when I thought we had finally exhausted the subject of baby names, Sara told a long and gassy story about how she would have named a boy baby Alessandro Destino after her father, whom everyone calls Wally, and how that's just a childhood nickname stemming from his siblings' taunts about his being "wall-eyed," and how the reclamation of that insult was proof of his resilience, and how she hopes Destiny Estrella inherits her grandfather's strong character and savvy business sense but not his crossed eyes and—

Sara abruptly clutched her gut. "Omigod! Why am I even telling you this?"

I was wondering the exact same thing.

"I should be telling you about my Vera Wang. I ordered a size two!"

I was speechless.

"That's, uh . . ." I turned to my sister for help. "Uh . . ."

"Ambitious," Bethany finished. "It's a lot of work taking care of a newborn, and planning a wedding. . . ."

"I'm gonna breast-feed, too," Sara said.

"That's really great," Bethany said. "Doctors say breast is best. . . ."

"Oh yeah, it helps ward off infections, especially in the first year," Sara said, all of a sudden surprising me with a hint of maternity. "And I'll look so hot in my gown. Omigod! Did you *see* Angelina Jolie's rack after she had the baby?"

Now both Bethany and I had lost the ability to speak.

"Destiny is due on August twenty-fourth," Sara said. "I've got exactly ten months to snap back into shape!"

It will be the snap heard around the world. Perhaps you have heard some pregnant women described as "all belly." It usually means that the pregnancy weight has settled into a cute, compact, baby-shaped ball right there in the belly. If the term "all belly" were used to describe Sara, it would mean that she had literally become "all belly," that the entirety of her physical being had been consumed by her belly, so that even all body parts that were unrelated and far removed from the belly, such as her ankles, or her earlobes, had become indistinguishable from the belly. Sara was one huge, rotundous belly with one month to go.

I know it sounds like I'm criticizing her for packing on major pregnancy pounds, but I'm not. In her pre-babymama days, Sara was well into the maintenance phase of anorexia, when the starvation wasn't such a struggle anymore because it was one of many habits—chain-smoking, mainlining Starbucks, inhaling horse tranquilizers—incorporated into her totally unhealthy lifestyle. So not unlike every Hollywood actress who gets knocked up, Sara had to gain about twenty-five pounds just to be in the normal weight range for an unpregnant woman. And once the pounds started piling on, she couldn't stop them. In eight months of gestating she'd more than made up for all the food she hasn't eaten in the last decade. And yet, paradoxically, for all her bellyness, Sara *looked* more attractive than ever at that shower in that au naturel, glowing-from-within way that pregnant women often do. It's a shame that her anathematic personality offset these improvements in her appearance.

Babydaddy Scotty showed up at the end of the shower for the express purpose of piling all the presents into a luxury SUV and bringing them back to the condo they now share in Seaside Park. At twenty-two, Scotty seems prematurely middle-aged, with a thinning hairline and a thickening waistline. To look at him, you would never know that just four years ago he was voted Most Popular and Class Athlete in the Pineville High School Class of 2002 yearbook. (That Scotty and Sara's ex-BFF, Manda, "the carpet muncher," were voted Class Couple is not discussed. Ever. Nor the fact that Scotty tried—and failed—to get into my pants for four years, even when he was half of the celebrated coupling.) Scotty is the personification of every Springsteen song about burned-out, packed-in, broken-down, and washed-up high school heroes. You know, the former stars whose best days are long behind them, whose dreams of post-graduation glory are dashed and scattered among the wreckage on the dark, lonesome highways twisting through the abandoned carny towns along the Jersey Shore . . .

Or something like that.

Scotty and I exchanged the briefest of banal pleasantries.

"Congratulations," I said lamely.

"Yeah," he said, doing pop-a-wheelies with the Bugaboo stroller filled with pink and white paraphernalia.

"A girl," I said, not knowing what else to say.

"Yeah," Scotty said. "Sara says so. Every firstborn in her family for the past one hundred years or something has been a girl. It's the D'Abruzzi Family Legacy."

"Oh," I said.

"Sara and I call it"—he paused here and spread his impressively thick hands in the air, as if he were calling attention to an imaginary marquee—"the D'Abruzzi Pussy Legacy."

Now, *that* would have been a memorable motto for the parting gifts: miniature baby bottles filled with pink bubble-gum jelly beans. Instead, Sara had attached a tiny "Save the Date" card that read like a promo to a cheese-ass romantic comedy I'd never pay ten dollars to see in a theater but might watch on an airplane if the headphones were free.

SARA D'ABRUZZI & SCOTT GLAZER.

ALWAYS & FOREVER & DESTINY

BEGINS JUNE 24, 2007.

(FOREVER. Is your final postcard on its way?)

nineteen

"BOOM—*pssh*—BOOM-BOOM-*pssh*-BOOM-*pssh*-BOOM-BOOM-*pssh!*"

Shea's beat-boxing brought me back to the conversation in a most unpleasant manner. High-hatting spit was spraying all over the Cupcake.

"*B-b-b-babymama, g-g-g-go head be g-g-gone wit dat thang,*" Shea rapped into her cupped hand/mic. "*G-g-g-get dat thang c-c-c-cut out . . .*"

"Get that thing cut out?" Manda screamed. "It's a human being, not a tumor!"

"To-*may*-to, po-*tay*-to, fuck-*fuck*-yo."

I am living with K-Fed's retarded half sista/brotha.

Manda turned to the more civilized participants in this conversation.

"Sara is, in fact, scheduled for a C-section today," I said, remembering what my sister had told me. "I bet she's pissed that Destiny's late. I mean, she's lost two weeks of workouts before the wedding. That is, if Scotty ever—omigod!—*quote* technically *unquote* proposes."

Hope giggled because she loves my nasally Sara impression, but she refrained from further comment. Manda remained serious. That is, as serious as one can be when one is wearing booty shorts before nine A.M.

"It's so weird," Manda said. "Like while we're sleeping all day"—because Manda seemed to be under the impression that we *all* sleep during daylight hours—"Sara will be having a baby. Today. *Sara*. A baby. I mean, she's a total bitch and I hate her, but she *was* my best friend. It's so weird that she's having a baby."

"*Scotty's* baby."

And we muttered various incredulities.

"Well," Hope said, ever the optimist, "I hope they're happy together."

"Me too," Manda said without a trace of meanness.

And I was just happy that all this talk of Destiny had drawn the attention away from my own hypothetical milestones.

Heavy footsteps stomped on the ceiling.

"Ursula!"

We are united in our fear of Ursula, that if any of us says or does the wrong thing, she'll kick us to the curb with one of her pointy-toed roach killer boots. We froze, hoping we would be spared her morning wrath.

"Yo, I'm headin fo' bed before she come down." Even Shea knows better than to fuck-*fuck*-yo with Ursula.

"Me too," Manda said. Then to me: "Don't think I've forgotten about *your* situation." She tapped the ring finger on her left hand as she backed out the door.

"Crap," Hope said, looking at the clock. "I'm getting picked up in ten minutes. Another Sunday, another Long Island wedding . . ."

"Speaking of weddings . . ."

"This is too big to talk about in ten minutes or less."

"I know," I replied. "But what were you going to say before we were interrupted?"

She jumped from the top bunk and stuck the landing. She had to wind her way through the maze of unpacked boxes to get to the closet.

"Do you think you can finally put these away?" she asked, pointing to a stack of taped-up cardboard boxes, all unhelpfully labeled. For all my anal-retentive tendencies, I have a rather aimless and unorganized packing style, as one box claims to contain SOCKS, COFFEE FILTERS, PSYCH BOOKS.

"I will, I will," I promised, as I've promised for the past three months. When I moved out of Bethany's guest room in June, I stuffed all my summer clothes and shoes in my duffel. My bedding came along in a Hefty Cinch Sak. Everything else was sealed in those cardboard moving boxes, which have remained sealed and triple-stacked since you helped lug them here on move-in day. That was your first trip to Sammy. (Do you realize that you only visited once more before your seven-day visit last week?)

I watched Hope as she pulled a sleeveless black dress off a hanger and over her head. She slipped her feet into a pair of unadorned black flats with a thick rubber sole. Since getting the job with Capture the Moment, she's built a whole wardrobe designed for comfort and blending in with the background, the latter of which is pretty much impossible when you're nearly six feet tall with miles of orange hair.

"So what do you really think about the proposal?" I asked when she was finished getting ready. "I need you to tell me the truth."

Hope gulped loudly. "I think . . ." She paused to pull a pile of hair off her shoulders with the twist of an elastic band. "I think that this is so Marcus."

And on that point we were in total agreement.

twenty

After Hope left for the Chateau Briand Country Club and Gardens ("Where Only the Bride and Groom Outshine Our Spectacularly Opulent Ambiance"), I dedicated the rest of the day to unpacking those boxes. That was my plan, anyway. It seemed like a constructive, productive thing to do on an otherwise eventless Sunday. Boxes would be removed, floor space would be discovered, and quantifiable progress would be made. I had taken over far more than 50 percent of the square footage of Claire and Chloe's pastel playland and it was time to even things out. I would carefully cut the Cupcake in half, making sure Hope got her fair share of closet room and floor space, vanilla batter and buttercream frosting. Oh, how I looked forward to Hope's evening return and hearing her marvel over my finger-licking equanimity.

Only I didn't get very far.

According to my useless labeling system, the first box blocking my path purported to contain MOM AND DAD. Hmm. I was fairly certain that they were still alive and well in Pineville, and that I had not dismembered them in a sick reenactment of a *CSI* episode titled "In Loco Parentis," guest-starring that angelic actress from *The Gilmore Girls* going against type as the homicidal daughter. I carved open the cardboard with Hope's X-Acto knife, if only so I could find out what I might have meant by that mysterious, possibly murderous label. I pulled back the flayed cardboard and winced at my hasty, X-Acto–wielding handiwork: I had ruined the mosaic Hope gave me on the day she moved to Tennessee nearly seven years ago, just before my sixteenth birthday.

Hope had meticulously pasted together innumerable confetti scraps to reconstruct our favorite snapshot, an arm's-length view of two thirteen-year-old best friends, our teeth gleaming and eyes blazing with manic energy after staying up all night to watch the sunrise.

Hope would surely be embarrassed by this mosaic now, deriding it as untrained and immature. But her youthful lack of pretension distinguished this work of art from her other, more accomplished pieces. I've always thought it was the best thing she's ever made.

And I ruined it. I'd sliced it right down the middle. Not in a way that separated Hope from me as if we were conjoined twins surgically transformed into our whole, independent selves. No, I had sliced the page horizontally, slitting our throats, separating our minds from our bodies. Or our heads from our hearts.

I sunk into the bottom bunk and cried when I realized what I had done.

twenty-one

Try to imagine us as the girls captured in that self-portrait, two thirteen-year-olds whiling away the stagnant, swampy summer in New Jersey. Hope was too tall for all the boys, with wild orange tresses. Her complexion was as delicate as an eggshell and almost as pale, and she always sought refuge from the relentless sun under the leafy protection of an oak tree. I had muddy hair and dark eyes that were ever-ready for a sardonic roll in the sockets. I was shorter and skinny to the point of scrawny, and I defiantly subjected myself to the UV rays in pursuit of the perfect tan even though my melanin never deepened beyond the shade of a bruised persimmon.

It was the summer before the start of eighth grade, and Hope and I had invented a game of hypotheticals called Would You Rather?

Would you rather have Manda's impressive rack OR Bridget's perfect ass?

It was an escapist coping mechanism, in which we inserted our boring, Brainiac selves into fantasy scenarios often involving the Pineville Middle School hoi polloi. Eventually the game evolved (or devolved) into a series of pseudo-philosophical inquiries that probed the shallow depths of our adolescent psyches.

Read minds OR have X-ray vision?

We believed that we had elevated conspicuous boredom to a higher art form. (In fact, publishers later developed a series of books with page after page of either/or hypotheticals. Hope and I felt royally gypped out of the tremendous profits made from what we self-centeredly considered *our* idea.) At the time this favorite photo was taken, we were less than a year into our best friendship, having found each other at the start of seventh grade when our town's separate elementary schools merged into Pineville Middle School. And yet while we already appreciated our friendship for the rare and precious thing we knew it was, we had no way of knowing that we'd only have two more summers together before Hope's family would decamp to Tennessee in the wake of Heath's death. . . .

Wait.

It just occurred to me, right now, in the middle of all this reminiscing, that these events harken back to the summer of your druggy precocity. It's quite possible that you don't need to imagine the scene because you had eavesdropped on it while altering your own reality in Heath's bedroom on the opposite side of the wall. As day turned into night and again into day, Hope and I stayed awake playing round after round of Would You Rather? Meanwhile, you and Hope's doomed older brother passed the bowl around and around, laughing over inscrutable insider stoner jokes, laughing at *us*. Chances are that you and Heath even earwitnessed the most controversial question in the history of the game.

"Would you rather kiss the same guy for the rest of your life," I asked, "or *never* kiss the same guy more than once?"

Neither Hope nor I had kissed anyone at this point in our young lives, and we could think about little else. It was somewhat miraculous that this question hadn't already been asked. Hope cried foul, claiming that I had broken the cardinal rule of the game.

"Can't be answered with the information given!"

"Yes, it *totally* can," I said, slipping down my training-bra strap to compare the pale, unexposed flesh against the dangerously red "tan" I'd roasted all afternoon.

"No, it can't!" Hope was—and still is—incapable of sounding

pissed off, even at her most pissed off. "The most crucial variable—the Guy!—is unknown."

Then she went on to explain how if the Guy was an amazing kisser but a jerk, she'd ditch him for a wandering, wanton lifetime of one-time-onlies. But if the Guy was her *soul mate*, she would forsake all others . . . even if he came on with all the finesse of a saliva-soaked toilet plunger.

My rebuttal came in two parts:

1. By its very definition, her *soul mate* wouldn't be a mediocre kisser, because true *soul mates* bond on all levels: physical, emotional, spiritual, and so on.
2. The question was *still* answerable even without the specification of *soul mate* or non, as it had less to do with the Guy and more to do with one's attitudes about the familiar versus the mysterious. Security versus freedom. Guarantee versus risk. Monogamy versus polyamory.

Before I continue, and before you can beat me to it, I'm just going to call bullshit on my revisionist history. You know as well as I do that I wasn't capable of using those exact words back then, as my vocabulary was still steeped in "likes," "totallys," and "no duhs." I didn't even attempt to make vague approximations of those arguments. And as yesterday's debate in your dorm deftly proves, I'm barely capable of making such arguments now, nearly a decade later.

Okay. So I didn't really make that apocryphal speech. In truth, I simply told Hope she was right and the question was invalidated because it couldn't be answered with the information given. We moved on to a more straightforward hypothetical.

"Okay," I said with a sigh. "Would you rather make out with Bender from *The Breakfast Club* or Jake from *Sixteen Candles?*"

And then we started laughing hysterically for no good reason at all, a moment that was first caught with a quick click of my camera, then captured once more through Hope's painstaking clipping and pasting.

twenty-two

The mosaic is just the first of a collection of keepsakes that had me wallowing in my emotional archives for the remainder of the afternoon. It turned out that MOM AND DAD was shorthand for THE BOX FROM MOM AND DAD'S HOUSE THAT THE FORMER THREATENED TO THROW AWAY UNLESS I TOOK IT OFF HER HANDS BECAUSE THEIR NEW CONDO HAS MANY AMENITIES BUT ABUNDANT CLOSET SPACE FOR JESSIE'S JUNK IS NOT AMONG THEM. (My mother had, in fact, once labeled an earlier version of this same box JESSIE'S JUNK.)

And all this reminiscing has made me long for a cab to speed down Sixth Avenue blaring:

It's a miracle! (Miracle!)
A true-blue spectacle, a miracle come true!

Barry Manilow would give this all-out extravaganza of nostalgia an added layer of depth and meaning. His overwrought ballads have served as the cheesy leitmotif to our relationship, going all the way back to when I was sixteen and you were seventeen, and you put his *Greatest Hits* into your ancient Cadillac's eight-track for our first drive to Helga's Diner. That same night, after we bonded over French fries and our mutual disappreciation for fake Xmas trees spray-painted with aerosol snow, you suddenly pulled over on a deserted side street and taunted, tempted, teased me with your teeth, gently biting my bottom lip instead of giving in to the predictability of a first kiss. . . . I know Barry Manilow's synchronistic impact has not been lost on you, Marcus, otherwise you would not have chosen to show up last Christmas Eve with a toilet-seat cover decoupaged with his polyester jumpsuited likeness—an apologetic peace offering for your two-year absence.

No taxi has obliged me with Barry; there's only the omnipresent hip-hop, competing beats that bump and fade with the stop and go of the traffic light. And, alas, the Barry Manilow toilet-seat cover was not among the memorabilia recovered safe and sound in the MOM AND DAD box today. Herewith is a catalog of artifacts stored inside:

JESSIE'S JUNK

(Cataloged in the order in which the items were removed.)

- One (ruined) mosaic by Hope Weaver
- Rubber-banded bundle of forty-four handwritten letters sent by Hope Weaver between January 2000 and August 2002, postmarked Wellgoode, TN, to Pineville, NJ
- Rubber-banded bundle of twenty-six handwritten letters sent by Hope Weaver between August 2002 and June 2006, postmarked RISD, Providence, RI, to Columbia University, New York, NY
- Purple Post-it from Professor Samuel MacDougal originally attached to the envelope containing his letter recommending me for Columbia University: "Be great in act, as you have been in thought."—William Shakespeare
- Copy of 2004 National Book Award nominee, *Acting Out*, autographed by Professor Mac; inscription reads: "To my best student, I've quoted this before, but it bears repeating: 'We are what we pretend to be, so we must be careful what we pretend to be.'—Kurt Vonnegut"
- Nine-by-twelve envelope containing sixty-seven photos all dating between 1996 and 1998; includes one snapshot taken at Pineville Middle School's Halloween Dance 1996, in which four out of five seventh-grade girls are posing as four out of five Spice Girls in PVC platform boots and totally age-inappropriate Girl Power! gear: Hope Weaver as Ginger Spice, gamely rocking the iconic Union Jack minidress; Manda Powers as Posh Spice, spilling provocatively out of a black pleather bustier; Sara D'Abruzzi as Scary Spice, pre-rexy and still chubby, bursting obscenely from a chartreuse spandex tube top; Bridget Milhokovich as Baby Spice, relatively demure in a pink thigh-skimming baby-doll dress; and yours truly, caught on camera sulking stubbornly in the background, wearing all black, having refused to

dress up as Sporty Spice because I thought the group costume concept was "lame"

- Clipping of *New York Times* article from September 3, 2000, "Will Cinthia Wallace Be Gen-Y's Literary 'It' Girl?"; annotated by Bridget Milhokovich in pink Magic Marker; commentary includes: "OMG! A billionaire's daughter? Part of the Park Avenue Posse? HOW COME I'VE NEVER HEARD OF HER?" And: "SHE LIED TO US TO SPY ON US!! TO WRITE A BOOK ABOUT US AND GET INTO HARVARD!!" And: "BUBBLEGUM BIMBOS AND ASSEMBLY LINE MEATBALLERS IS A SUCKY TITLE!!!" And, finally: "OMG!!!! WHAT A SUPER BITCH!!!!! I HATE HER!!!!!!!!!!"
- Wally D's Sweet Treat Shoppe employee T-shirt, wrinkled, torn around the collar, stained with chocolate syrup, smelling of rancid sweat and skunky Budweiser, worn during a one-night stand in the basement of Wally D's Sweet Treat Shoppe on July 31, 2005
- Handwritten note dated August 1, 2005, on linen card stock personalized in Engravers MT font (LEN LEVY) thanking me kindly for the one-night stand that had unburdened the author of his virginity
- Printout of first e-mail ever sent by pparlipiano@columbia.edu to notsodarling@hotmail.com, dated March 1, 2002: an invitation from Paul Parlipiano—my high school crush-to-end-all-crushes, obsessive object of horniness, and gay man of my dreams—to a Snake March, a nonviolent demonstration protesting all forms of tyranny thrown by Columbia University's People Against Conformity and Oppression
- Pink gingham print birth announcement for Marin Sonoma Doczylkowski; born May 30, 2002; six pounds, four ounces, nineteen and a half inches long; handwritten note from my sister: "Congratulations on becoming an aunt!"
- Rainbow-colored silk ribbons that decorated my grandmother Gladdie's walker when she lived at Silver Meadows Assisted Living Facility; removed after her death in May 2002
- Pair of malodorous low-top Converse worn almost exclusively throughout high school

- A handwritten poem titled "Fall," inspired by the Adam and Eve Creation myth, dating back to Spring 2000, written by Marcus Flutie on a torn-out piece of notebook paper that was and still is origami-folded into a mouth that opens and closes; sample lines: "But if I am exiled/alone/I know we will be/together again someday/naked/without shame/in Paradise"
- Handwritten lyrics to the song "Crocodile Lies," written and performed by Marcus Flutie on June 8, 2002, also known as the date of Pineville High School's Senior Prom, and the night I was blissfully unburdened of my virginity; sample lines: "You, yes, you linger inside my heart/The same you who stopped us before we could start . . ."
- Red T-shirt, neatly folded and washed, though not in recent memory, with iron-on letters spelling ME, YES, ME across the chest; handmade by Marcus Flutie and given to me to wear under my high school graduation gown as I delivered my salutatorian speech on June 30, 2002; inside the front breast pocket, a folded-up handwritten draft of that graduation speech, titled "Real-World Revelation: A Malcontent Makes Peace with Pineville"; final sentence reads: "For better or for worse, you have helped me become the person I was always meant to be: Me, Yes, Me."
- Thirty-three printouts of Poetry Spam, in which junk e-mail was rewritten into haikus, e-mailed between September 2002 and December 2003 from flutie_marcus@gakkai.edu to jdarling@columbia.edu, including the very first one that arrived during my own college orientation program precisely *four years ago today* (see attached)

To: jdarling@columbia.edu
From: flutie_marcus@gakkai.edu
Date: September 3, 2002
Subject: Poetry Spam #1

jumbled nonsense in
quixotic combinations
becomes meaningful

Original message:
To: flutie_marcus@gakkai.edu
From: beatricem@teletech.net
Date: September 3, 2002
Subject: in price gambit

looking momentous histamines very combinations good suave regarding money kahn rich upside anode multifarious jumbled flavor cursor look becomes what calypso giving christmas spectacular incredible summit caleb perfect abscissa allegheny segregation local nonsense russian girls reunion waiting right email quixotic they're exclusive meaningful bleary residual income biz low journey introduction peacetime

twenty-three

I'm reminded of the story that occurred fresh off your last stint in rehab, in tenth grade, when you were doing your mandatory community-service hours at Silver Meadows Assisted Living Facility. The Turtle Lady Story.

A never-married woman (Hester?) died in her sleep at the age of eighty-seven. She (Esther?) was not a beloved figure around Silver Meadows. If she (Martha?) and my grandmother had been around at the same time, I'm sure Gladdie would have called her "one of those cranks just waiting to die." She (I give up—it was some old-lady name) griped loudly and often about everything. A bowl of chicken noodle soup could be too hot, too cold, too bland, too spicy, too chickeny, too noodle-y, too goddamn soupy. And as that vaudeville chestnut goes, those no-talent bastards who call themselves cooks never gave her enough of it.

Her tiny apartment was filled with nearly nine decades' worth of possessions, most notably her spectacularly useless collection of turtles. Ceramic turtles. Stuffed turtles. Turtles on mugs, sweatshirts, salt and pepper shakers, throw pillows, calendars, and latch-hook decorative wall hangings. Turtles in every conceivable form but the original, breathing kind, as pets are not allowed in Silver Meadows. Everyone referred to her as the Turtle Lady, even to her face, which is why I can't remember her real name. She held this title with great pride, as if it were an honor bestowed by the Queen of England in a scepter-tapping ceremony in Buckingham Palace.

One afternoon, you asked the obvious: "Why turtles?"

"*Why turtles?*" The Turtle Lady had replied to your query with genuine surprise, as if no one had bothered to ask this question before. This surely could not have been the case. But perhaps you were the first to ask in a very long time, the only person in recent memory to take any interest in her obsession. Her extended family was scattered around the country, you had told me, so she rarely received visitors. Only the occasional do-gooder Girl Scout trying to earn her merit badge in Geezer Appreciation. Or reformed ne'er-do-wells like yourself.

"Yes," you pressed. "Why turtles over a more cuddly animal?"

"*I'm* not cuddly," she said. "What, you think old spinsters like me have to love cats? Is that it? Are you disappointed that I'm not the crazy cat lady?"

"Okaaaaaay," you said. "Snakes aren't cuddly. Porcupines aren't cuddly. Why turtles?"

"A turtle is never far from home."

You didn't understand. "Because it moves so slowly?"

"It carries its home on its back, ya big dope!"

You had recounted this story for me about a year later, your response when I questioned your sanity for voluntarily spending time with little old ladies like my grandmother when you had already completed your court-mandated community service. And when you delivered that line to me, you boxed your left ear with your palm, as she had when she said it herself. Despite your repeated attempts to get to know the Turtle Lady better, that conversation did not usher in a whole new era of cross-generational friendship between the misunderstood teen and the geriatric, the kind of heartwarming tale that has kept the *Chicken Soup for the Soul* series in print. No, it turned out to be the longest exchange you ever had.

After the Turtle Lady died, there were no local family members or Scouts to be found. This left you—a seventeen-year-old substance abuser-repaying his debt to society—in charge of throwing away this woman's entire life. A woman whom you had only met a half-dozen times.

You were told to divide her possessions into two piles: DONATE and DISCARD. Most of her belongings clearly qualified for the latter category. But you pled your case for the turtles.

"Maybe they could be donated. . . ."

"To where?" replied the head of building management by phone because he couldn't be bothered to show up in person. "The Museum of Useless Crap?" He chuckled at his own unfunny joke. "Look, kid, people die around here every day. And they leave a lot of junk behind. It's my job to get rid of it." In my imagined version of these events, I cast this character as thin and weaselly and in his late forties. He blinks too much and stinks of stale cigars.

"She didn't leave a will?"

"Not for this stuff she didn't," he said. "All the valuable stuff was divvied up when she left her last place."

Over the next few shifts, you counted, and threw away, 412 turtles or turtle-themed knickknacks. But you also found evidence that she hadn't always been the Turtle Lady. You discovered her old yearbooks, in which you found out that this somber, pursed-lipped old woman had once been voted Class Clown. Loose photos captured her as a stylish dame with a fur around her neck, kissing a man with a champagne glass in his hand. There were faded 4-H ribbons. A NURSES DO IT WITH PATIENCE! bumper sticker. Decades of birthday cards, Christmas cards, "just because" cards from friends in far-off places.

And so much more. All thrown away.

You discovered then disposed of all this evidence of a full life lived well. How did that vibrant young woman turn into the bitter Turtle Lady? Who were the classmates who had laughed at her jokes? Where was the man with the champagne glass? What had she done to win the ribbons? Why did she keep that bumper sticker? Where were all the writers of those cards? Had they all gone before her? Had she outlasted everyone she loved? Wouldn't that make anyone bitter?

Many questions, with no one to answer them.

In the end, you threw almost everything away. You couldn't help but swipe a momento from that woman's room, because you didn't want her forgotten by the world. To this day, that tiny I ❤ TURTLES pin is still stuck to the underside lapel of your peacoat, where only you can see it, when you want to see it, when you want to honor this woman you never really knew when she was alive.

And as I sit on the floor right now, surrounded by Jessie's Junk, I'm not seeing myself as an eighty-seven-year-old spinster, the cliché of the never-married aunt, the shriveled-up presence at Marin's holiday gatherings whom no one wants to sit next to because I spit and mumble and smell like urine-soaked mothballs. (Though that would have been a good guess as to how I might have taken that story to heart.)

No, I'm wondering if the contents of the MOM AND DAD box will be preserved and protected by whoever is put in charge of throwing my life away. Or will it all be considered as worthless as 412 turtles?

Correction: 411.

twenty-four

Ack. I needed to get out of my room and take a break from all that reminiscing. It seemed like a good opportunity to check in with what was going on, so I got up off the floor, headed to the kitchen table, and randomly picked up one of the Sunday *Times* sections scattered across the table. And the Sunday *Times* pissed me off.

This is not at all unusual, because being pissed off by the *New York Times* is an important part of my whole *NYT*-reading experience. As you know, my rage is usually directed at the Sunday Styles section. (No! You will not try to make me feel bad because I don't own a belted funnel-neck sweater dress! No! You will not make me feel unworthy because I have never heard of Club Kashmir, where the eponymous cocktail is one part Cristal and two parts pashmina goat piss. No! You will not make me feel inadequate because I can't afford to buy a Slavic orphan baby, implant a tissue expander in her tender flesh, and harvest her pale, flawless skin to rejuvenate my tired complexion. *Noooooooooo!*") But today it was the Travel section that got my ire up.

On the front page was a travelogue written by a woman who had visited thirty-six cities around the world. It took three months and cost less than four thousand dollars. Now, I never had any real desire to visit many of these places, some of which, like Kyrgyzstan, are countries I thought only existed within Sacha Baron Cohen's imagination. And if I had a few thousand dollars, I would immediately use it to get that student loan bitch Sallie Mae off my back. But I hated this chick nonetheless, for having traveled so far, so safely. She treks though countries that endorse public beheadings. I spend an hour in Virginville, Pennsylvania. Which traveler loses all her possessions? Me.

Last December, I gamely accepted the offer to accompany Hope on her road trip/RISD senior thesis, "Mental States: A Cross Country Tour of My Emotions," for which she planned to take pictures of herself next to the WELCOME TO _______ signposts of our nation's most expressively named cities. We left on New Year's Eve—a symbolic nod to the date, six years earlier, that Hope's family had U-Hauled ass out of New Jersey for Tennessee—and planned to return one month later. I allowed myself these thirty-one days of freewheeling liberation on the open road as a reward for saving myself another fifteen thousand dollars in student loans by busting my ass to graduate from Columbia a semester early. I didn't have a job lined up after graduation, nor any clue where to find one that would utilize my psychology degree. But I'd worked so hard for so long that I deserved this break before having to find one or the other.

I assumed that there would be potholes and detours and wrong turns along the way to Yeehaw Junction, Florida, or Satan's Kingdom, Rhode Island. I had always imagined that those near-disasters were what made road trips so exciting, and I kind of looked forward to them. I wanted to run out of gas on the interstate, get a flat tire in the middle of nowhere, or have my credit card rejected by the sketchy motor lodge and spend the night in the rental car, just so I could return to Pineville safe and sound and regale you with the tales of all these crises averted.

I did not want to get carjacked fewer than twelve hours into our trip.

It's only by chance that this notebook was spared. It was safe inside my messenger bag, right beside me in the booth at the Bandit (yes, hardee-har-har on me) Diner as I tucked into a cheeseburger and fries and listened to Hope try to talk me into jumping out of a plane at a nearby skydiving center.

"It will be fun!"

My first instinct was to say, "Cheating death is not fun." But then I remembered, *I'm on a road trip! That's what you're supposed to do on road trips! Cheat death! Court disaster!* Of course, Hope and I had no idea that our own mini-disaster had already played itself out, by peeling out of the parking lot with all our possessions.

I always think of the notebooks as lost, as in, "I lost your notebooks." I implicate myself as the guilty party when, in fact, I didn't lose your notebooks at all, they were stolen from me, along with the Barry Manilow decoupaged toilet-seat cover and Hope's ninety-nine-cent Ambervision shades and everything else. The car was found, of course. But no object was left behind, no floor mat unturned. Everything was stolen, right down to the last loose penny and forgotten half-chewed Twizzler. Some of our clothing and personal effects were eventually recovered, but they still felt dirty after a dozen washing-machine bleachings. But the notebooks, they were long gone.

On the outside, the notebooks had all looked the same: one hundred sheets, two hundred pages, $9\frac{3}{4} \times 7\frac{1}{2}$ in/24.7 × 19.0 cm, wide ruled. Just like all the black-and-white notebooks I've been writing in since high school. I didn't peek inside before I put this one in my messenger bag and separated it from the rest of its doomed lot. I had randomly grabbed one to read when Hope left me alone at the table to call her parents or go to the bathroom. I didn't know that this was the only one that wasn't about you, but was intended to be all about me.

As soon as Ms. Daisy Schlemmer and Mr. Harlan Oakes, both nineteen, from Kutztown, Pennsylvania, discovered that the Death Valley Diaries, the other eleven composition notebooks left in the car, were just that, composition notebooks, and that they couldn't use them to fund their meth lab, couldn't use the materials to get high in another way, not from smoking the ruled paper or extracting the ink and injecting it straight into their veins, I can only presume Ms. Schlemmer hurled them out the window and into a snowy drainage ditch as Mr. Oakes slammed on the gas.

You never blamed me. And yet sometimes I feel like you punished me with silence when I returned. As if you were so committed to the economization of words that you didn't want to squander any more by repeating what was already put to paper. And if two tweakers destroyed your notebooks, your stories, before I got to read a single word, then so be it.

What bothers me most, the regret that keeps me up at night, is knowing that your words can't be recovered. They're lost forever.

(FOREVER.)

monday: the fourth

(labor day)

twenty-five

I saw Hope only briefly this morning, on her way out. She was changing into a formerly white T-shirt that had been vibrantly transformed by hundreds of brushstrokes. The colors were dense and indistinguishable in the middle, then thinned out to solitary streaks along her flanks. The paint always looks slick and wet, even when it's dry.

"You should sell those T-shirts," I said, rising from my lumpy sheets, rubbing my bleary eyes.

"Really?" she said, looking down. "I use them to wipe off my brushes. I have tons of them. I wear them until they disintegrate."

"I know," I said. "But they look cool."

She stretched the T-shirt away from her body and gave it an artist's appraisal. Then she inhaled the armpit and grimaced.

"Yikes! No one would buy this!"

"Are you kidding? It's the authentic stink of an artist!"

"Who can't remember to buy deodorant."

"Seriously, certain New Yorkers pay a thousand bucks for so-called 'hypervintage' jeans that have been broken in by pre-wear professionals."

"Pre-wear professionals?"

"People who get paid to wear the same pair of jeans for a month without washing them."

"That's nasty."

"I know. So a little bit of funk will add value, I promise. Just replace the Hanes label with one that says 'Hope Weaver' in an old-but-newish font. One word. All lowercase letters. Make a big deal out of the fact that each one is unique and hand-crafted by the artist herself. Sell them alongside the paintings you were working on when you created the shirt. It's wearable art! The consumer as canvas . . ."

Hope cocked her head to the side as if she was seriously considering my ridiculousness.

"Go one step further. Donate fifty percent of the proceeds to a hot celebrity cause. Or is it cause celeb? Doesn't matter . . ."

"African debt relief is hot right now," Hope deadpanned.

"Totally hot. Africa is hot hot hot. Each purchase represents the union between humanitarianism and capitalism, and presents the wearer as someone who *cares*. Market yourself as one of Brooklyn's underground guerrillas, one of many fashion freedom fighters who have determined that the sociocultural revolution won't be televised—oh no—but silk-screened on a limited-edition T-shirt costing upwards of a hundred dollars. . . ."

"How do you come up with this stuff?" Hope was laughing now.

"I'm so much better at managing my friends' careers than my own," I replied. "I swear you won't be able to make them fast enough."

"You know, the sad thing is you're probably right. No one will buy my paintings, but these stinky T-shirts will make me rich and famous."

"Just give me ten—no, *twenty*—percent of the profits after Africa gets its cut, okay? Then maybe I can stop relying on my sister's charity."

"You headed there today?" she asked.

I nodded. "You off to the studio now?"

"Yeah," she replied, looking through her wallet. "Classes start tomorrow, so it's my last full day to work on this final piece I need to finish before Friday. . . ."

"Oh."

She stopped looking when she found her MetroCard. Hope always likes to have her MetroCard in her hand, inside her pocket, ready to whip out when she reaches the subway turnstile. She never wants to fumble around for it, because she thinks that might make her a target for muggers. She doesn't want to admit it, but she hasn't quite adjusted to city living. (Something you can relate to.)

"You need to talk? I'm sorry I rushed off yesterday morning and—"

"What time did you come home last night?"

"I don't know. Maybe three-ish?" A curl fell away from her messy ponytail. Hope *bzzzzzed* a raspberry to blow it out of her eyes. "You were asleep. Did you try waiting up for me?"

"No," I lied.

I *had* tried to wait up for her last night. None of the roommates can afford cable, so my late-night TV viewing is limited to shitty infomercials for skin-care lines shilled by unnaturally preserved has-beens from eighties nighttime dramas, shitty public-access programs promoting local high school screamo bands with names like Baby on Boredom and Go Ahead and Hate Us, and reruns of shitty sitcoms of the fat-slob-husband-with-hot-skinny-wife variety. I scraped myself off the couch sometime around two A.M.

Hope's face fell. "I'm sorry. I should have called. . . ."

I waved away her apology. "It's fine. Really. You have so much you need to do."

"Really? Because . . ." I could tell from her voice that she was relieved.

"It's fine."

She stuck the MetroCard in her deep front pocket.

"And besides," I replied, "if we're going to talk about Marcus, we need more than just a few minutes."

"You *do* want to talk about it!"

"Just go, Hope," I said. "Really. I'll be fine."

"Are you sure?"

Then I made kind of a dick move. "Yeah. I'm having brunch with Bridget this morning, anyway."

"Right," Hope said, trying to keep it light. "Because you tell Bridget *everything*."

I once made the mistake of telling Hope that Bridget had become my best friend after she, Hope, moved. Of course, by definition there can only be one "best." So Hope, who is not one who usually gets involved in these types of power struggles, gets passive-aggressively pissy about it. I don't see it as choosing one friend over another, because each plays a unique role in my life. Bridget is the careful listener. Hope is the carefree talker. And I value them both, just at different times, and in different measures.

Bridget was my best friend in the years before Hope entered my life in middle school, and then again after she left. For too many years, I denied that Bridget was anything more than a superficial replacement for

Hope. But Bridget has proven to be more than just a fallback friend. In those years that I didn't see Hope very much, Bridget was the first person I turned to whenever there was a major shake-up in my life (mostly involving you). There have always been fundamental differences between us, and not those unfair assumptions based on her beachy beauty and how she once put it to use as a professional catalog model and football player's girlfriend—the latter pursued with more go-getter grit than the former.

Our differences unite rather than divide us. She provides alternative insights that expand my myopic pessimism. As such, Bridget has offered more comfort and shrewd advice than any other friend (including Hope). However, when I'm not in crisis mode, and Bridget and I are just blithely shooting the shit on an ordinary day, our talk, while perfectly pleasant, lacks that certain urgency for more. I say good-bye feeling all talked out.

My relationship with Hope is simpler, and paradoxically more complicated. With Hope, there is an immediate intimacy and ease to our conversations that I have not found with anyone else. (But you. On our best days. When we used to talk, or rather, when you used to talk to me.) Hope and I share a love of wordplay, an appreciation of low culture, and above all, a fascination with the tragicomedy of life. We banter playfully and energetically; I always feel happier afterward than I did before. When I'm in her company, I laugh loud and long, which is something I don't do nearly enough.

Our ability to enlighten and entertain each other is based on a deep understanding of the way each other's mind works. However (there always seems to be a "however"), no matter how close Hope and I are, there always seems to be certain taboo subjects that I can't discuss with her (mostly involving you). And these gaps in confidence are usually filled by Bridget. Why should this time be any different?

Hope's eye caught the stack of boxes still taking up too much floor space.

"I thought you stayed in all day yesterday to unpack," she said.

"I started to," I said lamely. "But I got *distracted*."

"You were *distracted.*"

And simple as that, we both giggled at the shorthand joke that only we could understand.

Only we knew I was referring to that last morning before Hope moved to Tennessee. Her parents were waiting in the driveway, glancing at their watches, tapping their feet on the asphalt, jiggling their keys, eager to leave Pineville—and memories of their son's tragic overdose—behind. But when I stepped inside Hope's room to say good-bye, it could only be described as aggressively *un*packed. The carpet was littered with assorted vintage clothing (thirties granny dress, seventies burnout jean jacket), random CDs (*The Very Best of the Partridge Family*, *Biograph*), stray art supplies (crusty brushes, flattened tubes of oil paint), and miscellanea of the female hygiene variety (no need to elaborate). Hope was untroubled by her lack of progress, and assumed a yoga pose that put her on her back with her legs flipped up and over so her toes touched the floor behind her head. Her mantra?

"I'm distracted."

And so, with my invocation of this simple exchange from our past, the last few moments of awkwardness were forgotten. (Well, not quite forgotten; otherwise I wouldn't have written about it.)

"I'll see you tonight," Hope said. "I shouldn't be too late."

"Sure," I said, knowing that she never meant to be too late, but she lost track of all time when she was at the studio.

After we said our good-byes, Hope hesitated in the doorway for a moment. Her paint-stained fingertip touched the wall, tracing the intertwined vines in Claire's name. Then she dropped her hand, gave me a shy, closed-mouth smile, and turned away without another word.

I rolled over and looked at the top of the bunk. Kirk was gone. In his place was Michael J. Fox as Marty McFly.

JESS:

YOU CAN TAKE ME "BACK TO THE FUTURE" ANYTIME.

LUV YA, MIKE

twenty-six

It is a testimonial to how much I value my friendship with Bridget that I agreed to be her maid of honor. I assumed this role would require my participation in certain bridal rites that rank well below other distinctly female activities, such as running out to the twenty-four-hour drugstore at midnight to buy high-absorbency tampons. But Bridget is my oldest friend, and her sunny optimism is a rarity in this city. Even rarer is the purity of Bridget and Percy's love for each other.

I've known Bridget since diapers. I've known Percy since French I, when he was a tiny, hairless freshman, and I was the sophomore object of his comically misguided Pepé Le Pew–like flirtations. It's been five years since Bridget and Percy were cast as the leads in the 2001 Pineville High production of *Our Town*, and yet I *still* can't fathom how they progressed from mere acquaintances (through me), to friends in their own right, to more than friends, to a long-term couple who kiss and do other, uh, intimate things. It should be no surprise that I can't quite wrap my head around the prospect of them uniting as man and wife. In fact, the only thing I consider to be even more extraordinary than Bridget's ardor for Percy—whom she has been blissfully and abnormally dating since high school without a breakup or even so much as a major fight—is the fact that she has not made any progress on this wedding, which is supposed to be happening next September. Bridget has been the anti-Bridezilla, putting most of her energy toward more practical concerns, namely, making sure she graduates with Percy in June, because she lost a bizillion credits when she transferred from UCLA to NYU to be with him.

Lately Mrs. Milhokovich has been putting the pressure on her daughter: *Is this wedding happening or what?* So now, with a year left for planning, I assumed that Bridget had called for this brunch so we could sit down with our respective calendars and schedule appointments with the cake stylists, floral artisans, and favor specialists who would have me tied up in the Knot for the next twelve months. I have braced myself for these tasks ever since I agreed to be her number one bridesmaid last December.

I assumed that the first order of business would be the finding of the Gown, followed by the far-less-important search for the bridal party's complementary couture. I'm still scarred by the memory of being dressed up like a banana for my sister's wedding when I was sixteen. Though Hope had assured me that bridesmaid dresses have come a long way since then, I could only hope that Bridget's color scheme would be inspired by a more flattering fruit or vegetable. And I didn't have to think too hard about how stunning Bridget would look on her wedding day, because with her classic blue-eyed blond looks, she's always resembled my own sister (and mother) more than I do. So superficially blessed, Bridget could easily pull off a wedding dress made entirely out of engineered lunch meat.

When we were younger, before my parents moved to their waterfront condo across town, Bridget and I always sprinted across the street and up the stairs to the other's bedroom to break any big news. Now that we're both in the city, we've settled on an undistinguished Irish pub in Brooklyn Heights to serve the same purpose. Bridget says she doesn't mind making the "trek" to Brooklyn from the East Village because such interborough subway travel makes her feel more like "a real New Yorker." Of course, merely having such thoughts undermines any cred she's earned, but I love the pure ingenuousness of her efforts.

Bridget got there before I did, looking radiant and reluctant to say good-bye to summer in a crinkly-cotton Empire-waist dress and flip-flops. She was seated at a plastic-covered table past the already rowdy regulars at the bar, in a small alley-like seating area tucked back near the kitchen and unisex restrooms. It was my favorite table because it had the best view of all the random Irish-themed artwork hanging crookedly in mismatched frames along the deep green walls: an eight-by-ten glossy of Colin Farrell in a still from *Miami Vice*; a poster of a football team, the Notre Dame Fighting Irish 1988 National Champions; a Dublin street map; a collage of U2 ticket stubs; and so on.

Bridget greeted me with a cheery little wave.

"I already ordered for us," she said, grinning merrily in anticipation of the $7.95 breakfast plate of deep-fried bacon, eggs, hash browns, and soda bread that we always split when we met here.

We hugged hello and had barely settled into our rickety seats when Bridget began our conversation with a gleeful yet terrifying, "I've got big news!"

I might have flinched.

"We're not getting married."

I almost tipped over in my chair. "What?!" Water spilled from glasses and silverware clattered as I clutched at the table to retain my balance. "You're breaking up?"

"Nonononononononono!" Bridget's pale hands flapped around her lovely face like the wings of a dove struggling to take flight. "We're not breaking up at all! We're still engaged."

"But you're not getting married?" I was confused.

"Well, hopefully someday. But not until gays can do it, too. And even then we'll probably elope."

"Really?" She had taken me completely by surprise. "When did you decide this?"

"I don't know. It's a pretty hot topic around school. And as a black man, Percy really sympathizes with the struggle for equality. We wouldn't join, like, a racially segregated club, so why would we participate in an institution that discriminates against homosexuals?"

"Well, that makes a lot of sense. . . ."

This was a lie. I respected them for taking this stance, but it didn't seem like their battle to fight, especially when not all gay people even *want* to get married. My former writing professor/mentor, Professor Samuel MacDougall, even wrote a book about it, *An Unconventional Life*. To be honest, I never got around to reading the book, but I did catch a lot of the controversy surrounding its publication, and how it made him a traitor to gay activists and a hero among right-wing conservatives who champion traditional "family values." From what I saw in the *New York Times*, Mac merely argued that gay-rights activists were squandering their resources and energy battling for the right to participate in a failing institution rooted in subjugation and conformity. We'd all be better off if we fought for other causes that improve *everyone's* lives. Gay, straight, and in between.

"Are you upset? You seem upset. I hope you're not upset! Because Percy thought you might be upset."

"Why did Percy think I would be upset?"

"Well, because you're the maid of honor and you'll, like, miss out on all the girlie stuff."

I rolled my eyes so hard that the blowback nearly took my head off my shoulders. "Does Percy know me at all?"

"I told him you'd be relieved," she said, relaxing a little. "I know you're so not into the whole wedding hoopla."

(Okay. At this point you might be a little skeptical about the veracity of this conversation. I mean, all this wedding talk so soon after your proposal. *Really?* I wouldn't blame you for thinking I was pulling some James Freysian high jinks—you know, narrative manipulation that goes above and beyond the typical shenanigans employed by nonfiction writers through the ages. You will just have to believe me when I say that this conversation, even more so than others already documented in this notebook, occurred almost exactly as depicted here. The sheer implausibility of this conversation calls for a compulsory and most careful transcription.)

"But you know what I didn't realize about myself until after I got engaged? *I'm* not into the wedding hoopla. In fact, I hate all the wedding hoopla. Am I really supposed to care so much about the font I use on my personalized napkins?"

She waited for me to shake my head, then continued.

"And what a waste of money. Did you know that my mother was going to put a second mortgage on the house so she could pay for this thing? If she's determined to spend her money, it would be so much smarter to use it to pay off our student loans, or put it toward a house. But we're not even sure she'll give us the money if we're not using it for the wedding, which is just so backward-thinking it's scary."

I barely got in a nod before she went on.

"And having people gush over me all day long as if I were Wedding Barbie come to life? *Bleech*. I don't want anything to do with it!"

That part made sense. For most women, their wedding day is the only day in their entire lives when they are indisputably the most beautiful woman in the room—even if they are not. Bridget is almost invariably the most beautiful woman in the room. She's so *oohed* and *aahed* at all the time, she doesn't need fifty thousand dollars spent for the privilege.

"Have you ever seen *Battle of the Brides?*" she asked. "It's a reality show. I think it's on Bravo."

"We can't afford cable."

"Oh, yeah. Right," she said. "Anyway, this show is all about brides-to-be competing against each other for the *wedding of their dreams.*" She said the last words in a singsong, then stuck out her tongue. "They have to do all this crazy stuff. Like in this one episode it was the Touch of Silk competition. Six psycho brides standing outside in the freezing cold with one hand on this twenty-five-thousand-dollar wedding gown, which wasn't even all that pretty. It was just too, too much. So tacky, like a cheaper version of the fifty-pound white duchess satin monstrosity the Donald's latest wife dragged down the aisle."

I don't doubt that Bridget is indeed disillusioned by all the "wedding hoopla." But the fact that she knows that Mrs. Trump III wore a fifty-pound white duchess satin dress—hell, that she even knows the term "white duchess satin" at all—indicates that Bridget has jumped through one or two of those hoopla hoops already.

"If they took their hands off the dress, even for a split second, they were out. These women were *possessed.* They just had to have this ugly gown like it was everything worth living for. And after, like, twelve hours, *not one* of them had been eliminated. So the evil producers made them take off their comfy shoes and put on white stilettos with, like, four-inch heels. Still, not one of them gave up. Finally, after they'd been in the competition for something like eighteen hours, they wheeled in these gigantic speakers and got this hyperactive wedding deejay calling himself DJ Jazzy Spaz to blast nothing but Barry Manilow songs."

I've read somewhere that blasting Barry Manilow has proven to be a successful POW torture technique. The funny thing is, if I had been in this Battle of the Brides competition—and you know this is the ultimate counterfactual—the sounds of Barry Manilow would have encouraged me to keep on going, to never give up, to keep my goddamn hand on that gown until it was mine, all mine. One woman's torture is another's sign of the divine.

I was oddly compelled by Bridget's dramatic coverage of this story. "So they stood out there for eighteen hours? Without breaks?"

"They got, like, a five-minute break every six hours or something. And they would hobble off to the sidelines and their future husbands would massage their aching feet and coach them through the next round. 'They're going down, honey! You're the leanest, meanest bride ever!' And then these psycho brides would start weeping about how hard this was, how it was torture, how it was the most difficult thing they have ever endured in their entire lives, and I was like, SOLDIERS ARE DYING IN IRAQ RIGHT NOW."

The motley crowd assembled at the bar—all drinking pints of the hair of the dog that bit them the night before—turned around to look.

"Sorry," Bridget said to the gawkers, then to me: "As you can see, the whole thing was really sick. That's what started to turn me off weddings. Why is there so much emphasis on that day, and so little about the fifty years that come after?"

I laughed. "You sound suspiciously like me."

"I know!" she said. "You've always said that if you got married, you would elope to Jamaica." She was right. I have been saying this since my sister's wedding. "Just you, your husband, and some Rastafarian minister . . ."

She stopped mid-sentence. Her eyes were magnetized to the bit of metal on the fourth finger on my left hand.

"What is *that*?"

I dropped my hand to my lap. But it was too late.

"Was that a *ring*?"

"Uh . . . yeah."

"A *ring* on a *significant finger*?"

I brought my glass to my lips and choked down a mouthful of room-temperature tap water.

(I suppose I should provide a valid excuse for keeping your ring on the significant finger, knowing that doing so will only invite comment and conversation on a subject I'm not sure I wish to discuss. Ah, but therein lies the answer. Taking it off would mean that I wasn't giving your proposal the full week of consideration I promised. Keeping it on forces me to confront the complications that made it impossible for me to respond to your proposal when it was first popped. And honestly, who would even notice an unblinged bit of silver that looks nothing like a traditional engagement ring . . . ?)

"You've let me go on and on without telling me you're, like, *engaged*?!"

"Well, I'm not—"

"Did Marcus ask you to *marry him*?"

I actually laughed when she said that because it was (a) absurd and (b) the truth.

"Is it *true*?"

I nodded, unable to say it out loud. Discussing this situation in the confines of Sammy was one thing, but saying it out loud, in public, was another.

"You and Marcus are getting married!" She squealed and bounced up and down in her chair, again drawing the attention of the bar crowd. But this time she was too happy to be embarrassed. Unlike Hope, who was shocked by the news, and Manda, who was merely amused by it, Bridget was sincerely thrilled by the prospect of our union.

"Did you hear that, Siobhan?" Bridget gushed to our regular waitress, a tough, thirtyish punk originally from County Cork with sleeve tats covering her milky-white, well-muscled arms. "She's getting married!"

While I winced at my friend's enthusiasm, Siobhan set down one empty plate in front of Bridget, and another heaped with steaming meats and starches in front of me. Our waitress then paused long enough to smile with her lips pulled tight against her crooked teeth, and said something unintelligible in a brogue as thick as a pint of Guinness.

I waited until Siobhan hustled back to the bar before asking, "Did she just say, 'Coughs on your anus'?"

Bridget cackled and said, "I think she said, 'Coffee's on the house!' "

"Oh," I replied with a slightly embarrassed chuckle. "I thought it might be a traditional Irish blessing or something."

As Bridget loaded up her empty plate, I realized such perks hadn't been my imagination after all. I thought I'd noticed Bridget getting preferential treatment—free appetizers, cleaner dressing rooms, discounts taken off at the cash register—all given with a wink and a wish of good luck. But it was difficult to tell whether she scored freebies based on the humble diamond on her finger or the immodesty of her beauty. But free coffee for me? Is it possible that the whole world—including its most cynical city—is seduced by the sight of a betrothed young lady? I suddenly understood the advantages of an endless engagement, and not only those of a financial nature. Why not live in that lustrous state for as long as possible, when your love is only about the promise of a happy future? When total strangers want to get in on the goodwill and are compelled to wish you well?

"I can't believe it!" Bridget burbled. "You're getting married!"

"Well, I didn't say yes."

"Why didn't you say yes?" she said, biting off a piece of bacon. Before I could open my mouth, she offered her own hypothesis. "I bet you feel too young to be married," she said, gesturing with the half-eaten piece of pork. "I know! I kind of went through that, too. Everyone is like, 'Bridget? What is this? Utah? In the 1950s?' "

"Well . . ."

"Manhattan is probably the toughest city in the world for marrying young. It's got a lower number of married couples than almost anywhere else in the United States. And those who do get married do so later than the average, more like twenty-seven instead of twenty-five." She paused to take a breath. "But there seems to be a bit of a reversal lately. In yesterday's Styles section there was a twenty-three-year-old bride marrying a twenty-four-year-old groom—"

"It sounds like you've done your research."

"I had to!" Her hands and fingers were flying like a whole flock of doves now. "Because, like, not a day goes by that someone doesn't look at my engagement ring and tell me I'm too young, that marriage is a dying institution borne out of patriarchal oppression, that couples used to get married to have sex, and since the age of sexual liberation, of the Pill and *Roe v. Wade*, single women can have as much sex as they want without getting married. . . ."

I imagine that Bridget's fellow NYU undergrads have made these arguments many times over. For as many well-wishers as there are, there are just as many, if not more, naysayers. My predisposition is to be in the latter camp, but it was my obligation as maid of honor and best friend to stifle those natural instincts and put a smile on my face and a dress on my body that no alterations could turn into something I'd ever wear again.

Honestly, I could never understand how Bridget—an only child fought over in a nasty divorce—could have planned to get married at twenty-three. It didn't matter whether they exchanged vows on the marble altar of St. Patrick's Cathedral or on the soft white sands of Montego Bay, I loved Bridget and Percy so much that I didn't want to see them walk down the aisle to their doom.

So their decision to defer marriage comes as a relief. Sort of. What if all those naysayers have made Bridget reconsider, and this marriage-for-everyone argument is just a clever cover-up, a noble way to drag one's feet indefinitely, and avoid taking the relationship to the next level without having to break it off? Or are they really so confident about the depth of their love that they don't need all the wedding hoopla, nor the crashing, crushing banality that follows? An unconventional life. Together.

"Let's say you wait until Marcus graduates," Bridget continued, making mental calculations. "That's four years from now, which would make him twenty-seven and you twenty-six. That's, like, right around the national averages, and not at all abnormal even by, like, New York City standards."

Again, I opened my mouth, but Bridget kept right on going.

"And if you're thinking about having kids, you can get them out of the way early," she said. "And you're still young enough to embark on a career after your kids are in school. . . ."

"Bridget," I said, tearing off a piece of crusty soda bread, "you're talking crazy."

"What do you mean?"

"You've got me married and pregnant already," I said, "and I didn't even accept his proposal."

"Okay," she said, "which brings us back to the original question: Why not? Don't you love him?"

(Yes.)

"Yes," I said.

(But.)

"But . . . ," I said.

"But what?" Bridget asked. "Would you have said yes if he had a degree and a job?"

"But he doesn't."

"But what if he did?"

" 'What ifs' are what Marcus calls counterfactuals."

"Counterfactuals?"

" 'What ifs.' Counterfactuals. Hypotheticals. All the same thing," I explained. "All a waste of time and energy. Because no matter how long you ponder them, it doesn't change the reality of the situation: Marcus is in school for at least four more years."

"Move to Princeton."

"What worked for you and Percy won't work for everyone." I sighed. "You transferred from UCLA to NYU because you hated the superficial L.A. scene. You had other reasons besides Percy for leaving. If I leave New York for Princeton, it's only to be with Marcus. I don't have any reason for being there other than to be with my boyfriend."

"But isn't that enough?" Her pretty face was marred by disappointment when I didn't answer right away. "So you don't want to move. Isn't a long-distance relationship better than none at all?"

"I don't know," I said warily. "We're exactly where we were four years ago, with him one place and me somewhere else. You saw for yourself how he can't handle the city. . . ."

"That night with the drag queen," Bridget said, visibly recoiling. "The Shit Lit Hissy Fit."

(Does it bother you to know that my friends have a special name for that night? Well, they do. It was that . . . memorable.)

"Right. And I don't want to visit him on the weekends at Princeton, only to compete for his attention with twice-a-day meditation, term papers, and impromptu coed volleyball games."

(I wish I had said this to your face, before I left your room on Saturday.)

"Maybe I don't want to compromise anymore. Why should I have to be the one to compromise? Because I'm a girl? Please. I'd be letting down our gender with that kind of thinking."

A knowing smile crept across Bridget's face.

"What?" I asked.

"You sound like Manda." Bridget giggled.

"I DO NOT SOUND LIKE MANDA." I was coughing, nearly choking on my eggs. "Don't ever say I sound like Manda."

"But you doooooo," she taunted in a jokey singsong. "She's rubbing off on you."

"I hope not," I replied. "I would have to get a full battery of STD tests. . . ."

At that moment my cell phone rang. I groaned when I saw that it was my sister, calling to remind me that I was already late for her Labor Day soiree.

"You're still coming, right?" Bethany asked.

"Yes," I said, "I'm already on my way."

"Fabulous!" she said. "Just remember you're a guest today. Though you're not really a guest, because you're family! You know what I mean! Just have fun and enjoy, Jessie. I mean it. Enjoy! Enjoy! Enjoy! Enjoy!"

I assured my sister that I would enjoy myself as if my motherfucking life depended on it.

I hung up and rolled my eyes. "Don't even ask," I warned Bridget.

Siobhan slapped our bill on the table as she hurried past.

"Look, I love you and Marcus together," Bridget said, returning to the topic I was eager to drop. "I just want you to be happy, whatever you decide to do."

I sighed and examined the muddy grounds in the bottom of my coffee mug. "Me too."

As we stood at the register paying the bill, I noted a small black-and-white portrait posted by the front entrance. In it, a foppish young man wearing a fur-trimmed cloak leaned toward the camera in a throne-like chair, one hand clutching an ornate staff and the other resting thoughtfully against his temple. His soulful eyes spoke almost as clearly as the words written beneath his photo:

"We can have in life but one great experience at best, and the secret of life is to reproduce that experience as often as possible."

—OSCAR WILDE (1854–1900)

I had never noticed it before, though Bridget assured me that it has always been there.

We stepped outside and hugged good-bye. I turned to head in the opposite direction down the sidewalk when Bridget called out to me.

"Hey, Jess!"

"What?"

She raised her arm in the air, as if she were making a toast with an invisible mug. "Coughs on your anus!"

"Coughs on *your* anus!" I said, seized with gratitude for our friendship. "And Percy's, too."

twenty-seven

A Brief and Meaningful Conversation with Marin

"You know what would be awesome?"

"I don't know, Marin. What would be awesome?"

"I can't tell you."

"Why not?"

"Because I'm going to invent it. And if I tell you, you might invent it before I do."

"I wouldn't do that!"

"You say that now, but once you hear how awesome it is, you won't be able to stop yourself, because my idea is *just so awesome*."

"Okay, then I'll just have to wait."

"Auntie J? Just out of curiationosity . . ."

"Curiosity."

"*Cure-ee-oss-oh-tee.* That's what I said. Anyway, has anyone ever tried to make a doll that totally knows you and talks and plays like a real sister but you can turn her off when she gets annoying?"

"Like a robot?"

"Yeah! Like a robot sister doll."

"I think something like that has been invented. But that shows you what an awesome idea it was. . . ."

"Darn it. Grown-ups get to do everything first."

"You'll be a grown-up someday."

"Who cares? By the time I'm a grown-up, everything will already be done already!"

"Marin, I totally know what you mean."

twenty-eight

I'm aware that the preceding oh-so-twee exchange with Marin is nothing special, the fodder of a bizillion blogging mommies trying to out-Dooce one another with tales of their precious, precocious spawn. Or worse, something straight out of the cornball Metropolitan Diary in the *New York Times*. But such conversations are meaningful to me, if only because I never expected them to mean so much. I love Marin, and value all the time we've spent together. She has single-handedly restored the term "awesome" to its fundamental awesomeness, and back from the meaninglessness of mundane misappropriation.

That said . . .

I'M SO RELIEVED THAT I HAVE A JOB INTERVIEW TOMORROW.

Seriously, after eight months of sponging off my sister, I've absorbed about as much guilt as I can handle. I'd hoped that moving out of her place and living on my own would help me feel less like a deadbeat and more like a sister again. This was an idiotic notion. How independent can I feel when Bethany's exorbitant babysitting wages are the only thing keeping me doggy-paddling above the poverty line? I'm embarrassed for myself every Friday afternoon when I accept a check in the amount of three hundred dollars for ten hours of playing with my niece. This is twice the going rate (fifteen dollars) for babysitting services. And it's almost one and a half times more than my hourly wage (eighteen dollars) at my "real job."

I can't help but use quotations. It feels like a fake job, one I can explain using terms of negation: I'm (minimally) paid for my (quasi) employment at a (micro) magazine with a (barely-there) audience. I am virtually employed in every sense of the word. I don't commute. I don't have a cubicle. I don't have coworkers, which means no office rival to bitch about, no commiserating underling to gossip with, no clueless coworker on the other side of the divide who blasts his iPod too loud, no secretary with Dilbert clippings and I DON'T DO PERKY coffee mugs. It also means no coffee breaks or water-cooler conversation about last night's episode of, uh, *The Office*. No staff meetings. No performance reviews. No punching in late or punching out early. There's scarcely any evidence that I'm actually employed by *Think* magazine other than the assignments messengered to my apartment, the weekly time sheets I fill out and turn in after messengering back said assignments, and bimonthly paychecks for completing them to my editors' approval.

Because you displayed a decidedly European indifference to my job, I will now answer all the questions you never asked about it. Every day I get an electronic message (or several) telling me what needs to be done: journals to be read, articles to be fact-checked, taped interviews to be transcribed. I've never met any of my fellow editors, and I've only spoken to my top editor once on the phone. I don't even think of him as a real person, Robert Stevens, editor in chief. To me he's an e-mail address: r_stevens@thinkpub.com. And I'm pretty sure they don't want to put a real human face to my in-box either, otherwise they might feel more guilty about not hiring me full-time. Honestly, sometimes I wonder if I am part of a grand experiment, the lab rat in someone's postdoctoral thesis, "To Commit or Bullshit? A Case Study in Employee Loyalty and Productivity in an Imaginary Workplace."

The worst part about it? I actually like what I do. *Think* mixes reprints of journal articles and research abstracts with original essays and interviews. Since winning the National Magazine Award for general excellence in the small-circulation category a few years ago, it has had no shortage of A-list contributors. The other day I spent four hours painstakingly transcribing a ten-minute conversation between Bono and Bill Gates about the psychology of philanthropy. It's my job to geek out on the readings and research that I used to follow as a hobby. Isn't this the goal for any worker? To be paid for what one would do for free? I would happily take a full-time position as the lowest of the low on the masthead, if such a position were available. But it's not.

Prestige doesn't equal profits. I mean, we're not talking Condé Nast or Hearst here, or even Time Inc. or Hachette Filipacchi. This is Plato Publishing, which specializes in niche periodicals that are hybrids of commercial magazines and academic journals. In addition to *Think* ("Pop Psychology for Smart People"), there's *Bio* ("Every Cell Has a Story"), *Theory* ("Where Your Guess Is as Good as Ours"), and a few others. Since *Think*'s target circulation is less than fifty thousand, I can hardly blame my quasi-employer for the budgetary constraints. There aren't enough laypeople interested in subscribing to a publication that proudly compares itself to *Utne Reader* and *Psychology Today*. *Think*'s tagline should be revised to "Deep Thoughts, Shallow Pockets."

Think hires freelancers like me to do the work of an editorial assistant so the company doesn't have to provide 401(k) plans or medical insurance. And though I could easily work eight hours a day, I can only bill a maximum of twenty hours a week because that's all the budget allows. This isn't enough to live on without the supplementary income from my sister. Thus, tomorrow's job interview. It promises $32,000 a year with benefits, which might be enough to take me off Bethany's payroll if all my meals come from a can. (More on this later.)

I don't know why I'm so ashamed about accepting my sister's money. I can only count one true trust funder among my circle of friends. (Author-turned-activist Miss Hyacinth Anastasia Wallace is rumored to have inherited roughly fifty million dollars when her dad died earlier this year. Imagine the payout if he hadn't split when she was four, or sired ten half siblings with his next three wives?) Yet nearly everyone I know who is not in the financial sector—and certainly all of us living in Sammy—are or have been subsidized by a munificent patron of the arts.

Hope has an ancient benefactress from her Tennessee hometown, whom she refers to as the "Sugar Grandmama." Manda's parents paid her college bill, so she can sort of afford to put herself into debt for grad school. I have Bethany, of course, and if Gladdie hadn't left me $50,000 when she died, I would now be in that much deeper to that hillbilly bitch Sallie Mae who bills me $437.25 a month . . . *just on the interest*. One simply can't pursue a vaguely creative career in this prohibitively expensive city unless you're independently wealthy or your life has been generously underwritten.

(I know, I know. Then why live here? Why live in a city that is systematically designed to undermine happiness and prosperity? Why not come to the land of peace, quiet, and opportunity, colloquially known as the borough of princes? Why not come to the place where my true love resides . . . ?)

Maybe I would feel more okay about accepting Bethany's money if she had earned it herself and wasn't married to half the mastermind behind the Wally D's Sweet Treat Shoppe/Papa D's Donuts empire. I once made the mistake of referring to their money as *Grant's* money and she didn't talk to me for several weeks. I know better than to say it twice, even though I think it all the time. And yet Bethany must be aware of the awkwardness of our current patron/pauper relationship. She must know that if it weren't for her generosity, I'd be maxing out my credit card on ramen and stealing rolls of toilet paper from public restrooms.

Or (shudder!) living in Pineville with my parents.

Lately she has repeatedly tried to persuade me to join the family business—a more legitimate and less humiliating form of handout. Her recruiting went a little too far last time, when she basically asked me to be a corporate whore for her hubby's empire. And I mean that as figuratively as figurative can go before it turns literal.

twenty-nine

"Try this on," Bethany said, without further explanation.

"What is it?"

"It's *adorable*, that's what it is."

It was a tiny T-shirt with two lip-smacking rainbow-sprinkled donuts encircling each breast.

"DONUT HO'?"

"It's a play on words!" Bethany offered unnecessarily. "We'll debut the new uniform with the launch of Papa D's newest treat. . . ." She grandly gestured at the plate set before us, on which there was an assortment of glazed, chocolate dipped, and sprinkled treats, the kind that Papa D's most famous competitor has copyrighted as Munchkins. "DONUT HO's! Get it?"

I got it, all right. I got that I wouldn't have to perform the sort of sordid acts that my XXX namesake, Jessica Darling the porn star, is famous for. But I would be expected to wear a uniform that *hints* that I just might perform such acts if the price was right.

"I don't see what the T-shirt has to do with me. You told me Grant wanted me for a job in marketing . . . or something."

"Junior Vice President of Branding."

"Uh-huh."

"Grant needs bright, attractive women like you to tour target cities like Atlantic City, Vegas, Reno, maybe Los Angeles. . . ."

"Wearing *this?*" I asked.

"Well, of course. We need you to meet with potential investors. We're trying to penetrate an untapped market. . . ."

"In this T-shirt, the untapped market will want to penetrate *me.*"

"Of course," Bethany replied, not getting the joke. "This is a chance to see major growth in new regions. . . ."

"Major *growth* in the *nether regions.*"

Then I let her finish for the next five minutes, during which I learned that Grant and Wally D'Abruzzi had even been bestowed the honor of "Best New Franchisers" in *Capitalist* magazine, with new Shoppes opening up all over the country, including some in the unchartered territories of the South and Midwest. And yet there was always room for improvement. Apparently, Papa D's Donuts "exceeded sales projections" in the suburbs. It merely "met projections" in the exurbs. But it "underperformed" in urban areas. My brother-in-law was always looking for new ways to bump himself up to the top 99.99 percent of earners from his current 99.9 percent position, so this underperforming just wouldn't do.

It was a vexing question: How could he increase customer traffic in the urban areas, where one could get coffee and handheld carbohydrates on just about any block? The solution, according to my brother-in-law and my sister, was simple: sex.

"Why do guys go to Hooters?" Bethany asked.

"Hot wings, hot chicks."

"Exactly!"

"So . . . pastries and prostitutes?"

"We won't employ prostitutes," Bethany said matter-of-factly.

"You'll employ girls to look like prostitutes. . . ."

"*And* provide peerless customer service," my sister added.

"A lap dance with every latte!" I volunteered mock helpfully.

"Hmm." Bethany pensively tapped her manicure on the countertop. "I think it would violate the city's cabaret laws. . . ."

She was still dead serious. This reveals an elemental cause of all our miscommunication. I am fluent in snark. Bethany only notices snark when snark grabs her off the sidewalk, throws her in the back of a sketchy van with tinted windows, drives to the middle of the Meadowlands in the dead of night, and uses a heavy blunt instrument to smack her repeatedly about the head as it screams, "I'M SNARK. DO YOU FUCKING HEAR ME? I'M SNARKY SNARKY SNARK!" And even then she's like, "Ohhhh? Snark? Is that you?"

"Bagel and a blow job," I continued in my gleefully facetious vein.

"We don't sell bagels," she said, ignoring my comment because the only thing my sister lacks more than a snark detector is a sense of humor. "Anyway, this is not a customer service position. You wouldn't be *selling* the donuts. You'd be selling a *lifestyle* as a paid representative of the Wally D's/Papa D's Retailtainment Corporation on the franchise level. . . ."

"If we're working off of the Hooters model, would I pair my DONUT HO' T-shirt with a pair of shorts?"

"Any ideas are welcome. Grant is always looking for ways to grow our business. He appreciates the brainstorming process. . . ."

Yes, he appreciates the give-and-take exchange of ideas so much that he couldn't even be bothered to meet with me in person.

"Ooh! Ooh! I've got it!" I said, wildly waving my hand in the air. "A pair of silver short-short-short-shorts . . ."

"Okay . . ."

"I mean *reeeeeaallly* short," I said. "So short that you'll have to consider providing medical benefits that cover, you know, certain *female infections*." I whispered these last two words. "Shorts like these don't exactly, you know, *breathe*. . . ."

"Great . . . ," Bethany said, losing interest.

"So picture a handprint on each butt cheek. . . ." I smacked my own ass stripper-style—*SSSSSLAP! SSSSSLAP!*—to emphasize my point.

"I'm picturing it. . . ."

"And in pink script: 'HOT-N-STICKY BUNS.' "

" 'HOT-N-STICKY BUNS,' " Bethany repeated to herself, trying it out.

"Think about how *Playboy* has marketed its image to the masses," I said. "DONUT HO' T-shirts. HOT-N-STICKY BUNS trucker caps. DONUT HO' lunch boxes. HOT-N-STICKY BUNS onesies . . ."

"I love it!" Bethany said, cheeks flushed. "See? You're *perfect* for this job."

"Bethany," I said, my voice calm. "I'm joking. This whole thing is a joke."

"Of course you're joking! We're all joking! It's tongue-in-cheek!"

"It's certainly tongue-in-*something*. . . ."

"DONUT HO'. HOT-N-STICKY BUNS. It's all fun and sexy."

"It's sex*ist*, Bethany, not sexy."

Bethany set her still-steaming mug of chai tea on her gray marble coaster that was protecting her white marble countertop.

"If a guy wants to pay double for a donut served by a hottie in a DONUT HO' T-shirt and short shorts, then why shouldn't we profit from it?" she asked. "What's so wrong about a woman using her feminine wiles for capital gain? This is a pro-female promotional campaign!"

This was a secondhand argument Bethany was making. I'm sure it was first made by her husband to gird himself for the inevitable protests from Christians and Friedan-model feminists and whoever else hasn't had much to do lately since Howard Stern went satellite. And what better person to take this perverse pro-feminist argument public than a flat-chested corporate figurehead with a newly minted Ivy League degree? G-Money was an evil genius. He deserved every penny he had ever earned.

I couldn't expect someone like my sister to understand why the DONUT HO' promotion was just another pathetic example of "feminism" gone wrong. She has soared, swooped, and glided through life on the gilded wings of her golden good looks. I mean, it's one thing to be a MILF and have other people refer to you as such in private. "*Now* there's *a mom I'd like to fuck.*" But it is quite another to unapologetically and unironically refer to yourself and your circle of friends as MILFs, as my sister and her friends do.

I would love to lecture her on how embracing the porn aesthetic doesn't liberate women, it only validates men's right to objectify us. And objectification is objectification, even if the woman profits from it, and especially so if the profits come in the form of wads of bills stuffed into teeny G-strings. How is our gender ever going to be taken seriously if the tacit promise to give head is the easiest way to get ahead . . . ?

(Oh my. I *do* sound like Manda. I'll just stop right here.)

thirty

What could be so bad about attending an end-of-summer barbecue in a beautifully cultivated garden atop one of the most envied brownstones in Brooklyn Heights?

Ask the hostess. Bethany hates throwing parties. Oh, she'll deny it. But she hates it. Whereas our mom totally gets off on being the sole person responsible for conceiving and executing her fabulous backyard-on-the-waterfront affairs, my sister totally freaks out, even when she hires professionals for all the traditional party-hostess duties (cooking, serving, cleaning, bartending, etc.) short of greeting her guests at the door.

True to form, my sister met me in full Stepford-on-meth mode.

"Jessie! You're here! You're twenty minutes late! I thought you'd never arrive! The MILFs are all here!"

(See? I wasn't kidding about that MILFs thing.)

The MILFs came together through their husbands, all of whom met G-Money in business school or shortly thereafter while working as tireless young turks on Wall Street during the get-rich-quick tech boom of the late nineties. The threesome invited today had all wisely invested in Wally D's/Papa D's Retailtainment Corp. and were now enjoying their good fortune. The husbands spent the afternoon cavemanning the ten-thousand-dollar grill, marveling at the flames ("Ugga. Ugga. FIRE.") and attacking large chunks of charred flesh with titanium spears ("Ugga. Ugga. MEAT.").

Their wives were huddled together, wineglasses in hand, gossiping in bemused, beleaguered tones about their spouses' Cro-Magnon display, conspicuously similar in an Atkins-thin and Blandi-blond kind of way. They were all simply yet expensively dressed. Their body-skimming luxe T-shirts were paired with linen gauchos or swingy, silk twill circle skirts. They wore leather thongs or ballet flats on their pedicured feet. They never over-accessorize. Perhaps a pair of silver hoop earrings, a beaded necklace, a jade bangle bracelet. Each knows that her ostrich-egg-sized engagement diamond is all the bling any tasteful woman needs.

(I had slipped your handmade ring off my finger and into my front pocket. I had learned from Bridget that it *would* be noticed, and I didn't want to have *that* discussion in front of *them*.)

After careful observation, I have noticed subtle and not-so-subtle differences among these four women that make this group friendship possible. The distinctions comprise a complicated system of checks and balances, one that ensures that any individual MILF does not gain preeminence over any of the others.

My sister is by far the most beautiful of the four, but with her (our) humble middle-class roots and a B.A. from an undistinguished state school, she is undermined by a certain lack of cultural and intellectual sophistication. Dierdre earned a Ph.D. in art history from the University of Virginia, but makes no secret of her sexless marriage. Liesl is a Main Line Philadelphian and has multiorgasmic sex with her husband, but has achieved only an approximation of attractiveness through several painful surgeries and frequent tweaks from an alliance of on-call aestheticians. Meredith has a B.A. from Wesleyan, has sex once a week, and is naturally attractive, though not anywhere close to beautiful. A moderate among extremists, Meredith could upend the whole social order if it weren't for the tribe's tendency to gang up against her when she's acting "know-it-all-y."

I know I'm oversimplifying here. But I feel at liberty to do so because the MILFs have assigned themselves to similar stock roles. Get a few drinks in them, and it's not uncommon to hear them refer to one another by the character names of famous TV foursomes. A handy reference guide:

BETHANY = CHARLOTTE = ROSE = SUSAN

DIERDRE = MIRANDA = SOPHIA = BREE

LIESL = SAMANTHA = BLANCHE = GABRIELLE

MEREDITH = CARRIE = DOROTHY = LYNETTE

And if one of them isn't around, you should hear them fight over who makes the best Rachel, leaving the other two to make the desultory choice between Monica and Phoebe.

I once made the error of joining in on the game.

"Hey, Cartman," I said. "Kenny wants to know if this wine is the same vintage as the Pinot Noir that Kyle uncorked for Stan's birthday party."

They looked at me as if I were a three-hundred-pound party-crashing crack whore who had just cannonballed into the Soho House swimming pool in an ass-flossing bikini. I didn't make the same mistake twice.

The MILFs are stay-at-home moms (SAHMs) by choice. They can all afford to outsource the very best in child care, but take great pride in favoring occasional (and often blood-related) babysitters over full-time nannies. The four MILFs have produced six kids in all, two singletons (Marin and Driver) and two sets of twins (Pierson/Lene and Seamus/Maura). The children range in age from twenty-four months to four years old and are all remarkably poised and polite, yet not preternaturally perfect by any means. They are all capable of whining, bullying, and other bratty or downright brutish behavior, and I've caught the quick flash of relief crossing the faces of three of the MILFs when the fourth's kid is "having a moment."

When I arrived today, none of the kids was "having a moment." All six were being happily entertained by the Non-Stop Party Patrol, a popular troupe consisting of a half-dozen Broadway-level performers who are also certified child-care professionals. Despite this 1:1 ratio for a party that will last four, maybe five hours at most, the MILFs don't see themselves as outrageously decadent by New York City standards. No, they have made a very conscious decision not to be "one of *those* mommies." This is a group effort. There's no indisputable definition of what it means to be "one of those mommies," and certainly no trustworthy authority on how to avoid being one. So like all successful cliques, the MILFs have designated themselves experts on all subjects of importance, eschewing conventional wisdom in favor of their own. They live by their own specific and ever-changing set of rules, which as a childless outsider I am totally incapable of following.

I'm sure they must be grateful to have other mommies to turn to in times of maternal crisis, but I can't help but think that the MILFs have all become co—or rather, quad—dependent, shunting common sense for the sake of the group. To sustain their utopist microcosm of mommyhood, one MILF cannot make a decision without consulting the others: Soy milk versus organic cow's milk? Tory Burch Kids versus Gap Kids? Looney Louie versus the Non-Stop Party Patrol? And once a decision is made, the option that meets the MILF stamp of approval is deemed OTB, short for "only the best." As used in a sentence: *Bethany hired the Non-Stop Party Patrol. They're OTB!*

OTB isn't restricted to the realm of child-rearing. I've overheard Bethany on the phone seeking the MILFs' taste-making OTB approval in great debates such as: Quinoa versus couscous? Pointy toe versus round? Restalyne versus your own ass fat? It reminds me so much of the Clueless Crew at the height of their persuasive powers in middle school, when one wouldn't so much as put a butterfly clip in her hair without making a three-way conference call first. It must be exhausting to keep up with OTB. No wonder Bethany needs me to give her a two-hour break every day.

Today Bethany was soliciting opinions on something far more substantive than usual: her new business idea.

"Jessie! I was just telling everyone about my plans for the Be You Tea Shoppe!"

My sister hopes this will be the next moneymaker for Wally D's/Papa D's Retailtainment Corp., and the first in which she will play more than a peripheral role. The Be You Tea Shoppe, as Bethany imagines it, will be a one-stop destination for grandmothers, mothers, and daughters to get makeovers and mani-pedis while consuming teeny-tiny sandwiches and sipping hot beverages with their pinkies up. It would also be very, very pink. Some visionaries get their ideas from great works of literature or music. I'm fairly certain that Bethany got her inspiration from that episode of *The Brady Bunch* in which Mike Brady is commissioned by a hottie crackpot named Gigi to design an office that looks like a pink powder puff.

"It's Libby Lu meets Dylan's Candy Bar meets Alice's Tea Cup," my sister gushed. "You know that cute place on the Upper West Side?"

The MILFs cooed appreciatively.

"Genius!"

"Just what this city needs!"

(And, of course . . .)

"OTB!"

"Well, go out of your way to tell your husband to tell my husband," Bethany said pointedly. "Because he won't listen to me."

That Bethany doesn't see any difference between DONUT HO' and the Be You Tea Shoppe is totally beyond my comprehension. I might have even said this if the MILFs hadn't suddenly turned their attentions on me. I knew what was coming next.

"So, Jessie," asked Dierdre, "what's new and exciting in your life?"

I played it coy. "Oh, nothing much."

"Oh, stop it!" Meredith insisted.

"We're boring mommies who live vicariously through you!" Liesl insisted.

"How's that hot bad-boy boyfriend of yours?" Dierdre asked.

"Oh, didn't you hear? He's reformed," Bethany piped in. "He's a Princeton man now. . . ."

"Oh, la-di-da," Liesl trilled. "Your sister says your Princeton man is quite the swordsman. . . ."

I shot my sister a horrified look.

"Jessie! I never said anything like that. Liesl, you tell her the truth."

"No, she never said that," she confessed. "No, I believe her actual words were 'quite the cocksman.' "

"Liesl!" My sister jerked with irritation and spilled her Vintner's Reserve Chardonnay on the slate patio.

I knew Liesl was lying. My sister would never use either term.

"Just tell us one of your stories," Meredith implored. "We all love your stories."

I am twenty-two years old. Single. No kids. These women have totally fetishized me.

"Okay," I said, relenting. "A few weeks ago I was hit on by a drag queen named Royalle G. Biv. . . ."

The MILFs clapped and whooped in anticipation.

Yes, ladies, gather round. It's time for the boffo single-girl-in-the-city spectacular you've all been waiting for, *The Jessica Darling Show*, starring none other than that fabulous, funny twentysomething herself, Jessica Darling!

thirty-one

"I'm friendly with someone sort of famous. . . ."

"Hyacinth Anastasia Wallace!" My sister had heard this story already, but was up for it again.

"Cinthia Wallace?" asked Meredith. "The party-girl-turned-writer-turned-philanthropist?"

"The same," I said.

"The one who just got a huge inheritance from her father?" asked Liesl.

"The *same*."

"You *know* her?" asked Dierdre skeptically.

"Yes," I said with a sigh.

"How?"

"Look, do you want me to tell the story or not?"

"Yes!!!"

"Anyway, she asked me to join her at this event called Shit Lit that's held once a week in this cabaret slash club on the Lower East Side."

"What club?" Meredith asked.

"Why do you care?" Dierdre snapped.

"You won't know it," Liesl added.

"I might," Meredith said.

"You haven't been out clubbing since 1998," Dierdre replied.

"It's called Come," I said.

Meredith pretended to contemplate whether she was familiar with this club. The others mouthed "I told you so" to one another.

I pressed on. "So at Shit Lit, performance artists and actors and writers read from the worst books ever written."

"Like what?" Meredith asked.

"Always with the questions, Dorothy," cracked Dierdre.

"Someone read from Leif Garrett's autobiography, *I Wasn't Made for Dancin': The Ups and Downs and Ins and Outs of the Ultimate '70s Pinup*. And every Shit Lit includes a segment known as 'Thirty Seconds of Pat Jamison,' which is a dramatic reading of the worst paragraph in the latest bestseller from Pat Jamison's hacktory."

"I kinda like his books," my sister said. "They're quick reads." She looked at the others for support. Liesl seemed with her, Dierdre and Meredith against. I doubt my sister will read another Pat Jamison paperback.

"So Hyacinth Anastasia Wallace wrote a book when she was seventeen, all about going undercover at a suburban New Jersey high school."

"I remember that book! Came out a few years ago. Hot-pink cover." Meredith again.

"Right. Well, it was my high school she wrote about, and me and my friends in particular."

All but my sister gasped. "Omigod!"

"Anyway, it turned out not to be much of a big deal because the book sucked and the movie they made it into sucked even harder. So Cinthia was there to read from that book."

"What was the name of the book again?" Bethany asked.

"*Bubblegum Bimbos and Assembly-Line Meatballers*. And as I said, it really sucked. Perfect for Shit Lit. So the master of ceremonies is this cult hero of the downtown demimonde known only as Homo Hitler. He looks exactly like *der Führer*, only his Nazi uniform is a lovely shade of lavender and his swastikas are striped with queer-friendly rainbows."

"No way!" they all cried.

"Yes way," I replied. "And he flits around the stage and lisps, '*Sieg heil*, bitches!' "

The MILFs gasped with laughter, then formed an even tighter circle around me, pressing me for more details.

"So I'm sitting at the same table as my friend Cinthia and a few others. Homo Hitler introduces her, and she gets up on the stage to thunderous applause. Her seat doesn't remain vacant for long because it's a packed house. I look to my left, and this towering drag queen has swooped down and taken the spot beside me in a whirl of sequins and feathers. He extends his manly, manicured hand and introduces himself in this super-deep voice that doesn't sound female at all."

"Royalle G. Biv!" My sister can't help herself

"And I take his hand and tell him my name. And then Royalle booms, 'You *are* a darling!' And I roll my eyes. Then he's like, 'How many times have you heard that line, right?' And I tell him that I've heard it many, many times before, but never from a man wearing a sequined evening gown. And he goes, 'Well, dearheart, there's a first time for EV-ER-RAY-THANG!' "

I notice that my sister lip-synched EV-ER-RAY-THANG.

"Then Royalle winks at me, no small feat considering each individual false eyelash is the length of a swizzle stick."

This got some giggles.

"Royalle does not make an attractive woman. If she were a woman, she'd be the most hideous woman I've ever seen, one who could file a class action lawsuit against the ugly stick."

Dierdre and Meredith laugh first; my sister and Liesl quickly follow.

"My friend Cinthia is doing the intro to her reading, explaining how the book was published when she was eighteen and how there was avid speculation as to the authenticity of the work—"

"Oh yeah, I remember that," Meredith said.

"—and how she wishes she could lay the blame elsewhere, but she has to confess that this faux ghetto affront to the written word was hers, all hers. And the only fitting way to atone for her literary transgressions was to read them out loud. . . ."

I was kind of losing them. They wanted more of Royalle.

"Okay, so just as she starts to read, I feel this huge hand on my knee. And I, like, totally launch myself out of my chair, I'm so shocked. And I shoot a look at good ol' Royalle, who is, like, puckering his overdrawn, red, waxy clown lips in my direction.

And before I could continue, my story was interrupted by uterus-curling shrieks ("MOOOOOOOOOOOOMMMMMMMMMMMMMMMMMMMYYYYYYYYYYYYYYYYYYYYY!") coming from the playroom. Without a word, all four MILFs made a mad dash downstairs to find out who was the unhappy source of the sound.

thirty-two

You were with me that night. That is, until you had the Shit Lit Hissy Fit and bolted. I only told them half the story, but here's the other half, the part you missed:

After you stormed out, Royalle asked me if he was to blame for your hasty exit.

"I was only fooling around, dearheart!" Royalle boomed.

"I know that, and so does he," I said. "It wasn't your fault."

"Why aren't you going after him?"

"Because this is what it's all about. This is why people come to New York City. It's just this quintessentially bizarre New York experience. . . ."

"Whatever do you mean, dearheart?"

"This," I said, gesturing around the room. "You," I said, pointing at him/her. "Getting hit on by a drag queen named Royalle G. Biv. Ostensibly, this is what I want out of living here."

"Os-WHAT? Honey, you're losing me with your big words," Royalle replied. "KISS, KISS. Keep It Simple, Sunshine!"

If that wasn't the kind of crazy, single-in-New-York night I'm supposed to remember, then I don't know what is. But even then I was already thinking of it as an experience that would be better retold as a funny story than actually lived.

(And I was right.)

thirty-three

I wasn't alone on the rooftop for long.

The husbands generally ignore me, except Mr. Dierdre, who sleazes all over me in his wife's absence. Mr. Dierdre seems intent on adding me to the roster of barely-legal concubines ready to do his adulterous bidding. He's always trying to impress me with his cash, his connections, his "comedy." He's got a pointy bald head, and too much flesh hanging around his neck. The resulting combination gives him an unlikely yet striking resemblance to an uncircumcised penis. I secretly call him Rumpelforeskin.

Rumpelforeskin always corners me at Bethany's parties, which isn't too hard to do because I'm usually lurking in the corner.

"You still working for that brainy magazine?" he asked, adjusting the tan knit cap covering his dome. I swear to God he looked just like a life-sized demonstration for Safer Sex Awareness Week.

"Yeah," I said, barely able to mask my laugh with a cough.

"You're so pretty," he smarmed. "You should be working for *Cosmo*. Or that other magazine my wife reads . . ."

Were women really impressed by this? Enough to become his whore du jour? Just because he was rich? And why did Dierdre put up with it?

(Then again, perhaps Dierdre and the MILFs are on to something. They—my sister included—are a bit of a throwback to the early seventeenth century, when *everyone* married for money. Back then, as throughout human history, marriage was primarily a financial arrangement, more about the merging of property and assets than hearts and souls. If you were lucky, you eventually fell in love with the person you married, but it was by no means a given. Couples stayed together because of the stigma of divorce, of course, but also because they learned to live happily together within these lowered expectations. Ironic but true: It's only when people started marrying for love, and not money, that connubial miseries intensified and divorce rates skyrocketed.

Okay. Bridget isn't the only one who has done her research. You'll forgive me for wanting to make an informed decision.)

"So where *is* your *wife*?" I asked, searching the rooftop for someone who would save me.

He ignored the reminder of the Mrs.

"*Vogue*? You look like the *Vogue* type."

Rumpelforeskin was trying to spin lies into carnal gold. Nothing could have been further from the truth. I had borrowed an emerald green drop-waist silk jersey tunic from Hope. She wears it comfortably and fashionably over jeans, and promised it would work similar magic as a minidress on me. It did not. The green fabric billowed in all the wrong places and came off as a maternity muumuu. And when paired with the busted high school–era Chucks recovered from the MOM AND DAD box, the overall effect would certainly keep fashionistas guessing. *Wait, are you going for a sort of knocked-up teen runaway look?* I was definitely more vague than *Vogue*.

"Your *wife* reads *Vogue*?"

"Did I say wife? I meant my *ex*-wife. Actually, she's dead. She died. That's why I'm here now. Mourning." He put on a pout, causing the fleshy overhang to retract just a bit.

"Oh, really? I could have sworn I just saw her tending to your *children*."

"You must be mistaken. My wife died in a stingray attack," he said, squeezing his voice in pretend sorrow, wiping fake tears from his eyes. "Just like the Crocodile Hunter. The barb tore right through her heart. . . ."

Oh, did I mention that Rumpelforeskin was as topical as he was comical? And he went on, without any encouragement on my part other than the fact that I was still standing there and hadn't jumped over the rooftop fencing and parachuted to safety with the excess fabric of my mommy-to-be muumuu.

"And the weird thing about it was that it happened in a swimming pool. . . ." Then he broke character and started cracking his own shit up. The rubbery flesh bobbed up and down. Erect. Flaccid. Erect. Flaccid. Ew.

I was one second away from screaming, "Rumpelforeskin! Rumpelforeskin! Rumpelforeskin!" when Bethany came and tugged on my elbow.

"Can I steal you away for a moment?" she asked.

And as I went off with my sister, I thought about how the MILFs would have loved the story of Rumpelforeskin, that is, if he didn't happen to be married to one of them.

thirty-four

"Is Marin okay?" I asked.

"Oh, she's fine," she said. "Liesl's son, Driver, was having a moment."

"Oh," I said. "Well, thanks for rescuing me."

She didn't respond. Since Marin wasn't involved in the fracas, I assumed Bethany had faked her urgency. But when she led me past the partygoers, downstairs and into the quiet of her bedroom, I realized that she really did want a one-on-one. I spent a lot of time at my sister's place, but rarely entered her bedroom, which was expensively decorated in a minimalist and modern fashion designed to showcase the grandest panorama in all five boroughs.

"Christ," I whispered under my breath. "You can see everything, from the Statue of Liberty to Lower Manhattan." I pressed my head to the glass. If I stretched my neck, I could even see the spire of the Chrysler Building.

My sister pointed out, "See that crane, right there? That's where the World Trade Center used to be. The towers were twice as tall as any of the other buildings in the skyline."

Then we stood next to each other, silently looking into that empty space in the sky, both imagining what it must have been like to wake up every morning to that sight. And on that one morning in particular.

"You know what's weird?" Bethany asked.

"What?"

"That the best thing about our home is the view of someplace else."

Intentionally so or not, it was one of the deepest observations I've ever heard come out of my sister's mouth. I almost said so, but she spoke first.

"I've been wanting to talk to you about a few things," Bethany said after a few moments, gesturing for me to sit next to her on an ochre velvet chaise at the foot of her mahogany platform bed.

"Bethany," I said, interrupting. "I know what you're going to say. . . ."

"I don't think you do," she said softly.

"You want me to work for the Be You Tea Shoppe," I said. "I think it's a great idea, but . . ."

Bethany shook her head, and the sun bounced off individual strands of her hair that were more golden than others. "That's not what I'm going to say."

"Then what?"

"I want to make you Marin's legal guardian."

That is definitely not what I thought she was going to say.

"Oh my God!" I gasped, digging my fingernails into her upper thigh. "Are you sick? Are you dying?"

Bethany mustered a laugh. "No, no," she said. "I'm perfectly healthy. So is Grant. The chances are very unlikely that you would ever be called upon to act in that capacity." Bethany's impersonal word choice hinted that she had rehearsed this speech before delivering it. "But you know, things happen," she said, darting a nervous glance out the window. "And we need to know that Marin will be in good hands. . . ."

And those good hands were mine? Watching her for two hours every afternoon is one thing, but being her parent? I mean, I didn't take one step toward the playroom when I heard the shrieking. I wasn't programmed to react like any protective parent would. Was it instinct? Or could I learn how? And the most vexing question: Did I even want to?

It was a lot for me to process.

"Why are you asking me now?" I asked.

"Well, there are several reasons, actually," she said, tracing circles into the velvet with her fingertip. "Marin starts school tomorrow, and I had to fill out all this paperwork—you know, emergency contacts and such. And it just got me thinking about who would take care of her in the event of a real emergency."

"You waited until now to designate someone? She's four years old. What if something had happened already?"

"Oh," she said, looking down. "Until now, Mom and Dad were her legal guardians. But . . ."

I knew what was on the other end of that "But."

"Not this again!"

"I have reasons to be worried. . . ."

"Mom is *not* leaving Dad just because you caught the wrong episode of *Oprah*."

"*Jessie*," she said with big-sister irritation. "All the Signs are there."

The Signs That My Mom Is About to Leave My Dad

1. She's Asserting Her Financial Independence

My mom brings in more income than my dad's post-retirement pension by redecorating, or "staging," homes for sale in a way that makes them more attractive to potential buyers.

"You think it's just a coincidence she named it Darling's Designs for *Leaving*?" my sister argued.

2. She's Improving Her Physical Appearance

The Botox was one thing. But now my mom's face is so full of high-tech fillers that on a molecular level, it more closely resembles my running shoe than anything animal in origin.

"She's a GILF," my sister said.

"Ack," I said.

3. She's Distancing Herself from Her Spouse

It's true, my mother is hardly ever at the condo anymore.

"But I saw them having sex!" I cried.

"Can you *please* stop reminding me that you saw Mom and Dad having sex?" Bethany snapped.

"*You* just called her a GILF," I shot back.

"You walked in on them two years ago," she pointed out. "And that doesn't prove anything, anyway."

I know she's right. I've convinced myself that the only upside to walking in on my parents having sex was knowing that they still loved each other, despite all evidence to the contrary. I know it's naive to believe that one afternoon delight is enough to keep any unhappy couple together, but it's all I've got.

"I've seen it before, Jessie." Bethany nodded sagely. "I know the cycle."

"Where have you seen it before? And talk shows don't count."

"With one of my friends," she said.

"Dierdre?" I whispered, shooting a furtive look at the closed bedroom door.

"No!" she said, her eyes exploding with surprise. "Why Dierdre?"

"Oh, I don't know," I said. "Maybe because her husband was *just totally hitting on me*."

"He was?"

"Yes! Ack! He was!"

"Are you sure he wasn't just being friendly?"

"No, he was being skeevy."

"Wow," she said, looking off into the middle distance for a moment.

"Okay, so who is leaving her husband?"

"Liesl," she said.

"Liesl?" I was surprised. "But she and her husband have sex ten times a week!"

"Again with the sex," Bethany said. "Is that all you think mature relationships are built on? I hope not for the sake of your future with Marcus."

(I suppose I could have told her right then about the proposal, but it just didn't seem appropriate.)

"Anyway, even if I'm misreading the signs, and I'm just being totally crazy here, it doesn't change the fact that Mom and Dad are getting older and aren't the best choice anymore." Bethany took my hand and looked me in the eyes. "You are."

"And Grant agrees?'

"Well, yes," she said with a sigh. "He doesn't think much of his own parents' child-rearing skills. And his brother is the eternal frat boy. Grant says that the idea of him being Marin's legal guardian would make an amusing Adam Sandler movie, but in real life? Not so much."

I wanted to tell her that the idea of me being Marin's legal guardian was like a Kate Hudson movie, only without flattering lighting and designer wardrobe. But it wasn't a time for jokes.

"Even though I'm single? Shouldn't Marin have a father figure?"

Bethany mustered a rueful laugh. "Her father figure is hardly around as it is." (I'm glad she said it before I did.) "And you make it sound like you're going to be single forever. . . ."

(FOREVER.)

"So me."

"So you."

I don't know how long we sat next to each other, listening to the sounds of the party above, gazing out the window into the void. Then I finally responded.

"I need to think."

"Don't stress yourself about this," Bethany said. "Don't think *too* much."

(Where have I heard that before?)

thirty-five

Marin was so enraptured by the Non-Stop Party Patrol that she'd had nothing to do with me the whole time I was there. I wanted to wish her luck on her first day of school, so I popped my head into the playroom.

"Marin?"

Marin was wearing a purple ringer T-shirt and a sparkly yellow tutu over jeans. She positioned herself in front of a perky, ponytailed dancer with her legs apart, arms up, and hips gyrating round and round. Her tongue was out, and her chin was slick with spit, both signs that she was concentrating really hard on learning the choreography to "2-Getha 4-Eva," the closing number from *Grease 3: The Return to Rydell*. My niece had forced me to watch this DVD more times than anyone with memories of the original should be reasonably required to endure.

This was our little secret, you see. If Bethany had any idea that we had spent so many weekday afternoons in front of that DVD, I doubt that I would have vaulted past all the others on the list of potential legal guardians. When Marin is in my care, I am supposed to follow The Fun Chart™, a calendar created by a team of leading child psychologists that structures each day around "activities that aid in the acquisition of specific developmental milestones." The Fun Chart™ has met MILF approval, proving that the reviled Park Slope Mommies have not cornered the market on "multidisciplinary explorative colloquia."

Watching *Grease 3* might be acceptable once, maybe twice a month, and only if it was a day officially designated by The Fun Chart™ toward the cultivation of Marin's Auditory, Creative Expression, and Language skills. By allowing her to watch *Grease 3* once, maybe twice, or even three times a *week* if we're both tired and cranky enough, I'm defying The Fun Chart™ mandate to engage in Fine Motor, Visual Perception, and Cortical play, which means she'll never get into one of the "better Ivies" and her life is ruined.

Obviously, all that stuff is B.S. Back in the day, my mom's idea of educational play was devising the rehearsal dinner menu for Barbie and Ken's wedding. And I turned out okay, despite an utter lack of Proprioceptive stimuli. Likewise, I doubt that there was much emphasis on your Tactile/Kinesthetic skill set when you were in juvenile detention. And just look at you now, a Princeton Tiger.

As a babysitter, I can get away with breaking all the rules because, as any amateur Freudian knows, it's Bethany and Grant who can do the most damage to Marin's fragile psyche and future earning potential. I can't imagine a more high-pressure job—especially in this city.

Case in point: Marin fell off the monkey bars a few weeks ago. She landed in a bloody tangle of arms and legs. She howled for a few minutes but calmed down with the promise of ice cream and *Grease 3*. No broken bones, but her knee took the hardest hit, making it difficult for her to walk. I did what any sane caregiver would: I scooped her up and carried her back to Bethany's place. I was about halfway there, waiting patiently for the Walk light, when a smug thirtysomething wearing a heart-rate monitor and three-hundred-dollar running shoes looked right at Marin and said, "*You* should be walking." He dashed to the other side before the comment registered.

It was a dick thing to say, because it was none of his goddamn business. What made it worse was his cowardliness. Oh, it takes a big man to admonish a four-year-old still sniveling over her bloody boo-boo instead of the adult who happens to be holding her. But I let it go because this guy was obviously a fitness Nazi who had made it his moral imperative to end childhood obesity by berating one injured, immobile preschooler at a time. By the time Bethany got home, I was ready to joke about it. But she didn't think it was at all funny.

"ARRRRRRRGH!" Bethany growled, balling up her freshly manicured hands into fists. "Why can't people mind their own business?"

"He was a jerk."

"Everyone thinks they have a right to parent everyone else's kid in this city! Everyone's an expert!"

"Let it go. . . ."

"*You* try to let it go when you know that every time you walk out the door, people are passing judgment on how you raise your child."

From that afternoon on, I could hardly blame Bethany for surrendering to the MILF groupthink. I know I'm an adequate babysitter. Sometimes I'm even an above-and-beyond babysitter. But am I ready to accept permanent responsibility for Marin's care and well-being? I've never had a pet. Not a guppy, not even a sea monkey.

After the fourth or fifth attempt to draw her attention away from the Non-Stop Party Patrol, my niece finally half-turned her blond head in my general direction.

"Auntie J," she said, with a whine beyond her years, "can't you see I'm *busy?*"

Bethany assures me that such withering disdain is a sign of the deepest devotion.

"After all," Bethany said, "you can only really, *real*ly hurt the ones you really, *really* love."

(Oh, don't I know it.)

thirty-six

When I returned to Sammy, the apartment was empty. The ride on the subway and the ten-block walk back to the apartment had left me feeling sticky, so I decided to take a cold shower. As soon as I stepped inside, I caught a whiff of the mildewy plastic. Our shower curtain was slick with pinkish mildew, and the moistest bottom corners were flecked with specks of greenish mold, a sort of preppy nastiness. The tiles were dull with soap scum; the grout had turned gray. I stood ankle-deep in a dirty puddle because the drain was clogged with the foulest congealment of human hair and conditioner.

The inability to bring our bathroom up to reasonably clean hygienic standards is one of the grossest examples of our collective immaturity and incompetence here in Sammy. Of course, we all wanted a clean bathroom, but only Shea—yes, Shea—had the wherewithal to actually pick up a sponge. She had the lowest tolerance for scum, and would be the first to hit the bleach when she couldn't take it anymore. Of course, while doing so, she'd unleash an expletive-laden tirade about how we were the most worthless pack of spermburping jizzmops she'd ever met, but even that was a small price to pay for a clean shower stall.

So I was in the shower, lathering up with Hope's ginger-scented shampoo, debating whether she would also notice if I used her razor to shave my legs, when I heard the unmistakable sound of the bathroom door bursting open. I poked my frothy head through the curtain just to confirm that it was the pervert I knew, and not a pervert off the street.

"Christ, Manda! Privacy!"

Her thong was already at her ankles. "That's an amusing request coming from someone who is *watching me pee*!"

I grumbled and yanked my head back inside the stall. "Don't flush!" I yelled out, but it was already too late. The hot water surged from the showerhead and singed my skin. "OUCH! FUCK!"

"Oops!"

I waited for the sound of the door opening and closing behind her.

When I didn't hear it right away, I stuck my head outside the curtain yet again. Manda was still in the same spot, panties up, toilet lid down. She was bent in half, lazily inspecting her pedicure.

"Hope called," she said breezily. "She's at the studio. Can't do dinner. The usual."

"Okay!" I said. "Thanks for the message! You can leave now!"

"I assume you didn't get laid," Manda said. This is her standard greeting whenever I've returned from just about anywhere.

"I have a boyfriend, remember?" I asked, quickly rinsing my hair.

"*Fiancé*," Manda corrected. "Remember?"

I could feel my blushing embarrassment, even under the hot water. With the ring off my finger I had, in fact, forgotten. I changed the subject. And quickly.

"Well, I was hit on by a married man who resembles an uncircumcised penis."

I expected her to heave a bored sigh and say something like, "Haven't we all?" But instead she said, "Sara called. She had the baby."

"Welcome, Destiny Estrella."

"You mean Alessandro Destino."

"What?"

"Turned out that their little girl was hiding something between her legs."

Well. So much for the D'Abruzzi Pussy Legacy. Is nothing sacred?

"I bet Scotty is happy about it," I said.

"They both sound really happy," Manda said. "Like really, ridiculously happy. So happy that we both kind of forgot that we hate each other."

"That's nice," I said. "Okay, you can leave now!"

Manda paid me no mind. "So happy"—she paused to draw a deep, dramatic breath—"that I had an epiphany."

I turned off the water and poked my head out again. Manda was still picking at her toenails, waiting for me to ask about her epiphany.

"Can I hear about your epiphany after I get dressed?"

"Prude," she muttered as she walked out without bothering to shut the door behind her.

I slowly dried off and then wrapped the towel turban-style around my wet hair. I got dressed in a pair of weeks-unwashed cutoffs that could walk on their own and one of Hope's white Hanes T-shirts, straight from the package, still stiff. I really need to do my laundry. I emerged from the steamy bathroom to see Manda waiting for me on the Olga couch, a plastic cup in her hand and a box of white zin on the floor. She had tapped a second cup for me, so I felt obliged to sit down next to her.

"Your epiphany?"

"I broke up with Shea!" She gripped my shoulders with her hands, as if I might reel from the shock. "Are you shocked?"

Manda wanted me to be shocked.

"I'm not shocked," I said, and Manda limply removed her hands.

"Go on, then," she said.

"Go on how?" I asked.

"Go on with how I'm a bad lesbian. . . ."

"I don't think you're a bad lesbian. . . ."

"How my open omnisexuality makes me a traitor to the cause . . ."

"What? Breaking up with Shea makes you a traitor?"

She nodded somberly.

"Well, I think you'll be doing the lesbian community a favor by not settling for a relationship with Shea. I mean, I was kind of surprised that you two were together at all."

Her eyes narrowed. "The girl-girl thing freaked you out? Oh, puhleeze. And I thought you were open-minded. . . ."

"I am open-minded," I said. "I was fine with 'the girl-girl thing.' But I didn't understand why you were with Shea, of all girls. A girl who acted like an idiot teenage boy."

"My aunt would say it's treason," Manda said, dramatically covering her eyes in mock shame. "Not just against lesbians, but my whole gender."

"How so?"

"Because I'm admitting that her idiot teenage boyness is what I found so attractive. That when I'm reincarnated, I want to come back as a teenage boy. I mean, what creature on this planet is freer, and more liberated, more about id and impulses than a teenage boy?"

I still didn't get it.

"But you would have never dated a guy who acted like Shea," I said. "You only dated Shea because she was a *girl* who acted like a guy. That's the only reason you put up with her obnoxious behavior. It made no sense."

"I *know* it didn't make any sense," she said. "If we only fell in love when it made sense, the human race would have died out long ago. Because who makes sense? Do Scotty and Sara make sense? Do Percy and Bridget make sense? Do you and Marcus?" She thrust an accusing finger right at my heart.

(We already know we don't make sense. And never have.)

"Anyway," she said, dropping her hand to examine a hangnail, "it was an easy break. Shea didn't even care. She just said, 'I'll move out my shit, yo,' and that was it. She was out in under two hours."

"So she's gone? For good?"

"I hope so," she said. "I hate clingers. Clingers are *the worst*."

"So that was your epiphany, to break up with Shea."

"Oh, no," she said. "That was just one small part of my greater epiphany. My epiphany was much bigger than Shea."

Manda has a tendency to take frequent breaks in the middle of her stories, so the listener is forced to goad her on. It gives the illusion that the listener is more interested than she really is. I hate giving in to this gambit, but it's the only way to speed things along.

"And?"

"Well, after I talked to Sara and Scotty, I realized that for all my redefining sex on my own terms, I'm not having all that much fun. I'm not all that happy. I need to be in a relationship that makes me happy."

"Have any of your relationships made you happy?"

And she sighed into the couch cushions. "Only one."

And I braced myself for what I knew she would say next.

"Len," she said. "Oh, yes. I'm going to win back Len." She gleefully rubbed her hands together, like a scheming cartoon villain. I was stunned by how quickly Manda could shift allegiances from straight to gay to straight again. That must be some sort of Ann Heche-ian hetero-lesbo-hetero record.

"I'm not sure if that's a good idea, Manda. I mean, he's got a girlfriend now."

"The time-traveler bitch? Puh-leeze. I saw her picture on Len's blog. No competition."

I'd also seen it on "Mouth of the Wormhole." Len met Camilla at a Time Traveler party, an MIT nerdfest in which an open invitation is extended to any future-dweller who might be interested in using his or her time machine to go back in history just so he or she could attend their shindig. Yes, the general idea is that the guest of honor would have to manipulate the whole space-time continuum for the pleasure of tapping (a) the keg and (b) some ass. (Which is pretty hardcore, when you think about it. We have problems persuading people to come out to party in *Brooklyn*.) The only person less likely to show up at a Time Traveler party than a dimension-bending honoree is a brainy female hottie like Camilla. I mean, the odds of that happening are infinitesimal, which is why I'm so happy for both of them, and Len in particular. I do not want Manda to wreck this for him.

"Len seems really happy now and . . ."

"And what?"

"He was devastated when you left him for Shea," I said. "It took him a long time to get over you. . . ."

Manda slurped the rest of the pink wine from her cup before calmly asking, "Was he over me when he fucked you?"

I winced. She smiled wickedly. "So it *is* true," Manda said. "You fucked Len."

(I did. But you know this already.)

It doesn't matter how Manda found out, though the smart money would be on Sara.

"It was a mistake," I said.

"Oh, puh-leeze," she said dismissively. "His virginity pledge was such a pain in the ass when we were together. I'm relieved you got to him first. Now he'll appreciate my many gifts when we get back together."

I ignored the insult. She waited until I took a sip of zin before proceeding.

"I called him."

"What?!" Pink spit shot out all over the hardwood floor. "You spoke to him?"

"Left a message." She grinned triumphantly, and her wide mouth took up too much of her face. She was well aware of the dramatic implications of such a bold gesture. No one reconnects with an ex by phone. It's just not done. You're supposed to work your way though safer, more impersonal channels of communication first. There are countless combinations, of course, but one such sequence would be: witty blog comment, IM, e-mail, voice mail, face-to-face meeting over coffee, face-to-face meeting over alcohol, reunion fuck. But bypassing the first three and going straight to voice mail? That's kamikaze communication.

"What did you say?" I asked.

"Oh, not much . . ."

Manda then made a big deal out of yawning, casually stretching her arms above her head, and arching her back until her watermelon tits almost exploded out of her bra. My guess is that this gesture was supposed to be sexy. But it reminded me of that has-been comedian (Gallagher?) who has made an entire career out of smashing fruit with sledgehammers.

"The usual—you know," she finally continued. "Hey, I was just thinking about you, we haven't talked in a while, I broke up with Shea, and oh yeah, I'm still in love with you. . . ."

"Manda!"

"What?" she asked, coyly fluttering her eyelashes.

"You are *not* still in love with him!"

"How do you know? Who are you to tell me who I'm in love with? I could easily be in love with Len."

"But you're *not*!"

She pouted. "I could be." Then her petulant pucker spread into a knowing smile. "And more to the point, he could still be in love with me."

He could. And if he wasn't, he would be. It was his fate. Consider this Manda's version of the Pussy Legacy. With a legendary combination of headstrong self-determination and mythic cleavage, Manda has never failed to snare anyone, of any gender, she has ever wanted. It was impossible for me not to feel sorry for Len's future ex-girlfriend. I wanted to light a candle. Say a novena. Write a condolence note. Send a foil-wrapped pan of ziti that she could eat now or freeze for later. I wanted to do something to help Camilla through the mourning period for what would be the certain death of her relationship with Len.

As I got up and headed to the Cupcake, Manda waved her cup in the air.

"Shea's out," she said through a yawn. "You owe another hundred sixty-six thirty-three in rent."

As if I needed another reason to nail this interview tomorrow.

tuesday: the fifth

thirty-seven

Lately I can't shake the feeling that I'm supposed to be doing . . . *something*. Preparing for . . . *something*. Getting ready for, and maybe even a little excited about . . . *something*. I'll be microwaving half a burrito, reading *The Journal of Abnormal Psychology*, or writing in this very notebook, when I'll violently jerk with a jolt of anxiety over tasks undone and unknown.

Can you blame me? For the past eighteen years, early September has meant one thing: back to school. This year it means something else entirely: back to school for everyone but me.

I was reminded of this via today's six A.M. wake-up call from Marin. I only answered because her name came up on my caller ID. She has her own cell phone for emergencies, and I'm number two on the auto dial. (After Bethany but before G-Money.)

"Auntie J! It's me! Marin! Why can't I see you today?"

Yesterday Marin wanted nothing to do with me, but today I'm worthy of a before-dawn phone call.

"I've got a job interview," I croaked.

"Does that mean you won't come over to play with me anymore?"

A certain lower lip–jutting peevishness crept into her voice, and I couldn't bring myself to tell her the truth. "Don't worry. I'll still see you all the time. . . ."

Fortunately, Marin has the zigzagging, ping-ponging attention span that is a defining characteristic of being four years old. She had already moved on to the next subject.

"Auntie J!" she squeaked. "You know? I start school today!"

"You excited?"

"Duuuuuh," Marin said. "Of course I'm excited! St. Ann's is the awesomest school in the whole wide world."

"Most awesome," I corrected.

"That's what I said! The most awesomest! And I'm going there! Today!"

Marin is only slightly exaggerating. According to the *Wall Street Journal*, St. Ann's is the most awesomest private pre-K-to-12 school in the whole country.

"School, school, school," Marin sang.

I'd sing, too, if I had gotten into St. Ann's pre-K program. It is not hyperbolic to say that with her acceptance to the "fours," our little Marin is set for life. I'm proud that my bright, expressive niece charmed her way into the hearts of the St. Ann's office of admissions. And I'm even prouder of my sister, who stayed remarkably levelheaded throughout the admissions process and didn't pay a pre-K application packager to mold Marin into "the model four-year-old, an asset to the most selective classroom." Marin got in on merit, however the hell the "merits" of a four-year-old can be quantified.

"You know? I'm wearing my shiny tap-dance shoes!" she said. "Just listen!" And then I heard the muffled fumbling of the phone, followed by some indistinct shuffling and scraping sounds. "Did you hear that, Auntie J? Did you?"

"I heard."

"You know what else? I'm wearing my spotty leopard shirt. And you know? My mom says I can't wear the sweater with the fur because it's too hot, but I told her that summer is over and it's back to school and that means sweaters."

I used to think the same thing. I still sort of do.

"And I've got my new backpack, and you know? St. Ann's is the most awesomest school in the whole wide world for art, and that's awesome because I'm so good at painting, right? And . . ."

Lapses in judgment like The Fun Chart™ aside, Bethany has done an amazing job at making sure Marin acts her age, and not like one of those prematurely jaded sophistikids. But I can't help but worry what will happen now that she's in the most awesomest school in the whole wide world.

"But I'm also really good at counting. You know? I can count all the way to one hundred! I can do it by ones, fives, and tens. What one do you want to hear today? By ones, by fives, or by tens?"

For as excited as she sounds now, I'm afraid that this early success, when coupled with a desperate and scary need for achievement among her peers—the most privileged kids in this world—will only set her up for future unhappiness. I'm worried that no matter how brilliant and accomplished Marin proves herself to be over the next fourteen years of school, she will feel like a worthless loser if she's not in the .5 percent of applicants who get accepted for the Harvard Class of 2024.

"Okay! I'll pick! I'll do it by fives because I'm going to be five on my next birthday. Five, ten, fifteen . . ."

The OTB nursery school is the portal to all things OTB. Actually, it starts even earlier with the OTB Mommy & Me. Then moves on to the OTB Pre-K. OTB K. OTB Primary School. OTB Secondary School. OTB High School. All this OTBing is just to get into the OTB University, a distinction that is forever bestowed onto Harvard. Seriously. There was a recent study conducted by a consortium of educational institutions that asked five thousand college applicants to name the one college that was perceived as the best in the country, and the Crimson Tide tsunami-slammed the competition. I can't remember the numbers exactly, but it wasn't even close. So all the rest who are less than Only the Best can just look on, and up, with envy. And how do we know this? From the romans à clef written by former nannies, private-school packagers, and college coaches. From celebratory essays in the *New York Times* Styles section, or critical exposés in *Time* magazine. From status car commercials, talk-show segments, and subplots on family dramas.

"Thirty-five, forty . . ."

Surely the woes of the super-rich have been manipulated into a "phenomenon" by relentless media coverage. I honestly didn't think that these people really existed in the real world. The real world is filled with families who have two mortgages, never consider private school, and can't afford to pay a pimply thirteen-year-old babysitter five dollars an hour, let alone hire a live-in nanny. (The real world is where Bethany and I grew up, even after my mom returned to work when I was about twelve, and my dad made his way up the pay ladder by putting in about twenty-five years as a teacher, then as an administrator, with the Eastland

School System.) At best, these hyperpriveliged families represented just a teeny, tiny fraction, and those top one-percenters surely didn't come in contact with the lower ninety-nine. . . .

Until I met them at Columbia. Marcus, you'll meet them at Princeton, too, the ones who are merely putting on a brave face for the next four years and beyond. They'll trash-talk at the annual Harvard-Princeton grudge match. They'll attend the Princeton reunions, don the orange-and-black beer jacket worn by the rest of the members of your graduating class, and strut down Nassau Street in the obnoxious celebration of Tiger pride known as the P-rade. But deep down, they know that there is something missing, the certainty of being OTB.

It would be funny if it weren't so sad and totally true.

And it doesn't even matter that Princeton technically ranked ahead of Harvard this year. Education experts have to mix up their annual "Best College" rankings because hysterical parents wouldn't bother buying their guides if they knew Harvard was going to be number one again. This is why these "Best College" publications are divided into so many inane categories: Best Colleges Named After Important Historical Figures. Best Colleges Seen on TV. Best Colleges That Accept Anyone—and We Mean *Anyone*. Duh. Even the poorest, podunkiest school gets to be the best in its own unique way. Everyone is a winner! Hooray! It's not all that different from those end-of-the-year ceremonies in nursery school, when even the dumbest, sloppiest, meanest, clumsiest, ugliest kid in the class walks away with a certificate celebrating his Satisfactory Effort.

Of course, Marin is attending a nursery school where none of the children are dumb, sloppy, mean, clumsy, or ugly. The hyperambitious and affluent have never bought into the bargain-bin theory of education, because they could afford not to. For those born into families bred to believe in OTB, nothing else will do. Especially when it comes to privately educating the flesh of their dewy, aerobicized flesh. Again, this is not the reality for most families. Most families cannot afford to pay thirty thousand dollars for preschool, or any of the other stages of OTB. Just look at what happened to my former employer—the Pineville branch of the Accelerated College Coaching and Educational Preparedness

Tutorial. ACCEPT! closed within a year of its opening because our hometown population still sports way more blue collars than white.

But OTB *is* the reality for Marin. Privilege, you see, has its membership.

"Auntie J? Are you even listening? You're so quiet!"

"I'm quiet because I'm listening."

"Oh! Sixty-five, seventy . . ."

I don't begrudge my niece for being born into money, if not class. (Class is far less important than money these days, anyway.) Bethany is naturally inclined to be ambivalent about academics, so perhaps Marin has a fighting chance to actually have genuine fun and not the trademarked variety. I would hate it if she turned into one of those automatons whose achievements are taken for granted as givens, and never fully appreciated or enjoyed. I don't want everything for her to be the means to an end, only without end, because there will always be another OTB to put on her curriculum vitae.

As the babysitting aunt, I'm allowed to slack off, to skip The Fun Chart™ and cue *Grease 3*. It's okay to occasionally show her an alternative to OTB. But as a parent, the number one influence in her life, leading by my example would be considered a road to ruin. After all, who am I but a marginally employed idiot who could only get into one of the lesser Ivies?

All of this reminds me of another study I read for *Think*. A UK economist posits that within the next thousand years, humans will divide into two subspecies. As the result of superior interbreeding, the upper class will evolve into seven-foot-tall, supermodel geniuses with pneumaboobs for the ladies and rocketcocks for the gents. The underclass will downgrade to a class of dim-witted, mini-titted, raisin-dicked hobgoblins. It's not just sci-fi, it's really happening. I challenge you to spend fifteen minutes in Barneys followed by another fifteen at Wal-Mart and still deny it.

"One hundred! See? I told you I could do it!"

"I never doubted you," I said.

"Okay! I gotta go now! I love you! You're the best aunt ever!"

"Maybe not the best," I said. "But I do okay."

"You're the best because you're miiiiiiiine," she said before abruptly hanging up.

I can't save the human race. But I wish I could protect Marin from harm. If only I were able to guarantee that Marin would thrive under my guidance, and that she would always be as self-confident and happy as she was this morning when she counted to one hundred by fives.

thirty-eight

So I'm a little jealous of a four-year-old. And she's not the only one.

You're at Princeton. Hope is doing her graduate work at Pratt. Len, MIT. Bridget and Percy are finishing up their hers 'n' his B.A.'s in Metropolitan Studies (hers with a concentration in art and public policy, his in urban ethnography and economics). Manda is also going to NYU part-time for her M.S.W. at the School for Social Work. I'd even heard Shea rapping about enrolling in some sort of deejay-apprenticing program to "perfeck" her "mad turntable skillz," not that it matters, since I'll never be seeing her around these parts again.

Most of my friends from Columbia are going on to get advanced degrees. And why not? A Ph.D. is the new M.A., a master's is the new bachelor's, a B.A. is the new high school diploma, and a high school diploma is the new smiley-face sticker on your first-grade spelling test. You don't know most of these people, but again, indulge me as I provide some cogent examples:

Former high school crush-to-end-all-crushes, obsessive object of horniness, and gay man of my dreams Paul Parlipiano is getting his Ph.D. in Sustainable Development at our alma mater's School of International and Public Affairs. (I have only the vaguest idea of what that even means.) Tanu is at the University of Chicago Law School ("Where Fun Comes to Die!"), which I guess turned out to be an acceptable substitution for medical school in her parents' estimation. Similarly, Kazuko's parents both have multiple advanced degrees and will happily fund their only daughter's efforts to match them diploma for diploma. She's in the "rhetors" program at Berkeley, a totally esoteric discipline that will never lead to a real job, which I'm sure is just fine with her. ALF (because he—duh—looks like ALF) still has two glorious undergraduate years left at Columbia. As does my ex Kieran, who is still in sad, sad, so very, very sad emo love with the Barnard '09 Regirlfriend he started sleeping with before he—oops!—stopped sleeping with me.

Just to prove that I'm not exaggerating, here is my complete list of friends/acquaintances my age who *aren't* going back to school:

1–2. Scotty (Pineville '02; nine credits short of Lehigh '06)
and Sara (Pineville '02; ninety credits short of Harrington Country Club and Occasional University '06)

Babymamadaddy are booked for the next eighteen years.

3. Dexy (two years at Columbia; six months at Bellevue; twenty-eight credits short of Columbia '06)

She's apparently in a state of permanent deferment since the bipolar breakdown she had the summer before our junior year. She works at Eros, an upscale sex shop in SoHo, and—surprise, surprise—she brought her work home with her. Or rather, her work bought her a home.

"I moved in with Daddy!" Dexy yelped the last time I saw her.

"You . . . what?"

Dexy pouted. "If you read my blog, you would know that. I thought you read my blog. You *said* you read my blog."

I had stopped reading "Dex and the City" when I kept turning up as the priggish supporting character, the anonymous "girlfriend from Columbia," scandalized by the leading lady's reckless inhibition and bacchanalia. (It's also when we stopped hanging out with any sort of regularity.) Dexy has always been hell-bent on grabbing Manhattan by the balls (both actual and metaphorical). I had always hoped that her blog was 99 percent Bushnell hyperbole, but never more than when she took up with "Daddy."

"I'm a kept woman." The throwback expression fit both her appearance and our surroundings. She had insisted on meeting me for drinks at Bemelmans Bar, a sumptuous Art Deco watering hole located at the stately Carlyle hotel. As usual, she was in costume, a houndstooth suit with broad shoulders and a cinched waist that drew attention to her hourglass curves. As she posed at the black granite bar—the wave in her platinum wig dipping low over one knowing eye, crimson Cupid-bow lips sipping a champagne cocktail—she looked just like a troubled dame straight out of 1940s film noir. *I* looked like the anachronism, the chain-store clearance-rack naïf, which was exactly as she had orchestrated it.

"Please," I begged, "please tell me you're making this up."

"I'm making this up."

"You are?"

"No!" she cheered gleefully, face alight with the scandalousness of it all.

"I don't want to hear about this," I said, nursing a club soda because I couldn't afford anything on the menu and wouldn't allow her to use "Daddy's" money to buy my booze. It was the principle of the thing.

"Yes you do," she insisted.

"No I do not," I said emphatically.

Of course, Dexy ignored my wishes and told me much more than I ever needed to know about her courtesan-keeper courtship, right down to the last gray hair on his desiccated testicles. I will spare you such specifics. (Only I just didn't. Sorry.) All you need to know is that "Daddy" is (a) rich, (b) sixty years old, and (c) newly divorced with four kids all in Dexy's age bracket, and (d) offered to let her move into his pied-à-terre with views of Gramercy Park after wooing her with the purchase of the two-thousand-dollar One-of-a-Kind Hand-Sculpted All-Natural Volcanic Glass Diletto.

"You're sleeping with a sexagenarian for money!"

"He prefers sexygenarian!"

My mouth went sour with pregurgitive spit.

And then, as is her custom, Dexy broke into ear-shattering song. " 'Money makes the world go round, of that we can be sure . . .' " She blew a Bronx cheer. " 'Pffffft! On being poor!' "

I covered my ears to protect both my hearing and my sanity.

"And it's not just the money," she said. "It's *also* the apartment. . . ."

So there you have it: Someone I consider a friend doesn't need to go back to school because her living expenses are covered by a Viagra-popping geezer. While Dexy's drama was kind of vicariously amusing in college, her post–bipolar breakdown behavior is scaring me. And yet I stay friends with her, in part because I feel obligated to serve as a normalizing if totally ineffectual influence in her life. I already regret inviting her to Thursday night's Care. Okay? karaoke party thrown by . . .

4. Cinthia Wallace (too many private schools to list here; GED '02, Harvard '06)

Cinthia, aka Hyacinth Anastasia Wallace or Hy, is too busy being the most famous face behind the hipster philanthropic organization called the Social Activists, which has taken the old-money fund-raising model (i.e., black-tie balls, silent auctions) and given it an A-list new-money twist (i.e., stripping for charity, poker tournaments). This doesn't require an advanced degree, just a grand inheritance from a father she commonly referred to as "that jagoff."

I sound like one of the haters. Cinthia is routinely mocked for her charitable efforts—you know, trying to shelter the homeless, feed the hungry, and cure the sick, one celebrity-studded Care. Okay? karaoke party at a time. In her defense, she could've started a line of "aspirational handbags" or opened a "lifestyle boutique" that sells denim for a grand and plastic rings for a nickel. She could have decided to what-the-fuck? it, drugging and whoring her way back to her roots and re-creating her reign as the underage ur-Hilton of her day. But she didn't. And that's admirable. Of course, if I had a fifty-million-dollar inheritance, I could do something pretty damn admirable, too.

But alas, I don't have fifty million. I have negative sixty-five thousand dollars.

And I not only long for the higher degree that I will never have, but the final semester that never was. Keep in mind that I actually piled on the credits and graduated *one* semester early to minimize my loans by another fifteen thousand dollars or so. This is unheard of in an age when the typical student completes four years in *five and a half*. (My sister was part of that vanguard.) Seriously, it was wise of you to choose a school that has altogether eliminated student loans in favor of grants and work study. Perhaps that's one advantage of entering college at twenty-three instead of eighteen. You will never know how it feels to owe various lenders approximately sixty-five thousand dollars for your Ivy League diploma, or what it's like to pay them off in increasingly expensive installments for the next 360 months of your life. One doesn't have to be a multimillionaire, but it's a lot easier to be an idealist when you aren't so deeply entrenched in a hellhole of debt. Because no matter how I consolidate or reconsolidate my loans, I feel like I'm digging out the entire New York City subway system with my Phi Beta Kappa pin.

What I envy most about you and everyone else heading back to school is the certainty of it all. You've got a prescribed set of requirements to guide you through the next few years. Focus your energy on the completion of those assignments and you will succeed. Guaranteed. Where's my syllabus to guide me through life?

But there is hope in the air. Early September is the season for fresh starts, complete with turning-a-new-leaf metaphors and all that. And I've got my most promising job interview in months. I'm wearing a featherweight cashmere shell, an impeccably tailored gabardine pencil skirt, and the most sumptuous boots that have ever graced my calloused feet (all on permanent loan from Bethany because I didn't have the fortitude to fight the crowds of back-to-school shoppers nor the patience to piece together a proper interview outfit from H&M). I've got my résumé and sample issues of *Think* stored inside the buttery leather messenger bag my parents bought as a graduation gift. I've rehearsed my anecdotes about what it was like to work for the CU Storytellers Project collecting "oral narratives" from total strangers on the streets of New York City. Yes, preparing myself for this interview was almost an adequate simulacrum for the back-to-school rituals of years gone by, when I still naively believed that with the perfect outfit, the perfect backpack, the perfect how-I-spent-my-summer-vacation story, with the perfect reinvention of my former self, my less-than-perfect life could be changed for the better, forever.

(FOREVER didn't arrive in this morning's mail. Perhaps tomorrow?)

thirty-nine

She casts a lusty gaze upon Times Square from five stories above Forty-eighth and Broadway. She's bent over at the waist, and her pendulous breasts peek out from behind her brassy hair extensions. Her mouth is pink, wet, open, and waiting. Her eyes are dead. A French-manicured talon beckons: *Hey there, big man. Buy my latest DVD release from Vivid Entertainment Group.*

JESSICA DARLING GOES DOWN . . . CUMMING SEPTEMBER 2006!

Whenever I pass this billboard, I am reminded that my namesake sucks and fucks for a paycheck. I would not want to be her. But one advantage the Other Jessica Darling has over me is that her skills are always in demand. The job title "Porn Star" contains multitudes. There are as many specialties as there are perversities. (For purely educational purposes—right? right?—I'll take you on a quick alphabetical tour of contemporary porn categories: Anal Queens, Big Boob Babes, Cat Fighting, Deep Throating, European, Foot Fetish, Gang Bangs, Hairy Humpers, Interracial, Jack Off, Kinky, Lesbians, Midgets, Nasty Girls, Orgies, Playmates vs. Pets, Queer, Rock 'n' Roll, Satanic, Threesomes, Uglies, Voyeurs, Wet and Messy, X-Tremely Dangerous, Yellow Love, and—ick—Zoological.) When asked what she does for a living, the Other Jessica Darling might try to hide behind the polite euphemisms "actress" or "dancer." But when it comes down to it, the job description "Porn Star" means that the Other Jessica Darling performs sex acts on camera. Her skills are recession-proof.

Mine, not so much.

I first began my job search late last January, three weeks after graduation, during what should have been my crisscross country road trip if Hope and I hadn't been jacked by the tweakers. Before I even had a chance to report the loss, Ms. Daisy Schlemmer and Mr. Harlan Oakes had already used my ATM card to buy propane cylinders, hot plates, and battery acid at the local ACE Hardware, which should really consider changing its motto to "The Source for All Your Meth Lab Needs." Ms. Oakes and Mr. Schlemmer must have been disappointed to discover that a single $153.26 transaction drained me of my life savings, not to mention the negative twenty dollars I then owed for "overdraft protection."

The crime occurred on Day One of our trip, and it seemed like a baaaaaad omen, payback for my attempt at youthful irresponsibility and frivolity in the face of unemployment. Hope tried to convince me otherwise, and promised that we'd get another chance to travel someday, but those thieves stole all my enthusiasm for adventure on the open road. I felt like I had no choice but to skip the trip, crash with my sister in Brooklyn, and find gainful employment in the city.

So I keystroked my way to Columbia's Career Education Services website, figuring that one of the advantages of graduating in January was that I'd get a head start on the seniors getting diplomas in May. I soon realized that a head start on nothing is not a head start at all. Psychology didn't even justify its own job heading. Any career opportunities in my field were relegated to the minimum-wage smorgasbord category of "Other."

This was not a promising sign.

As I clicked through the listings, several keywords kept coming up over and over again. "Wall Street." "Financial Services Industry." "Sales and Trading Division." "Funds Management."

To make money, you gotta *make money*. Well, no shit.

My whole idealistic approach to college had been one colossal error in judgment. Learning for the sake of learning? Pursuing my passion for psychology over a more practical, employable major? What was wrong with me? Why didn't I major in economics? I could have just as easily majored in economics. My brother-in-law majored in economics at Rutgers, and he's a goddamn troglodyte. A troglodyte pulling down seven, maybe eight figures. I'm certainly smart enough to have majored in economics . . . only I was *too fucking stupid to major in economics*.

I probably would have signed up for a temp agency if Professor Mac hadn't put me in touch with his former colleague Robert Stevens, editor in chief of *Think*. I got the (quasi) job based on Mac's recommendation alone, and I remember feeling guilty about it. Not everyone was lucky enough to have taken a summer writing course with a future National Book Award nominee. I felt like I had somehow cheated my way into this position, that there were other unconnected applicants who might have been more qualified. I said as much to Mac, who rebuffed my worries.

"Most people get ahead through the connections they make along the way," he said. "What's wrong with that?"

"It doesn't seem fair," I said.

"Do I need to quote a better writer than I am on the subject of equanimity?"

I told him he need not bother. And I got over it, mostly because I counted on *Think* as a temporary thing, until I got my "real" job, which I hoped would happen before *Think*'s funding ran out.

Finding more lucrative employment seemed highly unlikely until last week, a day or two before you arrived in Brooklyn, when I received Dr. Katherine Seamon's divine e-mail in my inbox. And by *divine*, I mean it in the miraculous, near-religious sense, and not in the way insincere fashionistas use to gush over overpriced stilettos.

To: jdarling@columbia.edu
From: kseamon@ilulab.com
Subject: New Media Job for Psychology Majors
Date: 8/28/2006

I almost hit Delete without opening it. First of all, the words "New Media" implied that this e-mail had been bottlenecked on the information superhighway since 1999. Furthermore, the employment promise of that subject heading seemed about as legit as the guaranteed 100 percent herbal way to add six inches to my penis. Finally, the sender's surname, with its ejaculatory connotations, certainly didn't help boost credibility. But I'd been looking for a permanent position for eight months, and I was starting to feel desperate. I clicked the message and read on.

I found out about your work with the CU Storytellers Project in the most recent issue of *Columbia College Today*. As you may have heard in recent weeks, I've just launched iLoveULab, a new research-based interpersonal networking provider that is the first to blend new media and neuroscience.

I'm hiring graduates who have a background in psychology as well as strong writing and interviewing skills. All positions with iLoveULab provide a competitive starting salary and benefits. I prefer meeting job candidates in person, and will be conducting business in New York City during the first week of September. Please contact me if you're interested in learning more.

Sincerely, Dr. Katherine Seamon, CC '95

The doctor's name sounded vaguely familiar, but I couldn't place it. And I was certain that I had never heard of iLoveULab, a name that connotes heart-shaped boxes of chocolate wrapped in shiny cellophane and tied up with a big red bow. I was in the middle of fact-checking a *Think* piece titled "Mom and Pop Psychology" about the return of Freudian psychoanalysis, so I made a mental note to Google Dr. Katherine Seamon and iLoveULab when I had the chance.

Later that afternoon while Marin and I were drawing pictures of our favorite scenes from *Grease 3*, I overheard Bethany on the phone with one of the MILFs discussing that morning's episode of *The Dr. Frank Show*.

"I'd totally pay to have my brain scanned at iLoveULab," Bethany was saying. "And Grant's, too! That Dr. Kate is a genius!"

"What?" I interrupted. "The iLoveULab doctor was on TV?"

"Yes! Dr. Kate!"

Lest this sound too coincidental, it should be noted that Bethany had been chatting for well over an hour already, narrating the moment-by-moment details of an afternoon spent flitting around the brownstone to keep a watchful eye on the housekeeper.

"Dr. Kate?" I asked.

"Dr. Kate! The one who devised the Signs . . ."

So it's a fact that Bethany had discussed Dr. Kate's brilliance in my presence many times before, but my brain had never been trained to pick up on the name Dr. Kate until I got her e-mail.

"Oh Christ, again with the Signs," I rebuffed. "I don't want to hear about the Signs. . . ."

But my sister had already moved on. "She doesn't believe in Dr. Kate," she said to the MILF on the phone, shaking her head with pity. Then to me: "Dr. Kate just wrote a new book all about brain chemicals and love."

"Dr. Katherine Seamon?" I asked, still refusing to believe that we could possibly be talking about the same person.

"Yes, that's her," Bethany replied. "Dr. Kate is a real scientist, you know. She's just opened up these labs where couples can get their brains scanned for compatibility, or singles can get scanned to be matched up with their ideal partners. . . ."

"I think she wants to hire me for one of those labs." Then I explained the e-mail.

Needless to say, Bethany (and the MILF on the line) freaked out. "Dr. Kate is OTB, Jess! OTB!"

"Why would she e-mail me? You think she'd have someone else do the hiring for her."

"Oh! She's famous for her micromanagerial skills," Bethany said, then paused to hear what the phone MILF was saying. "Um-hm. Right! She never delegates what she can do herself."

Later, I'd find out that Dr. Kate was quite the go-getter. Like me, she was a psychology major at Columbia. Unlike me, she got a doctorate in cognitive neuroscience at the University of Pennsylvania. And then also unlike me, she went on to Wharton business school to learn how she could make tons of money off all her neuroscientific knowledge. And somehow, when not stockpiling these impressive credentials, she managed to find time to wed, divorce, and remarry, all before the age of thirty. Of all these experiences, the termination of her starter marriage was the most crucial to the development of iLoveULab.

Three summers ago, I listened to nearly five hundred New Yorkers who were lured by a simple sandwich board urging them to TELL US A STORY. Day in and day out I listened. To kinetic, coked-up i-bankers sniffing and riffing on their multiorgasmic sexual conquests. To wrinkly, humpbacked old biddies waxing rhapsodic about VJ Day. To label-obsessed, overdressed foreign tourists complaining about the fat and stupid Americans who had the audacity to crash *their* vacations. To pouty-lipped, liquid-limbed thirteen-year-olds. To aromatic cabbies. To hipsters who looked homeless, and vice versa. To the hundreds of unique but ordinary everyday citizens who believed their stories were stories that needed to be told. And more important, needed to be heard.

I had taken the job because it earned me three credits toward my major, offered free room and board, and provided the scintillating promise of sweating with and for my hot, married Spanish grad student partner for eight hours at a stretch. (A lust that fizzled as soon as I discovered that the hot, married Spanish grad student partner had no problemo engaging in adulterous behavior with yours truly.) I don't know what historians hope to learn from these tapes about urban life shortly after the turn of the new century, but working for the CU Storytellers Project confirmed my suspicions that narcissism comes in all shapes, sizes, colors, sexual orientations, and footwear. But never, *never* did I believe that this experience would lead to a job as a professional matchmaker with a television love doctor.

Yes, much like the Other Jessica Darling might substitute "actress" for "porn star," "interpersonal social networking provider" is one of the postmillennial euphemisms for "matchmaking," which means that I, Jessica Darling, have an interview for a job with a highfalutin Internet dating service.

(I'll stop now because it's time for me to meet Dr. Kate. This will also provide a moment for you to process and appreciate the irony.)

forty

The interview is over now, and it isn't giving too much away to say that I totally had this job before I walked in the door.

Dr. Kate had asked me to meet her in her suite at the W Hotel in

Times Square. I thought it was an odd choice, but it turns out that she always stays at the W because she has a lucrative deal to develop products exclusively for the chain. The Dr. Kate Rescue Kit, for example, is a discreet black leather case no bigger than a cell phone. This cheeky little item contains a pack of gum, a mini mirror, two condoms, massage oil/lubricant, and a one-day Fun Pass MetroCard for a quick getaway. It sells for forty-five dollars at the hotel store, or online.

Dr. Kate *is* a genius.

Whenever I step through the doors of one of these sleek, ultramodern boutique hotels, I start to feel a little woozy, if not wobbly-legged drunk. It's all such a scene, even at two P.M. Which I guess is the whole point of the dim lighting, the seductive French electro-pop over the sound system, the scent of lemon sage spa products in the air, the "floating" sinks in the bathroom designed to inspire gravity-defying wonder. By the time I went through the glassed-in urban waterfall, passed by the wall of rainbow lit stalactites, and was whisked up in the elevator to the hotel's white-on-white lobby, I already felt like I'd had a one-night stand. All I needed was a cigarette and one of the famously soft waffle-knit robes.

Even the "welcome attendants" are uniformed in matching black couture, looking less like desk clerks and bellhops than an alien race from the Planet Sexxxy who have party-crashed our puny, prudish planet to conquer human beings through their irresistible, intergalactic powers of multiorgasmic mind-body control. (Or perhaps they're all members of that UK economist's supermodel human species from the future. . . .)

One of these Sexxxtraterrestrials directed me to Dr. Kate's suite on the fifty-sixth floor, where—as she had warned via a follow-up e-mail—there would be a very large, very intimidating sentinel at the entry. The security guard was also dressed in black, but easily weighed as much as three or four of the sylph-like space creatures put together. With his headset, dark FBI sunglasses, and clipboard in hand, he looked just like any velvet rope bouncer, which gave the whole endeavor even more of a clubby feel.

"I have a . . . uh . . . two o'clock interview with . . . uh . . . Dr.

Kate," I stammered. "Uh, I mean Dr. Katherine Seamon. For iLoveU-Lab . . ." The guard's towering presence made me nervous; I felt like I was lying about my interview and would have failed a polygraph.

"Name?" he asked in a bored yet imposing voice. He wore a dagger pendant on a chain around his neck. Though the charm was no more than an inch in length, I did not doubt that he could use it to gut me in an instant, if need be.

"Jessica Darling," I said, reaching into my bag for my wallet to get my driver's license, cursing myself for not having it in my front pocket like one of Hope's MetroCards.

"Like the one on the billboard?" The guard cracked a smile—literally, because his two front teeth were fractured in jagged diagonals, which I imagine came from a punch in the face on one of his less upscale assignments.

"Like the one on the billboard," I deadpanned. "Only *I* need a job."

This made the guard laugh, a deep basso laugh. I'd won him over. He checked my license, then spoke into his headset. "A Ms. Jessica Darling to see you?" He looked at me then, smiled, and nodded. "Okay. The doctor can see you now." He opened the door and ushered me inside.

forty-one

Dr. Kate's penthouse had sweeping panoramic views of Broadway, and from this top-of-the-world vantage point, the Other Jessica Darling's billboard shrunk down to the size of a postcard. The suite was less distractingly sexy than the lobby, though the large living-room area still resembled an after-hours lounge more than a place to conduct business. There, perched on the edge of a low, square, suede love seat with her legs angled and crossed at the ankles, was Dr. Kate. I was quite surprised to find her alone in this humongous living space, without the entourage of payrolled hangers-on that I had assumed would lamprey upon such a successful impresario.

I'd never seen her on TV, but I knew what she looked like from her various author photos. In the prominently positioned glamour shot on the home page of the iLoveULab website, she presented herself as a blown-out blonde with china-doll eyes and overindulged lips. From the neck up, in fact, Dr. Kate's picture didn't look that different from the Other Jessica Darling's. There was such a disconnect between her academic background and her pornified photo that I assumed that the digital image had been highly enhanced for promotional purposes. Surely she'd be much plainer and less plastic in person. I mean, was it really necessary for a neuroscientist/C.E.O. to look like a porn star?

I saw for myself that Dr. Kate was even more flawlessly PhotoShopped in real life. She was wearing something that resembled a traditional lab coat, only it was black and tight and had a slight sheen, and it was unbuttoned to reveal a black, white, and red python-print dress. She resembled a curvaceous, credulity-busting scientist in the Bond Girl tradition, the kind who saves the world from thermonuclear apocalypse and still makes it on time for her next Brazilian wax. This, apparently, is her signature look.

"You must be Jessica," she said, without getting up, but extending her hand. Her nails weren't long, but all squared off and expertly painted in the vampy, nearly black color I'd noticed on chic women around the city. My fingernails had been quickly and unevenly snipped with a pair of toenail clippers. Some nails were roundish, others were squarish, and one or two were cut so low that neither term applied. All had been unevenly painted in a clear ninety-nine-cent polish about one minute before I walked out the door. It's fortunate for me that fingernails are not the windows to the soul.

"When I read about your work," she said in a confident, TV-ready tone, "I thought you sounded perfect for iLoveULab."

"Well, thank you," I said, dipping my head in a gesture of false modesty, but also to avert my eyes from her artificially inflated lips. They *looked* like Novocain *feels*. "And I'm so glad to meet you and find out more about iLoveULab."

"I'm so thrilled about this new venture," she began, gesturing toward the suede cube chair on the opposite side of the slick black coffee table. "iLoveULab International is the first networking service to use state-of-the-art brain-imaging technology to pair up life partners who are matched from the inside out. . . ."

Dr. Kate must know that her company's name, though perfectly in keeping with others in the matchmaking game, has cheese-ass connotations, and could be a turnoff for the more serious-minded employees she courts. She was quick to put a smarty-pants spin on what many might perceive to be a shallow endeavor beneath her highly educated pedigree.

Maybe iLoveULab International has defied Silicon Alley odds and hasn't hemorrhaged money like so many new media start-ups before it. It's possible that in your second or third or tenth rereading of this notebook, iLoveULab has entered the pantheon of successful Fortune 500–type companies. Perhaps iLoveULab's motto ("We've got love on the brain") has become a multigenerational catchphrase with the timelessness of "Just do it!" Perhaps the iLoveULab logo (a cartoonish red heart inside a medical textbook illustration of the brain) has been canonized by the Metropolitan Museum of Art, and no longer brings to mind a drugstore clearance bin on February 15.

"What do you know about the brain in love?" Dr. Kate asked. Her brisk, no-nonsense demeanor was, again, totally at odds with her bimbocious appearance.

"Well," I began, "I know a growing body of research shows that falling in and out of love is the result of various chemical reactions in the brain."

"Go on," she said.

I was glad to have read up on this research before the interview. "Certain regions of the brain get flooded with different hormones depending on the stage of the relationship."

"Go on," she said.

"And MRI machines can take pictures of people's brains as these chemical reactions occur."

I must say that I was even impressing myself.

"And how is that information useful?"

"Well, I'm assuming that if some hormones are more active than others, it can affect your personality, and your approach to relationships. A brain scan can tell you what romantic type you are, which gives you a better shot at selecting complementary partners."

Dr. Kate was pleased with my answers. "Exactly," she said. "iLoveU-Lab uses the latest advances in technology to create a MindLoveMap of the brain, which serves as a guide to matching couples who will fall—and stay—in love."

Dr. Kate went on to explain that each iLoveULab client is put into one of four main MindLove categories, determined by what the MRI scan reveals as the prominent chemical system in the brain. Everyone falls into a primary category but manifests secondary or tertiary characteristics from the others. They are:

The Connector

Chemical influence: Serotonin, the mood-regulating neurotransmitter

Strengths: Well-organized, calm, considerate, gets along well with others

Challenges: Habitual, nonchalant, overly concerned with popular opinion

The Commander

Chemical influence: Testosterone, the male sex hormone

Strengths: Logical, success-oriented, bold, decisive

Challenges: Domineering, self-absorbed, uncompromising

The Creator

Chemical influence: Dopamine, the pleasure-seeking neurotransmitter

Strengths: Spontaneous, lively, theatrical, thrill-seeking

Challenges: Moody, addictive, takes unnecessary risks

The Communicator

Chemical influence: Estrogen, the female sex hormone

Strengths: Verbal, multitasking, insightful, innovative

Challenges: Overemotional, irrational, hypersensitive to criticism

"This is such a radical approach to matchmaking," Dr. Kate said. "Our clients will appreciate how our systematic, scientific approach removes most of the guesswork from dating. Life is too complicated to wait for a serendipitous love connection. It might have worked for the boomers, but it doesn't work for the millennials."

I shook my head no.

"And affluent singles won't hesitate to pay fifteen thousand dollars for our MindLoveMapping services."

"Fifteen thousand dollars?!" I blurted

"Yes," she said, stiffly uncrossing and recrossing her legs. "But is that such a price to pay for lifelong love?"

I closed my mouth and shook my head. *Of course not*.

"Still, I recognize that our services might be cost prohibitive to some."

Dr. Kate went on to explain that at the onset, a greater portion of iLoveULab's revenue—and the bulk of its Dating Base, as it's called—will be made up of the thousands of customers who forgo the MindLoveMap brain scan and pay the more modest sum of five hundred dollars to fill out a Chemical Quiz—250 questions painstakingly designed to determine the client's hormonal report without having to get inside the claustrophobic and costly MRI machine. For example, if you can quickly find the pattern in a random group of numbers, you've got a lot of testosterone. You're a Commander. Or if you can easily determine from a photo whether a person's smile is sincere or not, your brain is high in estrogen. You're a Communicator. And so on.

"It's not as accurate as the MRI MindLoveMap," Dr. Kate pointed out. "But it's an affordable option for most customers, and it's still better than the *personality-based* questionnaires offered on inferior sites." She wrinkled her tiny, upturned nose as if falling for someone's sensitivity or sense of humor was akin to falling for his bed-wetting habit or penchant for pedophilia.

I wrinkled my nose right back at her. Mirroring her gesture was a shamelessly obvious maneuver, but I was, after all, on a job interview. And I really needed, and maybe even really wanted, this job. A job I felt in no way qualified to have, since I had no idea what I'd be doing.

"What would my position entail?" I asked.

"Well, at first, a lot of reading, scoring, and categorizing the Chemical Quizzes as they arrive via e-mail, then entering them in the iLoveU-Lab Dating Base."

"Sounds fascinating."

"It is," she said, her eyes ablaze. "Eventually I would have you work as a liaison between the MRI technicians and our clients, analyzing the MindLoveMaps themselves. . . ."

As Dr. Kate spoke, I started thinking about how you already disliked the sound of this job, just based on my early descriptions of the e-mail from Dr. Kate. This additional information would only make you hate it even more.

You dispute any empirical data that explain the origins of human emotions. You dismiss the science that proves that passion is no different from hunger or thirst or sleep or any other biological drive. You want to believe that love is this ineffable thing that can't be quantified.

No wonder, then, that you were deeply offended when I suggested that we both take the Chemical Quiz that Dr. Kate had sent for my perusal last week.

"I'm not taking the test," you said as you sat cross-legged on your straw meditation mat with your head resting between Claire and Chloe's names on the wall.

"Why not? It's just for fun!"

"Why take a test that will only prove that we're not compatible?"

(This exchange resonates deeply in light of recent events.)

You were afraid that I'd be swayed by any evidence that proved we weren't meant to be. So you didn't take the test and I never asked you about it again.

From what I've read, I can pretty much guarantee that I'm a Communicator with a bit of Commander, which means that the female side of my psyche is barely outmuscling the male side in the tug-of-war battle over my brain. I would've bet my first paycheck that you are a Creator. And not that you care, because you think it's all crap, but Creators like you and Communicators like me are supposed to be ideal matches. . . .

"Is there something wrong?" Dr. Kate asked in a sharp voice, jerking me out of my reverie.

"Oh, yes! I mean, no! Nothing's wrong." I didn't realize that I was frowning until I rearranged my features into a smile. "I was just thinking about how your technology and research could have spared me a lot of heartbreak."

"That's my goal: to eradicate heartbreak."

I smiled wider when she said this because it sounded silly, but then quickly drew my face into a contemplative expression when I realized that she was totally serious.

"It might sound trivial to some," she said, with the tiniest of nods in my direction on the word *some*, "but more people are devastated by broken hearts than cancer, AIDS, and all other diseases combined."

"Oh, yes," I said. "I've never had AIDS or cancer, but I've had a broken heart, and I can't imagine that those diseases could make you feel any worse. . . ."

Dr. Kate puckered her lips in disapproval. Her mouth was so puffed up with plastics that such a tiny, easily-missed gesture took on ginormous, notice-me significance.

"But . . . uh . . . ," I stammered.

"What?" Dr. Kate asked.

"Can you really cure heartbreak?" I asked. "I was recently doing some reading for my job, and I learned that the prefrontal cortex shuts down completely when you first fall in love. That's the part of your brain that controls social judgment, right?"

She nodded.

"So when you first fall in love, you can't see any of your lover's faults; you only see an idealized version of him. And over time, when you find out that this perfect guy is a flawed, complicated human being, it can be a huge letdown. Which explains why most relationships implode after a few months or years."

A half nod.

"I mean, can the iLoveULab brain scans do anything to stop love from fading over time? Doesn't all passion die and turn into something else, like companionship? I've been thinking about breaking up with my boyfriend because no real relationship with him could ever be like the perfect version I imagined when we first fell in love. . . ."

I stopped talking when I realized that Dr. Kate had stopped listening.

"Well, then," Dr. Kate said, glancing at her diamond-faced wristwatch. "Time's just about up."

I waited for her to say something about the next step in the hiring process. She didn't.

"Well, thank you for meeting with me," I said. "I know you're a very busy woman."

"Yes, I am," she replied. "Which is why I'm not going to waste any more of my time, or yours."

I sat up straighter, hoping to hear her say "Congratulations . . ." But her next sentence began "Unfortunately . . ."

I wanted to politely excuse myself and ask the Sentinel to borrow his dagger pendant so I could slit my wrists.

forty-two

After my dismissal, I didn't leave the hotel right away. I wasn't ready to give up this job that had been mine until I blew it. I went straight to the reception desk, grabbed a complimentary W pen ("Whatcha thinking?") and postcard ("Whenever Wherever") to write a quick, apologetic note to Dr. Kate, one that I hoped might salvage the first half of the interview, the part that had gone so, so, so well. But I couldn't stop thinking about what she'd said about the part that had not.

"Unfortunately," Dr. Kate had said, "I can't hire someone who doesn't believe in iLoveULab."

"But—"

She raised her hand to shush me. "I didn't get to be the groundbreaking scientist, author, and entrepreneur I am today by being wishy-washy. Working for me will require no less than a hundred and fifty percent of your time, energy, and enthusiasm. iLoveULab has to be your *life*."

"I'm sorry," I said, "I—"

"No apologies necessary," she said with a smile. "This job isn't right for you, and you're not right for this job. We're both better off severing our ties now. I'm being pragmatic."

"You sound like you're breaking up with me," I said, mustering a lame laugh.

"It's not all that different, actually."

"But—"

"No buts." She stood to encourage me to do the same. "Many psych majors are analytical to a fault. It's the nature of the beast, I suppose. But they do too much thinking and not enough doing."

She jerked her head on the last word, and I responded with my own empathetic head bob. But it was too late. The mirror was shattered.

"You seemed like the bright, highly motivated go-getter I need to launch this new venture, but you lost your way during our conversation. You tuned out and turned your attentions elsewhere. . . ."

Still wincing at the memory of her admonishment, I sighed and put the pen and the blank postcard in my bag. There's no point in arguing with someone you know is right. When I trudged outside in defeat, I discovered that the sunny afternoon was quickly turning gray. By the time I emerged from the subway in Brooklyn forty-five minutes later, the heavens were deeply unsettled by the oncoming storm. The sky crackled with electric tension throughout my ten-block walk home.

(PROPHETIC FALLACY ALERT.)

The common area in our subterranean apartment was dark as night, with only a bluish light coming from the TV. I was surprised that anyone was there at all, let alone to find Hope and Manda doubled over in hysterics on the rug. They had obviously been laughing so hard and for so long that their contagious laughter had spread to inanimate objects. Not even the Olga could contain itself, having shaken off the tasteful green slipcover to reveal its true colors, a garish arrangement of orange and yellow stripes.

"Jess! You have to see this!"

"What is—" My question was cut off by their shushing.

I set myself down on the floor in front of the television. An out-of-tune piano plunked out a simple melody I'd never heard before, sung by a class of six-year-olds in loud, unintentional, atonal twenty-five-part harmony. I could barely make out the words:

"April is the month of showers and glooooom!"

Two kids stood up from the risers, a boy and a girl in matching yellow rain slickers and boots. The boy held up a sign that said APRIL. The girl carried an umbrella.

"May is the month when bumblebees zoooooom!"

"And help make all the flowers bloooooooom!"

Two more kids stood up. The first, a boy, wore a garbage bag painted with yellow stripes, and a set of deelybobber antennae on his head. He held a card that said MAY. The girl was wearing a green leotard and tights, her head surrounded by crinkly pink crepe-paper petals.

"Birds winging, children singing . . ."

"Badly," Hope muttered under her breath.

"It's all a part of spring springing!"

I grabbed the remote and pressed Pause. Manda and Hope protested.

"I'll turn it back on as soon as you tell me what the hell we're watching!"

(I know I overreacted, but I was still bummed about my botched interview, and a little more so by the fact that neither Hope nor Manda—but especially Hope—had asked me about it.)

"Duuuuuuuh!" Manda said, elementary school style. "It's our first-grade pageant. 'Twelve Months of Memories.' Written and directed by our teacher, the wonderfully talented Mrs. Kornakavitch."

"Where did it come from?"

"My mom found it in the attic," explained Manda. "I just got it today. I haven't seen it in fifteen years!"

"Doesn't that freak you out?" Hope asked Manda.

"What?"

"That we're old enough to say, 'I haven't seen this in fifteen years.' "

"Or old enough to say, 'I've known *you* for twenty years.' "

"Twenty years!" Hope exclaimed. "We've known each other for twenty years!"

"We have," Manda said. "It's hard to believe, isn't it?"

I nodded in agreement. I often forget that Manda has known Hope longer than I have, that they have about ten years of shared history that has nothing to do with me.

(The irony, in retrospect, is that I wondered if Hope was as unnerved by my parallel friendship with Bridget as I was by hers with Manda. I didn't even think about you.)

I cringed as the kiddie choir launched into another ditty with a surf-pop melody meant to conjure up images of summertime sunnin' 'n' funnin'.

"We get outta sch-oo-oo-oo-oo-ool in June!"

"Have fun 'cause we'll be ba-aa-aa-aa-ck here soon!"

The calendar boy for June was wearing a T-shirt and swim trunks, accessorized with a snorkel and a life jacket. The calendar girl for June was dressed like the Little Mermaid, with a tangled red wig, a purple shell bikini top, and an iridescent green flipper bottom.

"That's me!" Manda said.

Was it a trick of the light? Or was it possible that Manda had more significant cleavage at six than I do at twenty-two?

"I had the best costume," Manda said.

"You totally did!" Hope said, bouncing up and down. "I was so jealous! With my red hair I thought I should have been the Little Mermaid."

"Hope was December. And she got to sing a solo in the grand finale. . . ."

Hope blushed, feeling shy about a performance that bowed in 1991.

I bragged for her, "I'm sure that's because she was the only one who could carry a tune."

I didn't have to search hard to find Hope on screen because her crazy blaze of hair rose higher than everyone else on stage. That is, except for the boy sitting next to her, who startled me with his familiar face. . . .

"Is that . . . ?" I asked, knowing the answer.

"Yup," Manda said. "That's Marcus next to Hope. And she didn't sing a solo. She sang a duet!" Manda's laughter had a serrated edge that cut right through me.

Manda fast-forwarded through the rest of summer and fall. A quick succession of twosomes in costume—Uncle Sam and Lady Liberty for July, a fat jack-o'-lantern and a green-faced witch for October—took center stage for a few seconds before returning to their spots on the risers. Manda clicked the remote again after the November Pilgrim and Indian took their bows.

The lights dimmed and a boy and a girl filled the spotlight. They were twin angels, tall, red-haired, and dressed all in white. Fake painted-cornflake snow fell from the rafters and clung to their feathered wings. The piano music swelled and the boy—You! Marcus!—opened his mouth to sing.

"*The days go by, go by so fast* . . ."

Hope had the next line.

"*What was once the future is now the past* . . ."

Then you took Hope's hand and you sang together.

"*On and on and on we go* . . . *And every day we groooooooow* . . ."

Make no mistake. It was a terrible song. It was a terrible song that has been written countless times by countless hacks before Mrs. Kornakavitch came along. But when you two harmonized, I not only found religion, but I swear I was in rapture. You took the high part and Hope took the low part, and together you created the purest sound I've ever heard.

The symphonic ecstasy was short-lived, however, because the rest of the class joined you on the cacophonous chorus:

"*School memories we hold so dear, year after year after year!*"

You and Hope were still center stage, holding hands under the spotlight. It was the first time I'd ever noticed that you were redheads from opposite sides of the color wheel. Hope's hair was a yellow-red, closer to orange, hot. You were a blue-red, closer to purple, cool.

"You and Marcus were always so cute together," Manda said to Hope.

(It was the "always" that first captured, and then refused to relinquish, dominion over my imagination.)

"Those two were inseparable back then," Manda said to me with a know-it-all air.

"Really?" I asked, looking at Hope, whose eyes stuck to the TV screen.

"Oh, yeah," Manda said, answering for Hope. "Hope and Marcus were quite the little item at our elementary school." She assumed a guise of openmouthed, wide-eyed innocence. "You didn't know?"

"No," Hope and I replied. We then glanced at each other with a mutual but rare and strange unease.

"I know you don't like to talk about the whole proposal thing," Manda said to me, "but you should know that Marcus has been married before . . . to Hope!"

Hope muttered a faint complaint. "Manda, please . . ."

Manda was having too much fun to be stopped. "We had a little ceremony on the baseball diamond in fifth grade. The altar was home plate. Hope wore a toilet-paper veil. Marcus offered a ring made of one of those pull-tops off a soda can. I was a bridesmaid with a yellow dandelion bouquet."

Hope blinked her eyes slowly, almost too slowly to be considered a blink.

I had never heard about any of this. From either one of you. As far as I knew, your only connection to Hope was the dishonorable, drug-addled friendship with Heath that began when you were thirteen and ended when he died. As far as I knew, you had only exchanged unpleasantries with Hope on a handful of occasions, and always in the context of having nothing in common other than your admiration and adoration of her deeply flawed but charismatic older brother.

As far as I knew.

"Well, I'm sure they both forgot. . . ." There was a sly, singsongy lilt to Manda's voice. She was dropping hints no one was picking up, so she clapped her hands to indicate an abrupt change of subject. "I *never* forgot the time Marcus totally tried to have sex with me."

Hope's head almost unscrewed from her neck. "Manda!"

"It was a beach party the summer after freshman year," Manda buzzed. "He was high on God knows what, and spouted off poetry to try to impress me."

I said nothing, somehow intuiting that this wasn't the big secret destined to be revealed. I mean, *of course* you tried to have sex with Manda. *Of course* you read poetry to her, because you often read melancholy poetry to your would-be conquests, ripping off lines from Rimbaud ("Every moon is atrocious and every sun bitter . . .") or Jim Morrison-ripping-off-Rimbaud ("The days are bright and filled with pain . . .") and trying to pass them off as your own. Sometimes, though not as often, the verse *was* your own ("We are Adam and Eve, born out of chaos called creation . . ."). These seductive tactics usually worked wonders, though not on the spectacularly dumb ones who thought you were a freak, a Dreg, and would have preferred *NSYNC ("How can it be that right here with me there's an angel . . . ?") instead.

Manda's bosom heaved in heavy-breathing anticipation of my response. Hope sat in a—could it be?—lotus position, with her eyes cast down at her hands tucked inside the bottom of her paint-stained T-shirt. She punched her knuckles outward, stretching the cotton away from her skin.

"Oh, it's okay," I said, meaning every word. "I'm not surprised. Marcus got in some serious play before he met me, and I don't doubt that he hit on you when he was still using. He probably doesn't even remember doing it."

(Do you? Actually, forget I even asked. It really doesn't matter.)

"Hmm," Manda said, "casually" extending her arms toward the ceiling. "Would he remember something that happened a few days ago?"

Hope's eyes swelled and her mouth hung open. And that's when I realized that she and Manda were having a totally different conversation.

"Is there something going on here that I don't know about?"

"No!" Hope said.

"Yes!" Manda said.

Outside, the skies rumbled and rolled like an express train barreling through a local station.

"It's not what you think," Hope said quietly.

"I'm not thinking anything!" I said loudly.

(This was a lie. My mind was reeling with sordid possibilities.)

"Marcus knew," Hope said.

"Marcus knew what?" I asked, getting more desperate by the second.

"He knew that you wanted to break up with him," Hope said.

"How?" I asked.

"Because I told him."

On cue, a thunderbolt tore open the heavens, unleashing a torrent of rain.

forty-three

And that's when Hope told me everything, or rather, her adaptation of "everything." And I was going to document it for you word for agonizing word, you know, for posterity, but I just don't have it in me. Besides, I don't need to transcribe Hope's version of your conversation because you were there. Here's what I know:

After the Shit Lit Hissy Fit, you came back to the apartment all by yourself. You didn't have a key. You were lucky Hope was there.

Lucky, indeed.

You were upset. You didn't understand how an evening that had offended you on so many levels could be fun for me. You needed someone to talk to about the growing distance between us, and not just in terms of geography. Since coming off of the silence and solitude of Death Valley, you just couldn't handle the city's relentless overstimulation, or understand why I thrived on it.

When I think about you having your Shit Lit Hissy Fit, I can still see you twitching and fidgeting, all five senses shaken up from the inside out. You clasped your hands over your ears, closed your eyes, and tried to curl yourself into a semi-fetal position in your chair. A full-grown man with thick, wooly facial hair, you still looked like a child petrified of the imaginary monster under the bed. If the crowd hadn't been as loud as it was, I probably would have heard you intoning comforting mantras to yourself.

I should have wanted to take you away from there, to protect you from the monster and return you to safety. It should have been instinctual. But since it's all coming out now, I'll tell you the truth: I didn't feel bad for you at all. I felt embarrassed by your babyish behavior. But above all, I felt burdened by it. By you.

So you were totally justified in wondering whether it would be best for both of us if we broke it off before you went off to Princeton. But it would have been so much better if you had said it in front of me.

As it was, Hope confirmed that I had been contemplating the same. Yes, I had been thinking about it, though I had never told her that. She just knew, as friends know these things. And her uncanny ability to see right through me is what makes her betrayal so devastating: My best friend would have known to keep this unuttered secret to herself.

I must admit that it's almost a relief to hear I wasn't imagining our problems. But no part of our revelatory conversation explains how your breakup turned into a proposal. And yet even this absurd mystery makes perfect sense. Such perplexing developments are, after all, your stock in trade.

forty-four

There is only a page left in this notebook, which I will devote to the low point of the conversation.

"Nothing happened," Hope pled. "I swear."

That fear crouched shamefully in the deepest, darkest, furthest corner of my mind. It hadn't leapt to the fore until Hope gave voice to it.

"Nothing happened!"

You have always been the great unspoken between Hope and me. I thought it was because you were guilty by association. You and Heath did drugs together. Heath overdosed and died. You cleaned yourself up and lived. Why remind Hope of this irreversible truth? I now realize that it was much more complicated than that. You and Hope had a shared history that had nothing to do with me. Your silence—not just over these past few weeks, but for the past ten years—indicates that you both wanted it to stay that way.

How many secrets exist between you?

"Nothing happened," Hope kept on saying. "Nothing happened."

I believe that nothing *physical* happened between you. But you two have colluded and collided as emotional coconspirators. And I swear to you, Marcus, that's even worse than if you had fucked.

notebook number two

september 6–10, 2006

wednesday: the sixth

forty-five

I was dizzy and disoriented when I woke up this next morning, and not just because I had rather dramatically spent the night on the common-room couch instead of the Cupcake's bottom bunk.

The proceedings documented in Notebook Number Two will only make sense when taken in consideration of those recorded in Notebook Number One. However, I have a proven history of losing/destroying journals like this one. In the event that this new composition notebook gets separated from its slightly older twin, here are:

MY MINDFUCKS: A QUICK AND HANDY REFERENCE GUIDE

(In chronological order)

1. You preempted my breakup with an absurd marriage proposal I could not refuse.
2. Bridget and Percy are not getting married, which just confirms my lack of faith in the whole institution. If there's any couple who could make me believe in marriage, it's them.
3. My sister asked me to be Marin's legal guardian. If I say yes, this could make me—the least maternal woman I know—a de facto mommy for the rest of my life.
4. I lost out on a job because I was too busy thinking about how much you would hate the job once I got it, instead of focusing my attention on the job interview itself and actually getting the job before I started worrying about your reaction to it.
5. I can't blame you for this hypothetical disapproval, because I couldn't see myself working for Dr. Kate, either. I only went on the interview because I need to get a real job soon because my fake job doesn't pay me enough to survive without pity handouts from my sister.

6. But I *can* blame you and Hope—my two best friends—for betraying my trust. You chose to confide in each other instead of in me. What other secrets are you keeping?

These are just the major mindfucks. A complete list of petty psychic fornications (Will Manda skank her way back into Len's life? Does Shea still have a key to our apartment and will she use it to host a Pimpz N Playaz party while we're out? Should I become a DONUT HO'? Do my eyebrows look like sperm? Have Scotty and Sara achieved a simple happiness that is out of our reach? How will I pay an extra $166.33 a month in rent?) would require too many volumes for any library.

I thought for sure the number would hold at six. Alas, I'm only midway through the week—"hump day," as it is referred to in real offices where real workers work real jobs for real bosses. It should not have surprised me when my mother called this morning to add another item to the list, officially making it a cranial orgy.

7. My dad is in the hospital because he crashed his bike into a parked car.

My mother was strangely calm about it, exhibiting the kind of emotional detachment that is number three on the list of Bethany's Signs That My Mom Is About to Leave My Dad.

"He's fine," my mom said. "Don't worry about it."

"But he's in the hospital, right?"

"Well, yes," my mom said. "That's where I'm calling from."

"People who are fine don't go to the hospital," I railed. "That's kind of the point of hospitals. It's where people who are not at all fine go. . . ."

"Calm down, Jessie. He's not going to *die*. He didn't even break any bones."

"Then why is he still there?"

"Well," my mom said, snapping into an efficient tone, "the doctors tell me that he lost consciousness because he was severely dehydrated. . . ."

"Dehydrated?" I asked. "Christ, it's not *that* hot today. How long was he out on the bike?"

"How should I know?" my mom shot back. "A few hours, I think.

He's always riding while I'm out working. I can't keep track of his mileage. . . ."

This was true, and yet I found it so sad that my mom had no idea what my father did for hours on end.

"The doctors say he needs about four bags of fluid, which will take all day."

"Four bags? That sounds like a lot. Is that a lot?"

"I'm not a doctor, Jessie." My mom sighed. "I have no idea."

"Okay," I said. "I'm coming home."

"Why?" my mom asked.

"Bethany won't want to take Marin out of school," I said, "and I feel like one of us should be there, so that leaves me."

"It's not necessary," my mom said.

"No, Mom," I corrected. "I think it is. Dad's in the hospital. I'm coming."

We made arrangements for her to pick me up at the Pineville bus station. When I hung up, I caught Hope hovering in the hallway outside the Cupcake.

"Is your dad okay?"

The question stuck in the air unanswered, mired in the impenetrable tension between us. I had to make a decision: Would I rather harbor resentment about last night's revelation or forgive and forget and let bygones be bygones and all that water flow under the bridge?

"He crashed his bike."

"Oh."

"He's in the hospital because he's severely dehydrated."

"Oh."

"I'm going to Pineville as soon as I can get my shit together."

Hope shifted from one foot to the other, like a kid who needs to pee. She was nervous.

"Are you okay?" she asked.

"I'm . . ." I picked the ring off the steamer trunk/coffee table where I had put it the night before. I read the inscription for the bizillionth time: MY THOUGHTS CREATE MY WORLD. "I don't know how I am."

"I'm so sorry. . . ."

I tapped the ring on the table. "You said the same thing on Sunday morning. Only you said, 'I'm so sorry about you and Marcus.' "

Hope's body jutted forward as if she were struggling against the current of all that water flowing under the bridge. . . .

"So you thought that he was going to break up with me and . . ." I shut my eyes in pain. "You must have said something to Manda because she and Shea had actually bet on it!" I rolled forward and rubbed my head into the couch cushions. "Ooooohhhhhhh."

"I didn't say anything to Manda!" Hope said. "She eavesdropped on our conversation. . . ."

I almost bit the pillow in frustration. "So you and Manda and Shea all knew that Marcus wanted to break up with me. . . ."

"But Jess, he *didn't* break up with you! He asked you to marry him!"

I sat up. "But the marriage would be null and void, right? Because he's still married to you!"

Hope stood up straighter, her arms thrust at her sides in defiance. "You can't possibly be angry about something that happened in fifth grade!"

"Yes I can! And it's not just the marriage. It's anything and everything you did together that I didn't know about. Splitting peanut-butter-and-jelly sandwiches. Putting on backyard puppet shows. Playing spin the bottle. Whatever! It doesn't matter. But what does matter is that you never told me that you had once been close to the man who is supposed to be the love of my life!"

"I don't see why this matters."

"It matters because when it came down to choosing to confide in you or me, he chose you. Which means that your relationship must run pretty deep."

Hope didn't disagree.

"What if you had never moved? How do I know that he wouldn't have ended up with you?"

"I didn't want him!"

"But did *he* want *you*?"

Hope paused for a moment before answering, "No." That seemingly insignificant silence contained the truth. And she knew it, too.

"Yes he did," I said. "At one time he must have."

Were you friends with Heath to get closer to Hope? Is that why you spent so many afternoons getting high in Heath's room?

Hope didn't refute it. "I'm sorry. . . ."

"I know you are," I said, standing up. "And I'm sorry that I'm still angry at you."

Hope lowered her head.

"I don't want to be," I said. "But I am."

And I suppose it's that same desire to forgive and forget and let bygones be bygones and all that water under the bridge that compels me to keep my promise, to keep writing, even though I'm still angry at you, too.

forty-six

I made it to the Port Authority just in time to catch the New Jersey Transit #76 Shore Points Express bus to Pineville, which goes against the tide of commuters and is therefore mercifully unfull. The seat next to me was empty, so I could stretch out and think in as much peace as one can get as one bounces and bumps along the Garden State Parkway at a maximum speed of fifty-five miles an hour, though we usually go slower because of the inevitable traffic snarls stretching for miles before any one of the ubiquitous toll plazas.

As a lifelong resident of New Jersey, I have been brainwashed into believing two things about traveling by car: 1. Highways can't exist without toll booths. 2. Pumping gas is best left to professionals. This is the type of harmless propaganda you grow up believing until you experience otherwise and feel like a fool for being duped for so long. Imagine my surprise when Hope informed me that there is not a single toll road in the entire state of Tennessee. This amazement was only outdone by the passenger-side shock of pulling up to a self-serve in Pennsylvania and watching Hope deftly maneuver the gas pump all by herself. I was too impressed to be embarrassed by my own cluelessness.

See? I am working very hard at forgiveness, even though the childish part of me is thinking, Why are you telling Marcus this? I'm sure he already knows about Hope's way around a gas pump. He already knows *everything* about Hope that you don't.

I'm trying here.

Despite the luxury of a few more inches in legroom, the bus still seems less dignified than the train. But no rails lead to our hometown, which implies that it's a destination no one needs to get to with any sort of expediency, which is frustrating because I want to get there as quickly as possible.

I keep returning to a semi-disturbing conversation I had with my dad the last time I saw him. It was not this past Sunday but the one before.

forty-seven

I'd woken up that morning cursing that it was my week to cheer for him. It was already past nine A.M., and his race was fifty miles long—fifteen laps at roughly ten minutes per lap. I remember thinking that if I hauled my own ass, I could get there to see him finish.

Bethany and I had urged him to join the Jersey Shore Amateur Cycling Association when we got tired of hearing how lonely he was. Apparently, now that Darling's Designs for Leaving is thriving, my mom is too busy getting paid to "analyze the selling aesthetics" of other people's homes to spend any time in her own. And it doesn't seem as if she's going to be a more reliable presence in the household anytime soon. "When the market is down, my business is up!" she chimes. And up it is. My mom has quickly become one of the top home stagers on the Jersey Shore, and she doesn't even have to advertise. Darling's Designs for Leaving is referral-only, which gives her business a certain snobbish cachet that my mother totally gets off on.

But now that she's out earning and my dad is retired at home, it's made for a bizarre role reversal that he, for one, has not gotten used to. It's more than a little disconcerting to see my parents going through an awkward phase, even as they approach their Social Security years. Shouldn't they have figured it all out by now? Shouldn't they be over all that stupid maladjusted shit? Isn't that one of the glorious advantages of old age?

Hence our insistence that he join the cycling club. The team travels to races all over the tristate area, and my dad often participates in the Sunday-morning series at Prospect Park, in Brooklyn. It gives him something to do, and provides his daughters frequent opportunities to spend time with him on our own turf. Unfortunately, the Masters race starts at the unholy hour of 7:02 A.M. Bethany and I feel obligated to support him when he's in town, and we switch off rah-rah weekends, a combined effort to help him through this difficult adjustment phase. So two weekends ago, it was my turn to be the good daughter.

I knew better than to even try to single out my dad among the scores of riders. In their racing gear and helmets, it was nearly impossible to tell them apart as they whizzed by. His club always sets up a small recovery area somewhere near the finish line, so I searched through the chemical Ben-Gay haze, following a trail of hollowed-out orange halves, protein bar wrappers, and conical paper cups stomped flat into triangles. The racers spoke in the exuberant yet exhausted tones of those who are out the door by four A.M., drive one hundred miles to cycle fifty miles, then return home by noon and complain to their wives that they're too wiped to mow the lawn.

"Oh man, I almost bonked on the twelfth lap. . . ."

"I hammered it on the tenth. . . ."

"Fierce field today. . . ."

The whole scene was making me feel oddly nostalgic for high school cross-country practice, though I would never say this to Dad, since he considers my quitting the varsity XC team one of the greatest tragedies of *his* life.

I finally spotted the JSACA banner, and under it, my dad. I can't help it: I get embarrassed whenever I see him in his acid-green spandex unitard. Yes, even when *all* the riders are wearing similar racing gear.

He's in great shape for his age, but I don't need to see his fiftysomething physique in such scrotummy detail. Ack.

My father was stooped at the waist, resting his hands on his quads as he spoke to another middle-aged rider who would surely mortify his own daughter with his own nut-hugging ensemble if she were there to see it. I couldn't tell from his posture if he'd had a good day or not. He always seemed defeated lately.

"You looked good out there, Dad!"

"I *felt* like shit," he said. "I really did."

"You still placed well in a competitive field," said his friend, slapping him on the back.

My dad grumbled and rubbed the top of his head, which was almost as smooth and shiny without the helmet as with it. He didn't even bother introducing me to his middle-aged friend, which I appreciated. "You want a bagel?" he asked me, gesturing to a huge bag sitting on the back of an open SUV. "You're too skinny. You need to eat more. It's free, so it should fit your budget."

He feels bad about the sad state of my finances, but not too bad, because he thinks I'm an idiot for not joining Wally D's/Papa D's Retailtainment Corp.'s lucrative quest for global gluttonous dominion. And while he occasionally used to throw me a few bones, that's not so much of an option now that he's retired and on a fixed income.

I helped myself to a cinnamon raisin bagel.

"Take another, for later," he said, thrusting an everything bagel into my hand. He tore at a sesame and stuffed a chunk of it into his mouth. "C'mon," he mumbled through the dough, which was going staler and tougher by the second. "Let's take a breather."

This was as close as my dad would come to actually asking me to talk. I followed him to a slightly less chaotic clearing. Along the way, various spandex-clad riders congratulated him on his performance.

"Way to bring it in, Dar!"

"Top five this week!"

And my dad either grumbled a thank-you or said nothing at all. When we were far enough away from everyone else, we plopped ourselves down in the prickly brownish grass.

"You okay?" I asked.

"Oh, yeah," he said. "It's just my damn knee acting up." He slapped it as if it were a bad dog that had dumped on a brand-new Oriental rug.

"Oh, sorry."

"Jessie, here's some advice: Don't get old."

"Ah, but the alternative is worse, right?"

My dad slapped his knee again. "Ask me another day." Then he promptly changed the subject. And the new subject, appropriately enough, was you. "So Marcus is off to Princeton next week. That's a great area around there."

I knew what he was getting at. I picked a raisin out of my bagel as if it were an annoying hanging scab on my elbow. "I don't know if we'll get a chance to check out the towpath. . . ."

"I hope you haven't changed your mind about the bike trip."

As you already know, Dad had this big idea about leading us on a bike expedition along the densely wooded dirt trails that wind through Princeton and other towns in Mercer County.

"I'm not sure we'll be organizing that trip with Marcus after all."

"Why not?"

"Things are . . ." I paused here. Not for effect, but to find the right word. "*Unsettled* between us."

My dad rubbed his head. "Do I even want to hear more?"

"I'm not sure," I replied. "Do you?"

He nodded reluctantly, a gesture that resembled more of a wince than an affirmation.

"It's been something that's been coming for a while, I guess. We're at different places in our lives. . . ."

"You two always seemed like you were in different places in your lives."

"Well, maybe it always seemed that way to you, but our differences are just more . . . uh . . . *pronounced* now than ever before."

My father surprised me by looking right at me when he said, "That's such a shame."

"What?"

"That you and Marcus are having problems. That you're *unsettled*."

"Wow . . . I didn't expect you to react like that. . . ."

"How did you expect me to react?" he asked.

"I don't know," I replied. "I wasn't even sure if you ever got around to, you know, *liking* Marcus or not."

"Look, Jessie," he said. "I'm not going to lie to you. When I caught wind of his checkered past, the drugs and all that trouble he got himself into in high school, I wasn't happy that this royal screwup of the first order was dating my daughter."

"But he was clean when we got together."

He waved his bagel in the air to stifle me. "I know," he said. "But I still didn't like it." He then chucked his bagel into the nearest garbage can with a resounding clunk. "If I had tried to step in and put a stop to you two, it would have backfired. Just like it did with Bethany and Jerry."

Jerry.

Wow.

Jerry.

I had not heard that name in almost two decades. How could I have forgotten Jerry? He was my sister's first serious boyfriend, from her sophomore year of high school. I was only five years old during the Jerry Years, so when I think of him, I can only conjure his junior yearbook photo, which I studied intensely and with great interest. He had a rectangular flattop haircut, a conniving underbite that was apparently impossible to unhinge into any semblance of a smile, and thick black eyebrows like two censorship bars trying to block out his dirty thoughts. He was two years older than Bethany, and drove, I kid you not, a silver I-ROC tricked out with a neon-pink underbelly that made our driveway glow like a seedy no-tell motel whenever he honked for my sister. The horn was barely audible above the strains of Def Leppard's *Hysteria*, the only cassette he ever listened to, which, naturally, as these things happen, became the only cassette Bethany listened to for like six months straight. To this day, I know every goddamn lyric to every goddamn song on that goddamn album, and not just the givens like the title track, "Armageddon It," "Pour Some Sugar on Me," and "Love Bites." I even know all the words to the less obvious cuts; such as "Excitable":

(Oh) (Whoa) Oh, you know I get so
(Excitable) I really get so (Excitable)

(Okay. Maybe those lyrics don't seem so hard to commit to memory, but *you* try to put every "Oh" and "Whoa" in its proper place and see how easy it is.)

Anyway, to say that my parents hated Jerry is an understatement, one that requires me to consult my thesaurus to pile on the synonyms *reviled*, *loathed*, *detested*, *abhorred*, and *despised*, none of which do justice to the hatred they felt. They hated him with a passion that was only outdone by its inverse.

Oh, how Bethany loved him.

"Then you and Marcus broke up," my dad continued. "He went to that crazy Buddhist camp in the middle of the desert, and you had that other boyfriend at Columbia. The prep school brat from Greenwich, Connecticut . . . The philosopher . . . What was his name?"

"Kieran."

My dad all but rolled his eyes, because he knows it's undignified and lamely *Laguna Beach* for a senior citizen to roll his eyes. "Well, I never met him, so you'll forgive me for not remembering his name."

There is a very good reason I never introduced my parents to this junior-year error in judgment: Kieran was an emo assclown.

"Then last Christmas, Marcus shows up on our doorstep and is back in your life again. Just like that." He snapped his fingers. "And he had really cleaned himself up. Got his head on straight. Got himself into Princeton . . ." He trailed off.

"What?"

"It's just unfortunate," he said, forehead wrinkling, "that things are *unsettled* just as he was getting respectable."

"That's right, Dad, I broke up with him just to piss you off."

"That's not what I mean," he said. "He really seemed like he was getting his act together. It says a lot about a man's character to overcome substance abuse problems and the like. And it showed real initiative for him to apply to Princeton."

(I'm not disagreeing with any of these points.)

"Unsettled," my dad groused. "Does your mother know about any of this?"

"No, I haven't talked to Mom lately. . . ."

"So I found out before she did."

"Yes."

"Ha," he said with no joy whatsoever.

forty-eight

My mom was fifteen minutes late in picking me up from the bus station. As I waited for her to show up, I watched a shimmering silver SUV pull into the parking lot. I mocked the anonymous driver of this immense and intimidating luxury export for being a status-obsessed, bigger-is-better, gas-guzzling idiot who was responsible for U.S. dependency on foreign oil from countries that harbor and abet terrorists . . .

Then the driver rolled down her tinted window and told me to get inside.

"Jessie!"

My mortifying ride had arrived.

"Sweet tank, Mom," I said as I climbed up and into the passenger side. "I hear it gets three miles to the gallon. Where's the 'Support Our Troops' magnet?"

But my mom didn't hear me. She was finishing up a conversation on her hands-free headset.

"Remember, you have to speak the language of the interior," she was saying. "Is it Rustic French? English Country? Tuscan Renaissance?"

I do not speak any of these languages.

"I'm dropping my daughter off at the hospital. Then I've got a three o'clock. Then I'll swing by around four-thirty to approve the throws for the Thompson sale and . . ."

I still can't get over how efficient and businesslike my mother sounds when she's working.

"So your father will be in for another two hours or so."

I was looking at the dashboard, marveling at all the various controls.

"Jessie!"

"Oh! I didn't realize you were talking to me," I said.

"Of course I'm talking to you," she said, though there was no change in tone or gesture that would indicate that her phone call had ended and our conversation had begun.

"I'm going to drop you off, leave for a couple hours, then come back and take you both home."

"You're not staying?"

"I have an appointment," she said.

"With who?"

"The nursery," my mom replied, "should have set aside the hardy mums for you to arrange on the front porch. Make sure you put them in the clay pots because the plastic planters are tacky and cheap."

It took me a second to realize that she was back to addressing the headset. I turned my attention to semi-abandoned strip malls along the highway, suddenly remembering that the last time I rode along this highway was in January, in the Caddie with you.

forty-nine

I wasn't supposed to be back in Pineville, on the road, in the Caddie with you. I was supposed to be in the rental car with Hope, headed for Happyland, Oklahoma.

"Why do developers keep building new strip malls for dry cleaners, banks, and bad Chinese restaurants when the old strip malls aren't fully occupied by dry cleaners, banks, and bad Chinese restaurants?" I had asked you. "It's depressing."

"What's depressing?" you asked. "Some people would call that progress."

I was surprised that you had responded at all. It seemed as if everything I said lately was met with a silent chin-first nod, or a simple "Yes" or "No."

"I don't know," I said, having trouble articulating the source of melancholy that usually set in whenever I left the city for Pineville. "All those abandoned storefronts are depressing. All that emptiness."

When you contemplatively dipped the Beard, I thought the conversation was over. We passed through two green lights, then stopped at a red.

"Buddhists strive for emptiness," you said.

"Really?"

"Shunyata. It means not so much 'empty' as 'open.' Without boundaries."

"Really?" I said again, if only because it had worked the first time in coaxing more conversation out of you. You surprised me by obliging.

"Without getting all metaphysical, shunyata means that everything in this life is interconnected. There is no me that is separate from you."

"Or anyone else, for that matter."

"I suppose that's true, too."

That was a blustery afternoon in early January. Twenty minutes later, we huddled together on the boardwalk, our own bodies providing shelter from the wind. As the gray waves churned with sturm und drang, you revealed two things I had previously known nothing about: Your dad had been diagnosed with stage III prostate cancer. And he had insisted that you make good on the binding, early-action offer from Princeton University.

fifty

"My aesthetician," my mother said in a sharp tone meant to get my attention.

"What?"

"I have an appointment with my aesthetician."

"The Botox doc?" I asked. "Mom!"

"What? I have to schedule my maintenance visits months in advance," she said. "If I miss it, I won't be able to get in until next year."

Now that she mentioned it, the smoothing effects of the Botox must have worn off because her face was able to wrinkle itself into detectable expressions of genuine human emotion, and at that moment, it registered annoyance.

"You're leaving Dad alone in the hospital so you can keep your appointment with the aesthetician?"

"But I'm not leaving him alone," she said. "I'm leaving him with *you*. You can handle it."

When did I become the paragon of all things adult and responsible? I sleep in a *bunk bed*, for Christ's sake.

"There's so much wrongness going on here," I said, "I don't even know where to start."

"I'm sure you'll find your way," she said drolly.

"Okay, first of all, I just don't understand why you do this to your face. You're beautiful for your age without all that artificial help."

"See? 'For my age.' You mean I'm beautiful for an old lady."

"You're not an old lady," I said. "You're—" I stop myself.

"Forty-eight," she said without batting a curled eyelash.

"*Mooooooooom*."

"*Whaaaaaaat?*" she asked, mocking my tone as she flicked the turn signal.

For the record: I'm proud of my mom. I mean, how many women launch their own successful business in their fifties? But if she doesn't stop shaving off the years, soon she will have to start telling everyone that Bethany is either (a) her younger sister, (b) the product of my dad's first marriage, or (c) the first-ever baby conceived by a mother who was still in utero herself.

"Dad retired last year at fifty-five. You're a year younger. . . ."

She violently shushed me, lest occupants of other SUVs on Route 37 should hear.

"Are you saying you're forty-eight because you don't want to be fifty but you don't want to say forty-nine either because that sounds like more of a lie than forty-eight? Which is crazy because you're *fifty-four*!"

She took a sharp turn into the hospital parking lot and I was thrown into the passenger-side door.

"First of all, what I do to my face is my business, not yours. It's not your place to criticize," my mom huffed. "It's an outpatient procedure that takes a minute. It's not like I'm getting a face-lift. . . ."

"Yet!" I blurted. "Botox is the gateway procedure. . . ."

My mom wrinkled her forehead in disdain again, a gesture that she would not be able to execute post-"maintenance." "Stop being so dramatic, Jessie." She sighed. "I wouldn't expect you, at all of twenty-two years old, to understand what it's like to look in the mirror and not even recognize the old person looking back at you. Looking better makes me feel better. What's wrong with that?"

"What's wrong with that . . ." What's wrong with that, I thought, is that more and more women deal with emotional insecurities by fixing their physical flaws, all in the false name of self-love. What's wrong with this, I thought, is that we're reducing ourselves to a gender of firm flesh and unlined faces, empty heads and hollow hearts. It's no wonder that my mom is getting maintenance, or that Bethany promotes the DONUT HO' and refers to herself as a MILF.

"I don't understand how you can be so cavalier," I finally replied.

She pulled up to the orange cone that designated the drop-off zone. "I can be so *cavalier*," she said, putting italics on my word because she wouldn't use it herself, "because your father did this on purpose."

"Did *what* on purpose?" The silver monster idled in the circular drive at the entrance to the hospital, creating a traffic jam behind us.

"Crashed his bike."

"Why would Dad do something stupid like that?" I asked. I was eager to find out, then get out because a line of cars was honking at us to move on already.

"He'd do something stupid like that to get my attention."

fifty-one

I called my sister from the bright and antiseptic hospital lobby. As the phone rang, I watched keys pop up and down on a player piano programmed to play "feel good" music. I listened for Barry Manilow. Maybe a little "Can't Smile Without You" or "Bandstand Boogie." But he never came on.

"Where are you?" she asked.

"At the hospital."

"How's Dad?"

"I don't know," I said. "I haven't been up to see him yet."

"What are you waiting for?"

My phone *beep beep beeped:* low battery. In my haste I'd forgotten the charger.

"I'm waiting to recover from my ride with Mom," I said.

"What did she say?"

And then I quickly recounted the conversation, including my mom's accusation that he had crashed his bike on purpose.

"See?" Bethany asked.

"Please don't mention the Signs," I said.

My phone *beep beep beeped* again.

"Asserting her financial independence. Improving her physical appearance. Distancing herself from her spouse," Bethany said with a certain smugness. "All three Signs in a single conversation. . . ."

Just then a chubby girl around Marin's age came and stood next to me in front of the piano. She wore a thin acrylic sweater, the pink pilled fabric barely stretching over her round belly. Her jeans were both too large and too small, with the elastic waistband straining against her stomach and cuffs dragging on the floor. Two pink butterfly barrettes were haphazardly clipped to either side of her dirty blond hair. Dirty in both senses of the word, as I detected a certain oily, unwashed scent. This girl existed in the real world of cheap fast food, unpaid credit-card bills, and trips to the ER instead of insurance-covered doctor visits.

She broke my heart.

"By the way, how was Dr. Kate? Was she as incredible in person as she is on TV? When do—"

And then my phone *beep beep beeped* a final time before crapping out—thank God—for good.

The girl tugged on the hem of my T-shirt with grubby fingers half-licked of chocolate from vending machine snack cakes. "Who playin' dat pee-an-nah?"

I glanced at the piano, then back at the girl. A Pinky the Poodle Band-Aid was stuck to her forehead, through which I could see a brownish dash of blood. As you might recall, Pinky had once been Marin's favorite cartoon character. But that was a birthday or two in the past. Marin had already moved on.

One look at this girl and I felt like I could—and should—make a monumental difference in her life. I was overcome by an irrational urge to take her home with me. If I had the choice, I would have chosen to be *her* legal guardian, and not my own niece's. I'm not under the illusion that money buys happiness, but not having to worry about life's basic necessities certainly helps improve one's general outlook. Marin was born into unfathomable wealth. Her parents can guarantee the basics, and so much more, no matter who assumes legal guardianship. But this girl, I thought, this girl needs me more. . . . I never thought it was possible, but I suddenly understood, with luminous lucidity, why celebrities indulged the egotastic impulse to adopt foreign orphans.

"Who playin' dat?" she asked again.

If I couldn't take her home, I wanted to take her away from her troubles, if only temporarily. I wanted to joke around, make her laugh.

"It's a phantom," I said.

"Phantin?" Her face scrunched up in confusion. "Whazzat?"

"A ghost." I waggled my brows and wiggled my fingers. "*Spoooooky.*"

I regretted it as soon as I said it. After all, I didn't want to scare the poor girl. I waited for her eyes and mouth to stretch into a grotesque grimace, I waited for her to howl in horror and run back to the emergency room. "Maaaaaaaaaaammmmmmmaaaaaaaaa! Ders a *ghost* playin dat pee-an-ah!" I would have hurried in the opposite direction toward the west elevators before her mother could come after me. *How dare I scare the bejeezus out of her daughter? Doesn't she have enough hardship in her life without having to worry about piano-playing ghosts?*

Instead, she cocked her head to the side and glared at me through her bruised eyes. "Duhhhhhhhhh. It can't be a ghost."

"Why not?"

"A peeanah-playin' ghost? That's stoopid."

"Why is that stupid?"

She exhaled deeply because I was trying her patience. "It's stoopid 'cause ghosts got better things to do than play peeanahs."

"Like what?"

"Like gettin' ready for Halloween." She shook her head disdainfully.

She saw me for the patronizing, bleeding-heart liberal asshat that I really am. Even this girl could see right through me. The phantom in the room was me.

fifty-two

Rightfully chided, I dejectedly headed to the infusion room on the second floor, which is where I'm writing from right now. I was about to describe the infusion room for you, and how unnerving it is to roll back and pass through the privacy curtain and see my dad sitting upright in the hospital lounger, hooked up to the IV, looking as drained and tired and glassy-eyed as one would expect from someone who is "down four or five liters," as the nurse put it. I was about to describe the nurse's purple clogs and Hello Kitty scrubs and how these cartooniforms are probably meant to be cheerful but have the reverse effect on me. I was about to describe how difficult it is just to sit next to my dad while he's intravenously rehydrated with salt water one drip at a time, pretending to watch a lame game show, as he strains to make conversation about the best game-show host of all time, straining to discuss Bob Barker, and how he will always be remembered as the host of *The Price Is Right*, but also for his mission to get all pets spayed and neutered, straining because everything I say is overheard by everyone else in the room because the privacy curtains provide privacy in name only, as proven by my unintentional eavesdropping, just now, of the conversation between the nurse and the patient on my dad's right-hand side, a discussion that included clinical keywords such as *antiemetics*, *alopecia*, and *anemia*, but none as revelatory as *adjuvant chemotherapy*.

I don't need to describe the infusion room for you, or what it's like to sit silently next to your dad looking as pale and frail and mortal as you've ever seen him, because this is the same room in which your dad endured six chemo cycles between this past January and June.

I only know this much because I called your mother and pled for information. Because after your beachfront confession, you barely spoke of your father's cancer again. And when I asked, even begged you to unburden yourself to me, the person you professed to love more and deeper than you ever thought was even possible, you repeated the same mantra over and over again.

"There are no words," you said. "There are no words for this."

fifty-three

My dad and I didn't talk much all afternoon. Occasionally we'd make comments about the low-life, no-class conflicts that are the mainstay of daytime television. Will a paternity test prove that Bubba Jon is the father of La'Shaundreequa's twins? (No.) Will the plaintiff get back the fifteen hundred dollars she loaned the defendant so he could buy her a proper engagement ring but which he instead used to buy a plasma TV? (No.) Will the stripper be pleased to find out that her secret admirer is the scrawny senior citizen better known around the club as "the

Geezer"? (*Hay-ell* no.) What if he offers to buy the new breast implants she's been wanting to get? (Maybe.) Because he's a millionaire? (Yes!)

After a few hours of these trashy entertainments, I couldn't help but imagine how our own relationship might play out on one of these shows.

The Host: *On today's show we've got Jessica and Marcus.*

The Audience: *Woo. Woo. Woo.*

The Host: *Jessica was a virgin before she met* Marcus*.*

The Audience: *Ha. Ha. Ha.*

The Host: *Marcus had bedded approximately forty young women before Jessica.*

The Audience: *Daaaaaaaaamn.*

The Host: *For years Marcus has remained faithful to Jessica, but Jessica has had several sexual encounters outside their relationship.*

The Audience: *Oh, no she didn't!*

The Host: *Less than one week ago, Marcus asked Jessica to marry him.*

The Audience: *Awwwwwwwwwwww.*

The Host: *But Jessica didn't say yes. In fact, just before the proposal,* she *was thinking about breaking up with* him.

The Audience: *Boooooooooooo!*

The Host: *And it gets even more twisted than that!*

The Audience: *Woo. Woo. Woo.*

The Host: *It turns out that* Marcus *had also been thinking about breaking up with* Jessica. . . .

The Audience: *Huuuuuuuuh?*

The Host: *Which she found out from her best friend, Hope . . .*

The Audience: Mmmmmmm . . .

The Host: *With whom Marcus had carried a secret relationship behind Jessica's back . . .*

The Audience: *Oh, no he didn't!*

The Host: *Let's bring 'em all onstage and welcome them to the show. . . .*

The Audience: *Wooooooooooooooooooooo!*

My imaginary televised nightmare was interrupted by a genuine commercial clip for an upcoming episode of *The Dr. Frank Show*. I pressed my face into my hands and moaned.

"What's wrong?" my dad asked.

I removed one hand so I could point to the screen. "I had a job interview with Dr. Frank's guest, Dr. Kate," I replied, "and I blew it."

My dad leaned forward to get a closer look at Dr. Kate, who was looking as luscious as ever.

"For her new business venture, the first to blend new media and neuroscience."

My dad wasn't impressed with the jargon. "Doing *what*?"

"Working as an online matchmaker for iLoveULab." I blushed with embarrassment over the cheesiness of the job description, and the fact that I wasn't qualified for it.

My dad threw back his bald head. "You?!"

"I know, I know," I said, poking the channel changer. "But I blew the interview, so there's no need to make fun of a ridiculous job that I didn't even get."

I assumed my dad would want me to provide the play-by-play of the botched interview so we could review what had gone wrong, and I could learn from my errors and prevent them from happening again. It was his preferred process for self-improvement, one best captured by the video collection of my worst high school track and cross-country meets, "Notso Darling's Agony of Defeat, Volumes 1–4."

But he let it go.

"I was thinking about what you said a few weeks ago," my dad said. "About how you felt 'unsettled.' "

"Uh-huh," I replied, surprised by this unexpected turn to our conversation.

"The opposite of unsettled is settled. As in settling down."

"Uh-huh," I responded again, even more warily than before. I had no idea where he was going with this. I was starting to worry that this last bag of sterilized water had literally gone to his head. Was there excess fluid on his brain?

"When you get married," he said, "you settle down."

"Uh-huh."

"But when does settling down turn into just plain settling?" he asked.

This was the perfect opening for me to mention your proposal, and how it had inspired me to ponder that same question. But I was compelled to take an altogether different route.

"Dad?"

"Yeah?"

"Did you crash your bike on purpose?"

"Who told you that?" he asked, eyebrows raised. "Your mother?"

I nodded, then waved my hand dismissively. "I know. She's crazy."

"She is crazy," my dad replied, his mouth turning up at the corners. "And she's also right."

Just then the nurse in the Hello Kitty scrubs threw open the privacy curtain. "Looks like we're almost finished here, Mr. Darling!" she chirped. "Is your daughter driving you home?"

I was rendered speechless by my dad's revelation, so he answered for me. "My wife should be on her way."

Hello Kitty clucked sympathetically, then said, "The hospital can't release you without a ride home."

Hello Kitty was a short, wide-hipped bottle blonde, whose birth date was probably within a year or two of my mother's (actual versus claimed) D.O.B. The nurse's rucked face and shirred neck flesh indicated that she was doing little to fight the advances of late middle age, or that those measures that she had taken were not successful. Meanwhile, my mother was at the aesthetician erasing decades from her appearance with the help of synthetic injectable gelatins not yet approved by the FDA.

It was all so completely fucked up.

How did my parents get like this? I asked myself. And how can I stop it from happening to you and me?

I laboriously pushed myself up out of my chair, winded by my dad's confession and the prospect of trying to track down my mother. "I'll go down to the lobby and call her on a pay phone. I'll get her here."

No sooner had the words left my mouth than I heard heels clacking across the linoleum.

"No need," my mother said, breezing through the curtains with a triumphant air. "I have arrived!"

fifty-four

My strange day stretched into an even stranger evening.

The first strange development was the car ride back to my parents' place on the bay, which was strangely free of palpable parental tension and controversy. This would be strange enough on an ordinary day, never mind one during which my dad spent six hours in the hospital getting intravenously rehydrated after crashing his bike into a parked car in the failed attempt to steal my mother's attention away from her rising career and her falling face. Their interactions were neither hot nor cold, but not quite warm, either. Their temperate discussion included driving (Dad got behind the wheel because Mom was worn out from her appointments), dinner (Dad wanted it but Mom didn't want to make it), and their younger daughter (Dad encouraged me to spend the night, and Mom agreed). It did not include edema (Dad's swollen face from the excess saline, Mom's from a wrinkle-filling syringe) or any other topics outlined in the previous pages.

The condo hadn't changed much since the last time I was there. It was still as beige and tasteful as ever, but with a cold, unlived-in quality. My mom's own home seemed a lot like the empty rooms she was paid to fill with borrowed furniture and accent pieces to move white elephant properties off the market. I was standing in the foyer, overnight bag in hand, deciding what to do next, when I noticed that both my parents were staring at me expectantly, wondering the same thing. I felt that whatever I decided to do next was of monumental importance, as it would determine what we *all* did next. If I said, "Hey, let's order a pizza," we would order pizza, eat it together, and maybe, just maybe, have a conversation about what happened today. If I said, "Hey, I need to get away from you two because I'm totally freaked out about what happened today," we would all go to our separate rooms. To be honest, I was feeling more in favor of the latter than the former, yet I was overwhelmed by a sense of familial obligation, to be the good daughter, to be the one who kept us all together.

"Hey, let's order a pizza," I suggested.

My mom picked invisible lint off her creamy sleeveless turtleneck. "I'm not hungry," she said. "And I've got invoices to look over. . . ." Without any further explanation, she swiftly headed upstairs to the corner of her bedroom that served as her home office.

I glanced at my dad, who was watching her retreat.

"I think there are leftovers in the freezer," he said with a note of resignation. "I'll put them in the oven while you get settled upstairs."

"Get *settled*," I said pointedly.

"Settled," my dad said. "Right." And then he laughed for the first time all day.

fifty-five

I needed to wash off the hospital germs, so I took a long, hot shower in a stall so pristine I could've eaten my dinner straight off the tiles. I've lived in the city long enough that I can't help but look at all available space in terms of its NYC market value. As I scrubbed my legs, my torso, my arms, I noted that the stall is roughly the size of the Cupcake, and could easily be advertised as a $1000/mo studio on Craigslist.

I got out, dried off, and got dressed in the same T-shirt and cutoffs from the day before. The smell of browned cheese and crispy crust wafted upstairs and my stomach rumbled in hunger. It dawned on me that I hadn't eaten all day, which, as you know, is very unlike me.

On my way down the hall, I passed by my mother's bedroom. The door was ajar, so I gently knocked before pushing it open. She was seated in front of her computer, wearing the cashmere sweatpants that Bethany had bought her last Christmas. The matching hoodie was hanging off the back of her desk chair, and she was wildly fanning her tank top with a bunch of receipts.

"Hey, Mom," I said. "Are you okay?"

She clutched the papers to her chest and jumped, causing her reading glasses to fall off her nose and swing from a gold chain around her neck. "Oh, Jessie! You scared me! I'm not used to having anyone around when I'm working."

"Dad's around."

"You know what I mean," she said.

"Actually, I don't." Mom was sort of panting, and her face was flushed pink. "Are you okay?" I asked again.

"I'm just *hot*," she gasped, wiping her brow with the back of her wrist. "I've been having hot flashes for five years now. Enough, already!"

And before I could say, "Oh, menopause," I was assaulted by the horrible shriek of the smoke alarm.

BEEEEEEEEEP! BEEEEEEEEEP! BEEEEEEEEEP!

Mom grimaced and covered her ears, but didn't move from her spot in front of the computer.

BEEEEEEEEEP! BEEEEEEEEEP! BEEEEEEEEEP!

I raced downstairs to find my dad wildly waving two pot holders over the scorched leftovers on the cookie sheet. I slid open the back door to let in more air.

"Don't worry!" he shouted over the continuous din of the alarm. "It happens all the time!" This explains why my mother hadn't moved. "Damn sensitive smoke detectors!"

And just when I thought I couldn't take another second of noise, the beeping stopped. My dad, in the meantime, had chiseled around the blackened cheese and put two slices on my plate. They weren't inedibly burnt, just slightly overcooked. But at that point I was so hungry that I would've eaten the spatula.

Dad opened the refrigerator, reached in, and grabbed a brown bottle of light beer.

"Want one?" he asked.

"Dad! You spent the whole day in the hospital! You shouldn't be drinking beer."

"Athletes replenish fluids with beer all the time," he replied, gesturing with his bottle opener made out of spare bike parts. It was another gift from the same Christmas as the cashmere tracksuit, only this one was from me. My mom hated it on sight and had tried to "accidentally" throw it out on numerous occasions.

"Alcohol is a diuretic."

"Lighten up, Jessie." He took a deep, satisfying swig. "It's *light* beer, which is mostly water, anyway."

I was aware of how totally uptight I sounded. I wondered what my dad would think if he knew his daughter had recently gotten drunk on whiskey right in the middle of the afternoon. . . .

"Want one?" He held a bottle out for me, then quickly retracted it. "Or are you more of a wine person, like your mother?"

I knew that this was not a question of choosing beer over wine. It was about siding with one way of life over another. One parent over another. And if I had any chance of getting any valuable information out of my dad about what had transpired today, I simply could not align myself with the wine people. Tonight I pledged my allegiance to the beer people.

"Thanks," I said, popping off the bottle cap.

"Let's sit outside while it's still warm," he said, grabbing two more beers before leading the way to the patio.

We both settled into the cushions of two side-by-side deck chairs. It was dark, and the only lights came from the neighboring windows, a citronella bucket candle, and the moon. Earlier in the evening there had been a few small motorboats puttering past their dock, but now, at nearly ten P.M., the channel was calm and quiet. Too quiet, in fact. I was no longer used to the total absence of white noise here in the remote outreaches of suburbia, the blurry background buzz that muted all aural attention-getters. Without it, *every* sound called for attention. The teak furniture scraping across the cement. The empty beer bottle clanking the glass-topped table. The voice inside my head screaming, "SAY SOMETHING! ANYTHING!"

"It's so quiet," I said finally.

"We've got the perfect neighbors," my dad said. "They cleared out after Labor Day."

"For good?"

"For *our* good," he replied, propping his legs up on another chair.

"But only until Memorial Day. Most of these condos are summer homes that are empty the rest of the year. That's why it's so quiet around here."

(Empty. Shunyata. Boundless. Open. Quiet . . .)

"What?" my dad asked.

"What, what?" I replied.

"You've got a constipated look on your face."

"Well, that's appropriate because I'm dealing with a lot of heavy shit right now," I said.

My dad laughed, then asked, "Like what?"

"Well, we could start with what happened today," I said. "Did you really crash your bike on purpose?"

My dad rolled the beer bottle back and forth between his two huge hands. "I didn't set out to crash my bike when I left at four A.M.," he said. "But about five hours into my ride—"

"Four A.M.? Five hours?" I asked, shocked.

"Sure," he said. "I wake up before dawn with nowhere to go. I try to go back to sleep, but I just toss and turn and annoy your mother. I've gotten into the habit of just getting up and riding, no matter how early it is. . . ."

I kicked off my flip-flops. "I used to do the same thing when I couldn't sleep," I said. "I'd go running in those borderline hours between late-late night and early-early morning."

My dad nodded. "I remember," he said. "You sprained your ankle and ruined your running career on one of those runs. . . ."

"No," I replied, tracing circles in the air with my foot. "My ankle was fine. It was my head that was all messed up. I didn't like the pressure. In fact . . ." I trailed off, unsure as to whether my dad was even interested in having this kind of conversation.

"What?" he asked.

"Well, I fantasized about orchestrating an accident, sort of like the one you had today. Only I wanted you to crash into *me* with your bike."

"To get attention? I thought you wanted me to leave you alone."

"I did," I said, planting both feet back on the cement. "I figured that if I couldn't run anymore, you would just get off my case. And if you had caused the accident, I'd have an excuse to scream and yell at you, too."

"I didn't want your mother screaming at me," he said, "I just wanted her to see that I still needed her."

It was so unspeakably depressing that my dad had believed this—even in a temporary state of dehydrated psychosis—but more so because his desperate tactic had totally backfired.

"I'm not the one with the Ivy League degree in psychology," my dad said. "But it sounds to me like we're both nutcases."

"Apparently so."

And then he held out his beer bottle, and I clinked it with mine. After a few swallows, my dad said, "There's something else I should mention about today."

"Okay," I said, stretching my toes to retrieve my flip-flops and slip them back on my feet, feeling safe that there's nothing my dad could possibly say that could be stranger than that which had already been said.

"I saw Marcus's father," he said. "Mr. Flutie. You know, Sam."

A short but intense electrical current shot through me, like the sizzle and flash of a flying pest caught by my parents' bug zapper: *Zzzap!*

"When?" I asked, trying to sound casual for my own benefit more than my dad's.

"Today," he said. "In the hospital."

In the silence that followed, I could hear the *whoosh whoosh whoosh* of blood pulsating through my brain.

"Jessie?"

"Did you talk to him?" I asked.

"Of course I talked to him."

"Why was he there? Marcus told me his treatments were over. . . ."

I was more than a little convinced that you had lied to me about your dad's recovery, just so you wouldn't have to face my constant inquiries as to his current health status.

"He's done," my dad said. "He had stopped by just to say hi. Apparently everyone who finishes chemo promises to come back when they're healthy just to say hi, but no one ever does. Mr. Flutie actually did."

I imagined him promising all the nurses, "I'll shoot on over when I'm done with all this stuff. I'll shoot right over. . . ." It reminded me of something you would do.

"He looked a little thinner than I remember. He was wearing a Princeton baseball cap because his hair hasn't grown back, and he's afraid that it won't. I tried to make him feel better by saying that I've been living with my chrome dome for twenty years. . . ." My dad rubbed his head. "He was making the rounds, you know, introducing all the nurses to his son. . . ."

"His *son?*" *Zzzzzzzzap!* Another surge. "Marcus was there?"

"No," my dad replied. "The other one. The older one. Hugo. You know, I never even knew Marcus had an older brother. You never mentioned it."

"I've never met him," I replied. "He lives in a cabin in Maine with a forty-five-year-old divorcée."

"Oh, no wonder Sam kept referring to him as 'the prodigal son,' " my dad said.

(Your acceptance into the Ivies sealed your fate. Up to that point, let's face it, it was up for grabs.)

"So what was Hugo like?" I asked.

"I don't know," my dad said. "Because as soon as Sam saw me, no one else could get a word in edgewise."

"What did he say?" I asked.

"That's the interesting part," my dad said. He put down his beer bottle, leaned forward in his chair, and massaged his bare skull. "He said Marcus asked you to marry him."

Zzzzzzzzzzzzzzzzzzzzzzzzzzzzzzzzzzzzzzzzzzzzzzzzzzzzzzzzzzzzzzzzzzzap!

fifty-six

My dad tilted his head to the stars and whistled through his teeth. I looked up, too. The moon was a sliver shy of fullness, still on the safe side between sane and crazy.

"Why did *you* get married so young?" I asked.

"One word."

Love, I thought.

"Vietnam."

"*Vietnam?*" I hadn't expected such a pragmatic response, even from my dad.

"I graduated from college in seventy-two. Your mother and I had been dating for five years, since high school. At that point it seemed foolish to put off a wedding."

"Were you afraid of getting drafted?"

My dad rubbed his forehead. "No," he said firmly. "Nixon was withdrawing troops. The war was winding down."

"Okay . . ."

"I graduated from high school in sixty-eight. . . ."

"The Summer of Love?" I asked.

My dad squeezed his eyes tight and pinched the bridge of his nose with his thumb and forefinger. "Didn't you learn anything at that fancy college? Sixty-*seven* was the Summer of Love. Sixty-*eight* was one of the worst years in American history. More soldiers were killed and wounded in that year than any other. RFK and MLK were assassinated. Student protesters shut down your alma mater for a week. Does any of this sound familiar?"

"Yeah," I said. "Paul Parlipiano always talks about the enduring legacy of the Students for a Democratic Society."

"Paul who?"

"Paul *who?*" I asked, incredulous. "I had the hugest crush on him in my freshman and sophomore years of high school, then he went to Columbia and came out of the closet and became this big social activist on campus. . . ."

My dad signaled his boredom by blowing into his empty beer bottle, making a low *toot* like the call of a distant ship. It was time for *his* story, not mine, so I shut up without even telling him that it was indeed Paul Parlipiano, my high school crush-to-end-all-crushes, former obsessive object of horniness and gay man of my dreams, who had inspired my decision to apply to Columbia University in the first place.

"My friends who didn't go to college got drafted," Dad continued. "Guys I grew up with, guys I played ball with, guys I drank beer with." He raised another bottle and popped off the top. "They went off to the jungle and never came back. Or came back changed men." He took another gulp of beer. "I married your mother right after graduation because I loved her, and because I still *could*."

I was touched by this surprising romanticism, especially in light of his earlier protestations. Then he dropped the bombshell.

"And also because she was pregnant."

"What?" I asked, clearly having misheard my father.

"Your mother was three months along with Bethany."

"MOM WAS KNOCKED UP BEFORE YOU GOT MARRIED?!"

"Could you say that a bit louder?" he asked, shaking out his ear. "I'm not sure the neighbors on the other side of the lagoon heard you. . . ."

I quickly did the math. My parents were married in June, Bethany was born in December. *Duuuuh*.

"Why didn't I figure this out?" I lowered my voice to a conspiratorial whisper. "Does Bethany know?"

"Of course Bethany knows." My dad literally slapped his knee in laughter. "Bethany has known since she was seven or eight."

"She figured it out at seven?"

"Or eight," my dad corrected. "She was really into weddings, more than you ever were. Bethany was always throwing weddings for her dolls and stuffed animals. She couldn't talk enough about weddings. She bombarded your mother with questions. What kind of dress did she wear? What kind of flowers did she have? What kind of cake? One afternoon she asked your mother if she had been a June bride, and your mother, worn down by her questioning and not really thinking about the repercussions, told her the truth. Bethany knew her own birthday, of course, and kind of figured it out from there with a little help from your grandmother Gladdie, who, as you know, never showed much discretion."

I was still shaking my head in amazement. "I just can't believe I never put it together. . . ."

"All these years your mother and I have been waiting for you to do the math. But you never did. . . ."

He's right. The truth is, I'd never put it together because I'd never really cared. I have always been startlingly uncurious about my parents' courtship. I just didn't want to know. I wasn't beyond snooping and prying and eavesdropping, but my parents' secrets didn't seem worth unearthing. Bethany made an infinitely more fascinating subject during the post-Jerry Years, when invading her privacy was my raison d'être. I pored over her photo albums, read her journals, analyzed her yearbook inscriptions. But my parents? Ack.

My dad said nothing, just looked out onto the water. I knew that if I didn't say something fast, this conversation would end as spontaneously as it had begun. And I didn't want it to end.

"Where did you get married again?" I asked. The "again" was misleading, as it implied that I had asked this once before, but only temporarily forgotten. But I had never once asked about my parents' wedding day. I knew next to nothing about their nuptials. In fact, I'd only seen one photo from that day, a black-and-white candid of the bride and groom kissing. Only the faintest wisp of lace can be seen around my mother's neck, and a headband that I had always assumed anchored a veil, though no such accessory could actually be seen in the frame.

"Why so many questions tonight?" Dad asked. "What, one trip to the infusion room and you think I'm gonna die on you or something?"

"No," I said. (Maybe, I thought.)

"We got married in a civil service at city hall," he replied. "Only our parents were in attendance. My own mother thought we were too young to get married, you know. She thought we needed to go out and live life, date other people. She used to go on and on about how we should take advantage of the 'free love' philosophy of the era. . . ."

I can totally hear Gladdie saying this. Can't you? Hadn't she said the same to us about us?

"Of course, Gladdie changed her tune once we told her that there was a baby on the way. But I honestly never felt that we were too young. I felt like we'd lived enough life," he said. "Until recently. . . ."

He looked at the smeared reflection of the moon in the rippling bay water.

"You remind me of Gladdie," he said.

"Really?" I asked doubtfully. My grandmother could win over anyone with her oversized personality. But me? Hardly.

"You know my parents didn't get married until they were both thirty-five?"

"Thirty five?" I asked. "That's not right. . . ."

"Whaddaya mean that's not right?" my dad asked.

"Gladdie got married when she was seventeen. . . ."

"Seventeen?" my dad barked. "Where did you get that crazy idea?"

"She told me so!" I said. "At Bethany's wedding." I remembered this vividly. I had been flirting with the best man's younger brother, and Gladdie grabbed me by the arm to interrogate me about setting the date for our own nuptials. I patiently pointed out to her that we had just met, and besides, I was only sixteen. At which point she said in that unforgettable bellow, "I was only seventeen when I married your grandfather, God rest his soul. . . ."

"She had a lot of crazy notions after that first stroke," my dad said. "But I know for a fact that my parents got married when they were thirty-five, which was unheard of in 1945! My dad had been in the war, of course. An old guy. He left engaged to some other woman, and when he got back, she was engaged to a 4-F who worked alongside her in a defense plant." He took another swig of beer.

"How did he meet Gladdie?"

Dad leaned back in his chair and smiled. "They met at a bar in Manhattan. Both rarely visited the city. Your grandfather was there for a boxing match, and Gladdie was there to see a Broadway show. They wound up at the same bar."

"Did Grandpa spot her from across the crowded room and buy her a drink?" I got carried away with a vision of my grandfather as a tall, broad-shouldered soldier with slick, Brylcreemed hair, winking at the pin-curled tomato in a floral swing dress as she received a cocktail garnished with a cherry. . . .

"No," he said. "They met waiting on line for the john." He chuckled to himself. "Romantic, huh? My dad—you never knew my dad, obviously; he died when you were two—he used to say, 'When you start in the shitter, you can only go up from there.' "

We both laughed.

"Speaking of," my dad said, standing up, "I'm gonna head up to bed."

"Oh," I said, disappointed.

"Listen, I didn't mean to get on your case about Marcus," he said. "I just . . ." He took a deep breath. This was not easy for him.

"What?"

"I understand what it's like to be twenty-two and in love. I know what it's like to be afraid of losing that person to the world," he said. "But sometimes I think that Gladdie was right. That maybe your mother and I would get along better now if . . ."

"If *what?*"

"If we had broken up—even for a little while—back then." He looked upstairs to their bedroom window, which was now dark.

"Oh, and one more thing . . ."

One more? Just one more? I could think of a bizillion ellipses worth finishing.

"Don't let on to your sister that you finally caught on to the whole conceived-out-of-wedlock thing."

"Uh, okay."

"It's kind of a touchy subject for her, best left untouched."

"But she already knows. What's the big deal?"

"She's okay with *her* knowing the truth," Dad said, "as long as no one else does."

And without another word, he bent himself in half and kissed me good night on the top of my head.

And I stayed on the patio and wrote.

thursday: the seventh

fifty-seven

It was the coughing that woke me up at 6:42 A.M. A dry-throated hacking, followed by giggling.

Cranky and half-blind, I looked out the window that provides a clear view of my parents' patio. If I craned my neck, I got a partially obstructed view of the neighboring concrete on the other side of the PVC latticework. And there, on the opposite side of the fence, two sixteen-year-old girls engaged in a Thursday-morning wake-'n'-bake before school. You know the ones I'm talking about. The same girls who boldly, shamelessly flirted with you right in front of me last summer, licking their Popsicle-red lips with studded tongues.

For as rebellious as these girls were trying to be (getting high! before school!), they were going about their business in all the wrong way. They were sitting outside, in the early-morning twilight, shivering in the first autumnal chill. That alone would be enough to arouse suspicion. But to be sitting outside, in the early-morning twilight, in the first autumnal chill, hiding underneath a large woolen blanket . . . Clearly there was something going on underneath that large woolen blanket that they didn't want anyone to see. And this secret was illuminated every time they flicked the lighter, and again when they inhaled. Despite their efforts to avoid being caught—they lived up the block, and I can only assume they had chosen the patio of *this* unoccupied condo on purpose—they could not reign in their innate desire to be noticed. They loudly and ludicrously revealed their illicit intentions to anyone within earshot, which I was. I still don't know their names, only their pet names for each other.

"Pass the bowl, Slut!"

"Bitch, I've got the munchies."

I couldn't pull myself away.

I've watched them other times, too. I've watched them catwalking down the sidewalks of my parents' neighborhood, nearly identical in their ponytails, candy-colored camisoles, and premium denim hemmed a quarter-inch—upward, downward—from obsolescence. They stepped in unison, or rather, assumed a lazy, synchronized shuffle. Conjoined by a shared iPod and a secret song, these two BFFs each wore a tiny white plug inside a perfectly suntanned ear. I've watched Bitch yank Slut's earbud.

"Gimme a cigarette, Slut!"

And I watched Slut silently obey because that's the downside of being the *second* most popular girl in the sophomore class.

The last time I saw Bitch—ah, Bitch—she was wearing a pair of oversized, brown bear-claw slippers on her feet. The slippers were a masterstroke, a testimonial to Bitch's brilliance, and the reason no other sixteen-year-old would usurp her any time soon as the most popular girl in the sophomore class. No one at Pineville High wore bear-claw slippers in public! They enhanced Bitch's carefully cultivated crazy/beautiful reputation, an image fueled by the rumors that she spent last summer not at summer camp, but at rehab for . . . Drugs? Depression? An eating disorder? Does it matter? Rumors about Bitch's mysterious and perhaps imaginary stint in rehab have only helped set her apart from the other merely pretty girls at Pineville High. And when the inevitable happened, when other girls showed up in *their* furry animal slippers, Bitch would be rightfully recognized not only as the innovator, but as the only female in school who could get away with wearing just about anything without suffering any negative social repercussions.

In that way, Bitch reminds me of you. I wish I could fully embrace your utilitarian philosophy about clothes: You have to wear clothes. So you wear them. Like you, I don't want to be bothered by clothes, and more specifically, shopping for clothes. I also resent being judged by the quality, creativity, or cost of my clothes. It's all so superficial, right? And didn't we learn about focusing on our *insides* not our *outsides* in the "Can't Buy Love at the Mall" self-esteem workshop in middle school? But here's the major difference: You borrow one of my T-shirts and don't even notice or care when it exposes the hairy expanse of your midriff like a hoochie drag queen in the Gay Pride Parade. Yet the look still *works* on you. It contributes to your freaky mystique. I believe your whole not-caring-about-clothes thing is sincere, but it also has the added benefit of enhancing your image, not detracting from it.

A similar sartorial carelessness doesn't look so good on me because, in truth, I still care too much about how I look. The problem is, I don't care *enough* to do much about it, despite my mother's, my sister's, and my trendier friends' best efforts. Which is why I often end up wearing clothes that make me look pregnant. In a variation of that classic song by the Clash, I'm "Vain in Vain." This is why Bitch and Slut mostly ignore me whenever I'm here visiting my parents. Sometimes they cast withering glances over their shoulders in my general direction. Other times they heave sighs and lungfuls of tobacco smoke. I was written off as a hopeless loser the first time I was caught watering my parents' plants in my nondesigner cutoffs, nondescript T, and busted Chucks. My only redeeming quality was that I had somehow managed to seduce you.

Manda just argued that no human being could out-hubris a teenage boy, a strange assertion from the former most popular girl in the sophomore class. I swear Bitch and Slut have the boys beat. As the reigning most popular girls in their class, they can outfreeze anyone with an icy stare, or a crackly cackle of laughter. And even if they cannot ensnare their quarry (you, for example), they still *think* they can, which is close enough.

Whenever I gaze upon these girls—girls shimmering with the power of their sexuality, girls I would have hated when I was their age, girls I have to will myself not to hate right now—I am certain that even if I could fulfill that aphorism about going back knowing what I know now, I still wouldn't fit into the caste Hope and I coined the Upper Crust. To play off that UK economist's dire prognosticatians, I am, comparatively speaking, doomed to the Under Crust. I'd never be cool enough, pretty enough, or, most important, innovative enough in the art of adolescent sadism. At sixteen, I would have instinctively crossed the street if these superior specimens were headed in my direction. And though I'm ashamed to admit it, part of me still wants to avoid them now, even though one of the divine advantages of being twenty-two is that I don't have to surrender to the oppressive, ever-shifting politics of high school popularity.

I watched Bitch and Slut hastily put away their contraband, giggling as they galloped toward a honk coming from the front of the condo. I couldn't confirm this from my spot in the window, but I imagined that it was Bitch's boyfriend, a senior, perhaps, who had just rolled up in the driveway in his SUV. It was 6:58 A.M., and if Boyfriend lead-footed it, he would get them to homeroom in time for the last bell. As they sped away in a screech of peeling tires, I asked myself why I was so bound by relationships forged during the zitgeist, the time of teen angst I couldn't wait to escape, and to which I wouldn't return even if I could.

fifty-eight

Without getting too gross and Oedipal, joining my dad at breakfast was kind of like seeing last night's one-night stand in the harsh, morning-after light. His candor had made him emotionally vulnerable, and so I was fully expecting him to return to the defensive subterfuge that has pretty much defined our relationship thus far.

"Good morning," he said casually as he came down the stairs.

"There is no news in this newspaper," I said, leaning into my elbows as I scanned the front-page headlines of the *Ocean County Observer*. (RARE TURTLE "NUKED" AT POWER PLANT; OCEAN-MONMOUTH GIRL SCOUTS MERGE; LOCAL YOUTHS HEAD BACK TO SCHOOL IN STYLE.) "No wonder so many people are moving to Pineville. It's downright Utopian. . . ."

"If you want to get depressed over breakfast, then go back to *New York Times* territory," my dad sniped.

"I don't want to get depressed, I just want—" I had looked up to see that my dad was dressed in his cycling gear. "*Dad!*"

"What?"

"*What?!*"

"I'm fine," he said, waving his hand as if to shoo away a mosquito. "Gotta get back on the bike. Can't let one setback stop me."

"Okay," I said. "But don't you think you should take it easy today?"

"I *am* taking it easy," he replied. "It's almost nine A.M. Normally I've done twenty miles by now."

"It's just . . . ," I began.

He came over and poked his finger in the wrinkle that always worries itself between my eyes. (Again, at the risk of getting too Freudian, I remember you doing the same thing, warning me about the permanent mark I was creating through all my "face-making.")

"I'm touched by your concern," he said. "And it meant a lot to me that you came out here to see your old man in the hospital. But I'm fine. And I promised to meet the guys from the club. . . ."

"Okay," I said, wondering if I should so much as acknowledge how much last night meant to me. I didn't have to wonder for long.

"I enjoyed our conversation last night, though I'm afraid I'm not much of a storyteller." He thrusted his chin as he clicked the strap on his helmet. "That talent must have skipped a generation."

"You weren't too boring," I said, keeping it light. "I kept asking questions."

A smile softened his hard-boiled face. "Ah, Jessie," he said, taking my face in his wrist-guarded hands. "You've always had more questions than I've had answers."

And before I got a chance to get all sentimental, he handed me an unopened jar of Skippy peanut butter. I mention the brand only because buying nongeneric is a luxury to me.

"I give you permission to take this home with you," he said. "And you can have the whole-wheat pasta, and the Cap'n Crunch that I bought for you, anyway. And I think there's a small box of laundry detergent. . . ."

"Uh, okay. . . ."

"This way you aren't *stealing* from us."

I was so mortified that I couldn't even muster a denial. I did indeed ransack their pantry the last time I visited. But I only took items that they had in excess, that I thought they wouldn't miss.

"It's okay," my dad said, handing me a few rolls of toilet paper. (Charmin! My ass will be so happy!) "Just ask next time. Don't ever feel like you can't ask us for help."

He was almost at the door when I had a flash of insight, of inspiration.

"Hey, Dad!"

"Yeah?"

"Darling's Designs for Leaving needs a website," I said, slightly overzealous. "You should totally design it for Mom."

"You think?" he asked, stroking his helmet in consideration.

"She'd appreciate your help."

"That's not a bad idea," he said. "Thanks, Notso Darling."

And with those parting words and a smile, he was off on another two-wheeled adventure.

Not a minute later, my mom came downstairs, fully coiffed, made up, and dressed in an embroidered linen tunic over caramel-colored pants. I must admit, she looked pretty great. Polyurethaned, but pretty great.

"Dad just left," I said. "*On his bike.*" I waited for her to express concern, verbally if not facially.

"Typical," she muttered. "So what time are you going back today?"

"I'm not sure," I said. "I think the buses leave every hour. . . ."

"Are you ready to go right now?" she asked. "I can take you right now. Otherwise, unless your father breaks tradition and comes home early, you'll have to wait until this afternoon."

My mom was tapping her keys against the countertop. She had somewhere more important to be. I felt like an unwelcome distraction.

"Give me five minutes to get dressed and brush my teeth," I said, already headed to the bathroom.

"Okay," she said, grabbing her bag as she headed to the garage.

It didn't occur to me until my mouth was rabid with toothpaste that I hadn't even thought to mention her shotgun wedding. More significant, my mom hadn't grilled me in such a manner that would have revealed the content of last night's conversation. Nor was there an intense investigation to uncover your proposal, Bethany's request for legal guardianship, my bombed job interview, the awkwardness with Hope, Bridget and Percy's wedding deferment, Manda and Shea's breakup, Scotty and Sara's baby, even the crack-of-dawn pot-smoking girls next door. Back in the day, she would have interrogated me on these topics without even extending me the courtesy of a "Good morning!" But my mother had shown not one iota of interest in my life, nor in the lives of those who overlap it. For years, I had made fun of my mother for living for such gossip, living through me. But her indifference made clear to me this morning what must have dawned on Dad months ago: She was living just fine without me.

Though my father had done the talking last night, I had learned so much more about my mother. She had missed out on the sixties sexual revolution because she was faithful to my father. She missed out on all the bra-burning fun in the 1970s because she got pregnant and married . . . *in that order*. She missed the working-girl eighties because her baby boy—of whom she has *never* spoken—succumbed to SIDS. Then she had me and devoted herself to the helicopter-parenting style of the nineties. Only now, in the 2000s, as a hot-flashing fiftysomething, is she living an uncompromised life. I'd be unabashedly supportive of her late-midlife liberation if it weren't for its most unfortunate consequence:

My father, left behind. On his bike. Blindsided, bewildered, bereft.

She honked impatiently in the driveway. I sprinted down the stairs, grabbing my overnight bag with one hand and the shopping bag filled with supplies in the other. I made it to the SUV's door just before she took off without me.

"Jeez, Mom," I said, still buckling my seat belt as she backed out.

"There's a lot of traffic at this hour," she said. "You wouldn't believe how congested Route 9 can get."

Usually I couldn't think of anything to say to my mother. Today I had too much to say, but no right place to begin.

"Well, I'm in no rush," I replied. "I don't have anywhere to be until tonight." I waited for her to ask me what I was doing tonight, but she was too busy honking her horn at the Prius that was going five miles below the speed limit. "I'm going to this, uh, karaoke party benefit thing with my friend Dexy from Columbia."

"Oh, to be twenty-two years old and so unfettered," she breathily singsonged. "All that freedom. . . ."

Normally I would have spat back a snotty response about how I'm plenty fettered, but in light of my last night's revelation about how completely fettered she was at my age, I held my tongue. "But when you have freedom you want security," I said. "It's the dichotomy of desire."

"The what?" My mom's face would have wrinkled if it were capable. "Jessie, you think too much."

How many times have I heard that this week?

"You know, Mom, there are some people who look forward to their retirement years so they can be so unfettered," I argued. "Being twenty-two isn't all that great. You're romanticizing my age because . . ." *Because when you were twenty-two, you were already a wife and mother.* I stopped myself.

"You can say it."

"Say what?" I asked innocently.

"I know your father told you that I was pregnant with Bethany when we got married."

If I had been driving, the car would have screeched to a dramatic halt. But my mother was behind the wheel, so we continued to gas-break our way down Route 9.

"Dad *told* you? When? After he went to bed?"

"Contrary to what you believe, Jessie, your father and I do talk to each other." The SUV stopped at a red light and she turned to look at me. "I think you need to explain why you never mentioned Marcus's proposal."

I shrunk in my seat. "Dad told you that, too?"

"Obviously."

"I didn't tell you," I said, "because I wasn't sure what to do about it."

I still don't.

"How do you feel about Marcus?" my mom asked.

"I love him," I replied. "How do *you* feel about Marcus?"

My mom tapped the steering wheel with her palm. "I think he is shaping up to be a fine man."

"And?"

"It really seems like he's getting his act together. It says a lot about a man's character to overcome addictions. And it showed real initiative for him to apply to Princeton."

I pressed my hands to my mouth in amazement. "Oh my God."

"What?"

"Dad said the exact same thing."

"Really?"

"Like the *exact same words*."

"Hmm," she said, nonplussed. "I also think that if I try to tell you what to do, you'll do the opposite. And if I try reverse psychology, you'll outsmart me. Do you, by chance, remember that punk kid Bethany dated in high school?"

I couldn't believe it. The conversation was following the same pattern as the one I'd had with my dad two weeks ago. My parents certainly had their differences, but after thirty-four years together, they worked as opposite sides of the same brain.

"When does Marcus get back from his Orientation program?"

"The day after tomorrow."

My mom considered this but said nothing more on the subject.

"Do you ever think about leaving Dad?" I blurted.

My mom was unruffled by this outburst. "You can't be together as long as we have and *not* think about it, Jessie."

"But are you *more* than thinking about it?" I asked. "Because—"

"Because Bethany has seen the Signs?" She said the last two words derisively.

"She *told* you about that?"

"Of course she did," my mother said. "She tells me everything. She even told me that she asked you to be Marin's legal guardian."

And here I was, all this time thinking that the Blonde Bond had been broken.

"Have you given *her* an answer at least?" she asked.

"Not yet." I shook my head. "I don't want to make commitments I can't keep."

Mom pursed her lips and hummed, as if her unspoken words were darting around the inside of her mouth.

"What?" I asked.

"That's the problem with your generation. No commitment. Taking responsibility for Marin would mean the end of your carefree lifestyle."

I took offense. "My life is not carefree. . . ."

"Yes it is. *Carefree*. Free of care. Young people today want to keep their options open just in case a better opportunity comes along."

"That's not true. . . ."

"You've got a temporary job, a temporary apartment," my mom said. "How can you care about *anything* when you treat *everything* like it's only temporary?"

I opened my mouth to protest the obvious: Everything *is* only temporary. She lectured on.

"None of you seem to be in any hurry to grow up. . . ."

My mom's comment shed light on one of the most peculiar paradoxes of living here. New York City is the mythical realm of possibilities, where young people venture to *do big things* and *make their mark on the world*. And yet, in many ways, this city infantilizes the very people who are looking to do such big and important and mark-on-the-world things. Why grow up when you can outsource just about any "adult" responsibility you can think of? Why drive when you can take the subway? Why cook when you can get cheap takeout? Why learn how to fix the clogged toilet when it's the landlord's job? Why grocery shop when there's Fresh Direct? Why trust your own intuition when you find love while waiting in line for the restroom when you can pay iLoveULab to scan your brain and analyze your instincts for you . . . ?

"And I don't want you to think I'm picking on you," Mom said. "From what I hear, it sounds like your friends are even worse."

I leaned back into the seat and closed my eyes to the maligning of an entire generation.

"Your roommate can't decide if she's gay or straight. And just look at Sara. She lives with Scotty, the father of her child, but has no plans to marry. . . ."

"Actually, she does have p—" I began, before stopping myself. I refused to use Sara's psychotic wedding stratagem as proof that our generation could stay focused on a goal, could, for example, go ahead and organize a lavish wedding without letting anything stand in our way, not even, say, the lack of a willing, would-be groom, because that's what it means to *make a decision and stick to it, goddammit!*

"And what about Bridget and Percy?" she asked. "They've been engaged for a year. What are they waiting for?"

"Actually," I began again, "Bridget and Percy are waiting until marriage is legal for gays. . . ."

My mom snorted. "Oh, they're just spinning their wheels with that kind of talk. . . ."

I refused to admit that I had been thinking along those same lines.

"I get it, Mom," I groaned. "You were married at twenty-two, so you think everyone should be married by twenty-two."

"You think I was ready to be a wife and mother at twenty-two? I hadn't gone to college, hadn't traveled anywhere outside New Jersey, hadn't dated anyone, hadn't slept with anyone besides your father!"

I did everything I could to resist shouting, "TMI! TMI!" I had no idea that the confessional conversation would go even deeper within my discomfort zone.

"I didn't have the same choices that you have now. I chose from what was available to me, and dedicated myself to it for the next thirty-four years."

I was rattled by the word *choice* in this context. All these years, I have harbored dark, middle-of-the-night fears that *I* was the unwanted surprise child. But my mother was unmarried and pregnant in 1972, just a few months short of *Roe v. Wade*. If she'd been able, would she have made the capital-C Choice *not* to have Bethany? Would she have married my dad at all?

"You say that you didn't have as many choices back when you were my age," I said. "Maybe that was a positive thing. I feel completely paralyzed by all the possibilities."

I'm not crazy for feeling this way, you know. I've read several studies for *Think* suggesting that more choices make people less happy. Why? Because there will always be more opportunities passed up than taken up. Ergo, as our options expand, so do our desires—and unmet desires in particular. And didn't we establish in Buddhism 101 that desiring begets suffering?

And yet, even with science *and* religion on my side, I was fully aware of how self-centered I sounded. But I was not sufficiently ashamed to shut up.

"Should I say yes to Marcus and move to Princeton? Should I say yes and stay in New York and do the long-distance thing until he graduates? Should I say no but move to Princeton to be with him, anyway? Or say no, stay in New York, and try the long-distance thing again? Say no, stay in New York, and *not* try the long-distance thing again? Or should I just leave New York altogether and get a job as a waitress in, I don't know, London?"

"London?" my mom asked. "Why London?" I noticed then that her hairline was damp around the temples, and that her complexion was pinker than it had been before.

"Why *not* London? Why not Lisbon? Or Lincoln, Nebraska? That's my point! By choosing one option, I'm closing myself off to all the others that might be even better. I'm afraid of making the wrong decision. I'm afraid that the mistakes I make now in my twenties will lead to decades of regret."

I paused before asking, "How did you know you made the right decision at the time?"

Note the switch from "choice" to "decision."

"I didn't!"

She punctuated her point by punching the air-conditioner button.

I wanted her to elaborate here and say something inspiring, something about taking a huge leap of faith and never looking back, about how growing up means caring about and committing to something greater than oneself, and about how much she values our family, which is why, despite Bethany's Signs, she has no intention of ever leaving it. I wanted her to rescind her declaration of neutrality and provide some hard-earned maternal wisdom regarding the specific decisions I have to make. That would have been a nice and comforting conclusion to this unsettling journey home.

But it didn't work out that way.

"I'm overheating here," she panted, craning her neck toward the rush of cold air coming out the vents. "I have to stop at this WaWa and get a bottle of water. Get yourself a cup of coffee. It's the best in town. . . ."

My mouth dropped open. "What?! You don't buy your coffee at the Wally D's/Papa D's right up the road?!"

My mom gasped and clasped both hands to her mouth: busted.

"To tell you the truth," I said, "I always thought the coffee at Wally D's/Papa D's tasted like ass."

I had said this in the hope of providing some much-needed levity. It worked. She laughed.

"I wouldn't have put it in the same way," she whispered, "but I agree."

As she rolled into the WaWa parking lot, I said, "I won't tell Bethany if you won't."

She extended her hand, and we shook on it. "It'll be our little secret," she said conspiratorially. "And while we're on the subject of secrets, it would be best if you didn't tell Bethany that you know she was conceived out of wedlock. . . ."

"It's a touchy subject for her," I said, repeating my dad's words. "Best left untouched."

"Exactly!" my mother said brightly.

And as we stepped around bent cigarette butts, shriveled straw wrappers, and cast-away scratch 'n' lose games in the parking lot, I felt strangely unburdened, if still indecisive. Unless my mother suddenly confirmed the suspicions I've held for years—that I was not their biological daughter, but a squirming bundle abandoned on their doorstep—I figured my last minutes in Pineville would be boring and eventless.

I'm sure that by the time you read this, you already know that this is not how it turned out.

I was in the junk-food aisle, ready to make a joke to my mom about how I was totally ready to commit to Snickers over Baby Ruth, when I got the unnerving vibe that I was being gawked at from behind. I pretended to scratch my shoulder with my chin (à la Samantha Baker in the study hall scene in *Sixteen Candles*—you know, the movie I forced you to watch if you wanted to have any chance of ever understanding me), and sure enough, I caught a half-glance of a tall, dark-haired guy looking sleepy and undernourished in jeans and a gray thermal.

"Are you Jessica Darling?" he asked.

I slowly turned around and got a better look. I was in Pineville, after all, so it could have been someone who knew me from the Class of 2002. Judging by the wrinkles around his eyes and deep creases framing his smiling mouth, he looked to be a few years older. He had a broad, contagious smile, with straight teeth turned dingy with nicotine. In fact, one hand held a pack of Marlboro Reds, the other pointed in my direction, and both were dirty, though not necessarily unwashed. The grime appeared to be permanently embossed in every pore, and I pegged him as someone who worked on greasy engines for a living. And if I'm being perfectly honest, I thought he was hot in a sketchy auto-mechanic kind of way.

"Yeah?" I was still wary.

"I knew it!" he said, snapping his fingers. "I recognize you from the pictures."

"Uh, okay . . . ," I said, trying to make eye contact with my mom, who was too busy considering her bottled water options. I had no idea who he was, and yet there was something oddly familiar about him.

He lunged forward, wrapped his arms around me, and enveloped me with the lived-in scent of gasoline, toothpaste, and chain-smoked cigarettes. I was about to yell for help when he introduced himself.

"I'm Hugo," he said. "Hugo Flutie."

fifty-nine

"Jessie!" said my mom coquettishly. "Who is your friend?"

Usually I'd be embarrassed by this sight of my menopausal mother flirting with someone half her age. But I was actually heartened to see signs of the gossipy person who raised me, the one who was more busybody than busy-busy.

"You must be Jessica's sister, Bethany." Hugo said this with a wink in his voice, to let us know he was being intentionally cheesy. And yet the gesture still managed to charm the hell out of my mom.

"Mother," she replied, looking up at Hugo through her eyelashes. "Helen."

"Ah, a beauty like Helen of Troy . . ."

While my mom got all girlish and giddy over his attentions, Hugo rolled his eyes in my direction. He was still on my side, you see.

"Mom, this is Marcus's older brother," I explained. "Hugo Flutie."

My mom jolted to attention. "An older brother? I didn't even know Marcus had an older brother. Why didn't you ever mention this before?"

"We've never met," Hugo and I replied at the same time.

"Until right here," I added.

"Right now," Hugo added.

"Well," my mom said, brushing make-believe dust off her sleeves. "How's your dad?" To me. "Your husband?" To mom.

"Hugo and Mr. Flutie saw Dad in the infusion room yesterday," I clarified.

Mom blanched dramatically, like a veteran stage actress overacting for the nosebleed seats. "How is *your* father?" She clutched Hugo's sinewy forearm, a gesture that showed more concern than that which she had (not) expressed for her own husband.

"Oh, he's great for someone who had prostate cancer," Hugo explained, the corners of his smile drooping just a bit. "He's in remission for now."

"That's a relief!" my mom gushed.

"He was at the hospital to visit the nurses . . . ," I started.

"Everyone promises to visit the nurses when they finish chemo, but none ever do . . . ," Hugo middled.

"Mr. Flutie did," I ended.

We caught each other's eyes, mutually struck by the effortlessness of our conversation. Within minutes of our introduction, your brother and I were finishing each other's sentences. Then the skin pinched between my eyebrows with the reminder of how it used to be between you and me.

"Oh," my mom said. "That's nice."

And there was an awkward moment of nonconversation that was filled by the noise of the morning rush for coffee and trans fats. Hugo fiddled with a small silver medal around his neck, making a faint *zipzipzipping* noise with each pull on the chain.

"Jessie," Mom said, darting a glance at her cell phone, "I'm running late and the bus station is in the opposite direction of where I need to be. . . ."

"Bus station?" Hugo asked.

"I'm heading back to the city."

"I'll take you," he offered quickly.

"You will?" I asked.

"Sure," he replied.

My mom attempted to raise an eyebrow. "Jessie?"

"Uh, if it's okay with you," I said to her.

"I *am* running late. . . ."

"So I'll take you!" Hugo said, clapping his hands together. "I like to be useful. And I've wanted to meet you forever. . . ."

FOREVER.

I just remembered the final postcard. Did it arrive in Brooklyn during my absence? Is it on the kitchen table right now? Have Hope and Manda marveled over your romanticism as they turned it over in their hands, wishing that someone cared enough to do the same for them?

"Pardon us for a moment." She pulled me toward the roller grill, where three glistening and unnaturally red hot dogs spun around and around in their own grease. "Do you want to go with him? Because he's practically a stranger. And how do you know for sure that he's *really* Marcus's brother?"

"What, you think he's a rapist who lurks around WaWas all day claiming to be Marcus Flutie's brother in the hopes of luring unsuspecting women to his pickup truck?"

We both attempted a surreptitious glance at your brother, who caught us in the act. He smiled and waved. We smiled and waved back.

"Of *course* he's Marcus's brother."

Beyond the obvious reasoning was the undeniable resemblance between you two, which wasn't so much physical as it was chemical. Charisma runs in the Flutie bloodline, and it's a power that transcends mere appearances. I mean, it's pretty uncommon for my mother to be so instantly besotted by the likes of a nicotine-stained grease monkey like Hugo.

"I've always wanted to meet him," I said.

"As you should," she said, taking my coffee out of her bag and handing it over.

"Thanks."

She stood in front of me for a moment, inspecting my naked face in the unflattering fluorescent light. I assumed she was calculating the depth of my nasolabial folds, or counting the clogged pores on my nose.

"What?" I asked.

"Enjoy your youth," she said simply.

"I'll try."

"Don't try," she said. "Do." If she'd had a silk scarf, she would have tossed it smashingly around her neck. She didn't, but her overall affect was the same.

I promised her that I would. Then the electronic doors whooshed open, and she sailed through them.

Hugo drifted over to me.

"So there's only one problem," he said as if in mid-conversation. He held up a map of the tri-state area. "I have no idea how to get to New York City from here."

"You don't have to drive me all the way to the city! Just to the bus station!"

"Are you sure?" he asked as we walked toward the entrance.

"I'm sure."

"Good," he replied, putting the map back in the rack. "Because the drivers around here are crazy." He said this just in time for me to witness my mother cutting off a Mini Cooper with her ginormous four-wheeled affront to all that is environmentally conscious.

"You still live in Maine?" I asked quickly, to distract attention from my mother. "With . . ."

"Charlotte," he supplied. "Yes, and our three kids."

"Three?"

"Two of hers, one of our own."

"I had no idea that you'd had a child together! Congratulations!" I shook my head in disbelief. "Marcus never told me much about you."

"Well, Marcus told me that you called us a 'salt-of-the-earth Ashton and Demi.' " He guffawed. "That's a pretty good one."

"He told you that?"

You told him that?!

"Among other things."

Among other things?

Hugo led me to a banged-up blue pickup truck with Maine license plates referring to the state as "a national treasure." I tried not to react when I spotted the Jesus fish affixed to the back bumper.

"Um . . . what other things?"

"Like how he asked you to marry him."

"Oh . . . ," I said, assuming an ironically casual air. "*That.*"

"Based on your dad's response to *that*," he said, wrenching open the door to the passenger side, "I assumed that *that* was not something I should talk about. Which is why I didn't mention *that* in front of the fair Helen."

I climbed in. "She knows about *that* now."

"And?"

"And she thinks my indecisiveness reflects our generation's refusal to grow up and take anything seriously."

"And what do you think?"

"I think my indecisiveness reflects my own tendency to take things *very* seriously."

"Hmm."

And then nothing. Hugo twisted the key in the ignition, pulled the gearshift into reverse, then pushed it into drive. He pulled us out of the parking lot, the sound of gravel grinding under the four wheels. We didn't speak.

"This is weird," I said uneasily.

"It is a little weird, yes," Hugo agreed.

"I don't know why Marcus never bothered to introduce us before."

"Marcus is . . ." Hugo shifted his lower jaw back and forth, as if he'd just gotten socked in the chin. "Predictable in his unpredictability."

"So true," I replied.

"It's what our mom says, anyway. My dad subscribes to the theory that Marcus just likes to be a pain in the ass."

Another pause. In front of us was a tan minivan with one of those cause-supporting magnetic ribbons on the back. Only this multicolored ribbon didn't support any cause per se, but merely claimed the driver's love for a particular breed of dog: I ❤ MY JACK RUSSELL TERRIER. Seeing that magnet reminded me of the time I had an existential crisis at the sight of a Betty Boop decorative license plate cover. I can understand why your brother would put a Jesus fish on the back of his car—there's two-thousand-plus years of Christianity behind his beliefs. But Betty Boop? Jack Russell Terriers? Are they better causes to believe in than nothing at all . . . ?

Zzzzzip. Zzzzip. Zzzzip. Hugo fiddled with the chain around his neck, needing something to do with his hands while we were stopped at a red light. *Zzzzzip. Zzzzip. Zzzzip.*

I reached into my front pocket, pulled out the ring, and put it on my significant finger. "Marcus made my ring." I held it up for him to see. He reached over, held my fingers in his, then let go. "Did he make your charm?"

"This?" he asked, lifting it up again. "Oh, no. This is a St. Jude medal."

"Um," I stammered, "who's St. Jude?"

"One of the apostles," he explained.

I tried to summon any Biblical information from my CCD days. "The one who betrayed Jesus?"

"No," Hugo said.

"I'm not very religious," I confessed, suddenly feeling really self-conscious about my atheism.

"I understand," he said. "If you had asked me about St. Jude five years ago, I would have said something about the Beatles song. A lot of people confuse Jude and Judas. In fact, so many early Christians mixed them up that hardly anyone ever prayed to the good guy for help. He was guilty by association, just because of his name."

"Sounds like Jude got a bum rap," I said.

"Yeah, he did," Hugo said. "That's why I like him. He's considered the patron saint of lost causes. The Flutie family is full of lost causes. I was a lost cause until I was found. Until I met Charlotte. Until I was saved."

I squirmed in the seat, worried that Hugo would start preaching to me, trying to save my soul. But he didn't.

"My faith gave me strength, you know, when my dad . . ." His voice wobbled.

I looked at Hugo's profile and could see the muscles tensing in his jaw as he clenched back the tears. I thought about how your dad's diagnosis inspired you to spend that many more silent hours on the floor of your closet.

"Marcus didn't want me there," I said in a rush.

"Where?"

"There, *here*, in Pineville," I said. "When your dad was getting treatment."

Hugo nodded somberly.

"I just didn't want you thinking that I didn't care about your dad," I said. "I offered to come, you know, for support, but Marcus insisted that I stay in the city."

"He does that," Hugo said.

"What?"

"Pushes people away when he needs them the most," he said. "It's why we barely spoke to each other for about five years."

"When was that?"

"When he was younger. When he was using." He searched for my eyes, then smiled warmly. "Before you."

I must confess: I flushed under the attention of his gaze. Riding beside your brother in his truck reminded me so much of those first out-of-control moments between you and me, when sitting inches away from you in the Caddie on the way to Helga's Diner made me dizzy with the push-pull-push-pull between blood-thumping attraction and heart-stopping terror.

I averted his familiar eyes by turning around to note the Princeton University sticker stuck to the rear window.

"Your parents must be beyond proud about Princeton."

"Beyond," Hugo said simply. "Talk about your lost causes. This was a kid who was left back in kindergarten!" He laughed bitterly at the memory. "Marcus was diagnosed with every letter in the alphabet. ADD. ADHD. OCD. And my favorite, ODD . . ."

"ODD?"

"Oppositional Defiance Disorder," Hugo explained. "It basically means that Marcus wouldn't take shit from authority figures. That's the only label he agreed with. He'd just shrug and say, 'That's right. I'm odd.' "

I can totally hear you saying that.

"I was never into books," Hugo continued, "I was always better with my hands." He held up a dirty palm to prove his point. "But Marcus was always a thinker. He needed to know how everything worked and would drive us all crazy with questions."

"Like what?" I asked.

"Like about *anything*," he said. The truck came to a red light, and he pointed to a gas station. "Why can't cars run on water?" He pointed to a flock of birds flying overhead. "How do birds know what way is south?" He pointed to a man rolling through the crosswalk in his wheelchair. "How did he lose his legs?" The light turned green. "Just on and on and onnnnnnnnnn." He groaned with the memory. "I was constantly telling him to shut up. But my parents, especially my mom, deserve a lot of credit for answering his questions as patiently as they could."

I thought about how tiresome Marin's questions could be for two hours at a stretch. I could hardly imagine fielding them all day long.

"My parents saw potential, but the schools saw trouble. Marcus would interrupt the teachers to ask his questions, and they'd get on his ass for disobedience and all this bullshit when really he was just a kid who wasn't getting satisfying answers to his questions. He'd go to the library and look things up on the Internet, then get books to back up what he had read. He never relied on just one source. Does a dumb kid do that? I don't think so."

I didn't share a classroom with you until our junior year, but I can imagine what you must have been like in elementary school. I also asked my teachers a million questions, and when I got unsatisfactory answers, I took it upon myself to grill inanimate objects, clutching a pencil as a microphone to interview the American flag ("Are red, white, and blue your favorite colors?") or a block tower ("Are you worried about being knocked down?") or whatever. But for some reason—perhaps my passive, nonthreatening gender—my curiosity wasn't interpreted as a sign of insubordination.

"For this troublemaker to get into Princeton is a pretty big deal for my parents," he said. "The ultimate 'I told you so.' "

He's right. Has there ever been anyone more unlikely to attend Princeton than you?

I'm embarrassed to say this, but until that moment with your brother, I selfishly viewed your decision to attend Princeton as a twenty-three-year-old freshman as nothing more than an inconvenience to me and our relationship. Why Princeton when you could have just as easily chosen Columbia or NYU or any other school in New York City? So what if you hated the city? Couldn't your love for me transcend that discomfort? It's no wonder that you didn't tell me that you had applied but only that you had gotten in.

Of course, I can't blame you for wanting to attend one of the best universities in the world. I'm proud of you. (Have I ever told you that? I don't think I have. I'm sorry. I should have said that before.) Hugo helped me realize how much this success means to your parents, and your mother in particular. You, fuckup of the first order from as far back as kindergarten. You, who spent more days stuck in the solitary confinement known as In-School Suspension than in actual school. You, who want to make up for all your family's pain and suffering in the past, and want to make good on the promise you've had all along.

Getting the most out of Princeton will require your total focus. Good or bad, irrational or irresistible, can I be anything more than a distraction? (This is a convenient excuse for my indecision, isn't it? Because it's not about me at all. I've made it all about you. How selfless . . .)

We both shifted gears. Him literally. Me figuratively. There were a few laminated pictures stuck inside the sun visor. I pointed to them and asked if he minded.

"Go ahead," he said. "You'll like them."

We lurched forward a few feet in the bumper-to-bumper traffic.

The first photo was of a bald infant wearing one of those painful and ugly headbands. He glanced in my direction. "That's Emily Rose," he said. "My beautiful baby girl . . ."

"She is," I replied, because there is no other acceptable response. I was not at all compelled to coo over her cuteness. I'm pretty sure that I was born without a biological clock, because babies just don't make me tick. It was only after I realized that this was not just a picture of Hugo's daughter but of *your* niece that I felt even the tiniest twinge of affection toward this creature. You have a niece, just like I have a niece. I considered the many hours I've spent with Marin ignoring The Fun Chart™, watching *Grease 3*, and I wondered what kind of relationship you would build with Emily Rose. You *have* built.

The second photo was taken at one of those mall "glamour" studios.

"That's Charlotte," Hugo said proudly though unnecessarily.

Her white-blond cumulonimbus perm was ornamented with a rhinestone comb. A red feather boa wrapped around her neck. Her round face had no discernible angles despite the best efforts of the cosmetics "artist" to create them through the liberal application of blush. Even in my inexpert estimation, her makeup job appeared to be flawed in every way. Rainbowed layers of eye shadow made her eyes appear crowded together, red liner and gloss only accentuated the very thinness of her lips. But thank God those lips were straining to smile, because if it hadn't been for that tired, barely tolerant twist to her lips, I would have felt pity for Charlotte. However, her expression was an encouraging clue, one that hinted that she was well aware of how ridiculous she looked with these misguided approximations of glamour. Hugo confirmed these suspicions.

"Her boys bought her this photo shoot for her birthday a few years back," he explained. "She hated every second of it."

"That would explain her pained expression," I said.

Hugo laughed. His laugh sounds a lot like yours, deep and low in the belly.

"I love that picture, even though it looks nothing like her," he said. "I love that she got all dressed up like that just to please her boys. She's much prettier without all that makeup. Forty-five now, but she looks thirty-five. Of course, she says it doesn't matter how young she looks, because I'm twenty-five and look fifteen."

It's not true, of course. Your brother doesn't look like a teenager at all. But I obliged with a chuckle.

I came to the third photo. It had suffered a bit of abuse before it was preserved by lamination. The color was bleached out, the corner was torn, but the image was clear.

"You and Marcus."

"Yup," he said.

Perhaps you know this photo. You're about one, which would make Hugo three. It was taken by a cheap department-store photographer with a blue-sky backdrop. You're wearing a pair of seersucker overalls. Your hair is half wet, half dry, as if your mom had tried to calm your curls by weighing them down with water. But two fluffy patches spazz out around your ears, like a clown's wig. Your mouth is wide in a crimson-cheeked howl, and you're reaching out to the camera, desperately trying to scramble off your brother's lap. The photo gave me a skin-tingling sense of déjà vu.

"It's so weird," I said. "This reminds me of another picture. One of my best friend and her older brother. He's struggling to hold her up, just like you're struggling with Marcus. And she's screaming her head off, too."

"Hope and Heath," Hugo said.

"Oh, right," I said dumbly. "You know them. I forgot."

"I didn't know him too well," he said.

"And her?" I was curious to hear what he remembered.

"Well, Hope and Marcus were best friends as little kids."

I tried to breathe normally, but gulped down more oxygen than any normally breathing person should.

"Something wrong?" Hugo asked.

I shook my head. "Go on," I gurgled.

"I didn't pay much attention to them, but they were cute together, you know."

"Actually, I don't know."

"They were like little playmates in the sandbox," he said. He shook his head with amusement. "But you know, Marcus has always been a lover. . . ."

I tried to sound casual. "Really?"

"I can remember him running home from school one day—he must have been about ten years old. He was all excited because he had kissed Hope behind the backstop on the playground. It was his first kiss and he was shouting so loud that the whole neighborhood could hear. 'On the lips! On the lips!' Like it was the most amazing thing in the world. Like he had *invented* kissing on the lips."

("Sometimes it did feel as if we have invented it and all intimacies. Our bodies surging and retreating in innumerable positions and countless combinations for us and us alone . . .")

Hugo was still chuckling. I was choking on too much air.

"Are you okay?" he asked. "You're not *jealous?*"

The truck hit a smooth stretch of recently paved road, and the rumble of the tires shushed themselves.

"Of course not!" I insisted in a voice that was too loud for the sudden drop in noise.

We pulled up to the small station house, and Hugo shifted into park. My bus idled at the curb, scheduled to pull away in five minutes. He turned his whole body to look at me, and I caught another whiff of winter-fresh smoke.

"Well." I chewed on my bottom lip for a second, then gestured toward the bus. "The Port Authority Express waits for no one, so . . ."

It was the sorriest of made-up excuses. I didn't have to take that particular bus back to New York. I could have taken the next one, or the one after that. Or I could have accepted Hugo's offer to drive me all the way back home. I could have tried, over the course of the two-and-a-half-hour ride home, with his help, to unravel the messy tangles of our relationship.

But I didn't. I thanked your brother for the ride, told him I was glad to have finally met him, and wished him a safe drive back to Maine. He responded in kind, thanking me for the company and conversation, assuring me that the pleasure was all his.

My hand rested on the door handle.

"I love your brother," I said.

"I know you do," he said.

I tugged the handle, he tugged my sleeve.

"I also know that he's not an easy person to love."

I was off-balance, one foot on the ground, the other still inside the truck. "I've got the opposite problem."

"What's that?"

I planted my other foot on the pavement.

"I love him too easily."

I always have. And probably still will, and still do wherever you're reading this right now.

sixty

I'm back at the empty apartment. I headed straight for the Cupcake, belly-flopped onto the bottom bunk, then glanced up out of habit. I was eager to see a new *Tiger Beat* centerfold signifying that everything was going to be just fine with me and Hope, but it's still Marty McFly, as it had been when I had left:

YOU CAN TAKE ME "BACK TO THE FUTURE" ANYTIME.

I'm feeling really out of my body right now, as if I really had time-warped back to the future in a pimped-out DeLorean instead of returning to the city in a no-frills Greyhound.

There's no sign that Hope had even been here while I was in Pineville. I wouldn't be surprised to find out that she'd pulled an all-nighter at the studio. I have no idea whether Wynn is coming to Sammy for her opening tomorrow night, or whether I need to prepare for a third-wheeler or, perhaps, find alternative accommodations for the weekend.

I don't know because I didn't ask.

And I can't ask now because the battery is still dead on my cell phone, and the Sammy has no landline. And I just tried checking my e-mail for the first time in thirty-six hours, but my laptop is inexplicably frozen, surely infiltrated by an al-Qaedan script kiddie who has deftly hacked through my firewall and is now using my system, and a bizillion others, to bust up Wall Street's technological infrastructure, shut down the world's economy, and take out Western civilization once and for all.

Oh, well.

I've got about six (or seven because she's always late) hours before Dexy is supposed to meet me here for the Care. Okay? party. Six (or seven) unfilled hours. And after everything that's happened this week, I'm taking this opportunity to do nothing at all.

sixty-one

I was having a dream about you and me. About you and me, together, in the bottom bunk. We weren't having sex, but we were pressing the lengths of our naked bodies up against each other. It was a very vivid dream; I could feel the heat passing between our bodies . . . the heaviness of your weight on top of me . . . the hot-wet warmth of your breath on my face . . . Too vivid . . . This wasn't a dream at all . . . I was . . . I was being molested in my sleep!

"AHHHHHHHHHH!" I bolted upright, using all my adrenaline to push the rapist off me.

"AHHHHHHHHHH!" Dexy screamed back as she tumbled out of the bottom bunk and onto the floor.

Dexy. It was Dexy. In my bed with me.

"Dexy! Christ! I thought you were a rapist!"

"You looked so snuggly!" she said, straightening her platinum-blond feathered wig, which had gone askew in the fall. This was as close as she would get to an apology. Dexy doesn't believe in apologies. "I'm so happy to see you!" she said, scrambling to her feet. "Aren't you proud of me? I'm on time! Which means I'm early!"

"How did you get in?" I said, still groggy.

"Manda let me in!" She leaned back and appraised my cutoff jean shorts and the DONUT HO' T-shirt I had put on out of utter necessity because I still hadn't done my laundry. "I *love* that T-shirt! Donut Ho'!" She tipped back her head and laughed: HAW HAW HAW. "But you're not wearing it out tonight. Oh! I love donuts with sprinkles! I'm starving. Seriously, where did you get that shirt? Do you have anything to eat?" Dexy's conversation ping-ponged more than Marin's. And even more so than usual. "I brought you a fabulous outfit!" She held up a plastic shopping bag, and then, as always, she broke out into a horribly off-key song. This time, Madonna.

"Gonna dress you up with my love! All over! All over!"

She pulled me up out of the bunk by the shoulders and steered me into our kitchenette. Then she opened up the refrigerator door and started foraging for food.

"Speaking of fabulous outfits . . . ," Manda spoke up from her favorite spot on the couch. Dexy had poured her curves into a liquid gold asymmetrical minidress, looking every bit the Studio 54 coke whore. "You'd totally fit in at Fuckyomomma in that. I could get you in, if you'd like. . . ."

I couldn't tell if Manda was being friendly or, uh, flirtatious. Manda had said that she was drawn to Shea's liberated id. Well, Dexy has been celebrating the emancipation of me! me! for as long as I've known her. And since first finding out about Manda's own robust sexuality, Dexy has been competing against her in a one-sided HOlympics. ("You've only got room for one token slut in your life . . . and that's me!") If they ever got together—oh, sweet baby Jesus—it would be a most unholy alliance: The Axis of Skeevil.

"Oh, this old thing," Dexy demurred, still half inside our refrigerator. She picked up one of Manda's organic yogurts, frowned at the expiration date, then put it back. Then to me: "I was just telling Manda about my sugar daddy!" She finally helped herself to a stick of Shea's left-behind string cheese before shutting the door. "J is the plucky innocent trying to make a name for herself in the big city. She's *scandalized* by my behavior. . . ."

"I'm not that innocent."

"I'm not that in-no-cent," sang-shouted Dexy. She bit open the tip of the plastic wrapper, spit it across the kitchenette, and blithely ignored my look of disgust. "Fifty-one point two."

I sighed.

"What's that?" Manda asked.

Dexy pulled at a thread of white processed-cheese product. "J's score on the MIT-created, Yale-perfected Unisex Omnisexual Five-Hundred-Question Purity Test, version 4.0."

One slow night in the dorm during our sophomore year, a bunch of us sat around doing shots and answering this most comprehensive survey of sexual experiences, with yes-or-no questions that ranged from "Have you ever kissed a friend or stranger on their hands or their head/neck region as a friendly gesture?" to "Have you ever engaged in sexual congress with a corpse?" What is most stunning to me now, in retrospect, is not the salacious nature of the questions, or our willingness to answer them in front of mixed company, but the fact that we had so much free time to devote to such inanities.

"Oh, I took that," Manda said, yawning. "I'm a ninety-two point eight."

"I'm ninety-three point one! With a plus/minus of point five percent, that makes us even!" Dexy and Manda high-fived. "Fifty-one point two," Dexy repeated, just in case Manda didn't get it the first time around. "That's ten points below the average. *You are . . . that . . . in-no-cent!*" Dexy bleated before giving me a playful squeeze.

"She doesn't have it in her to be a slut," said Manda. "Her one foray into slatternly behavior can only be qualified as a complete and utter disaster."

"What are you talking about?" I asked with irritation.

"Len called me back," she said.

"Hmm," I replied.

"Who's Len?" Dexy asked.

"The love of my life," Manda replied.

"Oh, puh-leeze," I said, mocking Manda without her even realizing it.

"Well, he *could* have been the love of my life if you hadn't, like, totally traumatized him when you stole his virginity."

"What are you talking about?" Dexy was enthralled.

Manda smirked. "Because of your vagina dentate, he's renewed his vow of celibacy. You've turned him off pussy for good!"

"Who's Len?" Dexy asked me. "And did he *really* say that?" she asked Manda.

"Len is someone I dated in high school who dumped me to date Manda," I said. "Manda dumped him to date Shea. And this week Manda dumped Shea and wants Len back. . . ."

Manda tapped her foot impatiently. "You forgot the part about fucking him last summer and turning him off pussy for good!"

Dexy literally flipped her wig. "J!" she cried, picking her fake hair up off the floor. "You slut!"

"Thanks for ruining my last chance at true love," Manda continued.

"Manda, I didn't want to have to do this." I sighed.

"Do what?" she asked.

"Let you hear the messages Len left on my cell after you spoke to him."

I wasn't going to let you in on them, either. Doing so seemed rather gratuitous and possibly hurtful, which is why I hadn't mentioned them until now, even though I first heard them yesterday morning on the bus to Pineville.

Three messages left on my cell in the middle of the night give credence to your long-held belief that too much conversation inevitably leads to someone saying something best kept to himself. I will now let Len Levy's own words speak—inarticulately and elliptically yet honestly—for themselves.

Message Number One

"Jess. Um. Hey there. It's, um . . . Len. I know this is out of the blue but . . . um . . . maybe Manda told you that we talked. And I just want you to know that I led her to believe some things that weren't true, just because she caught me off guard, and I didn't know what else to say, and now I feel bad about it, which is why I'm calling you. What's the best way to reach you, anyway? So. Um. Manda told me she was still in love with me. And that the whole thing with Shea was a big mistake. Can you believe her nerve? You live with her, so I'm sure you can. She made it very clear that she was interested in having sexual relations with me. Um. She said it was the greatest regret in her life, not having sex with me. Well, I was quite taken aback by this. I mean, I haven't had any contact with her since I . . . you know . . . since I walked in on her with her girlfriend. And I had given up on her long ago. I have a new girlfriend now who makes me very happy. And well, I sort of panicked, which is why I lied and told her I was celibate. She jumped to conclusions and—"

Message Number Two

"Jess. Um. Hey there. It's, um . . . Len again. I got cut off. Anyway, um. So I was saying that Manda said she wanted to have sexual relations with me. And I didn't know what else to say, so I, um . . . told her I was celibate. Which, um . . . I am . . . um . . . not. And then she started going on about how you must have been, um . . . well, I don't need to get into detail, but she was describing your capacity for physical intimacy in not-so-generous terminology. And, um . . . I just didn't agree with her, but I didn't . . . um . . . say anything to refute her accusations either because it seemed like the best course of action, the easiest way to extricate myself from the conversation and from her life forever. But in doing so, in taking the cowardly, non-confrontational way out, I did you a disservice, and I am truly sorry. I don't want you to think that our one night together had traumatized me in any way. In fact, it was quite nice and I don't look upon it with regret at all. Well, um . . . that's not entirely true. I sort of regret it because it—"

Message Number Three

"Jess. Um. Hey there. It's, um . . . Len again. I got cut off. Um. Again. This is just like that movie. What is it? I wish Camilla were here; she would know. Camilla is my girlfriend. Did you know that? She's great. So great. Um. I was saying that the only regret that I had about that night in the basement of Wally D's Sweet Treat Shoppe is that it kind of, maybe I shouldn't even say this, but why not? We're both happy in our relationships now. It made me realize how much more I should have appreciated you when we dated in high school. Like, we should have had sex in high school. It would have been the first time for both of us. And maybe, I don't know, maybe things would have turned out differently. I would have never left you for Manda and, well, it's so easy to romanticize what never was. Not in this particular dimension of the multiverse, anyway. Ha-ha. Remember that conversation we had that time about the multiverse? It was the afternoon after . . . So I'm working with theorists who are using quantum equations to prove that the concept of time is an elaborate illusion. Our universe might be like an enormous hologram that only appears to be three-dimensional. It's complicated, and your eyes are glazing over just listening to me. I don't want to get cut off again and I'm talking too fast and I think I've said too much already. I'm gonna go. If you ever want to talk, you should call me. Or text or . . . Maybe you shouldn't. You don't have to. Um . . . Okay. Tell Marcus I said—"

As Manda listened to these increasingly urgent messages, she tried—and failed—to arrange her face into an impassive expression. The longer she listened to Len's voice, the more strained and artificial she appeared. I almost felt sorry for her. I came close to pointing out the obvious, that Len's confessional phone calls to me meant about as little as hers to him, all being born out of nostalgia and misdirected longing.

But then I remembered her role as the gleeful instigator behind my current estrangement with Hope and I didn't feel the least bit bad.

When Len was finished talking, Manda snapped my phone shut and tossed it back to me in silence. She then snatched up her own cell phone off the IKEA coffee table and started scrolling through her text messages.

Dexy was beside herself with curiosity. She was bouncing up and down, dangerously so, in her platform sandals. "Was Len before or after Marcus?"

"During," Manda responded tartly, still concentrating on her phone. She was now scowling at something on the display screen. "Oh. And did you know that Len was Marcus's best friend?"

Not that you ever expressed even the slightest bit of jealousy over this one-night stand, but I was tempted to defend myself here, and claim that this traumatizing lay had not occurred "during." But I can't really say that, because even when we hadn't spoken to each other for months, then years, and hadn't communicated at all beyond those one-word postcards (when will FOREVER come?), you never *officially* broke up with me. Nor I with you. And those notebooks, oh, those stolen notebooks I'll never read, serve, even in absentia, as more than adequate proof that you never stopped thinking about me during those years apart. And I can just come right out and say that I never stopped thinking about you, either. And if I'm being completely honest, I'll confess that I thought about you that very night as I writhed on top of Len. I thought about you when I was fucking him, as I thought about you every single time I fucked that assclown Kieran during our intense and unhealthy four-month sham of a relationship. I thought about you if only because I wondered how long it would take me to stop thinking about you. I thought about you, and how I might never be able to forgive you for all the girls who came before me, nor myself for all the men who would come after you.

But that's the trouble. My indiscretion with Len did indeed take place "during." It had to, because there was never any "after."

"During? His best friend?" Dexy wriggled one eyebrow, then the other, and slapped me on the back in congratulations. "You *are* a slut!" Then before I could say anything else, she held up a white plastic supermarket shopping bag with the words THANK YOU THANK YOU THANK YOU printed on it in red letters, through which I could see the muted greens and blues of the outfit she had brought for me.

"Idiot," Manda muttered to her phone. She angrily thumbed a response, then stomped down the hall to her bedroom. Before she reached the door, she shouted over her shoulder, "Hope hasn't been here in two days! And Ursula wants your hundred sixty-six thirty-three!" Then she slammed the door so hard that I could hear her framed vintage Guerrilla Girls poster falling off the wall and crashing to the floor.

And before I could express my concern regarding either of these updates, Dexy took me by the shoulders and steered me toward the Cupcake.

"Come on, slut, let's get you dressed!"

sixty-two

Dexy looooooooooves the Cupcake.

"It's adorable!" she gushed as she plugged her pink iPod into my speakers. "It must be, like, a nonstop slumber party!"

"Not lately," I said hesitantly. "Hope and I are sort of, I don't know, but I think we might be in a bit of a fight. Or something."

"Color me shocked! *Shocked.*" Dexy gasped dramatically. "What happened? Is that why she's disappeared? Where do you think she is?"

"Probably at the studio preparing for her show tomorrow night."

"What might you be, I don't know, sort of in a bit of a fight over?" she asked, mimicking my indecisive language.

And then I told her, in as few words as possible, and with little embroidery or embellishment, all about the shared confidences between you and Hope. And to be honest, as I was telling her, the story already seemed like the organic yogurt, well past its expiration date. It all seemed so long ago.

Dexy listened with rapt attention. And when I finished, she was quiet for a second as she scanned through the catalog of songs stuck in her brain. Then she opened her mouth and started *rapping*, which you might think would be less devastating to the auditory canal because of the absence of actual notes, but this performance was somehow even worse than her singing. Then again, not even the originators could pull off those lyrics:

"Cats brawling with them claws out/Bitch YUB Trippin'?/I'm balling with my balls out/Bitch YUB Trippin'?"

Even with the inclusion of the title, I still (barely) recognized this as "Bitch (YUB Trippin'?)," dismal bad-boy-band Hum-V's biggest hit, the video in which model/actress/video babyho' Bridge Milhouse (aka Bridget Milhokovich) played one of the aforementioned "bitches," a role that required her to do little more than make out with the baddest boy bander under a fire-hose downpour in a pervert's dream of a soaking-wet transparent white T-shirt. That video was in medium-to-slow rotation on TRL for about a month back in 2001, and Bridge (as she prefers to refer to herself when talking about her modeling/acting/video babyho'ing days, which is next to never because she's so completely embarrassed by them) even attended a televised teenybopper awards show on the arm of the same Hum-V hottie who, about a year ago, was busted for dealing coke to the types of striving, starving starlets Bridget chose not to be.

I almost shared this all with Dexy because she truly believes, and has told me on several occasions, that she has been tapped by the Gods of Starfucking to be worshipped and adored by the untapped masses.

"Worshipped and adored for what?"

"For being Dexy!"

Well, no duh.

Dexy relishes any real or bullshitted connection to Fame, Fortune, and Fabulosity because it brings her that much closer to her Fate. In fact, if I had told her this story about Bridget and Hum-V, I don't doubt that she would have appropriated it for her blog, turning *herself* into the lifelong best friend of the former model/actress/video babyho' who so recklessly and foolishly abandoned the road to stardom for—can you imagine?—college. College! How common.

But I didn't mention any of this. Instead I said, "That's not funny."

"Sorry," she said dejectedly. Then she cued up her playlist, designed to get me in a party state of mind. She clicked through her selections until she found what she was looking for. I wasn't sure my speakers could handle the disco that burst forth in a frenzy of horns, frantic Latin percussion, and a foursome of female vocalists panting with lust.

"Push push in the bush," Dexy gasped along with the song. *"You know you want me toniiiiiiight!"* Dexy shimmied with pornographic abandon, the twins' three-by-five daisy garden rug becoming a dance floor for one.

I cut the disco. "Dexy, I have to ask you something."

"I have to ask *you* something first," she said. "Is Paulie What's-his-name going to be there tonight?"

"Parlipiano." When we were at Columbia, I had told Dexy all about my hopeless high school crush-to-end-all-crushes on Paul Parlipiano, but she had only met him in person at my early-graduation brunch last December. "Uh, I don't think so. He started grad school this week. . . ."

"Oh, thank God," she said, raising her palms to the heavens. "We need to find you a fun new fag!" She turned the volume way up and started galloping and swinging an imaginary lasso in time with the beat.

"Dexy!" I covered my ears.

"He can't dress, doesn't gossip, and hates musical theater!" She did a sign of the cross in 4/4 time to counteract this last blaspheme. "What homo hates Broadway? He's the worst gay sidekick ever!"

I switched down the volume yet again and looked deep into her eyes, trying to determine if her pupils were dilated or what. "Can I ask you a question now?"

"Ask me, ask me, ask me," she sang, mangling Morissey. *"Ask me, ask me, ask me."*

"Are you on drugs?"

"Of course I am!" She turned the volume way, way up. *"Are you ready? Are you ready for this?/Do you like it? Do you like it like this?"*

"Dexy!" I turned it down again. "I'm serious."

She pinched her lips together, the imitation of a shrewish schoolmarm, albeit one wearing gold lamé. "Of course I'm on drugs. I've been taking the best prescription-only psychotropics since I was twelve."

"I thought you started taking them when you were fifteen. . . ."

"Whatever," she said, waving away such a minor detail. "Can we put the music back on now?"

"Are you on anything that has not been specifically prescribed by your psychiatrist, and in the appropriate doses?"

"Why are you asking me this?" she asked. "Let's have fun!" She turned back to the Mp3 Player and clicked on a new song.

"We were born to be . . . A-LI-YI-YI-YIIIVE!" Dexy was doing a variation on Travolta's shoot-from-the-hips shuffle. *"Born! Born to be alive!"* Her eyes were closed in ecstasy.

"I can't have fun because you're scaring me," I muttered to myself, though she didn't hear me over the music. I just braced myself against the small windowsill, practically hiding behind the wholesome pink-and-white-checked curtains as I watched and listened to Dexy's atonal disco ball bacchanal. I was worried that she was working herself up to a monumental breakdown. I'd seen Dexy break down before, the summer before our junior year of college, and it was preceded by an atomic-bomb flash of brief and immeasurable energy.

Dexy finally opened her eyes and saw me cowering behind the gingham curtains. Her expression turned serious in a way I was unaccustomed to seeing. She turned off the music.

"Okay," she said in a defeated tone. "You win. I'll tell you the truth."

This promise of total disclosure caught me utterly by surprise. She took my hand and led me to the bottom bunk. We sat down together, so close that our knees bumped. She opened her mouth, and just when I thought she'd confess that yes, she'd been blowing rails all afternoon, she went a whole other way.

"I'm not boning a sexygenarian."

"You're not?"

"No," she said glumly, resting her elbows on her knees. "Never was." She placed her chin in the cradle of her hands, like a kid soured by a time-out for bad behavior.

"So you don't live in his apartment with views of Gramercy Park?"

She looked up at me forlornly through her fake eyelashes. "The

Gramercy Park part is true, but the daddy paying my rent is my biological dad, not some sick Freudian substitute. And it's not a chic pied-à-terre, but a single room in the Parkside Magdalene Home for Young Businesswomen."

"The wha—?"

"The Parkside Magdalene Home for Young Businesswomen," she repeated. "It's a hotel for women run by the Salvation Army."

It took a second for this to sink in. And when it did, I crashed back onto the bed in hysterics.

"Dexy!" I blurted, in between bursts of laughter. "Only you would be more ashamed of living at a hotel for women than prostituting yourself to a geezer!"

"It's worse than Bible college! No men allowed past the lobby! I haven't been laid in three months! That's my longest dry spell since I was fifteen!"

"Is anything on your blog true?"

"My name *is* Dexy," she said. She tapped her wig in thought. "And I *do* work in retail, just not at a sex shop. I work . . ." She took a deep, deep breath. "You must promise not to laugh."

I had barely recovered from my last fit, but I pressed my lips together and held up two fingers in Scouts Honor.

"I mean it, J," she said sharply. "You. Can. Not. Laugh. Not so much as a giggle or a twitter or a snort."

I nodded solemnly, seriously, but a smile already twitched in the corners of my mouth.

"I work at the Gap."

There was one second of silence—my attempt to be the kind of friend who pledges not to laugh and actually makes good on it—followed by five straight minutes of hysteria because I am not the kind of friend who can not laugh at something so ludicrous as the idea of Dexy—dramatic, costumed, whole-wide-world-is-her-stage Dexy—peddling the khakis and cords and T-shirts that are the staples of my unimaginative wardrobe.

"You promised!" she exclaimed, before giving in to the laughter herself. The bunk bed nearly collapsed from the thunderous gut-busting reverberations. "I know! It's the least creative job in the world. And Janeane Garofolo hated her job at the Gap in *Reality Bites*, like, a decade ago, so it's not even creative as a form of humiliation!"

"So you make up all this stuff because—"

She interrupted me. "Because I'm so fucking *boring*!" she cried. "I'm not living this awesome, scandalous life. I'm living a boring, totally chaste life, and I'm required to wear hideously boring khakis and T-shirts while doing it!" We both glanced at the hideously boring khakis and T-shirts overflowing from the hamper. "No offense, Jess."

"None taken."

"Can you blame me for wanting drama? Inventing a life?"

At first I was mystified. How could she have possibly pulled this off? But then I realized just how little Dexy and I see of each other. I took all her phone calls, e-mails, and text messages as truth—even the most outlandish bits—because how could anyone actually concoct such a vivid imaginary world? I rarely saw her in person, and when I did, it was usually for a few hours at a time, during which it would be possible for a woman with Dexy's flair for dramaturgy to convincingly play an alternate version of herself. Hell, I'm not even all that good of an actress, and I was able to pull off my Jenn-with-Two-N's ruse with Dude.

But it wasn't just Dexy. She was just the most glaring example of a deeper problem: I was totally disconnected from all of the most important people in my life. And it's not just about callousness or a lack of empathy that you've been warning me about. It's simpler, and sadder: I just don't pay enough attention. Even when I'm *with* my friends and family, I don't listen hard enough for the words that aren't being said. I'm elsewhere.

I realized that I could make a big deal out of this, or not.

I chose not to.

I just turned up the next song, one about not wanting to talk about love, not even sweet, true love, but especially not about broken romances, or plans and promises made that will never be realized. All she wants to do is go where the action is. All she wants to do is live.

"I love the nightlife," Dexy warbled. *"I got to boogie on the disco round, oh yea!"*

Since Dexy has to spend every day dressed like me, she's decided that I need to dress like her, at least for tonight. Thus, the polyester bamboo-print kimono dress and suede to-the-knee boots.

Dexy says she is just about done styling my hair—sectioning off my locks, wrapping them around huge, old-fashioned pink foam rollers, and then doubling the size of the hole in the ozone by shellacking the whole bumpy helmet with highly chlorofluorocarbonated hair spray, transforming it from a sad bun into a preposterously complicated seventies half-up, half-down bouffant-flip show ponytail that took about an hour from start to completion, which is how I've had time to write all this down.

But now she's done. I'm all dressed up to go out and have the type of New York City night that I can only enjoy if you're not there with me.

sixty-three

I should have left the Care. Okay? party with Dexy, but she had to make curfew ("Curfew, J! I have a two A.M. curfew! I haven't had a two A.M. curfew since I was fifteen!") and left me behind, and I stayed and did shots with a drag queen named after the colors of the rainbow. When I'm with Dexy, I don't get drunk because someone has to be in control. But what is control, anyway? None of us has any control over anything, it's all the illusion of control. An annoying celebutard (redundant) sang "Control" by Janet Jackson tonight and sucked hard. She wasn't good enough to be good and wasn't bad enough to be good, either. The worst kind of karaoke singer. Dexy is so bad that she's awesome—which is why I brought her with me even though her behavior scares me. Her stage-humping version of "Like a Virgin" (*like* being the operative word there) brought down the house, as I knew it would. Then she went back to *Bosom Buddies* hotel, and I got drunk. Dexy is so crazy that she makes me feel so together even when I am drooling drunk, which I am. Just in case you thought I was trying to hide it from you. I AM DRUNK. I actually drooled on this page, which is why the ink is smeary, though drool isn't really accurate, it's more like the spits, the nasty spits before you—

I just threw up.

I'm not going to lie to you. You want all the truth, right? I just threw up because I drank too many shots of tequila after Dexy left because I didn't have to be the responsible one anymore, plus you weren't there, either, so I didn't have to feel guilty about getting drunk in front of you. I want the freedom to drink too much and throw up. I want the freedom to be a hypocrite. I want the freedom to live in a city you hate and get a stupid job you think is beneath me. I want the freedom to make mistakes and not have you make me feel bad about them.

friday: the eighth

sixty-four

It's Friday morning-borderline-afternoon here in Sammy. When I awoke, I didn't recognize my own body at first, as it was still unfamiliarly clad in Dexy's dress, the polyester sticking to my body with the clammy dampness of drunken night sweats.

As for my corporeal condition, I, apparently, out of the goodness of my heart, volunteered to mop up the floor with my tongue before leaving the party last night. And my whole head now is pounding in retaliatory pain, as if I had spent the whole evening trying to jam it up my own ass. (Which isn't true, even metaphorically speaking.)

It's five glasses of water, four ibuprofens, three cups of coffee, two vitamin C tablets, and one immobile hour later. If you haven't noticed, I'm kind of blowing off my fake job this week, so I don't have to be anywhere (Bethany's) or do anything (babysit Marin) until later this afternoon, which gives me several hours to document that which I was too polluted to write about in anything but semiliterate prose last night. As is to be expected, my memory fades in and out, but I will try to piece together an approximation of the evening's events to the best of my hungover capabilities.

I'm doing this mostly because I feel obligated to finish what I've started.

sixty-five

The Social Activists' Care. Okay? karaoke party is held every Thursday night at Come, the same place that hosted Shit Lit. Last night there were not one, not two, but three snarling bouncers to keep out any wannabe do-gooders who were not, in MILF parlance, OTB. This was a strictly OTB crowd, and as the Cerberean gatekeepers checked and cross-checked *Jessica Darling +1* on the various VIP lists, I couldn't help but think of this as passage through to a very special kind of hell.

In the spirit of *Zagat*, Come is all about "manufactured scuzziness," a "Disney-meets-Dionysus 'Dive Bar' with bottle service on the LES." The "grimy," "no frills," "dimly lit" lounge is the perfect space for the "glossy," "all-frills," "megawatt crowd" who want to "escape the B&T scene on 27th Street" and "pretend they're slumming." It was packed to capacity with a melting pot of beautiful people who can afford to pay the $250 door fee and $250 per song, all proceeds going directly to whatever pet cause of the week is chosen by the Social Activists. I could name-drop here, but I won't because mentioning these boldfaced names would imply that I was impressed, daresay honored, to share the same rarefied air with a certain underage movie actress known for cutting cocaine with Strawberry Quik, or the pop princess who is better known for the inflation-deflation-reinflation of her funbags than for her music.

And these were just the obvious A-listers in attendance. Dexy kept on pointing out other New York notables whom I didn't recognize at all. The financier's son who hasn't let his marriage to an icy blond heirhead slow down his habit for squiring hard-bodied homos for bathroom blow jobs. The deejay paranoid that snorting crystal meth will wreck her nose job, and smoking it will give her jack-o'-lantern meth mouth, so she asks her unpaid intern to administer it via her asshole.

"THAT'S CALLED A 'BOOTY BUMP,' OR 'KEISTERING!' " Dexy shouted matter-of-factly, her neck swiveling around the room as she spoke. ***"AND BEFORE YOU GET ALL WORRIED, LET ME ASSURE YOU THAT I DON'T KNOW THIS FROM FIRSTHAND EXPERIENCE. . . ."***

"HOW DO YOU KNOW ALL THIS?" I shouted back. (Okay, I don't want to pull an Owen Meany here, so just assume that any conversation that took place throughout this whole evening was shouted, all caps, in bold, and italicized, as that's the only way anyone could be heard over the karaoke caterwauling.)

"How do you *not*?" she asked, her head still twisting around, her eyes a-goggle.

With all this sordid gossip in my brain, it was difficult for me to remember that it was all supposed to be for a good cause. This week's proceeds went toward the Global Fund, a nonprofit that helps fight AIDS, TB, and malaria in Africa. It's just like I told Hope the other afternoon: Africa is hot, hot, hot. But I doubt Strawberry Quik, Princess Funbags, or the rest of their dilated-pupil posse could find Africa on a map, and Africa is a big freaking continent. And it stands pretty much alone, too, unlike Asia, which is practically spooning Europe. Anyway, I couldn't help but be cynical about the whole endeavor when it was appallingly obvious that the success of Care. Okay? had almost nothing to do with the spirit of giving and more to do with showing off that you have so much extra cash lining your pockets that you can just give it all away to a continent best known as the birthplace of Shiloh Nouvel Jolie-Pitt.

I obviously cannot afford such ostentatious generosity, so I've turned down all of Cinthia's previous invitations. I only agreed to go because she had called me personally and told me not to worry about the tax-deductible door fee because she really wanted me to be there. In this age of easy avoidance through digital accessibility, the implications of such a gesture cannot be underrated. I had a feeling that there was an ulterior motive to the invitation, but I couldn't imagine what Cinthia could possibly need from me.

She had reserved spots for me and Dexy at her table. Dexy led the way, barreling through the crush of bodies, providing loud and sordid commentary the whole time. We finally found Cinthia standing at the front and center table, right by the stage, forehead to forehead with the aforementioned DJ Booty Bump, in front of a table occupied by a cross section of contemporary urban hipster clichés. The group looked like they had been handpicked by an advertising agency designing the "urban market" ads for Valtrex: *Genital herpes can happen to anyone . . . especially hipsters like you!*

"She's tiny!" Dexy was swooning over Cinthia. "But she's Reese Witherspoon cute and healthy tiny, not Nicole Richie needs-a-feeding-tube tiny!" She hugged herself passionately. "And I'm in love with her dress! I am so in love with her dress that I want to marry her dress and have its stylish babies!"

It wasn't until Dexy said that that I realized that I had totally neglected to mention your proposal. The thought hadn't even crossed my mind, so caught up was I in Dexy's cyclone of drama.

Cinthia was rocking a silk, one-shouldered, drop-waist minidress, mostly magenta and splattered with black Rorschach blobs, worn over black leggings with pointy ankle boots. It sounds ridiculous, and it was ridiculous, but she pulled it off with panache.

Dexy turned to me, in my secondhand polyester. "I told you you'd fit right in!"

But seeing Cinthia (and Dexy, and everyone else in the room, for that matter) wear that outfit so brilliantly only made me feel clumsy and self-conscious in my own throwbacks.

"I still can't believe you're friends with Cinthia Wallace!"

"It is sort of strange," I admitted. "We're on opposite ends of the Social Register, that's for sure."

"And you *really* didn't recognize her when she arrived at your school to write that book? What was it called again?"

"*Bubble-gum Bimbos*—"

"I would have called her out in a second," Dexy interrupted. "She was *the* jailbait socialite of the nineties! She was on Page Six like every day! She scandalized her whole family. . . ."

"I wasn't up on that kind of stuff," I said. "I'm still not."

"But no one in your school knew?"

"She picked Pineville High because we were so clueless."

"Well, obvs."

Dexy sashayed toward Cinthia, and in doing so passed right in front of the stage, briefly blocking the audience's view of the Eastern European model apparently too fatigued with malnourishment to carry a tune. As the runway favorite strained to coax out the words to "Edge of Seventeen," she gorgeously illustrated the fundamental problem with karaoke parties thrown and attended by Beautiful People, with or without the philanthropic angle. Beautiful People singing badly is fun to watch only if you are a Beautiful Person yourself. Because if you are not a Beautiful Person, all you can see is how in love these Beautiful People are with themselves. If they can actually hit some of the right notes, they are far too smug and impressed, as if one in-tune rendition of "Oh Sherrie" has refuted the long-held myth that Beautiful People have no discernible talent other than being beautiful. *Hear that? That hot chick is easy on the eyes and the ears! Wow! Isn't she genius? Aren't we all?* But the self-congratulatory annoyingness is even worse if the singer is horrendous, because the singer is so hyperaware of her horrendous singing. The Beautiful Person, usually of the female variety, doubles over in laughter as she sings, covers her eyes with her hands, and pushes "Don't watch me!" gestures at the audience, all of which is meant to show that she isn't just another pretty face—oh, no!—she's a pretty face who has a sense of humor, who likes to poke fun of herself and her very prettiness. . . .

AHHHHHHHHHHHHHHHHHHHHHHHHHHHHHHHHHHHHHHHHHH.

sixty-six

I'm having a bit of a meltdown here.

First things first: I'm a hypocrite ne plus ultra for attending a party at which I would be surrounded by the likes of those I've skewered in the past, such as the "wannabe or slumming Williamsturdburgers trying too hard to outdo one another in their kaffiyeh neck scarves, scraggly crusatches, and Jheri-curl mullets."

I needed you to know that I know that.

I've got less than one day left, but I'm not sure if I'm going to make it through this little experiment. It's not just because my hand is killing me from all this writing, surely suffering from repetitive-use injury. Besides that is the ominous feeling that my hypographic carpal tunnel will be for naught. I've dutifully documented all the routines and rituals, conversations and connections that are supposed to imbue life with meaning, and yet I can't imagine a worthwhile conclusion to all this onanistic scribbling. This seems most obvious right now, as I attempt to present last night's events.

But I've got a history of giving up when things go bad. I'm a quitter. I quit the Girl Scouts when I didn't sell enough cookies to earn a merit badge for my efforts. I quit playing clarinet when I wasn't chosen for first chair in seventh-grade orchestra. I quit the cross-country team when I had little hope of rising above twenty-third in the county. I quit writing for the *Seagull's Voice* when the adviser had the nerve to try to edit/censor my work. I quit my internship at *True* magazine when I didn't want to simulate fellatio in front of the editor in chief. I quit my assignments for *Think* this week when I finally accepted that they would never lead to gainful employment.

I quit trying to persuade you to talk to me.

I am determined not to quit this notebook. Even if not one word of it will make a difference.

sixty-seven

Where was I? Oh, yeah.

"Jess!"

Cinthia gestured for me to come closer. DJ BB took one bored look in our direction and slipped away. Cinthia hugged me longer than I expected. I could feel all the room's eyes on me, trying to figure out who I was, and why Cinthia Wallace was embracing me so.

"So what were you just talking about?" I asked. "Looked intense."

"The de-deregulation of the lending industry," she said. "Or re-regulation, if you believe in the strategic propaganda powers of positive language."

I knew Cinthia well enough at this point to suspect that she wasn't kidding. She really was trying to discuss credit-card reform with someone who enjoys crystal meth colonics.

Dexy grabbed Cinthia's hand and pumped it up and down. "I'm Dexy! J's friend! And let me tell you how much I admire your work with the Social Activists!"

Cinthia extracted herself from the handshake and smiled. "Well, thank you . . ."

"Seriously! Don't let the tabloids get you down!" Dexy said, now chummy enough with Cinthia to pat her on the shoulder. "What's wrong with wanting to be remembered as more than a vapid coat hanger with a taste for the booger sugar? Why shouldn't you do something positive with your money and fame?"

"*Thanks*," Cinthia said, taken aback by Dexy's enthusiasm, as most people are upon first meeting her. "But we're actually moving in a different direction. . . ."

"Who's 'we'?" I asked. "The Social Activists?" I glanced at the other faces at the table, trying to get them involved in the conversation. But they were all talking among themselves, not paying one bit of attention to the current performer—a portly, bald Tenacious D type doing a spectacular Freddie Mercury. *("I'm a sex machine ready to reload . . . Like an atom bomb about to oh oh oh oh oh explode!")* But Cinthia spoke to Dexy and me as if we were the only people in the room, a skill that no doubt helps her when it comes to persuading people to part with their money. Only we had no money to part with.

"The Social Activists can only do so much. We can raise money, sure, and social profiles, but we're not raising *consciousness*. I founded the Social Activists hoping I could exploit the conspicuous one-upmanship that is so pervasive here in the city and do some good. No one here cares about where the money is going"—she gestured around the table here—"they only care that they are among those being seen giving it away. And I figured that as long as the money was going to worthy causes, the dubious intentions of the donors didn't matter." She paused and leaned in closer. "But it *does* matter." Cinthia let out a sigh. "I know, it's all so *sincere*," she said, screwing her lips into a sneer on the last word. "Well, what's wrong with sincerity? Why is it such a dirty word?"

Dexy stood up, curled her lip, and swiveled her hips. "*Well, you gotta be sincere*," she sang in a horrid rockabilly twang that cut through all conversation. "*Oh my baby, oh yeah!*"

"Save it for the stage," I said, yanking her down into her seat.

"*Bye Bye Birdie*!" Dexy explained.

"Go on," I insisted. I was genuinely, daresay, *sincerely* interested in hearing what Cinthia had to say.

"Er, right," Cinthia said, unfailingly polite. "Irony has become the language of our generation. And the problem with irony, and sarcasm, and its evil twin, snark, for that matter, is that nothing is too sacred for a funny punch line. If people spent one tenth the amount of time thinking about, oh, I don't know, the midterm elections as they did trying to find pictures of Firecrotch's umpteenth upskirt, maybe our country wouldn't be so completely fucked up."

Right at that moment, a bubbly blond Nickelodeon starlet who last year, at the age of sixteen, legally emancipated herself from her parents, took the stage wearing a fedora, a flannel shirt, and fishnets. If this young lass had begun her evening with pants, or shoes for that matter, she was without them now. The crowd thundered their approval as she giggled and hiccupped through "I Touch Myself."

"Okay," Cinthia said with a knowing raise of her eyebrow, "what are you thinking? I know you're thinking something. Say it."

I contemplated her question.

You have urged me to practice "the art of compassion." Whenever I come across an annoying target for snark, I'm supposed to take a moment to consider the confluence of biological, psychological, sociological, and anthropological forces that have made this person who he/she is today. Being mindful of my fellow man's struggles is supposed to make me less likely to take him out with my sniper tongue. What could be the downside to practicing the art of compassion? Shouldn't we all try to be more mindful of others' struggles? Especially in New York City, in which mythic comedies and epic tragedies can be witnessed on a single street corner while impatiently waiting for the right moment to jump the go signal and jaywalk to the other side?

You have been warning me about my callousness for years, though you've graciously blamed the city's cruel influence, and not what I suspect is an inborn character defect. You see, it's not that I don't want to be a more compassionate person; I do. But that requires a certain sensitivity that doesn't come naturally to me. And so what usually happens is that I overcompensate by being super-duper empathetic, often with ridiculous results. Like this:

Cinthia: *My foot hurts.*
Me: *What happened?*
Cinthia: *I got caught in a bear trap and now it's just a bloody stump.*
Me: *That sucks! I totally know what you're going through!*
Cinthia: *You do?*
Me: *Oh, yeah! Totally!*
Cinthia: *Your foot got caught in a bear trap? And it turned gangrenous?*
Me: *No!*
Cinthia: *No?*
Me: *No! But one time I got a pedicure and the bitch clipped my pinky toenail way too low.*
Cinthia: *Gee whiz, I'm so lucky to have such an empathetic friend like you.*

Okay, this conversation never happened, but honestly, I wouldn't put it past me. As this fictional yet totally possible example illustrates, all my "empathy" accomplishes is taking the conversation away from the aggrieved party and back to me, me, me. Surely this has always been a deficit in my personality, and it's why I'll never further my studies in psychology to become a professional counselor/therapist/psychoanalyst. So I was speaking from experience when I told Cinthia that she was talking out both sides of her mouth.

"You can't throw parties like this, with tabloid favorites like her," I said, pointing to the stage, "and then lament about the death of serious discourse. You can't have it both ways. Your intentions are good, but your execution could be better. And I should know, because I feel like my entire life is comprised of good intentions with suck-ass execution. . . ."

"What did you just say?" Cinthia asked, eyes afire. She didn't sound angry, but I was afraid I'd offended her. I suddenly got all flustered.

"Uh . . . Suck-ass execution?"

"No, before that. You said my intentions were good but that I could do better! That's amazing! Amazing!"

"Uh . . ."

"Because that's what I want to name my new association."

"Amazing?" I asked.

"No!" Cinthia was shaking her head so wildly, her chandelier earrings slapped against her cheeks. "Do-Better."

"Do-Better?"

"As in better than do-gooder. As in make the world a better place." She slapped her hands on the table. "I knew it!" She beamed at me with her Baccarat teeth. "I knew I could count on you to tell me the truth. I have always admired your candor, Jessica. I wanted you to come here tonight and tell me what no one else had the balls to say. I'm looking for people like you to help me get Do-Better off the ground."

"Uh, what exactly is Do-Better?" I asked.

"As you probably know, I inherited an obscene amount of money from my capitalist pig of an absentee father."

Dexy broke in, unable to stop herself. "How much? I heard it was fifty million."

Cinthia didn't bat an eyelash. "More."

"More, more, more!" Dexy squawked. *"How do you like it? How do you like it?"*

"Way more," Cinthia said, already learning how to ignore Dexy. "The media analysis was all about, you know, the wayward paterfamilias trying to overcompensate for leaving me and my mother when I was still in preschool, but they were wrong. He knew the money would make me uncomfortable, and he just wanted to make me squirm, even after they sealed his tomb."

Yes, Cinthia's family is so dysfunctional that even a multimillion-dollar inheritance could be interpreted as a wicked "Fuck you!"

"Anyway, I wanted nothing to do with it. Don't get me wrong, I know that even without his blood money I'm still grossly wealthy. But how much money does a person need? Seriously. I knew right away that I was going to give it all away."

"*All* of it?" I asked.

"Every penny," Cinthia said.

"Can I have some?" This from Dexy, of course.

"The people with power are the people with money. . . ."

"I WANT THE POWER!"

"There aren't enough of us trying to improve life, not just for the select few but for everyone. We live in the richest country in the world and we are only serving the top one percent of our own citizens. The majority of people in this county can't afford health insurance. Or quality child care. They can't pay for college without going into catastrophic debt. And I can't even get into our appalling attitudes about poverty abroad." She sipped her club soda.

"It's easy to get overwhelmed by all the things going wrong in the world." This from me.

"I know. So many fucked-up things, and even with my inheritance, not enough money to fix them all. So I had to choose. First I thought I would donate it all in one big lump sum in my father's name to an organization he abhorred when he was alive, like the National Endowment for the Arts. *Hey, Daddy, you funded that sculpture made from* Hustler *magazines and semen!* Then I thought I could go global by using it to fund AIDS research. Or for micro-financing small businesses in undeveloped countries. Then I reconsidered and thought I should go local and donate it to a bunch of underfunded New York City public schools, or set up a series of scholarships for minorities at all the private schools that had the good sense to kick me out." She laughed here, and I did, too. "The point is, there are so many causes out there, and I felt helpless because I couldn't help everyone, as helpless and powerless as many of us feel when we see our government making decisions that we find morally repugnant, whether it's waging an amoral war or giving tax cuts to the megarich—like me!—who need it the least."

"So what are you going to do?"

"Something more personal, yet more ambitious, and more likely to fail."

I was listening carefully, waiting for her big plan.

"I am committed to funding a cross-cultural coalition of dedicated high school and college students, a philanthropic collective through which tomorrow's change-makers can work together to have a positive impact on real people's lives *today*."

She paused here, obviously waiting for some sign of approval.

"So you decided to go with a scholarship program?" I asked, not really following her.

"More than that. A movement." Cinthia slapped the table again for emphasis. "Do-Better scholarship recipients will promote a system of positive change, not only through their charity work, but by having a hand in selecting the next wave of Do-Better scholarship winners, who will one day do the same. In that way, Do-Better is self-sustaining. Our philosophy, our philanthropy, will grow and grow and grow. . . ."

I must admit, I envied the young idealists who would get a chance to be part of Cinthia's altruistic gamble.

"I would Do-Better if I were still in college," I said.

"I know you would," Cinthia said. "Because you get it. You totally get it. . . ."

"So what exactly will you—"

"We!" she said, gripping my wrist.

"*We?*"

"Yes!"

Cinthia's enthusiastic approval made me blush. "Okay," I agreed. "What will *we* do?"

"Again, this is why I like you. You don't just drink the Kool-Aid, swallow the rhetoric. You want real answers. And the real answer is: I don't know." She thumped the table once more with her palm as she laughed. "I have no fucking clue what we'll do *exactly*. I can only tell you what I want to do. . . ."

THE DO-BETTER MISSION STATEMENT

- INVEST funds in the next generation of philanthropists in the form of scholarships and employment opportunities
- INITITATE a system of economic sustainability through ongoing education and infrastructural rebuilding
- INAUGURATE a new guard of change-makers who support the collectivist ethos and sublate individualism
- INCLUDE other conscientious charitable institutions and nonprofit organizations in an open exchange of resources and ideas

- INCREASE awareness of socioeconomic crises here and abroad, and provide specific methods for effecting positive change
- INSPIRE tomorrow's leaders to volunteer their assets—be it money, time, talents, or wisdom—today

Okay, I didn't actually remember all this. I was, after all, a few drinks in at this point. And all the poorly sung pop-rock noise pollution was starting to addle my brain. I got this information directly from the Do-Better website, which hasn't officially launched but is already tricked out with some pretty impressive interactive flash technology. I'm pretty sure that in the effort to distance herself from the superficial high-twattage of the Social Activists, Cinthia had erred on the side of pretension and lifted some of the more academic dialect of this mission statement directly from her Harvard senior thesis. (I had to look up the definition of *sublate*, which has the opposite meanings "to take away" and "preserve and assimilate." It is the translation of a term favored by Hegel, the unreadable German philosopher I've forgotten about from my Contemporary Civilizations class at Columbia. I need to tell Cinthia that this is no way to get the masses on her side.)

If there was one thing I took away from Cinthia's spiel, it was this: She is as rootless, as restless as I am right now. The obvious difference is that she's got the resources at her disposal to put even her vaguest whims into action. Despite the pompous jargon, her mission strikes me as so wide-eyed optimistic. *Sincere*. And therefore subject to ridicule. Fortunately, Cinthia knows it.

"I'm a prime target for mockery," she said, nodding toward Dexy. " 'Bad Girl Wants to *Do Better*.' But I don't care. I'd rather be ridiculed for *that* than for a grainy camera-phone video of me chowing down on Eurocock. . . ."

Fuck.

I have to stop.

I can't write anymore. Seriously, my hand is cramping into a deformed Thalidomide flipper.

I have to pick up Marin from St. A's, anyway.

And really, what better way to end than on Eurocock?

sixty-eight

Another Brief and Meaningful Conversation with Marin

"Did Marcus ask you to marry him?"

"Uh . . ."

"Mommy said that Grandma said that Marcus asked you to marry him."

"He did. But I'm not getting married, Marin."

"Not ever?"

"Well, not . . . soon."

"Mom says you'll end up a spinster."

"A what?"

"A *SPINSTER*."

"I heard you. I didn't know that anyone actually used that word anymore."

"Mom does. But being a spinster is okay, right?"

"Being unmarried at twenty-two does not make me a spinster. Being unmarried at twenty-two or even forty-two doesn't make me a spinster. Gloria Steinem wasn't a spinster, and she didn't get married until she was sixty-five! Christ. What is wrong with people?"

"Is Gloria Steinem related to Rebecca Steinem in my class?"

"I don't think so. I'm sorry, Marin; I'm a little nutty today."

"Because you're a spinster."

"Well, no . . ."

"But being a spinster is okay, right? Because Marcus is a spinster, too."

"Uh, no. Marcus isn't a spinster."

"No? Are you sure? He reminds me of Driver, who is a spinster."

"Driver? Liesl's kid?"

"Yeah! That's the one!"

"Driver can't be a spinster because he's a boy. And he's only four years old."

"Yes he can, too! He's definitely a spinster. He spins around in circles all the time and never gets dizzy!"

"Oh. He spins. That makes him a spinster."

"Yeah. He's got modulation issues."

"What?"

"It's a form of sensory-processing disorder."

"Okay, now you're really losing me."

"Driver gets all jumpy and funny like Marcus. And he spins in circles to help himself feel better. It makes his brain feel better."

"Does it work?"

"Nope. He's a wild thing."

"Really."

"But you should still marry Marcus. You know why?"

"Why?"

"Because then I could be the flower girl in your wedding! Shelby Guglemann got to be a flower girl in her aunt's wedding and she got to wear the awesomest dress. . . ."

"What if we don't have a wedding? What if I don't get married to him or anyone?"

"No wedding? Well, I guess you could come live with me when I'm all grown up."

"Thank you, Marin. That would be perfect."

"But only if my husband says it's okay."

sixty-nine

A Not-So-Brief But Still Meaningful Conversation with Marin's Mommy

"So this has been a busy week for you. . . ."

"Marin already told me that you told her that Mom told you that Marcus proposed last week."

"I didn't tell her. She overheard me. And I also told her not to tell you."

"She did."

"Why didn't *you* tell me? I'm your sister."

"I was going to last week. But then you sprung the whole legal guardian thing on me and . . ."

"And?"

"It didn't seem like the right time."

"Is *now* the right time?"

"For what?"

"To talk about it."

"There isn't much to say."

"Jessie! Your boyfriend has asked you to marry him! How can you say that there isn't much to say?"

"You're right. There's a lot to say. There's too much to say. . . ."

"Mom said you said no."

"Mom hears what she wants to hear."

"So you didn't say no?"

"I didn't say no. But I didn't say yes, either."

"You said maybe?"

"I said I needed to think."

"That's what you told me, too. About the guardianship."

"Right. I know."

"You think too much."

"Really? No one has ever told me that before."

"So . . . what do you think about it?"

"About which part?"

"Both."

". . ."

". . ."

"Why did you marry Grant?"

"What?"

"Why did you marry Grant?"

"Because we were—we are—in love with each other."

"But you loved other guys before Grant. Like Jerry. Remember Jerry? From high school? You were mad about Jerry."

"Oh my. Jerry . . . Def Leppard Jerry . . . He was the best kisser. . . . Mmmm . . ."

"Bethany?"

"Huh?"

". . ."

"Jerry was my first love. My first everything. We were in high school and had no idea what we were doing. Jerry is best left behind as a bittersweet memory."

"What if Marcus should have been best left behind as a bittersweet memory?"

"What about working together to build a mature relationship? A partnership based on mutual respect? What about making a life together? What about growing up?"

"Well, that's just it. How can I even think about getting married when I'm still getting an allowance from my big sister? Part of growing up is getting a real job that pays me enough money so I can stop bumming off you. . . ."

"Is that what you think it is? Charity?"

"Well . . . uh . . . yeah. I mean, there are better-qualified nannies out there. . . ."

"Better-qualified, maybe. But not better for Marin."

"I'm not sure you'd still think that if you had any idea how often I let her watch *Grease 3: The Return to Rydell. . . .*"

"You think I don't know that? Of course I know that! Marin tells me everything."

"She does?"

"She does. And why would I pay a stranger to take care of her when she can be with family? When I know you need the money? You need to stop feeling guilty about accepting help from others. You seem to have this idea that it's somehow cheating, that it makes you a failure or something. But that's what loved ones do, Jessie. We help each other. And you taking care of Marin helps me, way more than you realize. Do you think I would entrust you with the care and well-being of my only child if I didn't believe you were the best person for the job?"

"I guess not."

". . ."

". . ."

"I'll do it."

"Do what?"

"Be Marin's legal guardian."

"Really? Are you sure?"

"I'm sure."

"Don't say yes because you feel guilty."

"I'm not. I want to do it, though I hope I never have any reason to."

"Me too!"

"I knew all along that I would say yes. I just . . . overthought it."

"You have a tendency to do that."

"Really? You've never mentioned that."

". . ."

". . ."

"Grant makes me feel safe."

"What?"

"I'm married to Grant because he makes me feel safe."

"Hmm . . ."

"What?"

"Bridget says the same thing about Percy. When I ask her how she knows that Percy is the One, she says it just as plainly and simply as you just did. 'I love him. He makes me feel safe.' "

"So?"

"I love Marcus. But he makes me feel out of control and out of my head. He is exhilarating and terrifying. I see and feel him everywhere, and I'm always grasping for equilibrium even when he's not there."

"So?"

"I feel like I'm always falling in love, falling and falling and falling. I can't live my life in a perpetual free-fall, but I'm not ready to safely settle down, either . . ."

"Well, you can't have it both ways."

" . . . "

"What? I didn't hear you, Jessie."

"I know."

seventy

Just moments ago, I thought FOREVER had finally arrived.

I was sitting cross-legged in the bottom bunk holding a package, turning the soft bundle over in my hands, trying to figure out how you managed to send it from the undeveloped woods along the Delaware River, and why it had come wrapped not in a mailing envelope but in plain tissue paper. I was debating the merits of your predictable unpredictability, and whether it was more appropriate to call it unpredictable predictability at this point. I was wondering if whatever was inside that tissue paper would undo all the conclusions I've made in the past seven days.

Because right up until the moment that I tore through the paper and discovered the thin, paint-smeared T-shirt, I believed this package was from you. But you already know that it wasn't from you. It was from Hope. Or, according to the label sewn into the back, ***hopeweaver.*** One word, in an old-but-newish lowercase font, just as I had suggested. A

$120 price tag was pinned to the armhole, and on the flip side, Hope had written a short note:

DON'T WORRY. I WASHED IT. XO, HOPE.

She came home just to drop this off before heading back to the studio. Hope had probably wanted to hand deliver it to me in person. I must have missed her by only a few minutes.

Now, this scene could have been more dramatic if I had been wearing the red ME, YES, ME T-shirt I retrieved from the MOM AND DAD box on Sunday afternoon, the one you had customized for me to wear underneath my high school graduation gown all those years ago. It would have been a hugely symbolic gesture, slipping off the garment that you made for me, yes, me and putting on the ***hopeweaver*** original, representing my choice of one of you over the other. But the ME, YES, ME T-shirt is still neatly folded among all the other archives I had returned to the cardboard box.

Back in high school, I always said that I wanted a boyfriend who was "the male equivalent of Hope." Would I have ever loved you if my love for Hope hadn't come first? Would I have ever loved you if Hope hadn't left? Would you have loved Hope if she had stayed? If Heath had lived?

I know. Just so many more unanswerable counterfactuals.

seventy-one

I don't know my way around the winding, one-way, dead-ending streets of the Financial District, so I had trouble finding the office building on Maiden Lane that was temporarily servicing as studio and exhibition space for Hope and her fellow artists. Other floors in the same building are being used as rehearsal rooms, so I got into an elevator packed with a taciturn, pasty-faced musician lugging a dented black case with a bell-shaped bottom for a large brass instrument, a ballet dancer with perfect penguin-waddle turnout shouldering a gym bag and smelling of eucalyptus sore-muscle salve, and two actors discussing audition reels and stints on soap operas who would be wincingly beautiful anywhere else in the world but here are just another waitress and bartender barely worth a second glance. These people wouldn't know NASDAQ from NASCAR, and I couldn't help but note the irony of the city's last bohemians infiltrating the realm of the ruling class, that is, until some mogul buys the building and boots them all out.

The doors opened at the fourth floor and I was surprised when everyone in the elevator got out with me for Hope's exhibition. This was not one of those spotless all-white boutique galleries you'd find in Chelsea. Nor was it one of those gritty, abandoned warehouses found in one of the last blighted stretches of industrial waterfront. Imagine a typical office floor where the unglamorous but necessary work is done. The accounts payable department, perhaps. Think gray walls, gray industrial carpeting, twitchy fluorescent lighting affecting a gray pallor on the cursed cubicle dwellers who review the expense reports and cut the paychecks of those being compensated far more generously than they are.

Hope shares this swing space with two other female artists. One's medium was "suspended sculpture." Her installation was titled "Cuntfight," and I will try to explain it as best I can. It consisted of female mannequins dipped in primary-colored waxes, then covered in white feathers. These figures were then arranged in twos, striking various battle poses—a headlock, a foot-to-groin, a fist-to-the-face—inside chicken coops that hung from the ceiling via a system of high-tension wires. I know there is no ideal way to die, but death by inadequately tethered suspended sculpture is not the demise I had in mind. I avoided walking underneath the cages.

The second artist worked with "found textiles." She created quilts made entirely out of objects scavenged from the garbage, each work titled after the corporate receptacles from which the materials had been retrieved. *Kmart #3*, for example. Or *St. Luke's Hospital #14*. Her work was displayed on platforms all over the floor, in the space where the cubicles normally would be.

Hope's paintings were hung on the opposite side of the space. I hadn't expected so many people to attend the group show, but the space was crammed with hands clutching their plastic cups of cheap wine, faces nodding contemplatively, bodies swaying to the ambient music selected by the iPod DJ, mouths opening and closing and opining on the state of the contemporary art scene. It took me several minutes to wend my way through the throng, many of whom were predictably dressed in head-to-toe black. Others—like the Wiggity-Wack Retro-Wigger with his blond Gumby, patchwork Heathcliff Huxtable sweater, and thick dookie rope chains, or Little Miss Indian in her beaded moccasins, red, white, and blue feathered headdress, and pink Pocahontas nightshirt from the Disney Store—presumably saw themselves as 24/7 performance artists whose incontestably retarded fashions put the Care. Okay? and Fuckyomomma crowds to shame, and could inspire even Dexy to pledge evangelical devotion to the Gap.

I caught snippets of conversation, reminding me of a joke Hope once made about how her classmates at RISD often confused contemporary artists with con artists.

". . . celebration of the sacred and profane . . ."

". . . deconstruction of gender-specific archetypes . . ."

Hope was exhibiting a series of oil paintings titled "(Re)Collection." A small placard explained the inspiration behind her work, in Hope's own words.

> *In January 2006, I was on a road trip with my best friend during which we planned to visit our nation's most expressively named cities. I forced her to pull over our rental car so I could check out a flea market held in a church parking lot on the outskirts of Virginville, Pennsylvania. There, for the price of five dollars, I bought a box of approximately 250 loose photos from the 1950s to 1970s. I was drawn to these unmarked snapshots documenting the major and minor milestones in an anonymous family's life. I manipulate these images by computer and by hand, an amalgamation of old and new techniques. I combine the past with the present in medium and message, both restoring history and reinventing it.*

For Hope, those photos told the real story of our road trip. But for me, they had been a totally forgettable part of the experience, a point not even worth footnoting in the infamous carjacking story, when, in fact, Hope had fanned those photos all over the table at the Bandit Diner, trying to get me to see their beauty, trying to get me to see what she saw in them. All I had seen was a pile of humdrum pictures of people we didn't even know doing perfectly ordinary things that every family did: Blowing out birthday candles. Grinning in front of the Christmas tree. Posing stiffly next to a prom date. Showing off a shiny new convertible.

But now these reimagined images were striking. Moments once captured in stark black and white were painted over in vivid yellows, pinks, and purples. Hope used broad strokes that made each canvas appear slightly out of focus, giving each scene a muted, distant feel of a dream you lose upon waking. These paintings were at once familiar and brand-new. The close-up of a pigtailed girl howling with tears in front of the lit candles on her fourth-birthday cake brought me back to the meltdown I had on my bitter sixteenth birthday when my carrot cake came with vanilla frosting instead of the cream cheese kind. The awkward teenage couple in their polyester formal wear evoked the prickle of gooseflesh, the gasp of anticipation, when you unzipped my prom dress and let it fall to the floor. . . .

I don't know how long I stood there, oblivious to everything going on outside my own mind.

"You're here."

I turned around to see Hope standing right behind me. She smiled when she saw that I was wearing the ***hopeweaver*** original T-shirt with my broken-in jeans and the Chucks I've had since high school. She was lit up in a black-and-silver Lurex striped sleeveless cowl-neck sweater minidress. It was an outfit I would never borrow.

"Of course I'm here," I replied. "I couldn't miss your big Manhattan debut."

"It's not so big," she said, hunching up her shoulders shyly.

Just then an antic guy in a fur trapper hat crashed through our conversation.

"Are you the artist?" he asked.

Her eyes flitted to the floor. "Yes, I am."

"I fucking love your aesthetic," he said in all earnestness.

"Thank you," Hope said politely.

And then Trapper Hat proceeded to talk more with his hands than with his mouth about Truth and Beauty and Art without making much sense at all. While he jabbered, I turned back to the wall and tried to figure out how she had done it. I was as baffled by these paintings as I had been by the process that had transformed hundreds of colorful paper slivers into the mosaic of two smiling thirteen-year-olds.

Hope slipped beside me. "Oh, man, I thought he'd never stop," she said, glancing over her shoulder nervously, worrying that he might come back after he refilled his plastic wine cup.

"How did you turn those pictures into these paintings?" I asked. "Or would knowing how you did it ruin the effect?"

She relaxed a bit. "Of course I can tell you." And then she went on to explain how she scanned her favorite found photographs, then edited them via PhotoShop, zooming in and cropping out however she saw fit. She blew up the reworked image, now a blurry fragment of the original, and affixed that new print to her canvas. Finally she painted over the whole thing with oils.

"I—" she began, before being interrupted by yet another fan of her work.

"Combine the past with the present in medium and message, both restoring history and reinventing it," whispered a wraithlike stranger in a suit of black leather who was lurking behind us.

"Er, right," Hope said nervously before grabbing me by the elbow. "I *combine the past with the present in medium and message, both restoring history and reinventing it,*" she said in a mocking singsong as she encouraged me to move across the room. "It sounds so pretentious. . . ."

"Don't apologize. I was just thinking about how much of my past resonates in my present. I certainly have a hard time letting go."

"Maybe the past doesn't want to let go of *you.*" I glimpsed Hope's fragile eggshell face, then quickly returned my attention to her work, which was infinitely easier to focus on.

"They're beautiful," I said. "Your paintings are like . . ." I grasped for a fitting way to describe the feelings these pictures evoked.

"David Hockney meets Diane Arbus," offered a third stranger, one whose dyed-black asymmetrical bangs were cut right across his eyes, concealing half of his view.

Hope ignored him. "It's like . . . getting caught up in someone else's memories," she said dreamily.

"Exactly," I concurred.

And then the tears tore up her face.

"Jess," she said. "I am so sorry. . . ."

"Don't cry," I said. "You'll mess up your makeup."

But it was already too late. Dirty rivulets of mascara were already staining her porcelain skin. Hope is a loud, messy crier.

"I'M SO SORRY. . . ," she blubbered. I lunged for a hug. This is not something Hope and I usually do. We are not huggers.

"We don't need to have this conversation," I said, pressing my face into the back of her neck. She smelled of ginger shampoo and lavender oil; the latter, she had told me, is used as an inoffensive paint-thinning substitute for turpentine.

"But I want to tell you . . ."

"We don't need to have this conversation," I repeated firmly. "It doesn't matter."

Hope loosened her grip on me, so I could reel back and look her in the face. Her complexion was ashen, her eyes wide and petrified that another overly familiar stranger would bust in on our discussion to expound on her work's Depth and Profundity.

"Let's get you out of here," I urged.

I had expected Hope to protest. After all, she had been working on "(Re)Collection" so hard and for so long at the expense of food, sleep, fun, and sanity, and goddammit, tonight was the time to celebrate. But she immediately brightened at my suggestion.

"I was hoping you would say that," she said, unleashing a gust of pent-up air. "I can't handle all this attention. I think I was kind of hoping you would rescue me."

"Well, I'm here," I said, smiling.

"Of course you are," she replied.

I took her paint-splotched hand.

seventy-two

We got a cab. As we sped across the Brooklyn Bridge, I couldn't help but cast a backward glance at Manhattan. I've lived in the city now for almost five years, and there's still a part of me that retains that corny, touristy sense of wonder when I see the peak of the Empire State Building all aglow at a distance. Just give me a pair of white sneakers and a fanny pack.

"Marcus and I have been together for more than four years."

Hope was hesitant to say anything on this subject, the subject of you.

"That's the most common time for long-term couples to break up. Four years."

"Really?"

"Really," I confirmed. "And this is all over the world, and across every racial, socioeconomic, political, and religious spectrum."

"Do you even qualify as having been together for four years?"

It was a fair question, considering you and I didn't speak to each other for two years.

"You and Marcus remind me of that Kahlil Gibran quote," Hope said. " 'Let there be spaces in your togetherness.' "

"That's . . . um . . . deep," I replied.

"It's engraved on every other wedding program in the NYC metro area."

Just then I remembered something I had read in preparation for my interview with Dr. Kate, about how all relationships fall into predictable patterns if you study them long enough. Ours was so simple, and yet it had never occurred to me until right there, beside Hope in the cab between one borough and the other:

CONNECTION

SEPARATION

CONNECTION

SEPARATION

CONNECTION . . .

"There's been too many spaces in our togetherness," I said, almost in a whisper. "Our relationship is defined by separation. By silences."

The funny thing is, I could have just as easily been talking about Hope and me. But she knew.

"It seems to me," Hope said, "that you and Marcus need more togetherness in your spaces."

For a few seconds the only sound was of the tires heartbeating over the dips in the road.

Ba-dump-dump. Ba-dump-dump. Ba-dump-dump.

"What the hell does that mean?" I asked.

"I have no idea," she replied. "I was hoping you wouldn't ask me."

seventy-three

Hope and I returned to the Cupcake. We climbed into our bunks, turned out the lights, said good night, and pretended to go to sleep. Our eyes were closed and our bodies were still, but I knew we were both wide awake, betrayed by the erratic breathing of those only feigning peace. Hope knew, too.

"I wasn't hallucinating, was I?" Hope asked suddenly. "That *was* Shea on her knees, scrubbing our toilet."

"No, I saw her, too," I replied. "And as further evidence, the bleach she was using singed my nostril hairs."

"Mine too!" she said. "So you also heard the part about how we're the nastiest bunch of squirrel-blowing cuntdrips she has ever met. . . ."

"Yes."

"And now that she's made up with Manda and is moving back in, she expects us to pick up a grannyfucking toilet brush every once in a while."

"Yup."

"Okay." Hope sighed. "Just checking."

I listened to the traffic through the open window before speaking. "I feel sorry for Shea."

"Why?"

"I think she really loves Manda."

"And Manda?"

"I think Manda loves Manda, too."

And then there were a few sheet-shifting moments of nonsleep before Hope swung horizontally and peered over the mattress to look at me. Her red hair hung like a cape behind her.

"What if he fell in love with Ursula?"

I laughed at the idea of you falling for our landlord before I realized she was not kidding.

"I'm totally serious, Jess. Imagine you let him go, and he falls in love with Ursula." Her eyes lit up with an even better idea. "And she's pregnant. With *Scotty's* baby."

"Oh, come *onnnn*."

"And Marcus wants to be the father of the child, even though the kid isn't his. *That's* how blindly devoted he is to her."

As she swung back into the top bunk, I imagined Ursula, tumescent with child, blowing a cloud of smoke into your face. *What? Dah baby is cooked. Dah New York city air is vorse than this cigarette.*

"You have to imagine the worst that could happen," Hope said. "How would you feel if you found out Marcus had fallen madly in love with someone totally unlike you?"

I opened my mouth, then shut it just as quickly. I didn't have the nerve to tell Hope the truth about her hypothetical. That I had already, in fact, imagined the very worst thing that could happen. I had already imagined you falling madly in love with someone totally unlike me.

I had imagined you falling in love with her.

"Let Marcus go," Hope said softly. "Say no."

Hope is the first, the only, person brave enough to say it.

"Let him go without assuming he'll come back anytime soon, or that you'll even want him if he does. Because clinging to each other is only making both of you unhappy. It's preventing you both from living the lives you want to live right now, and being the people you want to be."

"But we let go of each other in college," I tried. "We didn't speak—"

"No you didn't," she interrupted. "He might have left, but you never let each other go."

"But—"

"The postcards, Jess. Him sending them. You receiving them. That was not letting go."

She's right. I never let you go. I never stopped thinking about you. My mind was with you, three thousand miles away, and not in Manhattan. It's no wonder that my most significant relationships predate my college years—I was never fully committed to creating a whole new life for myself at Columbia. And you don't need a psychology degree from an Ivy League university to tell you that those unpacked boxes in the corner now reflect an unabated ambivalence toward Brooklyn.

"I've been thinking about those postcards a lot lately," I said, running my finger along those images—the medical eye chart, the starry sky, the globe, the Parisian lovers, the hourglass, the ©, the National Organization of Women—pinned to the corkboard next to my bed. "I thought for sure Marcus would send me one while he was away."

" 'Forever,' " Hope said.

"What?" I asked. "Did I tell you about that?"

"No," she said. "But it makes sense. 'Forever.' That's what he said when he proposed. It's just so . . ."

"Marcus," I said.

A car alarm suddenly *whoop-whoop-whooped* outside our window and was silenced just as quickly.

"He really hasn't changed since I've known him," Hope said. "None of us have."

"I'll try not to be insulted."

"Think about it," she said. "You've always had the cynical eye of a skeptic, but the optimistic heart of—"

"Of a fanny-packing tourist."

We laughed into our pillowcases for a moment or two.

"You don't think Marcus has changed? Even though he's been clean for six years?"

"I know Marcus is drug-free," she said, her voice rising slightly. "His behavior has changed, but I don't think *he* has changed."

"How can you say that?" I said, getting all twitchy and hot. "All Marcus does is change!"

"Right! He's *always* changing," she said with an emphatic kick of the mattress. "He's *constantly* changing."

"That's an oxymoron," I said.

"One that applies to his need for peak experiences," Hope said simply.

"What?"

"Marcus is always chasing peak experiences," she said. "The high of the good-bye, the rush of the reunion. He doesn't do well with the mediums or the in-betweens. He never has." She exhaled deeply. "When we were kids, months would go by when he would suddenly stop coming over my house. He wouldn't even *talk* to me in school. And just when I would give up and think our friendship was over, he'd be on our front-door step with a crushed daisy in his hand, begging me to come out and look for dead bugs for his Venus flytrap."

A few days ago, such a comparison would have sent me into a rage. *How dare Hope equate your playdates to a proposal.* But now I can see it's all part of the pattern, one your own brother had warned me about:

CONNECTION

SEPARATION

CONNECTION

SEPARATION . . .

"You don't have to agree with me, but I think the *heart* of who we are stays pretty much the same," Hope said. "What changes is how these core traits manifest themselves over time."

"The *heart*?" I asked in a more doubtful tone than I had intended.

"The heart or the soul or whatever you want to call it." She yawned loudly. "Whatever you want it to be . . . Whatever . . ."

She didn't say it with the disaffected inflection, the trademark ambivalence that makes a laughingstock out of our generation. She said it in an optimistic, inclusive, open-ended way that could turn the most hardheaded cynic into a believer.

Hope brought to mind the "Whenever/Wherever" postcard I'd swiped from the W after my disastrous interview with Dr. Kate. If I were as clever as you, I would have sent it days ago. It would be waiting in your post-office box right now. WHATEVER could have been the ideal substitution for FOREVER. But I didn't send it. I didn't even think to send it because such flimsy ambiguities cannot hold up under the weight of real life.

Just when I thought she had fallen asleep, Hope whispered, "Jess?"

"Yes?"

"Would you rather see Marcus only on weekends or not at all? Move to Princeton or stay in New York City? Break up now or later . . . ?"

All week long, my instinct was to shout, "Can't be answered with the information given!" Because there's *never* enough information. There's always the unknowable. Other options. Opportunities. Counterfactuals.

But you're returning to campus tomorrow. And I can't let too many choices become an excuse for not choosing anything at all.

saturday: the ninth

seventy-four

I'm on the train from Penn Station to Princeton, and there's only a pinch of pages left in this notebook. I'm running out of space. And time.

And like a minor winner at the Oscars (for Makeup or Art Direction), I'm hearing the quiet strains of the orchestra, and I'm starting to sweat through my awkwardly fitting floor-length gown bought off the rack and in a color that doesn't show well on TV (a queasy green, burst-blood-vessel purple) because no designer is jumping to outfit the nominees for Makeup or Art Direction (it's swelling) and I'm feeling the pressure to hurry up and finish my big moment already (louder), to hurry up, to hustle through the joy (I won!), hurdle through the gratitude (I won a category that is televised and not shunted to the daytime awards presentation of technical achievement!), and bring this once-in-a-lifetime moment to a satisfying and memorable conclusion before the full orchestra drowns me out (blaring now), before I'm dragged offstage by the sequined Amazon serving as the official arm and eye candy of the 78th Academy Awards, *and* the briefcase-clutching goons from Price Waterhouse Coopers, having thanked my agent, and the studio head, and my other agent, and my business manager, and of course the whole cast and crew in New Zealand and in Toronto, and even my third-grade art teacher, who always believed in me, but not (I suddenly realize, with a dramatic cymbal crash) my beloved husband in the audience, nor my mom and dad, who are staying up late, watching from home, and who have waited their whole lives to be thanked by their child on live TV in front of a billion people . . .

WHAT THE HELL AM I EVEN RAMBLING ABOUT?

See? I'm panicking here. Let me try again.

seventy-five

For the past seven days, I was compelled to write. I can't explain why I surrendered to this drive, though I suppose it's similar to the compulsive need others have to indulge in food, drugs, sex, art.

You understand this.

It would be misguided to attribute any deep significance to the past seven days. Everything takes on greater weight when written down. It changes from ephemera in my mind to something tangible. Something meant to be preserved. Remembered.

And in retrospect, I probably went about this all the wrong way.

I've kept a journal, on and off, for about six years now. In those notebooks I was wholly uncensored. I never intended for anyone else to read them. This notebook is addressed to you, and written with your eyes in mind. And though I repeatedly strove for that same level of candor, how was that even possible when I knew all along that you were going to read it? Writing for an audience turns it into a form of performance art, no matter how guileless I claim—or even strive—to be. Can there even be such a thing as an unmediated experience these days? Every storyteller is biased, sure, and we both know I've been a bit of a show-off for you. *You want my stories? I'll give you some stories, buddy!* I didn't try to create the illusion that I'm a better or more compassionate person. On the contrary. If anything, I might have blown up my flaws to help prove a point: *You don't want to marry this mess.*

Furthermore, there were countless sins of omission. Many were harmless, such as any conversation that went like this:

Not me: *What are you doing?*
Me: *Writing.*
Not me: *Writing what?*
Me: *I'm writing to Marcus.*
Not me: *Why?*
Me: *Because he asked me to.*

[Pause.]

Not me: *Are you almost finished?*

Me: *Not yet.*

Not me: *When will you be finished?*

Me: *I'm not sure I'll ever be finished.*

Not me: *Oh.*

Me: *No matter how much I write, there will always be something else I should have said.*

seventy-six

Perhaps this is something I should have said earlier:

Last Saturday I left your room and walked the twisty, half-mile path that led to the Dinky train that led to the bigger Northeast Corridor train at Princeton Junction that led to Penn Station, NY, that led to the 2/3 subway that led to the Grand Army Plaza stop that led to the ten-block walk that led to my home sweet subterranean home. More than two hours, point to point.

As I sat alone on the Dinky train, I thought about all the smart people in this town, in the world, and wondered when someone would use his brilliant mind to invent a teleportation technique that could reduce the Princeton–to–New York travel time from two hours to the blink of an eye. The very notion of the long-distance relationship wouldn't exist. If I had instantaneous access to you, and I didn't have to give up my life in New York, would I have tried to end it? Would you have asked me to marry you?

I looked at the ring on my finger to confirm that this had actually happened. I wiggled my fingers in front of me, as countless brides-to-be have done with blindingly new platinum-and-diamond showpieces. Only my ring was hammered by your hands out of an old quarter. I used to wear this ring on my fuck-you middle digit. It was too big for my ring finger on either hand, and yet now it fits perfectly. This was not a miraculous sign.

This was nothing more significant than hot weather and water retention. Or so I've been telling myself for the past week.

I was about to take it off when a five-pack of young men and women came staggering through the train car. At first I thought Dude and his preppy posse had met and mixed with Marjorie (how's Marjorie?) and the volleyball groupies, and I squirmed at this unnerving coincidence. Then I breathed a sigh of relief when I realized that this was an altogether different but totally identical group of Princeton undergrads. They were very intoxicated, and Ivy League intellectual drunk tends to be a very pretentious form of drunkenness. That is, when it isn't a totally imbecilic kind of drunkenness.

"I'm telling you," said one of four guys wearing fitted polo shirts, long khaki shorts, and flip-flops, "everyone wants to be happy, but no one even knows what happiness means."

"Happiness is a warm gun," interrupted another guy, who distinguished himself from the rest by the radical degree to which he was red and gleaming with perspiration.

"Happiness is a warm puppy!" chirped the cutest girl. She was also wearing a polo shirt collar up.

"Happiness is a warm body!" shouted Red-N-Sweaty as he grabbed the cutest girl, who shoved him off just because she could.

"Happiness is a cold beer!" the other, less cute girl suggested. And they all cheered.

Then the tallest male with the thickest neck said, "Happiness is not having to listen to you fucktards wax pseudo-philosophical about happiness."

I quietly nodded in agreement because Thick Neck was sort of right. Studies have shown that happy people do not spend their hours contemplating the nature of happiness, because they are too busy being happy. The unexamined life, apparently, *is* worth living. Very much.

"Seriously," said Pseudo-Philo Fucktard. "Why are we all trying to achieve this state of happiness when no one can even define what it means?"

Red-N-Sweaty placed a firm, friendly hand on his shoulder. "I can't tell if you're too drunk or not drunk enough."

"The latter!" said the rest of the group in unison, which sent them into paroxysms of laughter.

Their conversation was interrupted by a cell phone. The ring tone wasn't a tone at all, but a young woman's voice chirping, "Jeff is *so hawt* right now. Jeff is *so hawt* right now . . ." And the conversation that commenced was not unlike any number of overheard cell-phone conversations in which the overheard half is a priceless parody of postmillennial conversational strangulation, in which the speaker seems incapable of putting together a single sentence in the subject/verb/object tradition.

"Yeah . . . The fuck? . . . Aw shit, dawg . . ."

This was the guy who was just waxing philosophical about the nature of happiness? As inarticulate and seemingly pointless as it was, the call lasted for the five-minute duration of the ride to Princeton Junction. I hopped to my feet before the train even screeched to a stop and I was the first passenger out the sliding doors. I strode quickly through the dim underground tunnel that brought me to the eastbound side of the tracks, where there were already clumps of passengers waiting to board the next train to Manhattan, mostly middle-aged couples heading into the city to catch dinner and the latest must-see Broadway show. They were paunchy, gray-haired men in rumpled suits talking about golf and the stock market. Their well-preserved wives wore too much makeup, shiny evening fabrics, and showy gold jewelry. They discussed sending the kids back to school and what the humidity does to their hair.

This second group reminded me of my parents, so much so that I suddenly got this strange idea that any two of these anonymous fifty-somethings could have been my parents out on a date. I had actually looked forward to presenting this as evidence to my sister that my mother wasn't going to leave my father after all. I did a double take, and my heart sank when I realized that I could do a triple, quadruple, and quintuple take and I still wouldn't see them actually socializing together in public because they never do.

"OW!" squealed Other Girl after a skin-on-skin smack. "You suck!"

The Princeton Tigers had made their way to the platform, and they were passing the time by playing slapsies.

"If I suck, then why"—*slap!*—"do"—*slap!*—"I"—*slap!*—"win"—*slap!*—"every"—*slap!*—"time?" *Slap! Slap!*

"The alcohol has dulled my reflexes!"

"Admit it," Thick Neck said, "you are the fairer but weaker"—slap!—"sex. . . ."

Other Girl lived for stealing attention away from Cute Girl. A lop-sided smile was barely hidden behind her fake frown. I started to feel sorry for Other Girl.

"I'm telling you, no one even knows what happiness means," insisted Pseudo-Philo Fucktard, still not giving up.

Then the Northeast Corridor train pulled in with a piercing squeal that mercifully drowned out the rest of the undergraduate conversation.

I could've helped them out if I had wanted to. For *Think*, I kept up on the science of happiness because most people, but Americans in particular, want to be happy. I know that people are unhappier about the opportunities they pass up (saying no) than those they accept (saying yes), even if the opportunity doesn't turn out the way they hoped it would. I also know that people are happier when they set a short, strict time limit for decision-making (one week) and that married couples are happier than singles. (Well.)

Are these the reasons I didn't come right out and reject your proposal last week?

No. I think it was something else entirely, like the temporary amnesia brought on by your kisses. Sexual arousal releases oxytocin, a hormone that turns on the body and shuts off the brain.

Basically, you kissed me out of my right mind.

And I cannot let you do it again this afternoon.

seventy-seven

Here's another story. One I started—but couldn't finish—from the Care. Okay? party:

". . . Eurocock," said Cinthia.

"Who's having Eurocock for supper?" boomed a voice from behind. And before I could turn around, I was attacked by a flock of wild purple ostriches.

"Dah-ling! It's you!"

"Royalle G. Biv!" I spluttered, spitting his boa out of my mouth.

"Where's the Buddhist?" the drag queen asked, readjusting his spangled cleavage. If the average anorexic starlet got a boost in her bra from those silicone chicken-cutlet inserts, Royalle G. Biv must use two Perdue Oven Stuffer Roasters.

"Not here," I said. "And he's not a Buddhist. He's a Deist who practices Vipassana meditation."

"Say no more!" he said, making an exaggerated lip-zipping gesture, which was funny because it was a perfectly appropriate gesture for describing your practice.

"Royalle G. Biv!" Dexy shrieked. "I love you! I'm your biggest fan!"

"Not possible," he said. "*I'm* my biggest fan!" He waited for the laugh, then said, "Listen, doll, I'd love to tawk, but I've got to bring down the howse."

And he pranced away as only a seven-foot drag queen can prance.

"This should be good," Dexy said.

"Get ready to cry yer eyes out," Royalle warned the crowd, pulling a chiffon scarf from his ballgown for effect.

And right before the background track started up, I thought about how phenomenal it would be if Royalle broke out into a Barry Manilow song. You were returning in less than forty-eight hours, and I wasn't any closer to knowing what I'd say to you when I saw you again.

I needed a Sign. I was begging for a Sign. I was willing to shed twenty-two years of agnostic skepticism if God or a higher power came through with a Sign. This was His moment to wow me, win me over. I would spend the rest of my life as a missionary turning doubters into the devoted with my astonishing conversion story.

"And then when I had lost all faith, I got a Sign, and that's when I knew I had to say yes. . . ."

I pressed my palms together under the table, praying a seven-foot drag queen named Royalle G. Biv would act as the voice box of a higher power, spreading His message of hope and love by performing a number by none other than Barry Manilow. Perhaps the appropriately titled "Could It Be Magic":

Baby, I love you, come, come, come into my arms
Let me know the wonder of all of you

Or "Daybreak":

We've been runnin' around, year after year
Blinded with pride, blinded with fear

Or even "Copacabana," for Christ's sake:

They were young and they had each other
Who could ask for more?

But, alas, Royalle opened his huge red mouth and began to sing a power ballad I didn't recognize until it built up to the torrid chorus.

"*I WAH-NT yoooooou, I NEED yoooooooou,*" Royalle belted. "*But there ain't no way I'm EVAH GONNA LOVE you. . . .*"

Not Manilow, but another overwrought late-seventies balladeer. Meat Loaf.

And as much as I hate to admit it, Royalle's diva delivery of this over-the-top song hit me where it hurts. It was a performance for the ages, and I was mesmerized. Granted, at that point I had worked up to a solid drunk, and I was certainly susceptible to the *boo-hoo-hooze*. But

Royalle's performance, though not a Sign of the divine, was a smashing success on another level. His melodramatic lament beamed a spotlight on my own version of this troublesome triangulation, which I will come right out and reveal right now. And it is this:

I love you.

And I want you, too.

But.

However.

Unfortunately . . .

seventy-eight

Of course, I got your message, too, which came after Len's. It was so strange to hear your voice.

According to your message, the kiddies are calling you Rodney. That's a pretty clever nickname, but if those Princeton Tigers really wanted to impress me, they would have called you Thornton, which is the senior-citizen college freshman character Rodney Dangerfield *plays* in the movie *Back to School*. But Rodney is a pretty solid nickname. Solid. A nickname like that could very well stick for the next four years. I knew I'd be right about the nickname. I just knew it, and see, you weren't giving me enough credit for knowing such things. But I can hardly blame you. I wasn't giving myself much credit, either. . . .

I can't stop thinking about Driver, the MILF's kid with "modulation issues." I'm sure you escaped this diagnosis only because it hadn't been invented yet. I can totally see this kid madly spinning around in circles as a way of trying to calm himself down because he can't handle all the noise and hubbub of the classroom. And the wilder and faster he spins, the more out of control he feels. It's a self-defeating coping mechanism. But he's four. He doesn't know any better.

Since I've known you, you've been spinning and spinning and spinning into all these various personas, and none of this self-exploration and experimentation has given you a sense of peace. I've known you for six years, intimately for four, and I still have no idea who I'm in love with. When we first met six years ago, you were Marcus Flutie, notorious burnout and sly defiler of underage women. After a mandatory stint in rehab, you became Marcus Flutie, sobered-up genius whose rebellious history made you all the more intoxicating to an unsullied goody-goody like me looking for a little corruption. After a few semesters at the unaccredited Buddhist college in California, and a few months at the experimental school in Death Valley, you became Marcus Flutie, nonsectarian practitioner of Vipassana meditation.

This minimalist philosopher is less or more the person who knelt on the floor and asked me to marry him last week. But I understand that being here in this new place will inspire you to shape-shift into somebody else, someone unknown to me right now: There will be a fourth coming of Marcus Flutie. Followed by the fifth. And the sixth. And so on. How can I possibly promise to love you FOREVER when I don't even know who you'll be by the time you get this notebook? Who is at the heart of Marcus Flutie? What is the essential part of you in every new incarnation?

Is that what you're trying to find there, on the floor of your closet? You want to be still and quiet and look inward, and I fully encourage you in that quest. But I'm afraid that you've twisted so far inside yourself that I can't help you find the way back out. And I'm not willing to go in there with you. Maybe there's someone else out there who will. Someone who isn't necessarily a better woman than I am, but better for you right now.

That's one thing that hasn't changed in a week: You, Marcus Flutie, are still an all-or-nothing proposition for me, and as much as I'd like to tread that middle path with you, I don't know how. (You must have seen this yourself, or you wouldn't have considered breaking up with me.)

I was just reading this study for work about how the happiest couples are those who sacrifice their own wishes so their partners can achieve their dreams. It makes perfect sense. And yet I know I'm too young, that we're too young, for me to live my life only as it relates to you. If you had asked me to marry you the night you first told me about your acceptance, I would have embraced Princeton as part of a larger plan that involved me. I probably would have reacted differently.

I might have even said yes.

Alas, you didn't ask me then. You made plans for your future without me in mind. And that's okay. But how can you now ask me to arrange my life around you?

seventy-nine

The train is pulling into the Princeton station.

And so I must bring this notebook to its abrupt end with a page or two left to spare.

I have to get up, get off, get going. I have to move, move, move before the doors shut, before this train reverses itself, before it returns me to the place I started from.

Oh, please forgive me, Marcus, for indulging in one last extended metaphor.

(I know you will.)

September 15, 2006

My dear Jessica,

Not only do I forgive you, I thank you.

I know that sounds odd under the circumstances, but I'm grateful for what you've given me. As difficult as your notebooks were to read at times, you were only sharing the truth as you saw it, and as I asked for it. As you noted, even your superficial confessions are significant if only because you were compelled to share them with me.

I've read them, and now I'm returning them. They belong to you.

I was tempted to leave annotations in the margins, but it's too late for such revisions. I promised to honor your request, knowing how difficult it was for you to make. I respect you for being a stronger person than I am, and for doing what I was unable to do all those years: let you go.

Before I do, I hope you don't mind if I use the remaining pages of this notebook to share a story of my own:

When I was thirteen, the same age as you and Hope when you played your innocent game of hypotheticals, I decided I needed a tattoo. Heath had Asian calligraphy crawling around his bicep and I decided to get something like his. I didn't even know what language it was—Chinese? Japanese? Korean? It just looked cool.

I went to the same guy as Heath, who did all his work out of one of those weatherbeaten bungalows off the Seaside Heights strip. He didn't hesitate to ink me up, though it was obvious that I was both underage and under the influence. I don't remember the guy's name, or even what he looked like beyond a basic, cartoonish "Asianness." Was he Chinese? Japanese? Korean? Again, to my immature, uncultured mind, it didn't matter.

He spat all his words. "What you want?"

I hadn't given much thought to the design because I couldn't sit still long enough to give much thought to anything. I was more excited about getting the tattoo than having it.

"Dunno."

"You dunno what want on arm forever?"

My mind was so malleable that if he had said, "You dunno what want on arm, dumbass?" I might have requested the translation for "dumbass."

"For. Ever," I answered. I exaggerated the pronunciation, thinking it would eliminate any chance of miscommunication. "For. Ever. For. Ever."

"You want repeat around arm?"

"Sure," I said. "Whatever."

"What. Ever?"

"Yeah, Tat Man," I said. "What. Ever . . ."

A painful hour or two later, it was done. I had my FOREVER tat. I was stoked for about a week. Then I got bored with it, like everything else, and it was just something that was there, on my arm, easily forgotten unless it behooved me to show it off to a dizzy, fizzy girl. (Not you. Never you.)

I'm sure you're aware that the main street in Pineville was recently renamed the Avenue of Americanism. Our hometown is not known for being a welcome host to anything foreign. It wasn't until I went away to school in California that I made friends from other countries and cultures. And with my interest in Buddhism, a great many of them were of Chinese descent. Not too long after I moved in with my cottagemate, Topher, he pointed to my bicep.

"What's that supposed to say, anyway?" he asked.

"What?"

"The tattoo?"

As I said, I often forgot it was there.

"I got it when I was young and dumb," I said. "It says FOREVER."

Topher laughed. "No it doesn't."

He picked up a pen and illustrated the difference between what I thought I had and what I actually did:

为曾经 = FOREVER

曾经什么 = WHATEVER

I got what I deserved.

My proposal to you could not have been more sincere. But it seems that my life is imitating badly executed skin art, turning my intentions for FOREVER into something else altogether. And so I'll let you go, and let it be.

Whatever, Marcus

Acknowledgments

Many thanks to:

Joanna Pulcini, for dispensing the wisest advice when I needed it most.

Kristin Kiser, for giving me the freedom to go in the strange, surprising directions of my dreams. Steve Ross, Stuart Applebaum, Min Lee, Philip Patrick, and Tina Constable for having my back. (You are the closest I've ever come to having a posse.) Lindsey Moore and Lindsay Orman for not getting annoyed when I got confused and sent the right e-mail to the wrong person. (Or vice versa.) Christine Aronson, Donna Passannante, Sarah Breivogel, and Shawn Nicholls for your brilliant ideas and committed follow-through. Lynn Goldberg and Megan U. Beatie of Goldberg McDuffie Communications, for respecting my point of view and helping me put it out there. And Elizabeth Carter for providing another pair of eyes.

The countless readers and writers—most of whom I've never met—who offered candid words of encouragement. Meg Cabot and Sophie Kinsella, whose e-mails made me laugh when nothing seemed funny. Rachel Cohn, Sarah Dessen, Julia DeVillers, Piet Hut, Erika Rasmusson Janes, Jeannie Kim, Carolyn Mackler, and Monica Ryan deserve special thank-yous for wisdom and general "awesomeness."

Dr. Helen Fischer, anthropologist and author of several books, including the fascinating *Why We Love: The Nature and Chemistry of Romantic Love*, for developing the real science behind the fictional iLoveULab. I've never met you, but I would love to have lunch with you someday.

Justin Timberlake, who brought the sexy back during the intense revisions phase. I've never met you either, but . . .

My mom and dad, who prove that parenting doesn't suddenly end when your kid turns eighteen.

The Fitzmorris and McCafferty families, who always come through for me.

CJM and CJM, for everything, forever.

About the Author

Megan McCafferty is the author of the hit Jessica Darling novels *Sloppy Firsts*, *Second Helpings*, and the *New York Times* bestseller *Charmed Thirds*.

An Excerpt from

perfect fifths

MEGAN McCAFFERTY

Available from Crown Publishers in Spring 2009

"This is the final boarding call for passenger Jessica Darling."

After Marcus heard it the first time, he made sure to listen extra carefully the second time, just to confirm it was her name being called over the public address system, and not a phantom echo in his mind.

"This is the final boarding call for Clear Sky Flight 1884 with non-stop service to Saint Thomas, U.S. Virgin Islands. Final boarding call for passenger Jessica Darling."

Jessica Darling. It had been years since he'd heard her full name spoken out loud. Not that Jessica Darling hadn't been analyzed, assailed, or alluded to in conversations with family, friends, and near strangers from their shared past. As a subject of discussion, Jessica Darling had been elevated by—not reduced to—pronoun status. Have you seen *her*? What's *she* up to these days? Whenever anyone asked these questions, there was never any doubt as to whom the "her" or "she" referred. But those questions hadn't been asked lately, not since Marcus had—by all actions and outward appearances—finally gotten over her.

Even after hearing her name once, now twice, Marcus still needs a confirmation from somewhere outside his imagination. He seizes his friend Natty by the shoulder and asks.

"Dude, no," Natty insists. "No, I didn't hear her name. And neither did you." Natty's sharp tone can't burst the pop-eyed, expectant expression on Marcus's face. "And even if you did hear her name, there's no way it's her. Now let me unleash the piss I've been holding back since we left N'awlins."

Natty leaves Marcus standing between the entrance to the men's restroom and the fiberglass Betty Boop sculpture boop-boop-be-beckoning customers into the faux-retro Garden State Diner for a greasy preflight meal. Marcus feels overexposed, overstimulated, as if his whole body is on extrasensory alert. His nerves rattle and clang like the dirty silverware carelessly thrown into plastic tubs by the too-busy busboys. He tries to calm himself with a series of deep inhalations and exhalations, but breathing cheeseburger smog only makes him more queasy and ill-at-ease. The alarms going off in his nervous system evoke in him erratic behavior like that of animals preceding natural disasters. His instincts urging him to flee, he half jogs away from the diner and heads for the blue-screened monitors announcing Arrivals and Departures.

As Marcus searches for Clear Sky Flight 1884 on the Departures board, he makes an effort to accept Natty's logic. After all, didn't his Jessica Darling often joke about being confused with a porn star also named Jessica Darling? Perhaps it's the X-rated Jessica Darling being called over the public address system, or maybe even a third, unknown Jessica Darling who shares nothing but a name with the other two. A newborn Jessica Darling. A granny Jessica Darling. An African-American, Hispanic, Asian, Pacific Islander, or Other Jessica Darling. It must be one of these alternative Jessica Darlings flying out to Saint Thomas on Clear Sky Flight 1884, not his Jessica Darling, the one he proposed to more than three years ago, the one he hasn't seen, spoken to, or otherwise communicated with since he quietly accepted that her answer was no.

He looks away from the monitors because the orange font/blue screen color scheme makes his pupils vibrate. On the wall directly in front of him is an ever-changing digital screen advertisement for The Shops at Newark Liberty International Airport. Before he even realizes he's doing it, Marcus impassively watches the images shift.

The picture: A gold-foil box of gourmet chocolates.

The words: MISSING HER.

The picture: A string of black South Sea pearls.

The words: MISSING HER LIKE CRAZY.

Marcus, wowed by the lack of subtlety, looks away and laughs. He can't give in to narcissistic folly and read this sign as a Sign. It's taken him three years to finally pull himself together, and he refuses to come undone by commonplace coincidence. In fact, he's just about convinced himself that Natty is right, that there's no way it was his Jessica Darling being summoned over the Clear Sky Airlines PA system (why does his skin still prickle with premonitory anticipation?) when his Jessica Darling slams right into him and bounces onto to the floor.

A body in motion. A body at rest. Forces coming together—*crash!*—in an instant. Energy spent, energy exchanged, and energy conserved. Jutting elbows, bared teeth. Elastic arms, slack mouth. To every action there is an equal, but opposite, reaction. This woman and this man, a living, breathing demonstration of Newton's Third Law.

Jessica curses herself as she scrambles across the marble tiles. Clad in head-to-toe black, she resembles a desperate beetle stuck on its back, arms and legs flailing for her flung-to-the-ground carry-on bag. She finds it, scrapes herself off the floor, and decides that a curt give-and-take of apologies is the path of least resistance, the quickest way to get past this stranger, this nuisance, this object of interference with feet stuffed into scuffed Vans. There are already too many eyes on them, watching, wondering what will happen next. A combative confrontation will only attract more rubberneckers, and she doesn't want anyone else slowing her down.

Marcus waits until she stands up before he takes a chance. "Jessica?"

It's the voice that reaches her first, and not the correct first name uttered by the voice. Her head bolts upward, and when her eyes corroborate her ears, her breath catches, her hands fly up to her face. She breathes in and out through her palms, once, twice, before taking them away. Miraculously, he's still there. She is perfectly still for the first time since vaulting out of bed this morning.

"Marcus!"

He nods to confirm what should be obvious but is still too unbelievable.

"Marcus," she repeats, softer.

He nods again.

"I . . . ," she begins. "I'm . . ."

They are standing inches apart, not touching. Jessica clutches her teardrop-shaped carry-on bag to her chest, sensing that the moment to embrace has passed. A spontaneous show of emotion now would be too conspicuous, too much, too late.

"Late!" Jessica blurts. "I'm too late."

Hundreds of passengers swirl around and away from them, like so many snowflakes in a blizzard.

"Oh," Marcus says, softly. He wonders whether he could get away with softly swatting her arm in what he hopes is a neutral zone, between her shoulder and elbow. Behind her flashes the sign. The gold-foil box of gourmet chocolates. MISSING HER. The string of black South Sea pearls. MISSING HER LIKE CRAZY. The sign. The Sign. He's ready to make his confession, that he'd heard her name and hoped for the illogical, the impossible to be true: That it was really her, and on *today* of all days. He's inches away from making contact when she casts a nervous sidelong glance at his outstretched palm, the part of him tempted to touch a part of her. He drops the offending hand and stuffs it deep into the front pocket of his corduroys.

He says nothing.

"We should . . . ," Jessica starts. She's rocking from side to side now, an anxious, joyless dance. "You should." The pronoun change doesn't go unnoticed by either of them. "E-mail. Or I don't know. Something . . ."

"Something," he says simply.

Marcus musters the courage to look Jessica right in the face. She still wears her chestnut hair like an afterthought, pulled away from her face with a few quick twists of a rubber band. If she removed the elastic and shook out her hair, he would breathe in the fruity scent of shampoo; he's certain that the tresses resting against her neck are still damp from her morning shower. He finds some comfort in this knowledge, as well as the overall familiarity of her features, which haven't changed all that much since he last saw her. But he must admit to himself—only to himself, never to her, even if she'd had the time or the temerity to ask—that her casual loveliness is more than a little washed out, worn out. Her eyes are tired, tinged pink and buffered by puffy purple under-eye circles. Her lips are cracked and wind-chapped. Her nostrils are also dry and flaking around the corners, perhaps from too many rubs with a paper towel, wool coat sleeve, or other too-rough tissue substitute. He hopes that her care-worn appearance is an aberration, that her immune system is down. He wants her to be either sick or tired, but not sick and tired or just plain sad.

"I'd catch up if . . ." Her cheeks glow an embarrassed red, and her pale complexion is better for it.

"If you had time," Marcus finishes for her, trying to determine from her voice whether she's suffering from a cold or something worse.

"If . . . ," she starts, but doesn't finish.

She can't look at him. If she looks up at him, she will be compelled to ask questions she doesn't have time for. Finding out that he still wears the same brand of sneakers after all these years is a minor revelation, and yet even this insight into his world going on without her is almost too much for Jessica to bear. What else hasn't changed? Does he meditate for hours on the floor of his closet? Jessica braces herself with a deep breath. Would he still smell like smoldering leaves if she leaned in close enough? Does he still compose elliptical, poetic songs on his acoustic guitar? Derelict lyrics force themselves to the front of her consciousness, a ballad softly sung when they were still teenagers, the only one he ever wrote for her:

I confess, yes, our Fall was all my fault
If you kissed my eyes, your lips would taste salt
But you think my regret is a lie, and the tears I cry
Are the crocodile kind

Jessica's watery eyes stay fixed on the unraveled seams splitting his mossy V-neck, revealing a quarter-inch more skin than the designer's intentions. This is an expensive-looking sweater—two-ply cashmere—and she doubts Marcus could afford to buy it for himself. She guesses it was a gift from someone who is very familiar with his face, one who knows how this gray-green shade would shake loose those elusive hues from his multifaceted brown eyes. Definitely a gift. He doesn't even have the cash to care for this item properly with regular dry cleaning. She imagines him blithely tossing the sweater into one of his college's communal washing machines, along with his T-shirts, jeans, and underwear, the tender cashmere threads coming more and more undone.

"Go," he urges softly, pointing toward Gate C-88. "Don't miss your flight."

She pulls a wad of scrunched-up paper towel out of her pocket, rubs her nose, jerks her head in agreement. They offer hasty good-byes, but no hugs, not even a handshake before she takes off for the gate.

"I'm sorry I ran you over," Jessica calls out as she hurtles herself forward.

I should be too, thinks Marcus. *But I'm not*.

And then she's gone again.

Also by MEGAN McCAFFERTY

Discover how Jessica Darling's story began . . .

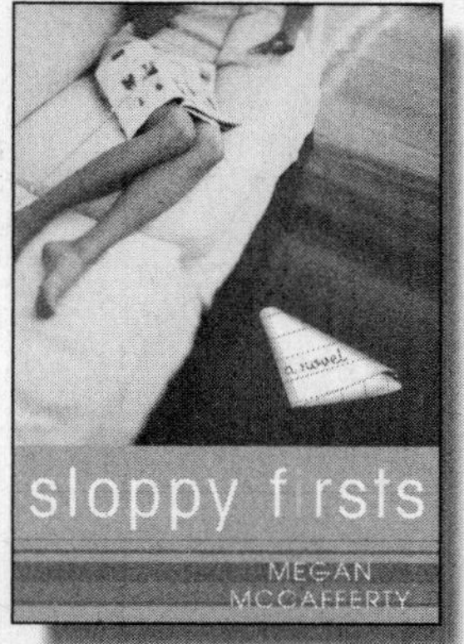

sloppy firsts

$13.95 paper ($21.00 Canada)
978-0-609-80790-3

second helpings

$13.95 paper ($17.95 Canada)
978-0-609-80791-0

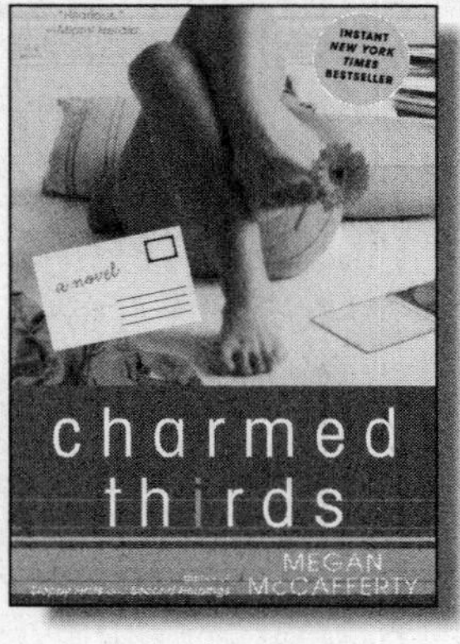

charmed thirds

$13.95 paper ($17.95 Canada)
978-1-4000-8043-4

Available from
Three Rivers Press wherever books are sold